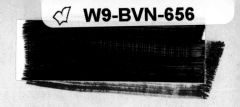

BRANDED

The Joe Noose Westerns
by Eric Red

NOOSE

HANGING FIRE

BRANDED

THE CRIMSON TRAIL *(coming Summer 2021!)*

BRANDED

A Joe Noose Western

ERIC RED

PINNACLE BOOKS
Kensington Publishing Corp.
www.kensingtonbooks.com

PINNACLE BOOKS are published by

Kensington Publishing Corp.
119 West 40th Street
New York, NY 10018

PINNACLE BOOKS and the Pinnacle logo are Reg. U.S. Pat. & TM Off.

ISBN-13: 978-0-7860-4681-2
ISBN-10: 0-7860-4681-3

First Pinnacle paperback printing: February 2021

10 9 8 7 6 5 4 3 2 1

Printed in the United States of America

Electronic edition:

ISBN-13: 978-0-7860-4682-9 (e-book)
ISBN-10: 0-7860-4682-0 (e-book)

To Anthony Redman
who loves violence in movies
but is one of the kindest people I know.

And to my wife Meredith
and our two dogs, Cider and Eggnog,
the most notorious outlaws in our house.

PROLOGUE

The kid was thirteen, younger than the others, but the only one who had killed a man. His outlaw pals Clay, Jack, and Billy Joe were all between eighteen and twenty-one years old; only one of them, Clay, knew his exact age. The others were runaways but the kid was an orphan who had never known his own parents. Even though he was the youngest, he had size on his friends, and at already six feet stood a head taller than any of the other three. If the boy had a name, he didn't know it, so Billy Joe, Clay, and Jack just called him Kid. The others knew he had been on his own since he could walk and like them, could handle himself. And the kid was a lot meaner. He hit harder in a fight. The Colt Peacemaker in the thirteen-year-old's fist was, of all of them, the only hand the gun looked like it fit.

The four youths were robbers, horse thieves, and petty criminals. Over the last year, the motley gang prowled like a scruffy wolf pack across the Wyoming, Montana, and Idaho territories, pulling random crimes and taking down small-time scores. Nothing heavy, kid stuff. Holdups of unarmed civilians the ruffians happened to encounter were their stock-in-trade. For the three years since they joined so-called forces, the young delinquents had stayed a step ahead of the law, avoiding arrest because their crimes were nickel-and-dime in nature, and law enforcement manpower was stretched too thin over the frontier to bother with penny-ante crimes. Plus most folks made them for kids. Kids with dumb luck. But their luck was about to run out.

Living hand to mouth, sleeping outdoors, roving aimlessly, by spring of 1865 the hooligans drifted to western Wyoming and had the poor judgment to try their hand at something bigger.

Tonight, the gang was moving up to rustling. The four young outlaws had spotted the small Wyoming ranch with the hefty herd of steer quite by chance when they had ridden off a washed-out trail and cut across a plain, trying to make their way south. It had been noon when the thirteen-year-old kid had spotted the stockade full of longhorns through a thicket of trees and whistled quietly for his friends. Clay had the idea first. Jack and Billy Joe said what the hell. The kid just shrugged.

None of the greenhorn outlaws had ever rustled cattle before or given thought to how such a crime might be managed or the stolen cattle sold even if it was managed; *rustler* just sounded good as a word and the young fools figured they could add it to their list of crimes that would be on their wanted poster one day. When they had one. It was a constant source of irritation to Clay that the gang didn't have a wanted poster. Nobody knew who they were and Clay wanted the gang to make a name for themselves. Trouble was, they couldn't think of one. Gangs usually had places or last names as the name of their gang and since the four weren't from anywhere and none of the boys knew their last names, coming up with a name for the gang was proving to be a challenge.

The youngest didn't care about making a name for himself for he was amoral and didn't care about anything.

The kid thought nothing of their crimes. The thirteen-year-old had no concept of right or wrong. Such notions never entered his thinking, or whatever passed for it inside his thick skull. He just did what he did to survive like he'd always done. The boy couldn't read. Had not had a day of schooling. Had never been in a church. He trusted in his own speed, strength, and violence. At twelve, he had killed a man and felt neither good nor bad about it other than glad it was the other guy who was dead, not him. The kid rode with the other boys because he just kind of fell in with them; he had no feelings about his friends to speak of; in fact, preferred to be alone. The thirteen-year-old was a brute, a rough figure of a human being God had sculpted out of clay but forgotten to fill in the features.

They waited until sundown.

When it was good and dark, the four young outlaws gave their horses a nudge with their spurs. Broke cover as they rode out from where they had waited out of sight in the woods. Drawing their guns, the gang kept low in their saddles and trotted out onto the grounds of the ranch, sticking to the shadows. The place was pretty big. A large buck-and-rail stockade filled with cows. A two-door barn adjacent. A farmhouse on the far side of the corral on the hill. Everything was quiet. The kid looked over the spread in the hazy moonlight and didn't see any people in the area. Just lots of steers in rows of shoulders and hind-quarters and longhorns stretching off into the darkness. One of his friends said something about them having so many cows they weren't going to miss a few but the kid couldn't hear or see who said it because he was riding in the rear and saw only the backs of the others' heads in the dim. They were riding around the stockade to find the gate and a way to get in, the thirteen-year-old guessed. He just followed the others' lead, not caring one way or the other.

The hooves of their horses squelched in the mud. The smell of cow shit was strong.

A slap of a hand on a mosquito made the kid's gaze snap front as Billy Joe wiped the bug off the flesh of his neck.

The kid grabbed the coil of rope in his saddle, not knowing how to rustle a cow but figuring a lasso was probably part of it.

It was almost too dark to see, but not quite. Resuming his inspection of their surroundings, the kid looked for any sign of people. A quarter of a mile off, the large timber ranch house sat atop the hill overlooking the buck-and-rail cattle stalls. A light burned in a kerosene lamp in a window but there was no movement. He couldn't see a living soul. The smell of cow dung and dirty cattle hides filled his nostrils. The lowing of the steers was intermittent; sounds of their penned movement covered any noise their horses' hooves made in the mud.

His friends' horses slowed.

The would-be rustlers rode up to a gate made of hewn wooden posts with a sign atop the youths would have read as Q-RANCH had any of them been able to read.

Fatefully, the kid regarded the *Q* letter's circle and squiggle and thought it reminded him of an upside-down hangman's noose.

Seeing the flash before he heard the gunshot, his saddle jerked downward as his horse dropped dead beneath him, tossing the kid headlong to the ground.

The thirteen-year-old hit hard but his skull was hard. Busy dodging rearing horses, the kid rolled out of the way to avoid getting trampled as hooves of the panicked animals came down and pounded the earth near his head. Then the boy was dodging the falling bodies of Clay, Jack, and Billy Joe as they got thrown from their saddles. The three good-for-nothing nags galloped off into the darkness in fear.

Before he could get up the kid heard the *click*s of the hammers being pulled back on three rifles, very close by. He froze. It was a bad sound to hear from a gun when you were on the wrong end of it. They were all surrounded.

The other boys heard the guns cocking, too, and knew when they were beat, so the four did the smart thing.

They all put up their hands.

Crunching of boots on dirt sounded on three sides opposite the cattle stockade. The steps were menacingly slow and deliberate. The people making them were cloaked in darkness, that deep country dark you can't see anything a foot from your face.

Exchanging glances, Clay, Billy Joe, and Jack looked very afraid of what would happen next. The kid, acting calm, figuring he would find out soon enough. None of them dared reach for their pistols.

Out of the darkness, the rancher appeared first. A tall and skeletal figure in a weathered leather duster, with long white hair. Hatred and meanness radiated off him. The old man's right hand was a mangled stump missing three fingers. It looked like an ax had been taken to it once. One of those digits was on the trigger of an immense double-barreled scattergun the left hand braced to his shoulder.

"Get their weapons." He spat. "Disarm 'em."

The rancher's sons, two boys the same age as the gang, appeared out of the shadows, holding revolvers. One was older than the other by a few years, it looked. Both boys were young and raw, but meant business. The older of them reached in and yanked the six pistols one by one from the hooligans' side holsters, handing them off in turn to his young brother. Neither of the rancher's sons said a word.

Walking ominously over to a fence post that had coils of rope hung on it, the father unslung four lariats and tossed them on the ground.

"Tie 'em up," the old man barked.

His two boys seemed reluctant to relinquish the grip on the revolvers they held on their captives by picking up the ropes, but their father raised his shotgun to his shoulder and stepped into position over the hooligans, sighting them down the barrel he moved back and forth aiming at their heads. "My boys is gonna tie you up now and any of you punks move a finger, I'll blow his head off and the head of the punk next to him. Savvy?" The boys on the ground nodded they understood. Finally, the rancher's sons put their captured revolvers on the ground, snatched up the ropes, and got to work.

His two sons clearly had experience roping steers and had the four young outlaws bound in just a few minutes. The kid and his friends were hog-tied by their wrists and ankles with their arms and legs behind their backs. The old man's boys were strong and rough and got their prisoners tied up with ropes quickly. The kid and his three would-be rustler buddies were soon facedown in the dirt, breathing soil. The rancher's sons had now retrieved the guns they had taken and were pointing them down at the prior owners, fingers on the triggers, looking like they knew how to use them. The boys followed their father's orders without argument as if he had them trained like animals. The kid thought they looked more scared of the skeletal old man than his friends were of having their own guns pointed at them.

"Get 'em over to the tree," the rancher said.

The kid had never seen anybody hanged before.

Tonight that changed.

Everything did.

The tree was big and dead, but it had a long, thick over-hanging branch that made for a sturdy gibbet when the old man threw the first coil of rope up around the branch. Then he tied off the rope with a mean yank; one end of the rope was already secured to the saddle of the first horse—all four horses were stupid and easily retrieved from the neighboring creek they stopped to drink at by the two young sons of the rancher—the other end he knotted into a noose. The kid wondered how the old man could knot a rope with the few fingers of his chicken claw of a mangled hand, but he did. The noose dangled directly above the saddle of the first Appaloosa, who stood chewing a carrot.

The elderly rancher finished with the first noose and let it hang, approaching the tied-up boys with a Grim Reaper countenance.

Somebody was about to get hanged.

The kid preferred it wasn't him.

His friends all exchanged terrified glances.

The rancher's two sons just looked at their father, keeping the pistols trained on the prisoners.

Instead of selecting one victim to be hanged, the old man threw some coal oil on a pile of coals in a metal brazier with iron cattle brands resting in it. Tossed a match. A *hiss* and *whomph*. The roaring uprush of flames splashed a hell-ish firelight over the scene. Flame and shadows bloomed on the menacing oak tree with the ropes dangling from the branch, empty nooses swinging over it.

The old man turned from the captured boys and didn't take one to be lynched. Not yet.

Instead, the old man grabbed a second rope. Tied a second noose. Threw the rope over the branch. Then knotted the other end to the saddle of another horse.

Then he made a third noose and tossed the rope over the branch. He tied that to the saddle of the last horse.

The kid's horse was dead, shot out from under him, and he didn't know if that was a good or a bad thing.

The minutes dragged on into an hour, the aroma of burning charcoal mixing with the rank stench of urine. The kid could see two of his friends had pissed themselves in terror. One of them was crying, snot smeared all over his screwed-up face.

The thirteen-year-old kid had nothing to say.

But his friends sure did. They were talking plenty.

"—Just let us go! Please! You'll never see us again!"

"—Take us to jail! Don't lynch us!"

"—Please don't hurt us, mister! We're sorry."

Sorry for what? The kid thinking the only thing he was sorry about was getting caught.

He knew the rest were wasting their breath anyway. Nothing his friends were going to say was going to get them out of this fix. The kid didn't care one way or the other. It was what it was. It was going to be over soon—he just wanted to get it over with. The thirteen-year-old felt the heat on his face from the coal brazier, felt the cold night wind on his back facing the dark stockade, but those sensations were all the kid felt.

"Get 'em up," growled the old man. He had returned and stood. "That one. That one. And that one."

The gaunt skeleton of a man lifted a crooked finger on his mangled hand to point out Clay, Jack, and Billy Joe. "Put 'em in their saddles. Throw ropes around their necks." The two strong rancher boys took the captives one at a time, both sons hauling the trammeled young outlaws to their feet. In turn, they dragged them to the tree and pulled a noose over each of their necks before pushing them by the ass up into the saddles of a horse. The old man had the huge scattergun in the faces of the kid's friends when the ropes were put around their necks. All the kicking and screaming didn't save the boys. Two were pistol-whipped to make them compliant and shoved onto their steeds. Moments later, Billy Joe, Jack, and Clay were perched in their saddles with nooses around their necks and all stopped resisting—if they fell off their mounts or their horse bolted, those nooses would break their necks, so none of the boys moved a muscle.

The two nameless sons turned and walked back to the kid, who could now see they were more scared then he was, especially the smaller of the two. Both lads were shaking with fear and close to tears and the kid wondered why, since it wasn't them being hanged. Four hands took his arms to pull him up.

"Not him." At their father's sharp barked command the two sons let go of the last boy lying hog-tied on the ground. The kid looked up at the rancher's towering silhouette framed against the leaping fire and black night sky, the old man's face one big shadow, a hole in the darkness looking down on the kid, who couldn't see the eyes he felt drilling into his skull.

"How old are you, son?" the old man asked.

"Thirteen," replied the kid.

"Just a boy. Too young to hang."

With that, the old man turned his back on the kid and walked over to the tree where the wretched three condemned youths sat like bags of shit on three horses with three ropes around the neck awaiting cruel vigilante execution. His two sons walked with him, one on each side, heads hung and shoulders slumped, like it was a march to their own gallows.

The kid couldn't believe his luck.

He'd slipped the noose.

His friends were about to swing but all the kid felt was glad it was them, not him.

The rancher asked the three young outlaws if they had last words.

All three cried for their mother.

Seeing his two sons were looking away, the old man struck them both hard on the heads with his fists, forcing their full attention to the hanging. "This is what happens to those who do wrong. Time you boys became men and knew what delivering hard justice means."

Pointing the ugly scattergun into the sky near the heads of the horses, the old man triggered both barrels, unleashing twin *kaboom* blasts into the heavens.

The three startled horses bolted.

Clay, Jack, and Billy Joe were jerked out of their saddles as the ropes snapped taut on the branch. Their bodies swung suspended in midair, boots kicking off the ground, bumping into each other like sacks of grain, necks stretching grotesquely elongated until they cracked. The fat one, Jack's head popped clean off and his decapitated body hit the ground with more blood than the kid had ever seen. Billy Joe and Clay got covered with it, eyes bulging and tongues lolling, spinning around and around on the ropes in convulsions until they hung limp on the nooses. The ground below them was stained with their waste as they evacuated. It was ugly. An ugly way to die.

The old man wasted no time, drawing his knife and

slashing the ropes, cutting the bodies down where they landed in a pile.

His two sons were traumatized. The smaller one buckled over and puked in the dirt, shaking like a leaf. The taller one just stood and wept. His body was heaving in sobs.

The kid just watched from the ground.

Walking to his boys, the father put a hand on each of their shoulders. "You're men now. I'm proud of you."

"Can we go home now, Pa?" the older son asked.

"Once we deal with the other one," the old man replied, swinging his gaze to the kid. The thirteen-year-old, all brawn and no brains, locked eyes with him defiantly. As the rancher family walked in his direction, he knew he was not going to get off that easy.

"Hold him down, boys." Faces smeared with dirt and tears, his two sons grabbed the hog-tied kid by each shoulder and pinned him to the dirt so he couldn't move. The kid looked up at the old man looming over him glowering down in judgment, his fearsome countenance inflamed by the angry blaze of firelight from the nearby coal brazier. Yet the old man spoke quietly with something like pity in his eyes as he gave the kid a considering look.

"Where are your parents, boy?"

"Don't got none. Never knew 'em if I did."

"Poor soul. Nobody ever taught you right from wrong. You're just a boy but you ain't ever going to grow up to be a man unless you learn good from bad. A man that doesn't know right from wrong ain't nothing but an animal, no better than cattle. And cattle get branded."

The old man lifted the fiery Q brand from the brazier. It glowed red-hot. Firelight reflected in his sunken mean eyes made them shine with hellfire. To the kid, he looked to be devil, not man.

"Open his shirt," the old man commanded.

The sons ripped open the kid's shirt, tearing cloth and popping buttons, exposing his muscular hairless unmarked chest.

The kid knew what was coming. Now he felt something.

Fear.

The fear grew to raw panic and terror with every inch closer the blazing cattle brand came toward his chest, the heat against his bare flesh growing unbearably hotter, until the old man pressed the red-hot brand into his skin. The sizzling *hiss* of his own roasting flesh filled the kid's nostrils as the smoke from his cooked skin billowed over his face and choked him. The searing blazing *Q* brand burned deep into the center of his chest, the old man leaning against the brand with both hands applying pressure.

As the kid screamed and cried and begged for it to stop, he thought he heard the two sons screaming, too.

It didn't stop. The kid felt the red-hot brand burn all the way through the bones of his chest to his heart and brand him to his soul. Then he went into shock.

Finally the old man lifted the brand off and tossed it on the ground. "Throw water on him." His two sons were hysterical with tears as they bum-rushed a water keg, lifted it, and poured the frigid liquid contents all over the kid, soaking him from head to foot.

The kid didn't move, splayed akimbo in the dirt, a charred and bloody *Q* scorched into the center of his chest. He was in shock and his lips were frothed and eyes rolled up in their sockets, revealing the whites.

But somehow the kid heard the old man's parting words:

"Every day of your life you will look at that brand and remember a man has a choice to make between right and wrong."

Words he would never forget.

When the kid's vision began to focus, his gaze had congealed with a cognition birthed in his eyes that was new, like a star born in the swirling cosmos.

"Put him on a horse."

The kid didn't know where the rancher and his sons found the horse, but somehow they put him on it and sent the mare off into the night with him slumped in the saddle. Then all he knew was pain and darkness until the sun came up and then all he knew was agony.

Long the pain lasted.

But that was a very long time ago.

Now, twenty-one years, three days, and five hours later, Joe Noose, the man the boy had become, was going to get his revenge for what they did to him . . .

CHAPTER 1

His retribution came one fateful winter morning in the unlikely guise of a little boy Joe Noose had never laid eyes on before.

It was December of 1886. The bounty hunter was presently employed as sheriff of Victor, Idaho. A group of badmen led by a very bad woman had killed all the lawmen in Victor. Noose had killed all the villains in turn. The town made him sheriff. Noose took the job only because of his horse. It was a long story.

Physically, Noose looked intimidating enough for law enforcement. Now thirty-four years old, he had grown to be a very big man who stood six foot three without his boots. He was built of solid muscle. The man's pale blue eyes had a steely gaze in a hard face with chipped ruggedly handsome features carved on a boulder of a head covered with thick brown hair. His hands were as large as cattle hooves and the biggest pistol seemed puny in his grip. He would have towered over his former self, the helpless youth who had been tortured, but that boy remained locked forever inside Joe Noose within his mighty frame, for his life began that terrible night long ago . . . the branding had burned a moral code into Joe Noose's soul—a code he'd come to live by.

Over the twenty-one intervening years, the man of action became a bounty hunter whose reputation across the western territories was bringing his dead-or-alive bounties in alive. Joe Noose had a brute instinctual sense of justice and always tried to do the right thing; his credo was never kill a man he didn't have to, but that hadn't stopped him from killing quite a few. He did what he had to do enforcing his own personal code of justice. Sometimes that was complicated. The bounty hunter dabbled in legitimate law enforcement and of late had worked as a Deputy U.S. Marshal and now a sheriff although the badge with the star on his chest was temporary.

The sheriff job ended the day his best friend, Marshal Bess Sugarland, walked into the Victor sheriff's office with the little boy and had him open his shirt. Bess had come with another young U.S. Marshal and together she and he had ridden over the Teton Pass with the child in tow. It was a frozen winter morning as the four of them stood in the warmth of the room.

Shutting the door to the sheriff's office behind them, Joe Noose showed Bess and her two companions to three chairs set in front of the wood-burning stove. The small room was cold and their breath condensed on the air.

She had still not introduced her fellow travelers to Noose. One, the rugged, brooding U.S. Marshal, the other the quiet, reserved little boy of perhaps nine or ten. Noose guessed Bess would make introductions in her own good time, knowing that they were here for a reason. The child seemed nervous and fearful and stayed close to the woman as she showed him a seat then took one herself and smiled at Joe. "The badge looks good on you."

"I'm just the interim sheriff while they find a replacement," Noose explained. "Bonny Kate's gang killed the last sheriff and his deputies before I did for them and the town needed someone to wear the badge. Seemed like the right thing to do when they asked me. You heard about all that fuss." A nod from Bess. "I have a deputy when I need him, which ain't often because the town's pretty quiet these days now that hanging business is done with. Best believe I got the situation in hand. But I'll be moving on soon, I reckon."

"Bounty hunter, then marshal, now sheriff. A body has a hard time keeping track of your movements, Joe," Bess joked.

Noose was glad to see she hadn't lost her ornery sense of humor, but was worried about the huge wooden leg brace she wore on the wounded leg—it was bigger than the one he last saw her wear, and he hoped that the bullet Frank Butler had given her to remember him by wasn't going to mean she would lose that leg. Bess saw him looking at her brace and looked crossly at him. "It ain't gangrene. I'm not losing the damn leg. Just got it jacked up again thanks to you when my horse fell on me while I was riding up the pass with my deputy, looking for you during the fires."

With a sigh of relief, Noose looked over at the lawman who had just sat beside her by the stove. The young man had a hard, angular face, an intense, dark gaze, and was watching Noose closely. "This him, your new deputy?" Noose inquired.

Bess shook her head. "No, my deputy is a greenhorn named Nate Sweet I left back in Jackson to man the U.S. Marshal's office while I came here. Somebody had to mind the store while I was away. Good man, Sweet is, lots of promise." She looked over to the officer with her. "This here is Marshal Emmett Ford."

Joe Noose gave Marshal Ford a long, hard stare—something was familiar about his face, but he couldn't quite place it. "We met before, Marshal?" Noose asked. "I seem to recall your face."

Ford held his gaze respectfully and shook his head, demurring. "No, sir. I don't rightly recollect so."

Noose shrugged. Maybe he was mistaken. He looked a question at Bess. Drew her gaze with him to the silent little boy bundled in coats, sitting staring into the fire. She spoke up. "The boy, we don't know his name because he won't talk. Marshal Ford brought the boy to me a few days ago. So I brought him to you. He's why I come, Joe."

His brows furrowing, not following her conversation, Noose went to the stove, where the pot of coffee brewed, filling the room with a warm, toasty aroma. Without asking if they wanted any, Noose poured two cups and handed them to Bess and Ford, both of whom accepted the hot beverages gratefully and sipped. The boy just watched the fire.

"Sit down, Joe," Bess asked politely. He did. He was about to hear the story and the reason for her visit. "I'll let Marshal Ford tell it. Go on, Emmett."

The young lawman cleared his throat and spoke plainly. "This boy was the only survivor of the massacre of his entire family near Pinedale. Father, mother, two sisters all cut to pieces and strewn about."

"Go on."

"They weren't the first victims of this individual. We think it is one man. Twenty-five people, families, men, women, children, have been butchered by this killer. The ones we know about, anyhow. He has been leaving a trail of bodies from the southern border of Idaho across up into Wyoming and I've been hunting him ever since the spring." The marshal spoke gravely. An intense, personal dedication to catching this killer was plain in his eyes. This was more than a job for Emmett Ford. It was a mission.

"Good hunting," Noose said.

Bess interrupted. "I came to you for a reason, Joe. So did Marshal Ford."

"What reason?"

Ford answered, "You're the best bounty hunter in the western states, Noose. Everybody knows that. There ain't a man in the world you can't track down and apprehend. I haven't been able to catch this killer on my own. I need your help. And there is a five-thousand-dollar dead-or-alive bounty on this individual."

"That's serious money," Noose replied, warming his hands by rubbing them together by the fire. "Very serious money. But the thing is, Marshals, I took a job as sheriff here in this town and gave my word I would perform those duties until a replacement is found. Nobody's arrived to relieve me yet, don't rightly know when they will. I'd surely like to chase down that bounty, but I have a job."

Rising to her feet, Bess's spurs jingled as she walked to the wall and leaned against it by the stove, fixing Noose in her persuasive gaze from an elevated vantage. "Only you can catch this man, Joe."

Noose raised an eyebrow in question, letting her continue. "You don't know the rest. This killer, he always leaves his signature. One you'll understand, Joe." Gesturing to the boy, Bess made the motions with her hands of opening her shirt. "Show him," she gently but firmly bid the child.

Swallowing hard, his eyes vacant, the little boy obediently unbuttoned his coat, then opened his ragged cloth shirt to expose his chest.

When Noose saw what was there, his eyes widened in raw emotion and he rose from his chair to his towering full height, staring unblinkingly at what was on the kid's naked, chicken-bone chest: *The brutal mark of a red-hot branding iron was savagely burned into the child's very flesh—half-healed and raw was seared a single upside-down letter . . .*

$$\partial$$

It was the same brand that Joe Noose bore forever on his own chest, a mark burned into him when he was little older than this boy, by the same brand, by the same man. He felt his own long-healed scar burn freshly under his shirt like a phantom pain, feeling again the white-hot agony of long ago. Noose was speechless as he just stared at the poor child looking up at him with hangdog eyes, displaying his disfigurement with shame.

His knuckles whitening, Noose's fists clenched at his sides in a murderous cold fury that made the cartilage crackle.

When his gaze swung back to Bess Sugarland, she held it confidently. "This is a job for you, Joe. Only you can stop this man."

Nodding, Joe Noose pulled the sheriff's badge off his coat and laid it on the desk.

Noose knew what he had to do. And he wasn't going to be able to wear the sheriff's star doing what he was about to do; no proper lawman could. The big bounty hunter currently employed as interim sheriff of Victor, Idaho, said good-bye to the badge. He was not going to be upholding the law when he caught up with the son of a bitch who branded him, because this was personal and when it was personal the only law was the Law of the Gun.

Lawdog never suited Noose much anyhow.

He just took the job for his horse but his horse was fine now.

Noose stretched his muscular six-foot-three frame to his full height and walked to the window, his leather boots and spurs creaking the floorboards until he stopped, looking out with his pale blue eyes distant and lost in thought. The wintery Idaho sunlight filtering into the Victor sheriff's office showed all the faded bruises and old scars on his handsome granite-block face. His breath condensed in the cold hair in a haze around his face, fogging the glass and clouding and obscuring the view of the town street— a wall that shut off his view as if to tell him his fate was inside the room, which he already knew.

Joe Noose felt Marshal Bess Sugarland's eyes on his back. His friend knew to patiently give him his time to think.

A branding mark the same as his.

Made by the same man, twenty-one years apart.

He had a lot of questions.

"Tell me everything." Joe Noose turned from the window to face Marshal Emmett Ford, fixing him in a hard unwavering gaze that demanded answers, all the facts.

Across the room, Ford stood by the small coal stove, having just poured himself a fresh cup of coffee. He met Noose's gaze without blinking. Despite Noose standing a head taller than Ford and having a hundred pounds of muscle on him, the marshal looked iron fit and was not intimidated. Ford was about Noose's age, rangy and lanky, a lupine cowboy face weathered by the elements. His intense brown eyes bored back into Noose's own as he took a sip of coffee and began his tale.

"I first heard about the branding murders three years ago, where I was posted at the marshal's office in Laramie," Ford said in his soft, even voice. "People passing through from the far north states brought talk with them about folks hacked to pieces who always had the mark of a brand in their chest, men and women. No survivors of any of these attacks, just branded bodies. Like somebody was leaving a message. Of course, the marshal's office got called in to investigate. The assumption was Indians. But that didn't make sense to me because there were no scalpings. It was the brand that made me know this was the work of a white man. Indians don't use cattle brands to mark their cows. Nobody at the U.S. Marshal's office listened to me, though, so I requested special assignment, set out alone, and went to track this murdering SOB down. Been on the bastard's trail ever since. But I come up short. So I'm coming to you."

Noose looked and listened as the wiry male marshal took another sip of coffee. Ford's face looked familiar somehow. But the man looked like a lot of people, not good- or bad-looking, face and hands suntanned from the outdoors; an honest, plain face. It was his eyes that made him different, the deep wells of a man who had seen things no man should see and live to tell. Noose liked that about him and felt an instant kinship with the marshal for unknown reasons he didn't quite understand that made no sense. Snapping his pale-eyed gaze back to Emmett Ford, he saw the Texas marshal was watching him intensely. Noose said: "Go on."

Ford reached up to adjust his weathered Stetson and shrugged in a rangy cowboy way. "Through '85 and '86 I tracked him through Idaho and Utah, then up into Wyoming. Came across bodies in every state. All of them butchered like steers. All of them branded. This villain he moved like a ghost. Nobody saw him." The Ranger spoke in a lazy twang, but Noose noticed that the drawl seemed to come and go as it did with some men.

"Where did you find this boy?"

"Wyoming. In Pinedale. South of Jackson. His entire family was . . . father mother, sisters. Two sisters, girls, at least I think. Honest, it was hard to tell who was who the condition I found them in. All branded. The boy must have got away during the attack, because I found him hiding in the food cellar, got away during the fight maybe because it was . . . well . . . a mess. He had the brand, but he was alive. I took him with me, had him riding with me, hoping he would start talking, give me some clues about the killer, but fact is, the boy ain't said a word since the day I found him. I had him on back of my saddle the last month but The Brander's trail, it went cold. I know he's out there, still killing, still using a red-hot iron to defile the human remains, but truth was I'd just about given up."

Ford's eyes lit up. "Then I hear about a bounty hunter who could find anyone, anywhere, who could track any man that walked on two legs." Ford nodded respectfully in Noose's direction. "I heard about you, sir."

Noose just regarded him evenly. Out the corner of his eye, he could see Bess smiling proudly at him. Ford went on.

"People say Joe Noose is the best bounty hunter in the western territories. Figured I needed help, and if anybody can track the branding killer down it would be you. So I come to find you."

"You did."

Bess piped up. "Marshal Ford came to the U.S. Marshal's office in Jackson and found me first, asked about you. Showed me this boy. Showed me, well . . . I knew this was a job for you, Joe."

While he had been talking, Emmett had also been watching Noose and Bess exchange cryptic glances, unspoken guarded exchanges about the man they were after during the ride. Finally, Emmett spoke up.

"You two know something you're not telling me." When they didn't respond, he added, "With due respect, we're all supposed to be partners on this."

The bounty hunter looked a question at the lady marshal and she nodded, so he shrugged. "Bess didn't tell you, Marshal, because she didn't feel it was her place to. Not until she spoke to me first. Reason is, me taking this job, it's personal. You see, it ain't just because I'm a good manhunter she come to me to track down this killer you're after. I've had dealings with him, a long time ago."

Emmett looked like he'd been slapped. "What the hell are you talking about?" he said.

Noose eyed Emmett evenly with a pale-eyed gaze. "I know who he is."

"So who is he?"

"Same man who did this to me." Noose bit the fingers of his gloves and tugged them off his hands. Then he unbuttoned his coat, then his shirt, exposing his bare torso. Displaying the old scar of the upside-down Q burned into his chest.

Turning pale, the young marshal gaped at the wound, getting his mental bearings until he put it all together.

"Get the picture now?" Noose said.

Emmett nodded. He seemed dazed putting it all together, going through a struggle to maintain his composure.

The bounty hunter closed his shirt and coat and pulled on his gloves.

"But . . . when?"

"Long time ago. Twenty years thereabouts. He was fifty, sixty, mebbe then, puts him seventy to eighty now. Old, but he's the one we're after."

"Who the hell is he? Who *are* we looking for?"

"An old rancher is the one who branded me. He had a mean and twisted sense of justice back then. Reckon he's gotten a lot crazier in twenty years. But it's him. Can't be but one man going around branding people with a *Q* brand iron. I know who we're looking for."

Emmett nodded. "He has a name of sorts, this killer. Some are calling him The Brander."

"It ain't his real name, but it'll do until we learn his true one."

"It's your turn. Tell me everything *you* know," Emmett said.

Noose had already told his story to Bess.

Now he told it to Emmett Ford.

Ten minutes later, the horrific account of his branding as a thirteen-year-old was finished. The young marshal was a level-headed, reserved man not given to displays of emotions. But Noose thought he saw moisture in his listener's eyes when he got to the part about the rancher's sons participating in the hanging and the branding.

"The old son of a bitch lost whatever wits he had, it looks like. Back then, he hanged my friends but just branded me because to him I was too young to hang. Now he's murderin' and brandin' everybody. What I'm saying is he used to have his own kind of moral code, but now he ain't playing favorites. From what you're telling me, his only code is *kill 'em all*."

"You really sure it's him?" Emmett asked. "The Brander."

"Sounds like it, but it's been a long time and we don't know nothing for sure."

The only thing Noose knew for sure was the fiend was escalating his predations. He slaughtered families of men, women, and children and the corpses were piling up. Only this little boy had survived, and he wasn't talking. He didn't have to. All Joe Noose needed to see was the sister branding weal to the one he bore to know who the killer was, who he had to be.

Marshal Bess was sitting with the little boy on her lap near the warmth of the stove, her eyes moving back and forth between Noose and Ford as they talked. Noose gave her a glance, touched by the tender protective way his friend was holding the child, a warm touch that promised no one would ever harm him again the way he had been harmed. That was Bess to the ground.

Switching his gaze to the silent little boy, Noose could not tell if Bess's ministrations had any effect on him, since the kid just stared into the crackling stove fire with a forty-yard stare. The flames danced in his blank eyes, and the pulsing glow of the small fire inside the grate played off his empty features. Noose knew that the little boy was intact on the outside, but inside was gone and not coming back.

His own branding scar began to itch and burn the way it did when it was telling him something. *There but for fortune.* This nameless boy could have been Joe, his scar was telling him—he'd just been stronger, or luckier, but for whatever reason was in a position to put down the fiend like a dog and be sure that the man they called The Brander never branded another living human soul.

So Noose stood across from the small boy, both with the *Q* brand seared on their flesh beneath their shirts, the adult and child version of the same victim.

Emmett Ford set down his coffee and walked up to Joe Noose and with his back straight looked him respectfully square in the eye. "Will you help us catch this killer, sir?"

Noose held Ford's gaze and shook his hand. "Yes, I will."

Jumping out of her chair, Bess swaggered over to the two men, screwing on her hat. "I'm going, too, Joe. Don't you think I ain't. This is the three of us."

No point in arguing with her.

Giving her a big cracked grin, Noose just nodded.

It was decided.

"Let's ride."

CHAPTER 2

The only thing Joe Noose would miss about being sheriff was the warmth of the office coal stove because where they were heading was going to be as cold as the moon for long weeks ahead on the deadly trail. At the end of that trail lay his oldest enemy, who at least would be contending with the same harsh and brutal Wyoming winter conditions his pursuers were. *It would warm up considerably for the old man when Noose sent him to Hell, hotter than a thousand red-hot branding irons.*

The three manhunters spent the rest of the day provisioning for the trip ahead, getting supplies and ammo for their weapons and reshoeing and otherwise tending to their horses. Joe Noose had to get his affairs in order, leaving the job of sheriff of Victor. The plan was to stay one night in Victor then ride out at first light.

The boy stayed behind.

The trail ahead would be dangerous, no place for a child who had already been through enough. Mountainous remote terrain. Temperatures below freezing. Likely gunplay. And a red-hot branding iron with a taste for human flesh. The bounty hunter Joe Noose and the two U.S. Marshals, Bess

Sugarland and Emmett Ford, would ride it together, fully armed, loaded, and locked down.

Noose took care of placing the boy in a proper home. After two months of being sheriff of Victor, Idaho, he knew everybody in town on a first-name basis, so Noose knew right where to go. He left Bess and Emmett behind to saunter across town down to the schoolhouse. There, he had a few words with the kindly teacher Sarah Jones, who agreed to take the boy under her wing and keep him fed and clothed under her roof until proper arrangements could be made. Mrs. Jones felt confident that the youngster would be adopted by one of the local families, because it was a town full of decent people. Thus, Noose found the lad a home with the generous schoolmistress of Victor, who showered the child with attention the minute he was introduced to her.

That done, Noose gathered his weapons. A Sharps large-bore single shot long-range rifle. Two .45 Colt Peacemaker revolvers. Two Winchester lever-action repeating Model 1886 rifles. Twelve boxes of ammo for each. And a bowie knife.

And went to the stable directly.

Copper looked up at him with bright, warm eyes alert to the call to arms. The big bronze-colored stallion exuded muscular energy and vitality, looking like it was itching for action. The bullet wound it had taken in the shoulder had fully healed. Its eyes were bright with anticipation of hitting the trail again with its owner. The steed needed action and was happy it was going to get it. *What took you so long? It's about time.* Its expression spoke. The horse was chomping at the bit.

So was Joe Noose.

"Boy, we got us a job to do."

The look Copper returned said *Let's do it.*

Saddling up, Noose rode his horse out of the Victor stable for the last time, trotting up Main Street to the general store. Where they were going there wouldn't be beds, so the bounty hunter needed to purchase a tent and lean-to to sleep in outdoors, as well as a few buffalo blankets to keep the cold out. Freezing to death on the Wyoming frontier in the winter was a very real danger, even with comrades. Every spring thaw, bodies of man and horse were discovered where they fell and froze . . . sometimes just bones. He swung out his saddle and tethered Copper to the hitching post, then went inside.

He was unsurprised to see Marshal Bess and Marshal Ford already there in the general store, purchasing supplies for the trip. Salted beef, coffee beans, dried beans, corn dodgers, and whiskey were in the process of being loaded into the saddlebags of their horses.

Noose lent a hand loading up the provisions, taking casual note of his saddle mates' firearms. Emmett Ford had a Henry rifle in his saddle scabbard, a big powerful gun used for hunting buffalo. He also packed the more accurate distance weapon, a Sharps rifle. His pistols were twin Remington 1875s. The bounty hunter knew his friend Bess was wearing her father's twin pearl-handled Colt Peacemakers, undoubtedly freshly cleaned and oiled—in her holsters, for she never went anywhere without them. Her regular Winchester repeater rifle was on display. Casting a glance at her saddle as he filled her saddlebag with supplies, Noose saw she had packed plenty of ammo.

The Brander, if that's what the old man called himself these days, had much to fear from the formidable firepower the three who were chasing him were armed with. It would give any sensible man pause.

The few last details taken care of, it was time to make tracks.

Noose wrote his resignation note and, explaining his departure, personally placed the note in the hand of Mayor Ralph Wiggins, who was sorry to see him go. His last act as sheriff of Victor was to promote his deputy Alan Mills to fill his post as interim sheriff until a permanent position could be filled. Noose guessed that probably wouldn't be anytime soon and that his deputy Mills would grow into the job and hold it for a long time. They shook hands. Noose wished him luck and it was done. He was back to being a bounty hunter.

After a good night's sleep in the local hotel, the three manhunters were rested, breakfasted, and saddled up as dawn broke over the town, ready to begin their ride across the Teton Pass.

"I'd like to swear you in again as a Deputy U.S. Marshal, like I did with Bonny Kate," Bess said, taking out a badge.

Noose smiled and shook his head. "Two marshals on this job is quite enough. Better I work outside the law on this one, Bess. You just tell me which way we're riding."

"Back across the pass to Jackson. Check in there, provision, and ride south to Pinedale, where the last murders took place. Figure it's two days' ride." Marshal Bess had it all worked out. "Figured you'll want to check the crime scene. We left it untouched."

"That boy's family, right?"

She gave a trenchant nod.

"Any idea which direction the old man rode after he killed them?" Noose watched Bess through the falling snow, his pale blue eyes piercing hers through the veil of snowflakes pouring over the brim of his big black Stetson.

She shook her head. "It snowed over. Savvied you'd be able to figure that out from clues at the scene and track him."

"You savvied right." He thought for a moment. "How long ago did the murders occur?"

"It's frozen solid out there, but looks like no more than a month."

"Means the old son of a bitch got a month's head start ride on us."

"You'll catch him."

"Not sitting here."

"Then we best get a move on."

"Yes, ma'am." Noose cracked a warm, broken grin at Bess and she lit right up. "Daylight is wasting."

The three spurred their horses.

They rode hard out of Victor.

Three hours south on the trail brought Joe Noose, Bess Sugarland, and Emmett Ford to the edge of where the forest fires had blazed across the mountains last summer until the early-fall rains had extinguished them. Noose slowed Copper to a trot, stunned at the devastation: tens of miles of forestation had been reduced to blackened cinders. Far as the eye could see, charred matchsticks of what once were pine trees a hundred feet high poked out of the snowbanks in dead columns of burned-out tree trunks that seemed to go on forever; the towering mountains, gorges, and ravines of the Teton Pass stood starkly exposed through the endless rows of scorched trees jutting skyward like porcupine quills everywhere Noose looked. The air smelled of burned wood all these months later. It was a sight to give a man pause.

All this magnificent forest lost because of lady outlaw Bonny Kate Valence, whose storied exploits had left a path of legendary destruction in her wake. Noose himself had started the fire to save her life so he could get her to the gallows to hang. He didn't have a choice—it had been his job. The bounty hunter did not tell his saddle partners he had tossed the match, as it would do little good. The forest would grow back. Bonny Kate wouldn't.

Certainly, it was a lot less dangerous riding back over the Teton Pass than it had been riding up it for Joe Noose—the fires were out and nobody was shooting at him as they had been then, a few months ago. The hairs on the back of his neck prickled as he remembered the hellish heat of those apocalyptic flames he had so narrowly escaped.

Today the ride was peaceful and quiet. The Teton Pass was preternaturally silent, just the whistle of the wind and sound of falling snowflakes and creak of their saddles. There were no birds, having no place to nest in the dead, frozen tundra. Noose, Bess, and Emmett didn't talk, lost in their thoughts in the sobering surroundings.

Midday on the ride, Bess reached into her saddlebags and handed Joe Noose three hundred and fifty dollars cash tied with a string.

"What's that for?" he asked.

"It's the bounty for Bonny Kate Valence for services rendered. You got her to the gallows. And the Marshals Service threw in an extra fifty dollars. It's what they would have paid the hangman."

"Thanks, Bess." He chuckled. "Reckon I earned that money." He took the pack of money and put it in his coat.

"Reckon you did." She smiled. "Put paid on it. You can deposit it at the bank in Jackson when we stop by the marshal's office in town, if you don't want to carry that much cash."

"I'll do that."

The lady marshal's brow furrowed. "I'm sorry, Joe."

"What the hell for, Bess?"

"For all the trouble that job and that woman gave you. Straight up, I was worried she was going to be a handful but I figured one woman couldn't get the better of you, even a hellcat like that. Not after the Butler Gang. Maybe I should have thought twice, but I was in a fair fix with her hanging scheduled in two days and Mackenzie and Swallows out of the picture. I leaned on you as a friend."

"That's what friends are for." The bounty hunter grinned. "Glad I could help."

"Well, sorry anyway."

"Bess?"

"Yeah?"

"I'd do it again."

"Joe Noose, you are some piece of work." They shared a laugh. She shook her head ruefully. "When that Arizona sheriff rode in with those men of his looking for Bonny Kate, I couldn't believe it."

"Then there was her old boyfriend."

"There was *somebody else* out to get her?"

"She was popular in an unpopular kind of way, let's just say."

"You must have had your hands plumb full."

"I dealt with them. And they got dealt with. I warned 'em. At that point, I was harboring a few sympathies for the woman. Figured maybe she got a raw deal from folks."

"You liked her."

"Not at the end. But at the beginning, yeah, she was good company."

"Did she—did you—?"

Noose looked at Bess square in the face, eyebrow lifted in question, a glint of humor in his pale eye.

She rolled hers. *"You know."*

"Not even a kiss." He shook his head with a smile.

"But I bet she tried."

"Yes, she did."

"That was a whole lot of woman. You and her alone on the trail, how did you resist?"

"I never mix business with pleasure."

"Bet you thought about it."

"Once or twice."

"God, I hated that woman's guts."

"She liked you."

"How do you know?"

"Bonny Kate told me. Said you and her were a lot alike."

"That'll be the day."

"Said you were both strong, independent women in a man's world who stood up for yourselves and such."

"What did you say?"

"I said she wasn't a shadow of the woman you were, and I meant it."

Marshal Bess Sugarland dropped Joe Noose's gaze, he saw her eyes had moistened, and that was the last they spoke of the late Bonny Kate Valence.

The three riders were the only movement along the rugged trail as they rode steadily upward toward the peak of the pass.

Emmett spoke up. "If we find The Brander—"

"Ain't no if. It's when," Noose replied.

"Good to hear you say that. When we do find him I mean to take him in alive."

"There ain't gonna be no taking him alive, Marshal. He's a sick animal. You put a sick animal down."

Emmett reined his horse abruptly. The other two halted their mounts. The three riders faced one another on the empty, desolate snowbound pass. "You mean to kill him?"

"Hell yes, I do."

"But you have a reputation for bringing dead-or-alive bounties in alive."

"This man is the exception."

Emmett shook his head firmly. "I'm the marshal and this is my quarry, Noose. I want this individual captured and taken back to Laramie and stood for trial. I want to question him."

"Shoot first, ask questions later."

"The problem with shooting first and asking questions later is the wrong man getting shot."

"I never shoot the wrong man."

Noose and Emmett locked eyes and the young lawman held the rugged bounty hunter's rough gaze. Tension flared between them like a struck match.

Bess cleared her throat. "Settle down, boys. Correction, Marshal Ford, you're one of *two* marshals on this job. Since I'm the marshal of Jackson, my authority supersedes yours in Wyoming and I agree with Joe Noose. We're after a mad-dog killer. My standing order is to shoot him on sight. And shoot to kill."

"I don't like it." Emmett scowled. "We're lawmen, not assassins."

"Duly noted."

It was two to one. Tensely hunched in his saddle, Emmett Ford didn't like this one little bit. His face was shadowed under the brim of his hat, but the bright winter sun caught the gleam in his eye of a man biding his time.

The trio rode on over the peak of the quiet Teton Pass, the trail winding downward now, revealing the sprawling winter landscape of the Jackson Hole basin spreading out below. Out there, the site of the last branding slaying lay ahead twenty-two miles due east. With luck, they'd pick up a few clues and hopefully catch The Brander's trail.

It was day one and already they had their differences.

CHAPTER 3

The crime scene was a log cabin.

A black speck on the white landscape visible from a half mile off.

It was a bad place, Noose could tell, even from a great distance. The vast silence of the wintery Wyoming snowfall normally brought a sense of peaceful stillness to the bounty hunter. But here it was a vacuum, an absence of life, the silence of death, and the still of the tomb. Black crows circled overhead and perched on branches, cawing, contributing to the atmosphere of dread; a murder of crows nestling in the branches.

Noose, Bess, and Emmett trudged their horses through the steadily falling snow piling up to the steeds' knees. It was slow going.

His guns holstered, Noose saw no reason to have his weapons at the ready—he knew there was nothing alive at the cabin.

Gradually, with each step of their horses, the place came into view.

The cabin was hand-built, sturdy but threadbare, in dilapidated condition. Part of the roof had caved in under the weight of ten feet of snow. The dangling icicles on the windows looked like frozen tears. The black shuttered windows and shadowed doorway resembled the coal eyes and mouth of a snowman or, the closer they rode, a skull.

Copper's muscular flanks shivered between Joe Noose's legs and not from the cold. The man looked at his horse and saw its ears were pinned back. Copper was spooked. Its big moist brown eyes were wider than normal as it kept a sharp wary lookout on its surroundings. Noose patted his stallion's huge, tawny neck and stroked its flowing golden withers. "Easy, boy."

Emmett dismounted first and strode up to the porch, checking to see if the U.S. Marshals order he had nailed to the front door was intact. It was. He efficiently circled the cabin on patrol, checking to see the windows and door were shut as he had left them. Noose and Bess remained in their saddles until Emmett trundled around the edge of the homestead, up to his waist in snow, then nodded things were to his satisfaction. "I closed the place up and put a 'No Trespassing by order of the U.S. Marshals Service' flyer up. Looks like nobody meddled with the place. Not like there was much to steal."

"This was where you found the boy."

"Yes, the only survivor. Hiding under the dead body of his mother to keep warm. I found them in the food cellar."

"Did you bury the victims?" Noose asked.

Emmett shook his head. "The ground was froze hard as rock. Couldn't get a shovel in. I left the bodies inside the cabin where they fell. Put ice on 'em figuring the cold would preserve the corpses for transport later. Then I sealed the place up and rode for Jackson to find both of you."

Dismounting, Noose and Bess led, then tied, their horses to a tree a hundred yards out. There were closer trees to hitch them, but the bounty hunter and the lady marshal both saw their mounts were nervous being near the house.

"This place gives me the creeps," Bess said quietly to Noose. "The horses don't like it."

"It's a place of death," he muttered.

"Not looking forward to what we're about to see in there."

"It'll give us clues."

"See you been giving the side-eye to Marshal Ford. You don't think he knows what he's doing?"

"Haven't spent enough time with him to gauge. So far he seems competent. Pretty much done what I'd have done. Smartest thing he's done yet is rounding me up."

"That's a fact."

Moments later, the friends had hiked back through the snow and stood with the third of their number next to the porch. Emmett waited patiently in the cold, giving a deferential nod to his female counterpart. "Other than the roof caving in on account of the weight of the snow, this place looks pretty much like I left it, Marshal."

"You cut sign when you first arrived?" Noose asked.

"There had been a snow dump. Saw faint horse tracks but couldn't be sure when they were made."

Noose considered that. "Direction?"

"Northeast."

"You rode northwest. To Jackson."

Emmett nodded. Noose watched him a long beat, then swung his pale gaze to the foreboding door of the cabin.

"The bodies. Show me." Noose nudged his jaw.

Walking onto the porch, sliding his Remington 1875 revolver out of his side holster, Emmett Ford took position by the front door and shot a warning glance back to his saddle mates. "It ain't pretty."

Noose stepped onto the frozen, creaking boards of the porch, caked with ice. Bess followed. Their spurs jingled. "It never is."

A sharp *crack*. Noose's hand shot out and grabbed Bess's elbow just as her boot broke a rotted board and her leg dropped through to the shin. With the strength in his one arm, the huge cowboy lifted her back onto her feet on the porch.

Emmett kicked in the door with a solid blow of his boot, and it swung wide. A blast of frosty chill air laden with the stench of dead meat rushed out to greet them.

The three entered the cabin, stepping into the stale, still atmosphere of the place. It was cold as sin. If Hell were known for lower temperatures, this would be the place.

Wind whistled in a high banshee keening sound with the gusts of snow falling through the hole in the roof.

The furnishings of the cabin were spare and few. A potbellied stove. A straw mattress. A chair. A table, now overturned. Every surface of the entire single room was covered with a film of frost, half the color of ice, half the dark burgundy color of blood that had frozen.

"Lordy," Bess gasped.

Four bodies lay strewn on the floor and against the walls. One man, three women. They were still covered with the chunks of ice that Emmett Ford had placed over the human remains to preserve them in the cold.

Emmett kicked a few pieces of ice away from the man, revealing his frigid body had been worked over with an ax, his legs chopped off below the knee, the wounds long cauterized with frost.

All of the victims had been branded on the forehead.

Each bore the scalded, seared Q brand on their foreheads, burned deep into their blackened flesh.

"How long were they dead?"

"The blood was fresh."

"You cut sign?"

"Said I did."

"You couldn't have been a day's ride behind the killer. Why'd you let him get away?"

"Because the boy needed medical. Had to get him tended to first."

"Fair enough." Cocking an eyebrow, Joe Noose looked out the window at the heavy pristine snowfall glistening with crystallized frost on the landscape outside, any horse tracks long buried under many feet of snow. "The snow probably covered up The Brander's tracks days before you got here, Marshal Ford. But horses ain't the only thing that leaves tracks . . ."

Bess looked up to see Joe Noose was staring down at the floor as he walked in a methodical trek of the room, pacing step by step first up one side, then down the same side, then taking a step to the side and repeating the process. His expelled breath condensed in twin funnels of mist out his nostrils like a snorting bull as he checked the crime scene with great deliberation. "What are you looking for, Joe?" she asked.

"Bootprints in the blood."

"Those bootprints could be mine," the other marshal pointed out.

The bounty hunter shook his head, brows furrowed as he walked the floor with a downcast focused gaze. "The blood was froze by the time you got here, you said. The Brander was stepping in fresh blood. Like right here."

Noose crouched down, looking at the large print of a boot in a frozen crimson relief.

Bess and Emmett crouched down beside Joe and studied the grisly bootprint. Noose traced it with the finger of his glove. "Man's boot. Size twelve. Chipped heel right here." Pointing out a visible crack in the heel, he looked at Bess, then Emmett. "We can identify this bootprint when we see it again, and identify its owner from it." Grabbing his bowie knife from his belt, Noose drove the blade through the weakened old boards, making several hard chops and cutting the foot-and-a-half-square section of the floorboards with the bootprint in the frozen blood free. He rose and handed the section of floor to Bess. "Wrap a blanket around this, pack it secure in your saddlebags. We're taking it with us."

Marshal Bess nodded, took it, and left, heading outside to the horses. Now they were alone, and Noose looked at Marshal Ford. "Who were these people, Marshal?"

"I don't know."

"The other people The Brander put his iron to and killed, who were they? What connection do they have?"

"None."

"You sure about that?"

"No. Just ain't found a connection between his victims yet." Emmett shrugged. Noose grunted. "You'll be the first to know."

"Joe!"

The woman's voice out on the porch brought the two men swiftly outside. She was crouched down by the floorboards of the porch. The section of floor with the bloody bootprint Noose cut was wrapped in a soft blanket beside her. Bess was digging something out of the porch floorboards with her knife.

An old broken boot heel.

Covered with a raspberry-colored frost of frozen blood.

"Looks like The Brander put his foot through the porch like I did, left a little something behind."

"Let me see that," Noose said. Bess handed the broken heel to him. "It's size twelve. Got to be from his boot."

"Unless he has a spare pair of boots, he'll be looking to get that repaired next town he comes to," Bess said. "If we get lucky, we got us a lead."

"But which direction did he go?" Emmett worried.

Noose looked out over the white landscape. "The snow covered any tracks. Which direction The Brander went after he left here is anybody's guess. It's a coin toss. But The Brander has been targeting farms and ranches and most of those are within twenty miles of some kind of town so the owners can get supplies. He needs to get that boot fixed. My guess is he's heading toward one of the towns in the area. Trouble is, there's a lot of towns around here north, south, east, and west. The Brander could have lit out to any of them . . . We might as well pick one, ride in, ask if anybody seen an old man missing three fingers of his right hand with a *Q* brand on his saddle, maybe had his boot repaired. First thing we got to do is pick up his trail. It ain't gonna be easy. We'll need luck, like Marshal Bess says."

The two marshals nodded. Emmett spoke up. "Now, I preserved this crime scene here for you to see, Noose, you seen what you need to see?"

"Reckon."

"Then, Marshal Sugarland, the next sheriff's office we pass, I'd like to alert them of the location so they can send some men to collect the bodies and give them a proper burial."

"That's the decent thing to do, and it's fine with me," she said, nodding. "Nearest Sheriff is Alpine, twenty-one miles northeast that way." She pointed. "Joe, okay with you, we ride northeast?"

The big hunter shrugged. "Until we pick up The Brander's trail, one direction is as good as any other."

The trio of manhunters mounted up.

The three rode out into the deep snowdrifts, twelve horses' legs pushing through snow coming up to their knees, burrowing a new trail where none existed.

CHAPTER 4

The *Q* branding iron is cold now.

The blackened metal tufted with snow.

The lone rider has it in his saddlebag, next to his Henry rifle and his ax. They are his tools. The brand is his signature.

It will taste flesh again soon.

The Brander grips the reins in a gloved mangled hand with three fingers missing. His long white hair falls over his shoulders around a face that is a frozen mask from the chill but he isn't cold.

His hate keeps him warm.

And it isn't far now.

CHAPTER 5

Over the next week, Joe Noose, Bess Sugarland, and Emmett Ford rode south past La Barge to Big Piney, broadening their search.

They had no luck in La Barge, a small settlement in the plains with a population of less than forty. The sheriff's office was closed because the lawman had recently passed away and the position in the remote outpost had yet to be filled. Given the lack of crime in that section of the boondocks it was not a priority, the bootmaker they spoke to told them, although he felt confident they would have a new sheriff come spring, or definitely by fall. As for the bootmaker, he had no requests for a heel repair by any man in since last winter, three fingers missing on one hand or not. And he had heard of no murders involving a cattle brand. The trio rode on, struggling to pick up The Brander's trail.

"It's like finding a needle in a haystack," Emmett said.

"Or a snowflake in a blizzard," Bess said.

"Keep riding," said Noose, not one for idle words like analogies.

Four days later, in Big Piney the three manhunters stopped at the sheriff's office and Marshal Bess reported the killings at the cabin thirty miles north. The sheriff was a weathered, stocky, rough-hewn man in his fifties named Bill Armstrong, who took the news with shock and wasted no time rounding up his deputy to ride north and retrieve the bodies. Armstrong told the two marshals and the bounty hunter no other such similar slayings had been reported in his jurisdiction—the Q branding would have been news—but acknowledged that with the harsh winter conditions, many of the local ranches and farms were cut off by the snows this time of year and communications were infrequent and poor. Bess told the sheriff that she and her hunting party were going to be on the trail until they caught the killer, and if he learned any information to relay it by telegraph to the U.S. Marshal's office in Jackson to the attention of her deputy Nate Sweet, for she would be checking in with him when their location permitted.

While in Big Piney, Noose, Bess, and Emmett asked questions at the grocery store. No sightings had been reported of an old man missing three fingers on his right hand. At the bootmaker, nobody fitting The Brander's description had come in to have a heel repaired on his left boot. In fact, the man had no business at all the past two weeks.

Before leaving town, the manhunters reprovisioned and reshod one of the horses, and then they were off into the ice-cold harsh snows of the Wyoming frontier.

The third night, they made camp in a canyon and sat around a campfire, trying to keep warm. The roaring flames kept back the chilling temperature as they ate a dinner of salted beef, hot beans, and coffee. Bess saw Noose staring into the fire, lost in thought, his finger under his shirt tracing the brand. She didn't ask, but the distant look in his eyes was unlike him, and she guessed he was thinking about another fateful fire many years ago and a flaming brand turning red-hot.

"The old fella that branded you. Can you remember anything more about him that could give us some kind of description?" Emmett asked Noose as they ate.

"It was a long time ago. He was old back then. At least he looked old to me. Remember, I was just a kid, and it was dark. Fifties or sixties, mebbe. Puts him seventies or eighties now. Suppose he could be in his sixties. Seems pretty old to be killing all these folks and covering as many miles as The Brander has been doing, but he was a tough son of a bitch then. Some men just look old. I recollect him as tall. Thin. Long white hair. And like I said, he was missing three fingers on his right hand. Looked like a chicken claw."

"That's a damn good piece of description for us to be looking for."

"A good start. Folks will remember a man missing all them fingers on that right hand."

"You said he had two sons," Bess reminded Noose. "Could The Brander be one of them?"

Emmett seemed to give that suggestion some consideration.

"They had all their fingers," Noose replied. "At least they did when I knew 'em. Weren't nothing but a pair of scared kids. Soft. We're looking for the father." He nodded decisively to himself, grimly resolved. "He was the crazy one."

As there was little civilization farther south until they reached Evanston a hundred miles away, Noose decided they had been heading in the wrong direction, so after a group discussion, it was decided the hunting party would turn around and ride east toward Green River.

Consulting a map, the three made note of the nearest towns and hubs of civilization north, east, and west, rejecting farther south as that was the direction the killer's previous victim had been and they saw no reason for him to backtrack. Otherwise, the branding slayings seemed to follow no logic or pattern besides the capricious bloodthirsty whims of the fiend committing them.

The trail of The Brander was colder than the frigid subzero Wyoming winter landscape the three manhunters rode through. Much of the time, they couldn't see ten feet ahead of them. Noose felt that symbolized their progress with their quarry.

Who would The Brander's next victim be?

Where would he strike next?

Wyoming was a big territory.

For all they knew, he'd already left Wyoming.

The progress with the horses was slow. Roads, when there were ones, were ankle-deep in snow for the horses. Trails, those they could find, were knee-deep. When they had to cross open plains, their mounts had to shove on through drifts that reached their bellies.

It was a guessing game as to the location of the killer they were hunting, trying to pick up his trail, but doggedly Noose, Bess, and Emmett persevered. With each fruitless day and more miles covered turning up nothing but a head cold, that determination grew.

The foreman at the corral in Smith hadn't seen any old man missing three fingers.

Neither did the wagon master on the road on the plain south of Bondurant.

Two bootmakers twenty miles apart in Freemont had repaired several broken heels, but the owners had all their fingers. Business for them at least appeared to be better than it was for their counterparts to the south.

"These folks that this guy you're calling The Brander put his iron to and killed, what's the connection?" Noose once again asked Emmett.

"None I've been able to tell. Does there have to be a connection?"

"The man who branded me didn't seem the type to do it for no reason."

"Even if there is a connection with the men," Bess pointed out, "that don't explain why he is branding the families."

"Reckon it don't."

Joe Noose, Bess Sugarland, and Emmett Ford rode on through the sleet and slush, bundled against the relentless snow that always seemed to be in their chests as if trying to push them back, to stop them from reaching The Brander.

It was the last week of December, and they had been on the trail for three weeks and two days.

CHAPTER 6

Holed up on his isolated farm during a blizzard in the middle of nowhere thirty miles away from anything had been driving Buck Dodge nuts with cabin fever.

The cowboy had been crawling out of his skin all morning. He paced the floor of his small hardscrabble house, his loaded carbine rifle close at hand. He was wrapped in three blankets over his coat and gloves and was still cold. The wind moaned through the planks of the walls. The broken roof groaned under the weight of four feet of snow. The hinges on the door rattled. The man was hearing things, and hearing nothing, which had become the same thing. His humble spread was socked in with snow. He couldn't shake the feeling of unease. Every ten minutes, Dodge cracked the wood shutters and looked out, checking if anything was out there beyond the vague outlines of the buck-and-rail fence and small barn buried under piles of heavy snow so deep it made them vague, unrecognizable shapes.

He saw no horses, no men; no intruders stood out against all the oppressive whiteness, no movement whatsoever but the ceaseless swirls of snowflakes.

There was nothing out there but the blizzard.

But Dodge could not shake the feeling something bad was closing in.

His dog Blue hadn't stopped barking the last two hours straight. Sounding the alarm about something. A big tough old mastiff and a good guard dog was Blue. The animal was the man's best friend. The hound didn't bark at just anything and whatever had him riled up today wasn't wildlife, a moose, or deer. It might have been wolves, but the dog's throaty vociferations would have run off any wolf pack by now. And Blue was still barking, the sound of each bark driving nails into the cowboy's skull.

Just as he was about to close the shutters against the dog's infernal barking, there was a burst of motion at a tree. He raised the gun only to see a murder of crows explode into the empty sky, wings slashing like black blades. Just birds. Boy, was he jumpy.

Dodge had been stuck indoors for the last week. The loneliness was getting to him. The man blamed his nerves on a bad Wyoming winter whose blizzard conditions and bitter subzero temperatures made it impossible to leave the farm and get to town. His larder was stocked with enough provisions, and there was plenty to eat and drink so that wasn't the problem. Being cut off was. Being snowed in made people landlocked in these parts. The roads and trails were too deep to ride any great distance. The isolation had the better of him and kept him on constant edge. The farm five feet deep in snow had become for Buck Dodge a prison with frozen walls.

At least his house was usually warm, his potbellied stove normally ablaze, filled with burning wood, keeping the two rooms toasty, even if the air was close and stale. But he was out of firewood. A cord of it was piled by the barn not a hundred yards from his front door, but today for some reason he was afraid to leave the safety of the house and go out there. Because it now was very cold inside and getting colder, soon he would be forced to go out or freeze to death.

The cowboy's ears perked.

His dog had stopped barking.

"Blue?"

Dead silence.

"Blue!"

Grabbing his rifle, Dodge went to the window and threw open the shutters. No barking came from outside. Something wasn't right.

He loved his dog. The cowboy decided to check it out. Shouldering on his heavy sheepskin coat and tugging on his work gloves, Buck Dodge took his rifle and stepped out the front door. A wall of snow and cold wind met him head-on in a frigid blast and he forged out into it, Stetson hat low over his eyes. Keeping the rifle leveled, he swung it right and left outside the house, but there was nothing out there. The arctic wind froze his bare ears even as it deafened him with its bitter howl. *"Blue!"* he yelled into the din, the volume of his voice swallowed by the wind. *"Who's out here? I'm armed!"*

The dog was chained around the side of the house to a railroad spike in the ground.

The hound's bark had been silenced.

Gripping his rifle, Dodge flattened against the side of his house and advanced sideways step by step along the wall. Snow and sleet blew into his eyes, and he swept his coat across his face to clear them. When he reached the corner, the cowboy leapt around, leveling the cocked rifle at . . .

Nothing.

The dog was gone. No blood, no signs of struggle, the hound was just not there anymore. *Had it run off, chasing an interloper?* Buck Dodge closed in with his rifle, checking for the dog's prints in the snow, but the prints he saw were not canine but human.

A man's fresh footsteps in the snow.

The tracks were leading around the other side of the house, away from him.

Buck followed the bootprints, his rifle held at the ready in his gloves. Again, he flattened against the right side wall of the shack, inching closer and closer to the corner to the rear of the house. When he reached it, he took a few hyperventilating breaths and leapt around, ready to fire and expecting to step into a barrage of bullets.

None came his way.

The tracks of the boots in the snow continued along the side of the house, then turned the corner.

The unseen son of a bitch was playing games with him.

Where the hell was Blue?

The smells of cold damp wood and snow filled his nostrils, but there was a new, strange smell.

Hot metal.

Flattening against the wall, the cowboy advanced with his gun toward the corner to the left side wall of his home, throwing glances left and right to be sure whoever the trespasser was didn't ambush him from back the way he came. His boots crunched on the snow as he passed the rear window of the house. Turning his head, he snuck a quick glance through the glass window into his shack.

Crash!

The red-hot branding iron smashed through the window

in an explosion of shattering glass and pile-drove against the bare flesh of his face, the blazing *Q* sizzling into his flesh, searing the mark of brand into his features in a cloud of steam and smoke of burning skin and hair!

In a hideous high-pitched scream of agony, Buck Dodge staggered back, stumbling into the deep snow, hands dropping his rifle as they went to his face, white-hot burning pain enveloping his head.

Writhing on the ground, he heard the fast footfalls running across the floorboards out his front door and crunching louder on the snow as his assailant rushed up to him. *"You son of a bitch, you burned me, you dirty son of a bitch!"* Dodge shrieked, pulling his hands away to see the shadowy figure standing over him, an undefined blur of blackness because the cowboy's eyelids had been scalded shut over his eyeballs.

All Buck Dodge could see was the glowing red curlicue getting closer and closer, feeling the unbearable heat of the metal intensifying on his face until the brand pressed against his skull and he smelled the smoke of his own roasting flesh and his own tortured screams filled his ears.

Ten minutes later, The Brander wipes his rusty hatchet clean on the white snow that isn't soaked with blood.

His victim is in pieces.

He has chopped him up after using the branding iron to interrogate him, repeating his single question over and over until he got his answer.

The fiend's work is done here.

Now his next work waits to be done and his question has been answered, where he needs to go to do it.

Having left its signature, the brand, its business finished for now, is extinguished in the cold snow with a steaming *hiss*—the metal goes black, cold, and dead, waiting to burn again. And again.

Walking out into the snowstorm, the tall skeletal figure disappears into the swirling snowflakes, then in an unseen *creak* of saddle, *clink* of stirrup, and *clop* of hooves is gone.

CHAPTER 7

A hundred and fifty miles south in Jackson Hole, Wyoming, Deputy Marshal Nate Sweet, whom Marshal Bess had left in charge of the U.S. Marshal's office in her absence, was thinking this was not what he signed up for.

The laconic thirty-year-old lawman with the Johnny Appleseed complexion and steady disposition found himself this morning having tea with the five women from the Jackson Hole Women's Auxiliary at the town council offices off Broadway. He sat on the sofa sipping cold tea in the plush office surrounded on all sides by five bossy middle-aged councilwomen whose perfume was as suffocating as the weaponized estrogen sucking the air out of the room. The ladies, a major political power in the town of Jackson who pretty much ran things municipally, were in a foul temper. As a group, they were none too pleased that their handpicked female marshal Bess Sugarland, the representative of their gender they basically bullied into office as the first female U.S. Marshal in Wyoming, was absent from her post. The ladies were even less pleased that a young *male* marshal, a deputy at that, occupied it. Sweet privately admonished himself for not getting Bess to write a letter explaining the reasons for her absence on the hunt of the branding killer, because none of these councilwomen bought his explanation, no matter how many times he patiently explained it to them. The deputy was trying his best to be polite, but a gunfight with both hands tied behind his back and no bullets in his gun would have been more pleasurable and less effort. These women never shut up, he couldn't get a word in edgewise, and Nate Sweet didn't know how much more he could take.

"When *is* Marshal Bess going to be back in Jackson?" demanded Eleanor Rittenhouse, a pushy aristocratic woman from Philadelphia who had a ranch in neighboring Solitude and served as council treasurer.

Sweet returned her accusatory gaze politely. "For the third time, Mrs. Rittenhouse, I do not have that information. Marshal Sugarland is out on the trail on a dangerous man-hunt and has advised me that it could take weeks or months before they subdue their quarry. Before Bess left, as I have said several times already, she left me in charge as interim marshal to perform all marshal duties in her stead."

"How do *we* know *you're* not *lying*?" snapped Florence McCoy, a heavyset matron who was city council president and let everybody know it.

"Excuse me?" Sweet blinked.

"How do *we* know that Marshal Bess has not been *forced* out of office just because she's a woman!"

"By who?" This kept getting more ridiculous.

"By the Jackson Gentlemen's Business Bureau, that bigoted cabal of *men* in this town who everyone in this room knows pulled strings to get our woman marshal thrown out and replaced with a man! Sending *you* to oust her. How do *we* know this isn't another *male conspiracy*?"

"That's silly." Sweet was getting a headache trying not to laugh.

"We don't think it's silly at all, do we, ladies?" Heads shook gravely. Murmurs of assent. Florence stirred her colleagues up with her melodramatic aria of pompous rhetoric. "As *president* of Jackson Hole Women's Auxiliary, I say if it *walks* like a duck and *quacks* like a duck then by God, it *is* a duck. Now, Marshal Bess is not *physically* present in Jackson being town marshal and *you*, Deputy, wear *her* badge and sit in *her* seat, and I say that is empirical evidence of a *conspiracy* by the male establishment."

At last, Sweet understood why Bess complained so much to him about the daily town politics she had to deal with as marshal. As her deputy, his interface with the public was strictly procedural and town politics was his boss's department. But now that Sweet was getting a taste, he gained even more respect for his boss with the political nonsense she had to contend with. Out of respect for Bess, Sweet kept his temper since she always did, and didn't raise his voice. "It just isn't true, ladies. Ask anyone. I have nothing but respect for Marshal Bess Sugarland, she's the finest woman and finest lawman I've ever met. It's an honor to be her deputy. She is totally dedicated to her job and this town. She's out on temporary assignment, but she's coming back and when she does, you'll all be happy. Take my word."

"Well," Eleanor huffed. "We can't ask Bess. She's not here."

"She's not here because she's on assignment."

"Marshal Sugarland did not tell us anything about that."

"She didn't have tell you anything about it. It's marshal business."

"So we're just supposed to believe this because you say so? Who put you in charge?"

"Marshal Bess did."

And so it went, around and around. Thoughts of using the councilwomen for target practice did cross Sweet's mind.

An accord of sorts was ultimately arrived at after three wasted hours when Deputy Marshal Sweet informed the fine ladies of the Jackson Hole Women's Auxiliary that he was, in fact, in touch with Marshal Bess on a periodic basis by way of telegraph; she checked in with the Jackson U.S. Marshal's office from time to time out on the trail whenever she came upon a town with a telegraph. The council battle-axes managed to extricate from long-suffering Sweet a promise that, at the first available opportunity, he would get Marshal Bess to telegraph a personal confirmation to the Jackson Hole Women's Auxiliary that she had indeed made him marshal in her stead, and she would indeed be returning when whatever business was so important it required her to abandon her loyal constituents was completed. Sweet knew Bess would be pissed being asked to report to the women's council who she believed were as big a pain in the ass as Sweet did— *he knew her telegram would consist of three words: kiss my ass*—but the deputy was at the point where he would agree to anything to escape the clutches of the councilwomen.

When at last he got out of there in one piece, Sweet felt a surge of relief as he hit the frigid cold fresh air of Broadway. The temperature had dropped to below freezing in the few hours he had been at the council meeting, and despite the bright sunshine he was freezing his ass off. It was a beautiful Wyoming day, though, so the deputy took his time strolling through Jackson. He enjoyed the hike back to the office, even though the streets were covered in knee-deep snow and he was chilled to the bone. Sweet was rattled by those council broads and being outside cleared his head. This job was tougher than it looked.

Three months ago, Nate Sweet was a fresh recruit who had been assigned by the Cody U.S. Marshals Service headquarters to report to Jackson to serve as new marshal Sugarland's deputy after she had replaced two other marshals killed in the line of duty the month before. Sweet was cocky and overconfident, excited to begin his first assignment after his training, but things between his new boss and him got off to a bumpy start. First, Sweet didn't know *he* was a *she*; Cody headquarters neglected to inform him that the marshal he would be reporting to was a woman— perhaps so he didn't turn the assignment down—how was he supposed to know he'd be working for a woman? So first thing meeting Bess Sugarland and seeing she was of the fairer sex (and a fine specimen to boot) Sweet had shot his mouth off about her gender, made some dumb remarks, and got his ass chewed by her but hard. Marshal Bess, young Sweet learned in the first five minutes, was a tough-as-nails experienced no-nonsense lawman who took no shit from anybody, especially her deputy. One tongue-lashing was all it took; Sweet respected and feared Bess from day one. It took him a long time to live down the initial bad impression he made with her, but the rookie was eager to prove himself to the lady marshal. The forest fires on the Teton Pass gave him his chance, and when Deputy Sweet saved Marshal Bess's life and pulled her out of the raging inferno, their respect had become mutual. Since that day, the marshal and her deputy had been a team in Jackson. Bess Sugarland and Nate Sweet had become good friends, a friendship built on the foundation of trust the lawmen's lives depended on each other. It was nothing romantic—they worked together—Sweet wouldn't cross that line, but Bess was a beautiful woman and that didn't mean he didn't think about it from time to time.

But he had a job to do and that came first.

Everything was going just fine until a month ago when that Idaho marshal Ford showed up with that branded kid and wanted Bess to find Joe Noose to catch some villain he was after. Sweet hadn't met Noose but heard enough stories. Bess got all worked up about Noose needing to see the branded kid right away but she didn't say why. Problem was, the bounty hunter was over in Victor being sheriff so she and the other marshal and the boy rode straight out that day over the Teton Pass. It all happened so fast. Marshal Bess made her decision, grabbed her guns, saddled her horse, gave Sweet some orders, then off she rode with her companions and left Sweet minding the store. That was Bess Sugarland to a T: fast and decisive.

But now here he was, Deputy Sweet was marshal of Jackson now, at least until the real marshal got back. It was a thrill to wear the new badge and bear the weight of that responsibility the badge bestowed for a few days. Townspeople looked at him with new respect on the street. It was uneventful. He basically ran the office, filed reports, dealt with a few local disputes, pretty much what he did before.

And five days later, Bess returned, only to leave again. She showed up riding over the Teton Pass with the same marshal and the big tough man Joe Noose Sweet got to shake hands with for the first time. They'd left the kid in Victor. It was not to be a long stay for Bess, Noose, and Ford—it was just a whistle stop before they headed out again on their manhunt. They had stopped off just so Bess could gather a few maps and brief her deputy, getting him up to speed on events.

Bess had good news and bad news for Sweet.

The good news was he was going to get to wear the marshal badge awhile longer, possibly for a few months.

The bad news was she was going on the trail with Joe Noose and Marshal Ford to catch an evil killer, she could be gone for months, and Sweet would be on his own minding the U.S. Marshal's office. Could she count on him? she wanted to know.

Of course she could, he said, and meant it.

But when Marshal Bess rode out with the big bounty hunter and that other marshal, Sweet felt a knot in the pit of his stomach now that public safety in Jackson, Wyoming, was going to be on his watch and he had no backup. As far as law enforcement in town, he was top cop. As her horse disappeared into the distance with her two saddle companions, Deputy Nate Sweet was already wishing Marshal Bess Sugarland was back.

But the deputy marshal took comfort that he certainly wouldn't have to worry about the lady marshal's safety with her big friend around.

Today, two months into his tour being U.S. Marshal of Jackson, he was settling into the job. Nate Sweet walked the streets and felt finally it was *his* town. He had adjusted to the lonesomeness during the long months without Bess, and townspeople were getting used to him. As he walked down Broadway on the freezing cold snowy Wyoming day, he looked out at the gigantic crags of the Grand Teton mountain range rising majestically against the sky, and Sweet felt like he just *belonged* in this place. He'd earned his badge or had started to. Sweet wasn't a greenhorn rookie anymore. While he looked forward to Bess coming back and taking over again as marshal, Sweet believed he could perform the job she trusted him to do until she did return, confident he would not fail her.

A few folks riding horses and wagons traveled past him in the bitter conditions. Sweet caught snippets of conversation on a wagon and heard a name dropped in conversation, a name he'd been hearing a lot the last week or so . . .

"Puzzleface."

There was someone new in town.

Two gamblers were walking by, one of them talking about losing a lot of money playing cards with a person called Puzzleface, who was getting himself a reputation, it seemed. Sweet just caught a piece of the conversation before he turned the corner, but this character with the odd name sounded like a nefarious individual who was drawing attention. Whoever Puzzleface was, people were talking about him.

On Main Street, Sweet went into the dry goods store and grocer to buy some coffee beans for the marshal's office. He was surprised to see Sally Kinkaid at the counter paying hard cash for a large stock of food and supplies. Sweet thought he had recognized her horse and wagon parked outside the grocer on the street; as far as everyone knew Sally couldn't be shopping for groceries when she had no money to buy anything and nobody, not even the grocer, would extend her any more credit. Sally was a single mother who lived with her three small children a few miles out of town on a small run-down farm; the family was destitute because her husband had died the previous summer. Everyone in town was concerned with the welfare of Sally and her children and how they would even survive this hard winter with no money. Now here Sally was, Sweet saw, spending money buying enough groceries and provisions to see her entire flock through the winter. Nate was delighted that the poor woman had a run of luck and told her so.

"Sally, happy to see things have turned around for you," Sweet said. "Looks like you and your kids are set for the winter. Folks were getting worried about you. How did you get the money?"

The rugged farm woman looked very happy when she smiled at him. "Somebody give it to me."

"They gave how much to you?"

"Fifty dollars. A proper Christian miracle."

"Who? Tell me so I can buy him a drink."

"He said his name is Puzzleface. He was riding into Jackson. Passed our farm on the way, saw us and the children out in the yard, and walked up and handed us the money. He just gave me the fifty dollars. Puzzleface said I didn't have to pay it back. I don't know what we would have done. We didn't have no supplies. We'd have starved this winter."

"Who is this Good Samaritan?"

"Never laid eyes on him before, Nate." Unlike Bess, Nate was uncomfortable being addressed other than by his Christian name, so to everybody in town he wasn't Deputy Marshal Sweet or Deputy Sweet, just plain old Nate.

"Funny name. Puzzleface. Did he give a last name?"

"He did but I disremember. Puzzleface he goes by I'm guessing because he has a big scar on his face."

Sweet helped Sally and her kids load the supplies on the wagon with Charley White, the grocer, and they both waved as the wagon pulled out up the street.

"That woman and her kids are nice people, they deserved that luck. That don't happen every day, somebody just giving you fifty dollars." Charley shook his head. "Wish it did."

"And giving it to a poor family who needed to eat, asking for nothing in return." Sweet smiled. "I'd like to meet this Puzzleface guy."

When they were back inside the grocery store and Deputy Sweet was grinding fresh coffee beans from the big metal mill by turning the wheel, he asked Charley White about Puzzleface. "What do you know about this individual?"

"I've been hearing a lot of different things about this Puzzleface from my customers, Nate. Everybody seems to have met the man or has a story about him to tell. Some of it good, some of it bad."

"How bad?"

"You know that big train robbery on the Union Pacific Railroad that got held up last month?" The deputy nodded to the grocer. "Well, some folks here in town are saying Puzzleface pulled the holdup, got away with a lot of loot, in cash."

"Has Puzzleface come in here?"

"No, not just yet. But folks seen him around. With that scar and all he's hard to miss."

Deputy Sweet was very intrigued. "Do you know where this stranger is staying?"

The grocer shook his head apologetically. Nate took his bagged coffee and paid cash. "I'll ask around. People have seen him. Anybody new in town gets noticed, especially with a scar on his face."

Deputy Nate Sweet figured he better have a conversation with the new guy in town.

First he had to track him down.

CHAPTER 8

Stopping off at the U.S. Marshal's office, the place lonely without his lady boss, Deputy Sweet put away the coffee, grabbed his Winchester, locked up, went to the corral in back, and got on his horse. He rode off down the street through the snow, figuring he'd check out the Jackson Hotel and see if the new arrival was staying there.

The hotel clerk told him nobody named Puzzleface or anybody fitting his description was currently registered at the establishment, but on the deputy's way out, a ranch hand said he had seen a man with such a scar eating lunch alone at the local restaurant Mary's Pantry earlier in the day. Sweet asked the worker for a description of Puzzleface and was told the man was dark-haired, of medium build, average in every respect, save for a jagged scar on his face.

Riding over to the diner two blocks away, the deputy questioned the cook and waitress couple who owned and ran the restaurant if they remembered seeing a man with a scar earlier that day. Mary Johnson sure did—she would not soon forget the man with the scar who had left her a generous twenty-dollar tip for a seventy-five-cent lunch.

Her husband, Bob, confirmed the man with the facial scar had eaten alone, been very pleasant, wore no gun belt, and didn't appear to be armed. Mary added Puzzleface was a very sensitive person; she could see it in his eyes, and she was never wrong about people. Who cared about a scar?

Mounting up, the deputy rode down Cache Street to canvas the bars on Pearl Street, checking if Puzzleface was throwing his money around there as well. He rode past two wranglers on their horses. He recognized the men as part of the crew on a ranch south near Bondurant, stopping to ask them if either had seen a man named Puzzleface with a scar who was new in town. One of the wranglers said a lot of folks have been asking that. When Sweet asked him what he meant, the cowboy just shrugged and said he'd heard people have been asking, is all.

The information that he was not the only one looking for Puzzleface should have been a clue for the deputy, but he didn't catch it at the time.

Sweet rode on. The snow was really coming down in a huge dump, and the lawman was freezing his ass off in the subzero weather, but his adrenaline was pumping.

As Deputy Nate Sweet rode down Main Street, he felt the blood rush to his loins, experiencing the same thrill he did losing his virginity because this was another big first time for the rookie lawman, conducting his own investigation tracking down an actual individual, hunting a man down. Now he had to use his brains and think, like Marshal Bess would. *Take inventory* was her pet phrase, which meant *look at the facts you knew*.

Who was this mysterious Puzzleface? What did Sweet know about him so far? Only that the man had come to town giving away money to needy folks. If the talk was true that Puzzleface had robbed a train, it made sense he'd be in Jackson—outlaws on the run routinely hid in Jackson Hole because the bowl formation of the valley and the natural protection of the surrounding big mountains made it a good place to hole up in; the only easy way in or out was the pass and rivers, and the area offered many natural hideouts to elude law enforcement. Was Puzzleface an outlaw and train robber? Did his guilty conscience over his ill-gotten gains have him going around giving away his stolen loot? Was Puzzleface like Robin Hood, stealing from the rich and giving to the poor? The more Nate Sweet's overactive imagination thought about Puzzleface the more interested he was to meet him.

After a five-minute ride he reached the town square, dismounting in front of the Silver Dollar Bar, the largest saloon in Jackson. The sign was painted in big gaudy gold letters. Coal oil lamps inside cast a burnished inviting glow on the stained-glass windows. It was already after six and getting dark out; the deputy marshal was technically off duty and could have a drink if he wanted one, but thought he'd canvas this place first. Tied his horse to the buck-and-rail hitching post alongside many other horses whose owners were inside. Deputy Sweet bundled himself through the swinging saloon doors into the warm boozy embrace and rowdy atmosphere of the drinking establishment and gambling hall. The Silver Dollar was a big joint with saddles instead of barstools for customers to sit on at the bar by the brass footrail. Cigar smoke hung in the air. It was good to get out of the cold.

The deputy looked around for Puzzleface. To his right, five card tables filled with poker, blackjack, and faro players stretched off into the darkness at the back of the room in the lamplight of the smoke-filled saloon. To his left was the bar itself, populated by a bunch of cowboys slumped over their beers and whiskeys.

Figuring he'd check the bar first for Puzzleface, Sweet shouldered up to the rail and looked left and right down the faces of the cowboys in profile to him. He stared at the drinkers one by one, until they felt his eyes and looked straight at him so the deputy could see their whole faces. A few gave him the side-eye, one looked back in challenge, but the deputy made sure the silver-starred badge on his chest caught the light, so the rednecks quickly backed down.

None of them had a scar on their face.

"On the house, Nate." The bartender Wilbur, a big, bearded barrel-chested ex-trapper who stood across the bar, had slapped a shot glass in front of him, ready to pour the bottle of whiskey already in his mitt.

Just as Deputy Sweet was about to ask Wilbur if he'd seen anybody fitting Puzzleface's description, the lawman was ambushed.

Two sets of hands slapped him on the back heartily as six members of the Jackson Hole Gentlemen's Business Bureau came out of nowhere to surround him on all sides. These men were the middle-aged wealthy financiers and property developers who owned much of Jackson—or, since most of Jackson Hole was government land with only 15 percent private ownership, *behaved* like they did. These rich men who owned ranches in the valley were sporting men of leisure and outdoorsmen who liked to hunt and fish. The Silver Dollar bar was their unofficial clubhouse where this overgrown boys' club loved to smoke and drink—and it was here that the men directed their efforts toward their primary raison d'être: protect their Man's World from the assault of Radical Feminists, namely their wives. For among other dubious accomplishments, the Jackson Hole Gentlemen's Business Bureau also happened to be the *husbands* of the ladies of the Jackson Hole Women's Auxiliary and they hated everything their wives stood for. It was a grand enmity that was shared in equal measure by their spouses; even as at home the couples shared wealth and meals and family, generally loved one another, and were happy for the most part.

Crowded in by the men of the Gentlemen's Business Bureau, Deputy Sweet found himself trapped and glad-handed. He knew it was part of his job that he had to be nice to the Jackson bigwigs, but he could hardly believe after escaping the wives, he'd been collared by the husbands. At least with the men he'd get drinks instead of tea.

As Emil Rittenhouse bought drinks all around after ordering a bottle of expensive Scottish whiskey that would have set back Sweet a month's salary, he poured the deputy a stiff drink, as Stephen McCoy shoved an expensive Cuban cigar in the lawman's mouth and lit it up as the six men lifted their glasses and a toast was made to town marshal Nate Sweet.

The deputy didn't toast. "Thanks, gentlemen, but Marshal Bess is the marshal, I'm just her deputy taking over for her until she gets back."

Some of the men laughed derisively and rolled their eyes, sharing dismissive looks clearly directed at Bess, which Sweet did not appreciate.

He let it go, tried to be politic. "Good whiskey. Thanks, gentlemen."

Rittenhouse patted Sweet on the back. "I just want to say that speaking for all of the men here, we've felt a whole lot better about things since that marshal Bess left and you took over as marshal now we got a man wearing the badge."

The other men said a chorus of "Hear, hear."

"It's temporary," Sweet said through clenched teeth.

"Let's make it permanent."

The insults to Bess from these fat asses had gotten Sweet riled. He wanted to get away from these insufferable fools before he said or did something he'd regret. The good booze in the high altitude had gone straight to Nate Sweet's head, and as his inhibitions slid away, so his blood boiled over the disrespect these men dared show toward Bess to *her own deputy*. It made his knuckles itch to connect with something. If they kept it up, bigwigs or no, somebody was going to get hurt tonight.

Sweet took a deep breath. "You don't understand, Mr. Rittenhouse, it's like I explained to your wife"—*a disgusted look from Rittenhouse*—"Marshal Bess is out on the trail on a manhunt and while she is gone I am deputy marshal until and just until she gets back. But while I have the temporary powers and authorities of a marshal, I am not now or ever have been a United States Marshal. I'm still a deputy. Bess Sugarland is the U.S. Marshal of Jackson. Everybody clear on everything now, or do I need to write it down for y'all?"

The fat cat's faces just laughed and whispered insinuations with good ol' boy gusto.

Stephen McCoy, the group's unofficial leader, took Deputy Sweet by both shoulders. "Nate, you're a good kid. What if we told you that we all here want *you* to be U.S. Marshal in Jackson? We want a man wearing the badge, we want you wearing it. We will triple your salary from what it is now. Yes, we know in the U.S. Marshals Service the salaries are fixed, but we will supplement that income with outside revenue streams from stocks to property. It's all perfectly legal. The Gentlemen's Business Bureau can make all that happen. In ten years you'll own your own ranch. Be one of us, our man. You want to be town marshal, say the word."

"That sounds like a bribe." Sweet shrugged McCoy's hands from his shoulders.

"Think of it as a promotion."

"I work for Marshal Bess Sugarland, for the last time, gentlemen, get it through your thick heads."

"She must be a real bitch to work for to have you so whipped."

"Consider your next words very carefully, mister." The deputy rubbed his knuckles.

McCoy grabbed Sweet's shoulder again, roughly this time. "U.S. Marshal is a man's job, Nate. Bess Sugarland's a woman. You got a dick, she doesn't. You have balls, son. Use them."

"Get Marshal Bess Sugarland's name out of your mouth before you find my fist in it." Deputy Nate Sweet's eyes narrowed dangerously, fists clenching at his sides, deadly cool.

"*What* did you say to me?" The bigwig was offended.

"You heard me."

Drunken McCoy screamed in Sweet's face. *"Screw that bitch marshal and f—"* The deputy's fist shot out, slamming McCoy in the jaw and knocking him cold with one quick, short punch. The unconscious bigwig was caught by his friends, who eased him to the sawdust-strewn floor. None of the businessmen had the guts to meet the tough eyes of the deputy.

But somebody in the saloon did.

Nate Sweet looked up and saw a gambler at a nearby table putting down his cards to watch the fight, and the cowboy looking straight at him had a jigsaw scar running down the side of his face as their eyes met and locked. Sweet stepped over Stephen McCoy and walked straight over to the card table, looking down at Puzzleface, a friendly authoritative smile on the deputy's face.

"Let me buy you a drink," the lawman said.

CHAPTER 9

"You must be Puzzleface," Sweet said.

A few minutes later, Deputy Sweet and Puzzleface were propped at the bar, facing each other affably.

"Don't believe everything you hear about me," the man replied with a friendly, self-deprecating smile, and offered his hand. Sweet shook and found Puzzleface's handshake agreeably warm. "My name is Bill Taylor. Some call me 'Puzzleface' Taylor. I'm here to tell you personally, Marshal, I ain't the man they say I am."

Deputy Sweet nodded, not sure how to respond, so he poured shots of that good expensive Scotch those Gentlemen's Business assholes had left when they fled the saloon the moment before. The two raised a glass in toast and drank, then Sweet poured two more shots. While doing so, he was considering the impression the stranger who had come to town made on him.

The man looked in his thirties. Puzzleface wasn't short, wasn't tall, of medium build and height, a confident gait, and had a dusty elegance. The air of a dandy. The man before him wore a well-tailored black coat over a silk vest, a ruffled shirt, suspenders, elegant, and worn if polished cowboy boots. No gun belt was visible. A weathered Stetson with a brim that had lost its shape sat near his hand on the bar. He had something of the riverboat gambler in appearance and took pride in his grooming.

His face drew all your attention. Behind a heavy beard and waxed mustache Puzzleface Taylor had a fine bone structure, generous lips, and surprisingly sensitive brown eyes in a delicate face marred by the jagged scar making a jigsaw cut running from his left cheek through his top and bottom left lip to the chin. The scar was the first thing you saw and it gave you a harsh first impression, but you got past that when you saw the eyes, and those soulful eyes pulled you in. Sweet wanted to ask the stranger where he got the scar, but didn't.

He said he wasn't the man they say he is? the deputy wondered. *What kind of man is he, then?*

"Need to ask you a few questions, Bill. It's my job."

"I didn't rob the Union Pacific train, if that's what you want to know. I don't carry a gun and don't know how to shoot one if I did. Never stole nothing in my whole entire life."

"Fair enough. Can anybody vouch for your where-abouts the day of the train robbery two weeks ago?"

"Hell yes. Everyone at the R.E. Miller Ranch over in Solitude where I've been staying for the last month certainly can. Ask anyone works and lives out there and they'll all tell you today's one of the first days I've left the ranch in weeks."

"Those are nice clothes. You look flush. What do you do for money, Bill?"

"I play cards."

"You're a gambler."

Nodding, Puzzleface patted the bulge of a deck in his vest pocket.

"Is that what brings you to Jackson?" Sweet changed the line of questioning, knowing without evidence of a crime, which there didn't appear to be, Puzzleface didn't have to answer any questions about where he got his cash any more than those Gentlemen's Business Bureau crooks did, and Sweet was sure there was a lot more to arrest those boys for.

"I like this town."

"No law against being in town."

"I ain't here to cause trouble."

"I didn't say you were."

"Other folks might tell you different. Some people got funny ideas about me."

"That's not the concern of the U.S. Marshals Service, Bill. Ideas do not fall under our purview. Deeds are our only concern, specifically misdeeds. Has anybody threatened you here in Jackson?"

"Not in so many words."

"Anything you want to report?"

"No."

"If anyone threatens your person, you come to me, you hear? I run a peaceful town."

Puzzleface nodded cautiously. "So what *have* you heard about me?"

"Heard you've been giving money to strangers."

"Folks is only strangers until you know 'em." He smiled. Puzzleface's voice was mellifluous and pleasing to the ear.

"Why are you giving people money?"

"To help them out." Puzzleface sounded sincere. His

eyes betrayed a kindness that nullified any aspersions to his character.

"No law against that."

Looking at Puzzleface, Deputy Sweet still felt he had no idea who he was. He was so fascinated by the scar-faced man he did not realize he had been staring until the stranger, unnerved by the lawman's stare, downed his glass a little too quickly.

"Thanks for the drink, Marshal Sweet." Puzzleface stepped away from the bar. "Better hit the trail and get back to the ranch before I have too many and fall off my horse." He gathered his heavy overcoat from the chair at the card table and started for the doors to the saloon.

"I'll walk you out." Sweet nodded, grabbing his hat. "I gotta get back to the office and lock up."

The two men stepped outside onto the cold snowy night air. It was full dark, and Cache Street, a hundred yards past the Silver Dollar Bar, dropped off into pitch-blackness. The bite of the chill oxygen cleared their heads and started to sober them up. They unhitched their horses and climbed into the saddles. Puzzleface flipped the reins and rode his gray palomino down Cache and Deputy Sweet was turning his stallion in the other direction when he heard the hooves stop.

Halting his horse, Puzzleface looked back over his shoulder. "Most people ask how I got my scar. You didn't."

"None of my business."

A beat.

"Okay, how?"

"It's a long story," said "Puzzleface" Bill Taylor with a grin like it was his standard routine, departing on his horse down Cache Street, swallowed up in total darkness as the sound of hooves faded.

A gunshot rang out.

Shattering the wintery silence, the single sharp report came from down the dark street where Puzzleface disappeared. There followed a high-pitched cry of pain and thud of a falling body muffled by the snow then galloping hooves of a bolting horse.

Startled, Deputy Sweet urgently swung his stallion and gave it spur, drawing his Winchester rifle as he charged down Cache Street.

Sprawled on the snow, Puzzleface lay sobbing, bleeding from a gunshot wound to the shoulder. He was alive.

Dropping from his saddle, Sweet knelt beside the wounded man and quickly examined the gunshot, determining the bullet had gone clean through the right shoulder and the wound itself was not fatal. The bullet hole on the front shoulder was huge and ragged, indicating an exit wound, so Puzzleface had been shot in the back. "You're gonna be okay, Bill. Hang on. Gonna get you on my horse to get you over to the doctor at the infirmary." Puzzleface was bawling in pain, his overcoat soaked with blood that was spreading in a blackened pool on the snow he lay on. The deputy made several careful attempts to lift the wounded man and get him on the horse, but couldn't pick him up because every time Sweet touched him, Puzzleface recoiled in agony, kicked and thrashed, and only wept harder. Starting to shake uncontrollably from blood loss and the terrible cold, his life kept draining on the snow like red paint on a white canvas. The stranger didn't have much time left, the deputy realized. If the wound wasn't treated by the doctor in the next few minutes, he'd bleed out.

"Sorry, friend." Deputy Sweet closed his fist and socked Puzzleface in the jaw, instantly knocking him out, and the wounded man stopped resisting. It was the second person the lawman's good right had rendered unconscious this night.

Now that Puzzleface was limp as a noodle, Sweet lifted him effortlessly in his arms off the street and eased him onto his stallion, slumping him in the saddle. The deputy noticed how light and featherweight the man was to carry. Climbing into the stirrups in the saddle behind his passenger, the lawman swung the horse around and galloped recklessly across the snowy ice-slick street east toward the local clinic.

Riding through the night transporting Puzzleface to the doctor, the young deputy marshal vowed to nail the cowardly gunmen who shot an unarmed man in the back once he identified the shooter, just as soon as he figured out who Puzzleface was and why somebody would want to kill him.

Soon the answers would astonish him.

Luckily that night, a capable new doctor named Jane Stonewall had recently relocated her practice from Victor in Idaho to Jackson. Dr. Jane's clinic provided excellent up-to-date medical treatment for the community, and the dedicated physician worked all hours.

Holding the collapsed Puzzleface with one arm in the saddle, Deputy Sweet held the reins in the other and steered his horse at a fast gallop across Broadway to Pearl Street. His saddle leather was drenched in blood, black in the moonlight. A few people out on the cold night had to dodge out of the way of the lawman's stallion to avoid getting trampled.

Five minutes later, Sweet pulled his horse to a halt by the whitewashed one-story wooden building of Dr. Jane's offices on Pearl Street. The light of the coal oil streetlamp flickered across a sign that read JACKSON CLINIC on the front door.

Deputy Sweet dismounted and gathered the slumped figure of Puzzleface off the horse, carrying the light load of the wounded man in his arms to the front door. His arms were occupied so he kicked to knock.

"Coming," a female voice said inside. The door was opened by a woman of about thirty, wearing spectacles and a clean shirt and white smock. Her hair was pulled back over a hardy face and her intelligent gaze was direct and observant of his. Dr. Jane's hazel eyes flashed in concern at the sight of the blood-splattered man in Sweet's arms.

"This man needs help, Doc."

"What happened to him, Nate?"

"He's been shot."

"Bring him in. How bad is it?"

"He's bleeding out. Somebody shot him in the back." Doc Jane stood aside to let Sweet pass to carry Puzzleface into a tidy functional hospital room in the glow of several coal oil lamps. "Put him on the table. Careful." She gestured Nate to a table and helped him lay the unconscious wounded man on it. Dr. Jane had already opened the medicine cabinet and was quickly snatching up handfuls of bandages and bottles of solvents.

The deputy looked down at the diminutive scar-faced man who was chalky pale from loss of blood. "Can you do anything for him, Doc Jane?"

"I need to take a look at that bullet wound first."

"It went right through from the looks, so you don't have to dig any lead out."

"Do I tell you your job? Here, help me get his coat and shirt off."

Carefully leaning over Puzzleface, Dr. Jane's strong fingers undid the buttons of the bloody overcoat and laid it open, then gently began undoing the buttons on the gory shirt, and Deputy Sweet helped her peel the sticky cloth away from the man's naked torso.

"My word," Doc Jane gasped in surprise.

Deputy Nate Sweet stared speechless.

The exit wound was a nasty, gory mess of rent flesh.

But that was not what caused their astonishment.

The blood from the bullet wound dripped down over two firm bare female breasts.

Puzzleface was a woman!

CHAPTER 10

The day was cold and sharp, sunlight scintillating off the crystallized frosted surface of the vast unbroken carpet of snow on the prairie as the three riders traversed it. Off to the west, the snowcapped granite peaks of the Yellowstone mountain range rose jaggedly against the roof of the blue cloudless sky. Joe Noose, Emmett Ford, and Bess Sugarland rode side by side, as they had for weeks. Their condensed breath and that of their horses left clouds of steam in their wake. It was a beautiful morning, the ground even beneath the snow under their horse's hooves, and the day was peaceful so far.

They were not alone.

A huge herd of elk, several hundred strong, migrated across the tundra. It was an impressive sight to behold. The animals were big and healthy with their brown and gray winter coats, rows of antlers like moving forests on all sides of the horses. The pack of roaming wildlife did not fear the horses or riders who gave them no reason to fear them. The trio of people relaxed and enjoyed the spectacle of the vast elk herd. Noose was pleased to see that his friend Bess wore a beaming smile on her happy face.

"So after you got branded, what happened?" Noose turned to look at Emmett when the marshal spoke. His companion was watching him attentively.

"What do you mean?" The bounty hunter shrugged. "I hurt like hell for months."

"I mean after that. What did you do?"

"I damn well sure didn't rustle any more cattle, I can tell you that. Straightened out pretty quick, I guess. Suppose that night knocked some sense into me. The hard way, I reckon, but I was a hardcase. Heading down a bad road. Getting branded got me to thinking a lot. And one thing led to another."

"Worked regular jobs, huh?"

"Recall I moved from Wyoming to Idaho then Utah, got as far as Texas but it was too damn flat and hot that far south so I come back Far West. This place fits my body, maybe because of the elevation. Worked all over as drover, laid rail on the trains, broke horses. Did that through my teens. But I stayed out of trouble."

"What got you into your line of work?"

"The pay. Mostly."

"When did you become a bounty hunter?"

"What makes you so interested in my life story, Marshal Ford?"

"Call me Emmett. We've been riding together for a month now, figure that oughta put us on a first-name basis."

"Call me Joe, Emmett. So why you asking me all these questions?"

"I'm not interrogating you but your story is damn interesting. A man goes from a teenage cattle rustler to becoming the best tracker and manhunter in the western states. That's quite a few big strides for a man to take in his life."

Noose shrugged. "I didn't want to get branded again,

or hanged, not after seeing what an ugly thing that was, so first I started working straight jobs. It didn't stick. I found I had an aptitude for fighting, more than others. I was big and able to knock down or put down most men and always could. And there was a place for my skills that didn't involve wrongdoing but doing good. Seemed that was my place in the world. For years after I got branded I never raised a hand against a man unless I had to, like to defend myself. But I saw that other folks couldn't defend themselves, so started raising my hand to the people they needed to defend themselves against. It helped those folks when there was nobody but me to be their fist. So what I was good at, what was right and what was wrong, my place in all that, it all started to make sense."

"You ever go back to that ranch?"

"The old man's ranch?"

"Yes."

"Nope. Never did. Never wanted to." His gaze grew distant. "May need to now."

"Everything circles back around, don't it?"

"I reckon it does."

"Hell, Joe. It was twenty years ago. That ranch probably ain't even around anymore."

"The old man is."

Noose looked over to see Bess listening in on the conversation. He cocked a disapproving eyebrow to her eavesdropping.

She just shrugged and smiled. "That's more than I knew about you yesterday, Joe."

"You already know all you need to know about me, Bess."

"Oh, I'm not so sure. Emmett here is getting you to open up more than I ever can."

"Bess, you do not want to hear me run off at the mouth."

"A little running off at the mouth might do you good, Joe Noose."

Copper snorted, blowing his lips out, wagging his head and nodding his snout as he chewed his bridle; all three of them laughed because even though the beautiful gold horse was probably just clowning, damned if didn't seem like it agreed with Bess that Noose should share about himself more.

"Whoa."

Noose reined Copper to a sudden stop. Bess and Emmett pulled their horses to a halt behind his. The three were at the edge of a shallow ridge, a long grade leading down into a narrow valley bordered on the other side by a rise leading to a higher ridge, the landscape blanketed with unbroken snow. His eyes squinted, the bounty hunter was looking far across the valley.

At the top of the ridge was a man on a horse.

The lone figure sat tall and skeletal in the saddle, his long white hair visible even from this distance. He was just a dark stick figure in all the white turbulence of the growing snowstorm, hard to make out but instantly recognizable all the same. His presence seemed to fill the valley.

"That's him," muttered Noose. Snatching his field glasses from his saddlebags, he put them to his eye.

"How can you be sure?" asked Bess, dubious this could be the man they were after.

Focusing the lenses with his gloved fingers, Noose found the solitary figure in the oval optics, which magnified him to head-and-shoulders proportions. The man was aged, wearing a ragged yellowed duster that enveloped his lanky, bony frame like a shroud. It was an old man from his aspect, his windblown long white hair obscuring his precise features, but his eyes shone bright with mania, staring blankly off in profile—it was unclear if this man saw them. Still, the bounty hunter couldn't be 100 percent sure it was The Brander. Noose panned the binoculars until the old man's saddle came into his field of view, and what he saw strapped to the saddlebags confirmed his suspicion:

The black metal rod of the Q *branding iron.*

"That's The Brander, all right." He passed off the field glasses to Bess. She peered through them across to the opposite ridge. "Look at the saddle. The branding iron is plain to see."

"Hot damn, I think you're right. Joe, you made him."

"Gimme those." Confounded, Emmett grabbed the binoculars and had himself a look. His voice was hoarse with emotion when he spoke. "Son of a bitch. We found him."

"If we are all three agreed we have identified our target"—Noose swung his arm around to snatch his Sharps long rifle from the saddle scabbard, socking it to his shoulder—"let's take the son of a bitch out."

"Don't shoot him!" snapped Emmett.

"Why the hell not?" growled Noose, side-eyeing the marshal from the gunsight of the massive rifle.

"He's too far. You'll miss."

"I never miss. Back off, you're throwing my aim breathing down my neck."

"He's gotta be four hundred yards away. In this wind, at that range, it's an impossible shot given these conditions. No matter how good a marksman you are, friend, it's even money you'll miss. Then The Brander will know we're onto him. I don't think he sees us, Joe. Let's use that to our advantage. I say sneak down this hill on our horses and come up behind him. Use the element of surprise while we have it."

Joe Noose kept the rifle to his shoulder, judging his aim as he calculated for windage, elevation, and bullet drop, his finger itchy on the trigger. Bess's hand touched his long barrel and pushed it down carefully but firmly. "Joe, Emmett's right. Let's get closer. Then decide whether to shoot or chase him down. We're too far."

With a grunt, the big bounty hunter spun the heavy long rifle around his hand like a toy, sliding it into his saddle scabbard in one smooth move. "Follow me," he said, spurring Copper over the edge of the ridge, down into the valley. Bess and Emmett's horses fell in behind him.

Descending the downgrade was long and easy, but the snow was heavy and deep. Copper's powerful legs pushed through powdered drifts up to its chest, dredging a path that made the two lesser horses behind it easier to plow through. Noose patted the neck of his golden horse appreciatively, hearing its hard breathing of exertion and seeing the snorted exhalations condensing in the frosty air; the tough, loyal horse of his would ride for its master until its heart burst.

For his part, throughout the ride, the bounty hunter kept his eyes fastened to the lone figure of The Brander astride his dun stallion on the high ridge ahead. He must not have seen the three approaching riders, for he had not changed position; either that or he was waiting for them. Noose had a bad notion that Emmett was right about the distance being too far to shoot and the necessity of getting closer to get a clean shot—The Brander may have realized the same thing but rather than going to them, he was waiting for them to come to him—once they were in his killing range, he'd whip out his rifle and pick them off like fish in a barrel in the narrow open valley. Here, the deep snow made quick escape impossible and anywhere they dug in they'd be exposed to his fire from the position he presently occupied. He had the high ground.

Three hundred yards to reach The Brander . . .

Another hundred yards, and they'd all be in shooting range of each other . . .

Joe Noose couldn't take the chance.

Hauling on his reins, he swung Copper in a sudden sharp turn and urged his stallion fast forward, hard right. Swinging a look over his shoulder, he saw Bess and Emmett, alert to Noose's surprise maneuver, quickly turn their horses to follow him into the trees. Hooves pounded the snow, kicking up clouds of powder that obscured the three figures. It took only a minute's hard ride for the bounty hunter and the marshals to reach the protection of the tree line, a hundred yards back from where anybody could take an accurate shot at them.

If the marshals objected to the improvised change in tactics, neither voiced it.

Once the horses were safely inside the cover of the trees, Joe Noose steered the reins and rode Copper through the trunks of the large conifers in the direction of The Brander. It was a tactic—the dense forestation obscured their approach. Noose looked back at Bess and Emmett following him in single file formation—both marshals had their pistols out. With his glove, the bounty hunter gave them terse hand signals . . .

—Bess, advance on my right.

—Emmett, advance on my left.

—I'll ride down the middle.

The strategy was to execute a flanking maneuver and come at their quarry from three sides. While none of the trio could see the terrain where The Brander last stood, he would not be able to retreat in their direction without heading straight into their guns. For the second time in ten minutes, Noose drew his rifle; this time he pulled out his trusty Winchester repeater that he preferred for close work. The gun was already cocked and loaded.

Copper kept an even, careful trot, somehow knowing to walk as silently as an Indian.

The forest was dark even though it was daytime; the snow-covered canopy of trees let in less sunlight than usual and it was as cold as an icebox.

The bounty hunter saw the trees part ahead, branches heavy with snow opening up on a view of more frost-covered trees. As he rode his horse through the forest, he still could not see The Brander. If the fiend hadn't fled or otherwise repositioned, he should be fifty yards dead ahead.

Noose swung his gaze to one side then the other, eyes on his comrades.

To his right, Marshal Bess edged her horse deliberately through the trees fifty yards out, riding determinedly forward with one hand on the reins, one hand holding her Colt Peacemaker barrel up.

To his left, Marshal Ford had moved over thirty feet, his Remington 1875 pistol held by his waist, throwing a glance to Noose now and then, watching him as carefully even as he watched for their approaching prey.

The sound of their horses' quiet hooves and their own breathing were the only sounds that reached their ears in the eerie winter stillness.

The three manhunters advanced through the forest in a loose phalanx. Ahead, more trees.

Now and then, Noose had to duck or get hit by a snow-encrusted branch, dangling icicles, or frozen pine needles.

When avoiding these was not possible, he got a cold slap in the head but his grimly set face, covered with snow and sap, stayed pointed straight and did not flinch.

His horse put one hoof after the other.

Sunlight twinkled through the branches ahead.

They neared the ridge where they had seen The Brander, just on the other side of the trees, forty feet away.

Putting his gloved hand up, Noose quietly tugged the reins to halt Copper. Looking left and right, he saw Bess and Emmett stop their horses quietly. Nodding to them, he pointed to the ground. The three dismounted with maximum stealth, boots reaching the snowy forest floor without a stirrup rattle, saddle creak, or spur jingle. They were good.

With Joe Noose leading the way with his Winchester jammed in his shoulder, sighting down the barrel, the three advanced in a triangular formation.

The bounty hunter raised his hand showing one finger . . .

Two fingers . . .

Three fingers . . .

On the three count, the trio burst through the branches from three directions, ready to shoot at the slightest provocation.

The ridge was empty.

The Brander was gone.

The first heavy-caliber round exploded a fist-sized hole in the trunk of the tree beside Noose's head before any of them heard the shot, showering wood shrapnel.

All three dived face-first in the snow, flattening on the ground. By now the rifle shot—*a Henry, judging by the volume*—echoed directionlessly around the ravine in a fading *boom*.

Instantly, Noose fired blindly over the edge of the ridge

from the ground, wasting a bullet drawing return fire to pinpoint their quarry's position.

Sure enough, another rifle report came from below, from the north, to their right.

Noose, Emmett, and Bess exchanged tactical glances. *They knew where he was.* Carefully, keeping their heads down so as not to get them shot off, they crawled on their stomachs through the snow with their weapons to the edge of ridge to sneak a look. *Muffled thumps.* They heard the distant galloping hooves on the snow below before they were able to look over the ridge and see the fleeing distant figure of the old man, duster flapping, galloping swiftly across the vast snowy valley—nothing but flat white space as far as the eye could see in either direction . . . and on it he was a shrinking speck leaving a trail of hoofprints and clouds of kicked-up snow in his wake.

From here, the three could see the northern side of the ridge they couldn't before—it was a steep but smooth downgrade leveling off at the valley floor—the escape route The Brander just took.

"Get the damn horses!" roared Noose.

"Let's get after him!" yelled Bess.

"Don't let him get away!" shouted Emmett.

In unison, the trio jumped up, bolted back to their horses, and quickly remounted them. They took off in a hard gallop through the trees out onto the ridge and down the grade. Noose was in the lead, Bess behind him, and Emmett brought up the rear. As the ground dropped away, the horses took the snowdrifts in long powerful strides and the manhunters hugged their saddles. In moments, they were down in the valley in hot pursuit of their escaping quarry.

Riding point, Noose squinted into the blowing snow to

spot the tracks of The Brander, his horse's hoofprints the only demarcations on the unbroken snow and easy to follow. Giving Copper some spur, the bounty hunter drove his powerful golden steed even faster. He heard Bess's and Emmett's galloping hooves right behind.

Far in the distance, dead ahead, the tiny speck of the fiend pulled away from them. Twin quick minuscule flashes, like sun reflecting on metal. Two bullets buzzed past the bounty hunter's head, startlingly close considering the distance they were shot from. Lucky shots perhaps, but Noose now suspected the maniac could really shoot.

Nothing to do but return the favor . . .

Cocking his Winchester, levering it by spinning the entire rifle around his hand, Noose straight-arm fired it in front of him in one glove. Then fired it again. And again. Glittering smoking brass casings ejected from the breech of the gun as he blasted it over and over at his slippery distant target. Behind him over the sound of Copper's galloping hooves he could hear Emmett's hollers of protest but Noose didn't care—he had plenty of bullets banked so he kept firing them and kept shooting. Maybe he'd get a lucky shot, too.

Across the vast snowy tundra, the three figures of the manhunters rode. Very far ahead, the single lone figure they chased rode faster than they did. The sun gleamed off the blinding white snow of the valley.

CHAPTER 11

By the time Noose arrived at the edge of the woods where The Brander had escaped by riding up into the hills, there was no sight of the fiend, but the hoofprints of his horse were plain enough. The bounty hunter spurred Copper and the horse barely slowed its speed as it took the hill in great galloping strides, steered by the big man on his back tugging the reins right and left as he followed the trail of hooves with his keen eyes.

Snow exploded in big bursts as Copper relentlessly plowed through drifts ranging in height from its knees to its chest.

Swinging a glance over his shoulder, Noose saw Bess and Emmett on their horses barrel through the tree line at his rear, fifty yards behind.

Walls of fifty-foot conifers draped with frost and icicles came at him. Using his muscular thighs in the saddle, Noose steered his horse through the obstacle course of sudden dense frozen forestation. It was getting harder to discern The Brander's tracks between the trunks with all the roots and foliage on the ground, so the bounty hunter slowed his horse to a propulsive canter, keeping his own head moving in a steady left-to-right scan of his surroundings, eyes constantly on the move to check if his quarry had broken off to the side—what he would do in that position.

All he saw was woods . . .

Snow and trees . . .

Glimpses of robin's-egg-blue sky above the forest canopy . . .

Sunlight twinkling through frosted branches . . .

A gleam of sunlight on metal.

The world exploded in gunfire, Noose already levering and firing his Winchester as the first bullets came. Spurring his horse, he dived from the saddle, hitting the snow in a somersault, rolling up to one knee, quick-firing his Winchester repeater at the general area where he saw the glint of gunmetal . . . when he saw the muzzle flashes, he sharpened his aim, but The Brander had taken cover.

Leaping off their horses, Bess and Emmett moved with crack precision efficiently tying off their horses on a branch and ducking behind two opposite trees.

Bam! Bam! More shots came at them from deep in the forest.

"Don't kill him!" Emmett yelled to Noose, who was getting tired of hearing it.

"Killin's the bullet's business, Emmett!" the bounty hunter hollered back, and returned fire.

Bess and Emmett both aimed their pistols around the trees they'd hidden behind and fired at their unseen nemesis.

That was when Noose noticed The Brander's shots were going wide, and the bounty hunter knew damn well the fiend could shoot better than that.

Noose threw an alarmed glance at Copper, standing out

in the open directly in the line of fire. His gold stallion watched him fearlessly, but he saw in the animal's gaze awareness of the danger it was in this close to the gunfight.

Two bullets exploded near Copper's hooves, but the brave horse with nerves of steel hardly flinched.

The Brander was trying to shoot the horses!

If that dirty miserable son of a bitch shot the horses, not only would Joe lose his best friend in the world, he, Bess, and Emmett would be stranded on foot fifty miles from nowhere out in the open wilderness and would probably die of exposure.

"Get the horses out of here!" Noose roared.

Bess and Emmett shot him alarmed glances a hundred feet away taking cover behind trees getting struck by The Brander's bullets. They looked to their horses and then back at Noose, who knew there wasn't time for them to figure it out.

"Cover me!" the big cowboy yelled, breaking cover like an artillery shell fired from a mortar, running as fast as his feet would carry him for his golden stallion. He needed to get to its side in a big hurry.

Instantly getting the picture, like a well-oiled machine, Bess and Emmett leaned around the tree trunks and blasted away in the fiend's direction with their pistols, laying down heavy covering fire. Gun blasts exploded in the clearing in staccato strings of earsplitting reports. Unless he was suicidal The Brander would have no choice but to duck for cover with no chance to return fire while the marshals' relentless fusillades of rounds came at him, if he didn't want to get his head shot off.

Snatching Copper's reins in one hands, his smart horse already on the move, Noose scrambled out through the open clearing in a dead run for Bess's Appaloosa and Emmett's pony, both horses rearing and pawing the air in panic as the bullets flew around them and exploded on the ground. Bess and Emmett continued to pound The Brander's position with lead. Grabbing the reins of his friends' horses in his free hand, Noose hurriedly untied them and went rushing off into the dense forest, pulling three horses in tow. Behind him, the onslaught of the marshals' covering fire was a nonstop battery of rounds booming through the trees.

When Joe Noose had the horses a safe enough distance away behind the protective cover of three tightly packed thick-girthed pines, he began to tie the horses off so he could get back into the fray. He noticed the gunshots had stopped and became worried his friends had been hit. But before he could draw and reload, he heard hurried footsteps and whirled to see Bess and Emmett rush out of the woods up to him.

"He stopped shooting," Bess gasped. "I don't know if we got him or not. I don't think so. Emmett thinks he saw him riding the hell out of there like his ass was on fire."

"That right, Emmett?"

"I saw a horse. It was pretty fast. I say we mount up and get on after him, check for his body back at the clearing, follow his tracks if we don't find it."

"I have to agree with Emmett, Bess."

"Saddle up, boys."

The bounty hunter and the marshals swung into their saddles and proceeded in single file formation at an urgent clip back toward the clearing where they just had the skirmish. The air stank of cordite and gun smoke that still hung in the air. Noose rode two horse lengths out in front, using his legs to stay on Copper's saddle, keeping his hands free to maintain a full grip on his cocked and loaded Winchester socked to his shoulder. He was looking down the barrel of the Winchester—swinging the muzzle back and forth in a steady sweep of the immediate area, his finger tight on the trigger, ready to shoot anything that moved on two legs. Patrolling at a quick, brisk trot, his horse passed the clearing where they exchanged fire a few minutes ago and traveled on. Behind, Bess then Emmett followed with their pistols drawn, reloading shells. Seventy-five yards onward, Noose looked down his gunsight at a heavy fallen log filled with bullet holes. The snow behind it had been disturbed, showing the indentation of a man who had taken cover behind it before taking flight. That man was long gone.

The Brander was in the wind.

The tracks of his horse trailed away, placement of the hooves in the snow widely spaced, indicating long strides, showing it had left in a big hurry at a full gallop.

"He's on the move. Heading west. *Yee-hah!*" Noose gave Copper some spur and the bronze-colored stallion charged off after the other horse.

The marshals drove their steeds after the bounty hunter, and three horses and riders broke off at a full clip together onto a flat plateau.

Right as a gale-force gust of sleet and snow hit them head-on and it was a whiteout.

Snow-blind, the three manhunters and the horses they rode didn't see the drop-off until they had ridden over it. The animals' hooves went out from under them and three tons of horseflesh became airborne. The plateau ended sharply as the ground suddenly fell away in a sheer ninety-degree slope, pitching the horses head over heels down a steep incline with the riders in the saddles. It was a soft landing in the five-feet-deep fresh snow but the animals somersaulted through the drifts. Blasts of dislodged snow flew everywhere. The horses bellowed and grunted and the people hollered and yelled. Down, down, the horses and riders on their saddles tumbled, out of control, rolling over and over in a tangled knot of legs and heads and hooves, unable to stop or right themselves. Finally, the horses just slid on their sides the rest of the way. Then they were at the bottom.

The trio scrambled out from under their steeds as the horses unsteadily righted themselves and man and beast climbed to their feet and brushed off the snow.

"Everybody okay?" Noose shouted.

"Yeah."

"Shit. Yes, I'm okay."

Noose looked up and saw the stallion.

The Brander's dun horse stood three hundred yards away, saddle empty.

A set of human tracks, black as specks of pepper on the pristine white landscape, led into a rise of snow-packed hills that surrounded them, scattered with trees and patches of woods.

After checking that their horses were okay, at Noose's hand signal the two marshals and the bounty hunter made off on foot.

Moments later, the driving gusts of snow had covered The Brander's tracks and his trail had vanished again.

Swapping glances, the trio decided to split up and head off in three directions.

Their three figures disappeared west, south, and north into the snowstorm and the blizzard became a battle-ground.

The Brander spots the pile of dried timber on the ground, sees it suits his purposes. Reaching into his heavy duster, he draws out the canister of coal oil and splashes it on the wood. Taking out a box of matches, the fiend strikes one in a flash of sparks, tosses it on the pile of wood, and watches the wood ignite in a burst of flames.

He jams his cold branding iron facedown in the fire . . . in ten minutes it will be red-hot.

Noose smelled a fire. A fire in a snowstorm made no sense, but the acrid stench of the smoke of burning wood and a coal oil accelerant was unmistakable as it stung his nostrils. The bounty hunter advanced cautiously through curtains of snow, his Colt Peacemaker drawn and its hammer cocked. All around him was a wintery wasteland of white falling flakes with opaque outlines of trees behind translucent veils of flurries. His boots crunched through the unbroken crust of snow as he trudged on, his eyes snapping back and forth from his surroundings to the ground, searching for boot tracks.

The dim glow of the fire bloomed to his left, appearing as a palpitating orange light he figured to be two hundred yards off. As he started for it, out of the corner of his eye to the right something caught his attention.

Noose saw a figure.

His heart began pounding like a sledgehammer in his chest.

There he was!

The man who branded him, a phantom, stood beside a tree not moving a muscle. One arm was raised and the glove clenched an object that looked like a gun.

Noose instantly dropped to one knee and aimed dead center in the figure's chest, leveling his aim on his pistol with his left hand gripping his right gun-hand wrist. *"I got you dead to rights, old man!"* he roared. *"Drop your weapon and raise your hands! Surrender and the marshals and I will take you in unharmed. But if you don't throw down your weapon by the count of three, I will chop you down! One! Two!"*

The hazy figure with the weightless gravity and spectral aspect of a ghost did not comply.

"Three!"

Squeezing the trigger three times, Joe Noose fired the .45 in a rapid string of shots, putting them square in the figure's chest. The triple *boom*s echoed throughout the valley, startling birds from the trees.

Lowering his gun, the bounty hunter squinted in surprise.

The Brander had not moved.

He was hit. Had to be dead.

But he was standing.

"What the—?"

Quickly raising his pistol, Noose loosed off three more loud rounds into the head and chest of the figure a hundred yards away, but as the smoke cleared he saw the bullets had not felled the fiend.

Who didn't shoot back.

Knowing something was amiss, Noose switched guns, holstering the empty Colt, then, pointing the loaded Colt, rushed the figure. By the time he was ten feet away, he saw it was no man at all, just his coat and hat hung on the branches of the tree. The bounty hunter's shots had all hit their mark . . . the wind whistled through the holes in the flapping cloth.

And too late he realized what the coat was.

A diversion.

Feeling the sudden heat at his back, Joe Noose rounded

as The Brander attacked him from behind, a large skeletal figure flying at him, clenching the red-hot branding iron in both gloved fists, the glowing *Q* coming right at Noose's face. He was looking into the burning eyes of his oldest enemy behind the waving long white hair. Startled, the bounty hunter raised his arm to protect his face as the brand slammed against the coat on his forearm, instantly searing through the cloth.

It wasn't the pain of the brand burning through the cloth toward his skin that incapacitated Joe Noose—it was the crazed eyes of the old man he remembered so well that sent raw fear shuddering through his body, turning his guts to jelly, immobilizing his limbs into a state of paralysis. His hand was trembling so badly he couldn't work his pistol, his trigger finger not responding to his mental commands. Then The Brander was upon him, clenching the searing branding iron with both hands and leaning his bony shoulders into it, as Noose covered his face in terror. The stench of the old man's body odor came back to him and made him choke. He smelled in the fiend's foul breath the aroma of a corpse. Somehow Noose got a punch off into The Brander's shoulder, hitting him hard enough to stagger him back so the hot brand came free, leaving a flaming curlicue of charred and cindered cloth and setting the arm of Joe's coat on fire. As the old man stumblingly regained his balance, Noose tried to beat the fire out on his gun arm while firing his pistol twice at the same time, but his shots went wild as the flames spread to the shoulder of his heavy coat. As shots blew chunks of bark out of a tree, The Brander dodged to the right, disappearing into the driving sheets of snow.

Afire, the bounty hunter leapt onto the ground, covering the burning arm of his coat with his body and rolled twice in the snow, dousing the flames while still gripping his pistol—but as he rolled onto his back and tried to rise, a boot stamped down on his gun wrist, pinning his gun hand to the icy snow as a second boot kicked him hard in the chest, pressing him flat.

The Brander stood over him, a tall and terrible figure, the gusting wind wreathing his face in swirling sleet as he stared down with an omnipotent gaze through the blowing trestles of his long white hair . . . and lowered the red-hot branding iron toward Noose's face. The red-hot *Q* spat off searing heat, steaming in the frozen air. It was burning his cheek, about to touch flesh. Past the glowing coil, the bounty hunter's bulging fear-filled eyes saw the psychotic whorls of The Brander's eyeballs reflecting the blazing metal like the Devil himself.

Joe Noose did something he had never done before in his entire adult life.

He screamed.

To his own ears, the scream didn't seem to come from his own body. It was detached—a raw sound of helpless panic and terror of a dying animal—surely not him.

Now Noose felt as he did when he was thirteen, helpless against this man, and no matter how big and tough and strong he'd grown up to become since what that old man had done to him, no matter how many men he'd killed or taken down, here he was again with the fiend about to brand him like an animal and there was nothing he could do.

You're only as good as your worst day.

"Noooooooooooooo!" Joe Noose cried at the top of his lungs, seizing the rod of the brand in his free hand and wrenching it away from his face as he swept one of his legs into The Brander's knee, knocking him off-balance. Noose forced the red-hot brand down into the snow, where

it sizzled in a funnel of steam. Staggered, the fiend used both hands to try to wrestle the branding iron away from the bounty hunter, the force and momentum helping Noose stumble to his feet. Then the two adversaries were locked in hand-to-hand combat fighting for the implement, each clenching the rod with both gloved hands, struggling to scald each other with the incendiary Q. The bounty hunter could not believe The Brander's strength; Noose was bigger and younger and had much more muscle than the skeletal figure he battled, but psychotic rage gave the fiend adrenaline-fueled physical power.

With a roar of fury, Noose slammed the iron brand into a tree trunk with The Brander still gripping onto it.

The metal bent on impact.

Noose hammered the pole again and again against the tree trunk.

On the third punishing blow, the branding iron broke in half.

Staggering back, The Brander looked at the broken branding iron he clenched, halved, in each hand. When his ghastly bereft gaze raised to Noose, his eyes were horror holes. The hideous high-pitched shriek of total insanity that escaped his throat was bloodcurdling.

Facing his oldest foe, Joe Noose again found his feet cemented to the ground. He knew he must attack the fiend now, punch, kick, stab, hit him with everything he had, but The Brander had him in his thrall and the bounty hunter couldn't fight back.

The sharp rifle cracks came loud and close. The bullets whistling through the air made The Brander duck.

With a last look of bottomless hate over his shoulder to Joe Noose, The Brander hissed and fled into the white vortex, his duster flapping around him as he vanished into the snowstorm.

Joe Noose was just standing there when Bess and Emmett came running out of the snowfall behind him and reached his side, and he stared with a vacant unblinking gaze into the emptiness of the winter void where his worst enemy had retreated.

"Are you okay?"

"Yeah."

"Did you get him?"

"No."

"Joe . . ."

The shaken Noose had already turned with shoulders slumped and walked away in defeat back toward his horse.

Chapter 12

Noose awoke.

It was so dark.

He lay on his side in the lean-to, wrapped in several woolen blankets beneath his buffalo-hide covering but was cold to the bone. His body was stiff, an ice block. His arms and legs didn't respond to his commands, and the numbness and tingling in his limbs and extremities made him feel immobilized.

It was so quiet—too quiet; unnaturally so.

For long moments the big bounty hunter lay with his eyes open, head against his saddle, opening and closing his hands and rotating his ankles, working the circulation back into the fingers and toes of his extremities. As the minutes passed, he watched the clouds of his condensed breath forming in front of his face, making ghostly shapes like atavistic spirits of the wastelands. A sense of foreboding made him uncharacteristically ill at ease, filled with a free-floating dread.

His eyes were good and usually became accustomed to the dark quickly, but not tonight. His vision was not adjusting to the darkness. The canvas of the lean-to was barely visible two feet away in the gloom.

The silence was deafening.

Something was wrong.

Gritting his teeth, Joe Noose willed himself to sit up and raise his arms, forcing blood into his hands. The effort it took was immense and the body shock of the subzero night temperatures sleeping out on the open plain made him gasp as the buffalo skin fell off his shoulders.

Too damn quiet.

His gloves were already on. Noose quickly massaged his fingers, getting them working, then reached over to grab his Winchester repeater. He cocked it and the sound of the round jacked into the chamber woke him all the way up.

Pushing out of the flap of his lean-to, the bounty hunter stepped out into the night air. As he did, he saw why it was so very dark.

There was no moon tonight.

The lightless world was engulfed in stygian gloom. The sky above was a black void he felt weigh down on him like an unseen yoke over the buffalo skin he had draped over his massive shoulders. Looking out at the horizon, Noose could not see where the sky met the mountains, everything impenetrable black down to the ground below his feet, a negative space below his boots as if he were standing in starless space.

He saw his breath condensing before his face and that was about it.

Panic not in his nature, Noose chose to use his other senses, moving by feel. Clenching the repeater rifle in his gloved fists, he slid his forefinger through the trigger guard. Noose knew the camp and the proximity of things by memory and habit, a lifetime of training to always know his surroundings.

The tree where the horses were tethered was to the right, twenty paces away.

Bess's lean-to was straight ahead, fifty paces.

Emmett's lean-to was to the left, fifteen degrees, a hundred and ten paces, by the dead tree.

Check the horses first.

Joe Noose began walking through the campsite. Five paces. Ten. Fifteen. Putting out one hand, his fingers touched the side of Copper's head where he knew it would be for he remembered exactly his horse's position.

Copper did not respond to his master's touch with warmth or surprise, just breathed in and out, as if the stallion was asleep, or in a trance. Noose could feel the horse's steady gaze but that gaze was somehow strange and detached, the warm brown eye he could feel but not see was staring past him, not at anything. It had to be the bitter cold.

Now check on Bess.

Dislocated and disconcerted by the complete darkness, the bounty hunter still retained his bloodhound's sense of direction; without using his eyes, he went by touch, measuring twenty paces to the left and soon reached her tent. Listening hard, he heard no snoring or breathing inside.

Touching the barrel of the Winchester to the cord running from the stake in the ground, Noose traced it to the canvas tent, then opened the flap with the muzzle.

Still no sound, sleeping or otherwise.

The tip of his boot crunched on a box of matches on the ground.

Picking up the box, the bounty hunter drew a stick.

Noose struck the match.

It sparked in a flash of flame that illuminated the tent in a hellish firelight.

Bess Sugarland lay on her back beneath her blanket, head against her saddle. Face the color of white marble, her bulging eyes were wide open and staring.

A hideous fresh charred mark of the Q brand was burned into her forehead!

The smoke of sizzling flesh hung in the air.

She was dead.

"Nooooooooooooooo!" Noose cried.

And suddenly he was grabbed from behind when a powerful arm wrapped around his throat, pinning him in an iron grip. The heat against his upper back was instantaneous and agonizing as he felt something pressed against his spine with superhuman force, then felt it sear through his flesh, spine, heart, lungs like a scalding spear until Noose saw the red-hot metal head of the Q branding iron burst out his chest in a cloud of bloody smoke and knew that he, too, was dead!

Then Joe Noose woke up, hearing himself cry out.

Outside his lean-to came the sound of two pairs of running footsteps, moving like stink in his direction. The sounds of guns being cocked rang out.

"Joe!" Bess shouted in alarm, through the flap of the tent first, pistol drawn as she fell to one knee beside Joe and stared in his face. "What happened, Joe? Emmett, check the area!"

Outside, Marshal Ford's running footsteps circled the lean-to, then the steps slowed. "Clear! Is Noose okay?"

Dazed, shaken, in the twilight between sleep and waking, Noose looked at Bess groggily and saw her shock and confusion at seeing him truly rattled for the first time since she'd known him. "Are you okay, Joe?"

He nodded, embarrassed. "Bad dream."

"Joe . . ." She sighed, something in her eyes that looked to him a lot like disappointment. "Pull yourself together."

Rising, she holstered her weapon and stepped out of the tent. The bounty hunter heard the marshals' receding voices.

"What happened?"

"Nothing. Get some shut-eye."

He heard his two comrades return to their tents, then it was quiet again and dark, but even though it was not as quiet and dark as his terrible dream, the peace and gloom brought him no comfort as they usually did. That safe space had been invaded.

Noose didn't sleep the rest of the night, just lay with his eyes wide open, watching the dark top of the lean-to, waiting for it to brighten, yearning for sunrise.

When it came the following morning, the three travelers moved out before the sky was fully light. They made a quick breakfast at the campfire and were saddled up and back on the trail. Joe Noose was glad to be on the move after his horrific nightmare. The three cups of coffee did little to relieve the exhaustion that clung to him after his bad night's sleep.

CHAPTER 13

By early afternoon, it was a relief for the three travelers when they found a local road heading north where an occasional if regular traffic of horses and wagons had cleared ruts in the snow, making it an easy trek for the horses.

Noose rode beside Bess.

"I never seen you rattled before, Joe."

"I ain't rattled."

"If that's what you being rattled *ain't*, Joe, I don't want to see you being what rattled *is*."

"I just want to catch up with this man."

"Because it's personal."

"Hell yes, it's personal."

"Don't let it get *too* personal. Like my daddy always told me, gunplay ain't personal, it's business. The business is shoot to kill, otherwise be shot and killed. You can't get hot in a gunfight. Can't let your emotions affect your reflexes. You need to be cold. Draw down and drop him."

"I know. But thanks for reminding me." Noose nodded and fell back to ride alongside Emmett.

"We all need reminding sometimes. That's what friends are for, Joe," she called back.

Bess was riding in the lead, Noose riding side by side with Emmett when the bounty hunter started up a conversation.

"So how long you been a marshal, Ford?"

"Joined the Utah U.S. Marshals Service five years ago next July."

"You from Utah?"

"From a lot of places. Idaho mostly."

"Been trying to place your accent. I figured you was from Wyoming."

Emmett looked at Noose a beat. "Does Wyoming even have an accent?"

"To my ear."

"I spent time here, but not as much as other places."

"Decided on a career in law enforcement, huh?"

"It fit me."

"What made you join the U.S. Marshals Service instead of, say, become a sheriff?"

He shrugged. "Why did Bess?"

Noose laughed loudly. "The town made her!"

"I heard that." Bess swung her head around with a tart grin and winked.

Emmett chuckled.

"Why did you?" Noose asked again.

The marshal shook his head. "I come from a long line of lawmen, Joe. Granddad was a sheriff. Pecos County, Texas. My dad was a sheriff out in Grange, Idaho, where I did a lot of my growing up. Wasn't much of a doubt I'd become a lawman. But I couldn't see myself stuck in one place as a lawdog, Wanted a job that would take me around this big country. The U.S. Marshals offered that. So soon as I was eighteen I enlisted in the calvary, did my four years at Fort Smith up in Boise. Saw some Indian action.

Made sergeant. After I got discharged, I put my papers in for the Marshals. My lieutenant's brother was a U.S. Marshal and he put in a good word for me. Been posted in Pocatello ever since, that is, until this."

"Got any brothers or sisters?"

"Three sisters. I'm the youngest. All three are married. One moved to Texas. The other two live in Idaho near where we all grew up.

"You married?"

"No sir. Not yet. But I mean to one day, have kids, raise a family, after I see how all this falls out."

"Why The Brander?"

Emmett threw Joe a confused glance. "What do you mean, why?"

"You've been hunting The Brander on your own for two years now, I reckon, right?"

"Right."

The bounty hunter's steady gaze considered his saddle mate. "It's a mission for you, I can see that. The Brander is a very bad and dangerous individual who needs to be stopped, that's a fact, and I respect your commitment. What got you onto his trail? There's a lot of badmen in the West. What I'm asking is, what gave you a hard-on for this one?"

"He killed a damn dog."

Noose looked at Emmett, who sighed and explained. "The son of a bitch branded that dog, burned him to death. The dog didn't do nothing. March of 1885, me and two fellow marshals came on what we figure was The Brander's first branding kill. Killed the entire family out in Provo, husband, wife, little daughter, and son, branded all of 'em. But it was the dog lying there with the brand in his side. I don't know, Joe. It put a fire in my belly. Right then

I knew I was gonna get that mean murderous son of a bitch if it was the last thing I did. I asked for the assignment and headquarters in Cody authorized it and gave me my orders. So I went after him."

"That led you to Bess. Which led you to me. Which led us here."

"More or less."

Emmett saw Noose watching him with that unsettling perspicacious pale gaze that drilled through his head, probing his character and taking the measure of him; the man seemed to see right through him. Noose's gaze unnerved everyone. "You ask a lot of questions, Noose."

The bounty hunter just grunted. "I like to know who I'm riding with."

"Now you do," said the marshal.

Noose didn't reply.

They were on the road to Wind River, fifteen miles ahead, one of the larger towns for a hundred miles in any direction. Once there, the manhunters' plan was to talk to the sheriff and inquire if he had any information on The Brander's whereabouts. They also intended to check with the local blacksmith and see if a man missing three fingers on his right hand had brought in a broken *Q* branding iron for repair in the last few days. The damaged brand was a new lead. Knowing the fiend would need to have his signature murder implement repaired directly, the trio's logical intention was to check area blacksmiths to pick up their quarry's trail again. Bootmakers no longer needed to be interviewed, because Noose had seen The Brander's boots up close and personal, and both had heels. After a month on the trail, it was time to reprovision and pick up some ammo in Wind River as well. Bess was desirous of a bath, so they thought they would all stay the night at the best local hotel and enjoy a good hot meal before heading out again the next morning. The prospects of a little relaxation raised the spirits of all three.

As they rode on down the road, the three manhunters passed occasional travelers heading in the other direction. A freighter wagon. Two ranchers on horseback. Two cowboys riding together. As the men approached up the road, one of the two individuals pulled his hat down, but it seemed a casual gesture, so Noose, Bess, and Emmett barely glanced at the two riders as they passed before turning a bend in the road out of sight.

The two cowboys were a hard-bitten man in his fifties named Mason Cole with bitter, shifty eyes and his older laid-back saddle mate, Carl Stokes. Cole had become clenched with violence and Stokes gave him the side-eye.

"Son of a bitch."

"What is it, Cole?"

"I know that man we just passed."

"Which one?"

"That big bastard just rode by is the bounty hunter son of a bitch who caught me and took me in and cost me ten years in the territorial prison in Laramie. His name is Joe Noose."

"Joe Noose? That was him?"

"That was him."

"It's been ten years, you can't be sure."

"Biggest man I ever met. Face I'll never forget. That was him, all right."

Stokes whistled. "I know Noose by name. He has a fearsome reputation."

"Back in '63 had me a thousand-dollar dead-or-alive

bounty on my head for that stagecoach business and Noose was the son of a bitch who collected it. Jumped me outside of Cheyenne and got the drop on me. He don't shoot people he figures he don't have to, but he tied me up on my saddle and rode me three hundred miles to Laramie. On my belly slung over a saddle three hundred miles over that rough ground was like getting punched in the stomach every five minutes the whole way. I ain't shit right since. Judge gave me ten years. The Laramie territorial prison was hell. Hell, I say. All on account of that man we just rode past."

"He didn't recognize you?"

"Nope, had my hat down after I saw him, so he did not see my face."

"What do you intend to do?"

"Son of a bitch."

They rode on another mile.

"Son of a bitch."

"Let it go, Cole. You're out now."

"Ten years I was in. Ten years that man cost me."

"Ain't nothing you can do about it."

"Hell, there ain't."

"Okay, my big-talking friend, just what *do* you intend to do?"

"Get me some payback is what I intend to do. I'm gonna put a bullet in Joe Noose's damn heart."

"You're just talking."

"Am I?"

"Leave it, Cole. They say nobody gets the drop on Noose. Supposed to be, he's too damn fast."

Cole gave an ugly laugh. "You think I'm stupid going toe to toe with a stud like that? Hell no, Stokes. I'm gonna shoot him in the back."

"He'll see you coming."

"Noose ain't as good as they say he is. Only reason he got the drop on me ten years ago was my stomach complaint had me distracted. Lucky is what he was. Today, his luck runs out."

"You're seriously going to go heels with that man?"

"Turn these horses around. I'm gonna kill him in town."

"I want no part of this, Cole. You're a friend and all, but this score is yours to settle, you're on your own. I'll be at Steamboat Kate's."

"I'll meet you there in a few hours. Tell that new redhead to keep it hot for me."

The two cowboys faced each other on their horses. Stokes looked sadly at Cole. "Don't do this."

"I had a dead-or-alive bounty on my head. That bounty hunter should have put me down. Money was the same. Wouldn't have had to deal with me now. Yessir, Joe Noose made one mistake: taking me in alive instead of dead."

"Adios."

The two riders rode in opposite directions.

CHAPTER 14

The three manhunters rode into the small town of Wind River, Wyoming ("pop. 354"). They came to it right on the main road. A settlement of one- and two-story buildings and stores was on a main street that turned off the road that they presently traveled on. It was more people than they had seen since they left Victor weeks ago, and the crush of humanity was welcome.

Noose, Bess, and Emmett trotted down the central street past the stable and feed store, soon passing a saloon, hotel and brothel, and several corrals. Wind River was an outpost that passed for civilization in these remote parts. The lady marshal saw the town was not as developed as Jackson, Wyoming, but on its way; in ten years, it might become a proper little city. Many of the structures were unpainted and weather roughened; little alleyways led off the thoroughfare. Along what passed for a boardwalk, dozens of towns-people bundled against the frigid weather and went about their business; they were taking care not to put a foot wrong in the broken sections of the planking or places where it simply hadn't been added. Trappers and cowpokes rode back and forth up and down the street on horses or in wagons, selling their wares or buying supplies. The air was filled with the sounds of horse hooves and the *clatter* and *clink* of carriages.

"You figuring on talking to the sheriff first, Bess?" Noose looked over at his friend the lady marshal.

"Logical first stop. We should while we're here."

Halfway down the street, they rode up to the single-story unpainted wooden building with a porch and next to a window with iron bars, a hand-painted sign that read WIND RIVER SHERIFF'S OFFICE on the side of the door. The trio of manhunters dismounted, tethered their horses to the fence, and went inside.

One look around and Noose made up his mind that all sheriff's offices look the same. Next to a small cell and woodstove, across from the gun rack and opposing deputy's desk, was the sheriff's desk, and behind it sat the man himself. He was affable and rough-hewn, an older gentleman, who had farmer's hands and outdoorsman's untamed beard, so Joe guessed this was a part-time job for him. Then again, not much crime probably happened in these parts. The man wore a drover's coat over a checkerboard shirt stained with mud, some of which tarnished the badge on his chest. Despite his rural aspect, the lawman seemed friendly enough when he greeted the three travelers who just walked in. "Howdy, I'm Sheriff Winston Potter. What can I do for you folks?"

Bess stepped forward and did the talking. "Sheriff, I'm Marshal Bess Sugarland out of Jackson and this is Marshal Emmett Ford from Pocatello. Joe Noose here is our tracker. We're on the trail of a murderer. A vicious killer who brands his victims."

"With a branding iron?" The lawman looked mortified and Noose already knew he would be no help.

"Correct. I'd like to ask you if there have been any killings in your jurisdiction that match that description?"

"Gee. Gosh. I'd sure have remembered. No, I don't—let me think."

The big bounty hunter stifled a yawn as he watched the slow-witted sheriff tug on his scraggly beard, trying to think, and knew his time was better spent elsewhere. "Bess, while you and the sheriff are conducting your business, I'm going to talk to the blacksmith we passed, then check out the stables to see if they remember seeing our boy."

"I'll find you in a few minutes, Joe."

And the bounty hunter was out the door.

Mason Cole was on foot. His present position was half-way down the block from the sheriff's office. The vengeful ex-con had tailed the bounty hunter and two marshals over some distance until they rode into town. Giving them five minutes' lead, he followed on his own horse then hitched it near the town sign near the main road where he had first recognized Joe Noose.

Then Mason Cole waited.

He'd waited twenty years, figured he could wait another few minutes. For the first time since the badman remembered, he enjoyed the wait because the weight of two heavy Colt Navy revolvers, fully loaded, cleaned and oiled, hung in his side holsters and the man he had dreamed all these years of settling up with was nearly in his crosshairs.

—Joe Noose, you got a big surprise coming when you get shot in the back.

A few minutes earlier as Cole watched the trio dismount at the sheriff's office and go inside, he stood by the feed store in the shade of the porch overhang, letting his mind go on a tear.

—Noose, you gonna look down and see that big hole in your chest is a bullet exit wound and realize all that blood everywhere is yours but you won't know what hit you. Not at first.

As his hands tickled the hafts of his holstered pistols, leaving a trail of sweat from his bloodthirsty glee, Cole hung back and waited for his moment when Noose was alone. Then he saw the unmistakable figure of the giant cowboy exit the sheriff's office and walk up the block.

Mason Cole followed him.

—When you fall to your knees, Noose, you'll look up and see the man who shot you in the back walk up to you and look you in the eye and say, Remember me, *and you'll be looking up the black barrel of my Colt Navy knowing it's me who killed you when I shoot you between the eyes and blow your Goddamn brains out!*

His eyes locked on his big target, Cole shadowed Noose as he walked into the blacksmith's stall and had some words with the man. The ex-con closed in step by step, blending in with the passing townspeople, looking like nobody in particular and got himself into killing range of the bounty hunter, who didn't see him because he was pre-occupied with some important business that wouldn't seem so important a few minutes from now.

Mason Cole wiped runny perspiration from his face with his yellow kerchief and licked his lips, wondering why his face was so wet yet his mouth was dry.

—Get ready!

* * *

The blacksmith put down his sledgehammer and walked up to Joe Noose, who stood by the counter of the stall. "Help you, mister?"

"I'd like to know if a man brought in a broken cattle brand for repair. The brand was shaped like a *Q*. The customer had three fingers missing on his right hand."

"How is that any business of yours?"

"I asked you a question."

"And I just asked you one."

"My name's Joe Noose. I'm a bounty hunter. I'm working for two U.S. Marshals and we're hunting a killer who uses that brand."

Noose looked at the rough-hewn bearded tradesman, covered with sweat from the burning coal brazier by the anvil. He towered over the smaller man, but the blacksmith clenched a sledgehammer in his scarred fist and showed no fear holding the bounty hunter's gaze. Along the racks on the frame of the stall hung forged chains, yokes, hooks, and cattle brands, but none Noose saw had a *Q* on them.

"How do you know the brand was broke?"

"I broke it."

"That ain't my problem."

"What *is* your problem?"

"I don't like people asking about my business or my customers."

"Problem here, Joe?"

Noose turned to see Marshal Bess had walked up beside him on the left. Marshal Ford sidled up to the counter on his right. The blacksmith looked at the woman lawman who looked back hard. "I'm U.S. Marshal Bess Sugarland and this man works for me. He asked you a question about whether someone paid you to fix a broken *Q* brand and now I'm askin' and I require you to answer or me and Marshal Ford here will drag your ass over to Sheriff Potter and lock you up because this is an active murder investigation and you ain't cooperating. Do we understand each other, friend?"

"I ain't fixed no broken brands."

"You sure?"

"Ain't seen no three-fingered men, neither."

"Why didn't you say that in the first place?"

"Because I didn't like the way this big guy was lookin' at me."

Bess chuckled not in a nice way. "Well, ain't how he looks at you that should concern you because he looks at everybody that way. It's him hitting you that you want to worry about. Have a nice day, sir."

Leaving the blacksmith's stall, Noose, Bess, and Emmett headed down the block toward the stable.

As they rounded the corner, Noose saw a flash of yellow, thought he saw a man with a yellow kerchief standing watching him, then duck out of sight, but when he looked again there was nobody wearing anything yellow among the passing people.

"Hold up," Noose said. Something had caught his attention. His two companions stopped where he did and followed his gaze to a building down a side street.

The Wyoming chapter of the Cattlemen's Association was on the edge of town. A large barn and stockade had several small offices in an unfinished wood structure. The organization had a small staff that managed the supervision of all the cattle ranches from Casper to Evanston.

"What are you thinking, Joe?" Bess asked.

"I'm thinking it's time we find out what ranch that Q brand belongs to. There can't be more than one. The

Wyoming Cattlemen's Association keeps a register of all the ranches in the territory and keeps their brands on record."

"Yes, it does," agreed Emmett.

"Our next stop," said Bess.

The three manhunters walked down the street to the entrance of the Cattlemen's Association and went through the door, unaware they were being closely watched.

Mason Cole had been reaching for his gun, having a clean shot at Joe Noose's back when his target was arguing with the blacksmith five minutes ago, then those damn marshals showed up out of nowhere and the ex-con missed his opportunity to kill the bounty hunter. It was suicide to try it with the two lawmen present because they'd shoot him dead.

Cursing fate, Cole hung back, leaning against the wall across the street in the shade of the overhang, where he blended in with the crowd. It was freezing but he was sweating. Wiping perspiration from his forehead with his filthy yellow kerchief, he noticed his hands were shaking from nerves. He willed them to be still, settled down, and kept watch on the three people across the street talking to the blacksmith. Shortly whatever business needed to be conducted was finished, and Noose headed off down the street in the company of the two marshals. When they were two hundred yards away, Mason Cole began to follow from an inconspicuous distance. His mean eyes locked on the big man's back were squinting and stinging because Cole wasn't blinking—no way he would miss the moment when the three split up and the bounty hunter was alone again . . . when he, Cole, would strike. He guessed the bounty hunter and the marshals weren't leaving town anytime soon. They were here on some kind of business, probably chasing a bounty, and were making a lot of stops, probably seeing if anybody had seen whomever they were after.

Mason Cole told himself all he had to do was be patient, wait until Noose stepped away from the others—a man has to eventually: everybody needs to take a leak at some point.

He'd get another shot at Joe Noose.

Inside the Wyoming chapter of the Cattlemen's Association, the three manhunters entered a large warehouse room, well appointed for the rough-hewn town. The room was lined with bookshelves stacked with records in volumes and loose- or bound-paper form. The place had a musty, cozy atmosphere, due to the comforting warmth of the wood-burning cast-iron stove against the wall, and the pleasurable aroma of hot coffee bubbling on the burner. A single clerk labored at a desk in the middle of the room.

"Let me do the talking," Noose said.

Bess made an ushering *be my guest* gesture with her glove, and she and Emmett followed Noose to the desk where the ruddy young clerk in a bow tie and spectacles sat going over papers. He looked up with a friendly smile, taking notice of the two silver badges on the man's and woman's chests. "How can I help the U.S. Marshals Service?"

Noose stepped forward, taking off his hat, and spoke in a serious tone of voice. "We're trying to find the ranch that a particular brand belongs to. Would you have that information?"

"Mostly, yes. Can you describe the brand?"

"It's a *Q*. Shaped like the capital letter."

"*Q*, eh? That's common. There may be more than one. But if it's in Wyoming, we should have a record. Well, let me look it up. Give me a few minutes."

The clerk stepped away from his desk and went to a large shelf lined with dusty leather-bound volumes and selected one. He pulled it down, set it on a back table, and began thumbing through the pages while the three man-hunters waited, exchanging uncertain glances.

The clerk finally stopped at one page. "I found a Bar Q ranch. Owner is one Abraham Quaid."

Noose raised an eyebrow. "In Wyoming."

"Correct."

"Would you have a location for the ranch?"

"Yes. It says here the address for the Bar Q ranch we have listed is in Consequence."

"Where the hell is that?"

"Let's take a look at the map." The clerk gestured the bounty hunter and two marshals over to a ten-foot map of Wyoming that was framed on the wall. Adjusting his spectacles, he found Wind River, their current location, with his finger, then traced his finger left and up on the map until he located a designation in a remote area for a place called Consequence, Wyoming.

"It's about a hundred and seventy miles northwest of here. Middle of nowhere, actually. Closest town is Consequence, five miles from the ranch itself. It's quite a ride from Wind River."

"You're sure about all this?"

"Well, this individual Abraham Quaid listed as the rightful owner filed the ranch and brand in July 1830, fifty years ago. Nothing to say the place is still there. But they use a *Q* brand, or used to."

"Still do," Noose said grimly.

"Hope this was of help to you folks. Help yourself to some coffee over by the stove if you have a mind to. I have to get back to work. A lady cattleman named Laura Holdridge at the Bar H Ranch is planning a giant longhorn drive to Cheyenne for the big Cattleman's Association auction. Her husband just died, so there's a lot of paperwork I have to do to get the ownership transfers of all those cows in order. Got to get back to work. Good day, Marshals."

It was damn cold outside and a lot warmer inside the Cattlemen's Association building. It was good to be out of the elements, so the three manhunters went over to the stove and poured themselves coffee, talking things over.

"He has a name now."

Emmett and Bess looked at Noose, wondering what he meant. He went on. "The man who branded me has a name. The Brander has a name: Abraham Quaid."

Bess nodded.

So did Emmett, with a heavy sigh. "Good to know."

Joe Noose's gaze had a distant look, his eyes filled with storm clouds. "I need to go to the ranch. The ranch that belongs to that brand."

"You never knew where it was until now?"

"No."

"No idea?"

"Wyoming, I figured, I guess."

"All these years you never gone back, Joe?"

"No reason to. Until now."

Noose was not being truthful; he could have found it, could find anybody anywhere on the planet, but the ranch where he was branded was the last place he ever wanted to set foot again. The very thought of going there created a disagreeable sensation in him.

Fear.

Joe Noose was a man afraid of nothing.

Except, it seemed, the old man who branded him; the one time in his life he was helpless, tortured, and victimized. Noose felt his stomach go queasy and a weakness in his limbs at the thought of returning to that damned ranch.

Yet somewhere, deep inside, the bounty hunter had always known he would one day return to the place where his soul was forged by the branding iron, and he felt destiny pulling him there now.

Marshal Bess was watching Noose closely and seemed to intuit what the voices of inner demons were saying to him, but her steady supportive gaze said *I'll be there, right beside you.*

The other marshal tugged laconically on his Stetson and pulled his beard. "I think going to that ranch sounds like a total waste of valuable time that we should be getting after this killer," Emmett sputtered. "Okay, so the old man came from there, but he sure as hell ain't there now, in the first place. Plus we got no idea where it is, in the second place."

"I think we'll find some answers there," Noose said.

"We'll ride there directly, first thing tomorrow," Bess stated.

It was decided.

The trio separated a few minutes later to canvas the town and question the locals; it would save time if they split up and spoke to the owners and employees to see if they had seen the three-fingered man who now had a name besides The Brander. Noose would talk to the stablemaster, Bess would talk to the grocer and gunsmith, and Emmett would talk to the owner of the feed store and any other places in that part of town.

As Noose was walking away alone, he turned into an alley leading to the stable.

And Mason Cole knew this was his moment.

The ex-con crossed the street and followed the man whose guts he hated into the alley, tailing about fifty feet behind. And as soon as he was in the alley, Mason Cole drew both pistols and took aim at the dead center of Joe Noose's back.

Joe Noose whirled, his right hand sliding his Colt Peacemaker out of his holster, finger on the trigger but not squeezing it, the clean action of the slide of the draw once the barrel cleared the holster and was up, pushing the top of the gun under his flattened left palm pulling and releasing the hammer and shooting the bullet—Joe Noose fanning and firing took a fraction of a second less than it would have taken for him to squeeze the trigger, but that fraction of a second cost Mason Cole his life.

The .45 round punched a dime-sized hole in his heart.

Cole was dead before he hit the ground.

Joe Noose didn't like killing a man.

But he didn't hesitate when he had to.

His reflexes were still good.

After The Brander gave him that case of nerves, it was good to know.

Damn good.

CHAPTER 15

Her hot bath felt exquisite.

Bess Sugarland was sunk in the big copper tub up to her neck. Beside her, a large boiling pot of water sat on a chair. The steam fogged the windows of the cozy hotel room, past the curtains.

It had been a month since she had been able to bathe, out on the cold, rugged trail, and if the water wasn't black, it felt like it should be. Right now, she luxuriated, felt the searing water relax her tired, knotted muscles, laid her head back.

She took another swig of whiskey from the bottle on the floor beside her; it was good local scotch malt, and burned her throat going down in a good way, giving her a glow all over. She'd forgotten about life's pleasures.

It was good to be alone.

She liked the men she rode with like brothers, one anyway, but a girl needed alone time.

Her inebriated eye caught the glint of the U.S. Marshal's badge sitting with her clothes atop the comfortable mattress and clean sheets she could not wait to climb into.

It was good to take the badge off.

A girl needed to be a girl sometimes, even when she was a lawman.

As Bess blissed out in the steam, her tensions melting away in the hot tub, her mind wandered back over the events of the long day.

The day had ended with a literal bang when Joe Noose shot a man who was gunning for him. The bounty hunter had immediately identified the corpse as one Mason Cole, a decade-old dead-or-alive bounty he had delivered to Laramie back in the day. From the looks of things, the man had spotted Noose someplace and come for some payback. Bess reflected that her friend Joe must have to live his life looking over his shoulder for the men he brought in alive on dead-or-alive bounties coming after him someday; it was the cost of doing business of how he made his living. Noose had to appreciate the risk that some of his bounties would want revenge, must know it would be safer and easier to kill them rather than leave them alive where they could retaliate—killing them was perfectly legal in a dead-or-alive bounty—but knowing all that, Joe Noose still stuck to his code about bringing in the men alive when he could. With that insight, the lady marshal's admiration and affection for her friend grew greater.

It had been a brouhaha today when the bullets started flying. Sheriff Potter had come running and though he may have made a doddering first impression, the lawman took a hard line about gunfights in his town of Wind River and conducted a hard-nosed investigation that involved a tough interrogation of Joe Noose. Luckily for Joe, a witness came forward: a stable hand was coming out of the barn just when Mason Cole drew his guns to shoot Noose in the back and saw the whole thing when Noose drew first and shot his attacker down in self-defense. The stable hand's story matched the bounty hunter's, two U.S. Marshals vouched for their companion's character, and for Sheriff Potter the case was closed.

After that, Noose, Bess, and Emmett checked into the town's one fine hotel and splurged on a hot steak dinner and a lot of drinks. For the first time since they lit out on their journey, the three of them relaxed and laughed and enjoyed one another's company as friends. The steaks were excellent.

Afterward, drunk, happy, and ready to sleep in a real bed, the trio retired to their rooms. And Bess Sugarland repaired to her long-dreamed-of hot bath where she now slumbered peacefully in the comforting water.

She had sweet dreams that night.

It would be the last ones she would have for a long time to come.

Chapter 16

The cattle were lowing.

Three hundred head of steer stood in the Wyoming winter valley in the dead of night.

The solitary wrangler Lonny Seed had the shit detail, the graveyard shift. Six hours from midnight to sunrise, sitting on his frozen saddle in the middle of the herd, keeping an eye on the stock. Here Lonny sat, straddling his pony, in the middle of the steers. The night was almost pitch-black from the fingernail moon carving a snick through the fuzzy winter clouds overhead. Hulking bodies of the cattle were mountainous shadowed shapes looming across the frozen tundra on all sides of his horse, disappearing off into the darkness where they could be heard but not seen. The stink of cow shit was gag-inducing.

Christ, it was cold.

The cowboy's bones were chilled to the marrow.

Hugging himself, Lonny felt a series of uncontrollable shivers shudder through his system—with his running nose and hacking cough expelling condensed breath into the arctic cold, he knew he was getting sick.

Casting a surly sidelong look to his left, he saw the

distant tiny light of the kerosene lamp in the crew tent three hundred yards away at the eastern edge of the herd— a lone beacon in the void like a solitary star in the sky— where the other six wranglers and ramrods were warm and asleep under their blankets. He was anything but, out here in the frozen hell.

What was the bitterest pill for Lonny Seed to swallow was that not two months ago the cowboy had been sitting on a horse looking out over a herd of prime steers twice the size of this that he and his gang *owned*—*stole*, to be precise, but those cattle were theirs and he had an equal share—he'd been a damn cattle baron or as close as he'd ever been to one. Now, through the cruel workings of fate, Lonny no longer owned any cattle and had been reduced to hiring on as a two-bit wrangler tending another man's herd so he could earn enough money to eat. How far he had fallen in so quick a time. His lonely, miserable post allowed him plenty of time to wallow in self-pity.

Only when he noticed the fumes of condensation billowing up from his chin around his face, did Lonny realize his teeth were chattering and he'd been cursing under his breath.

The only good thing about the damn subzero temperatures was the cattle didn't budge. It was too cold for them, too. And them not moving was a good thing because in the black of night, a hundred tons of bulls could flatten you and your horse if a few of them started moving, because they could barely see you in the daytime and were blind in absolute dark like this.

Presently, Lonny Seed realized he was not alone.

There was somebody else out here in the herd with him.

His first reaction was relief, figuring the foreman had sent one of the other ramrods out to split the shift.

"Jones? Flaherty? That one of you boys out there?" he called into the ubiquitous gloom. Nobody answered. "Hannerty. Cable?" Still no answer. Lonny squinted out at row after row of shadowy bovine backs, looming like a range of lumpy hills into the dim. And he saw all the horns. Jutting forests of long, jagged steer horns, far as the eye can see.

A few of the cattle shifted position.

Somebody was pushing through the steers, on foot, coming his way. But Lonny couldn't see who, only the displacement of the steers indicating the interloper's position. Involuntarily, the wrangler's hand touched the stock of his holstered Colt Navy. "Who's out there?" Again, no answer.

The cowboy caught just a glimpse of the glow before it disappeared, a radiance like red-hot metal.

Swinging in the saddle, Lonny looked left and right, drawing his pistol and not taking any chances. The sound of the cattle hooves thumping the hard frozen ground was becoming more audible. His sneaky brown eyes slid left and right, seeing nothing but cows. Cursing himself for letting his nerves get the better of him, the cowboy took a deep breath and tried to settle down in the saddle. He had hours on his shift to go yet.

His stiff half-frozen hand clenched and unclenched on the stock of his Colt revolver, his fingers too numb to return it to his holster.

He saw a flash of glowing metal.

Felt the white-hot burning anguish explode through his tendons and flesh of his hand, looking down in horror as the pistol flew from his grip to see the branding iron pressed against the back of his glove, the glove erupting in fire. Then, as he swatted at the flames on his glove setting his hand aflame, trying desperately to pull the glove off, the tall thin black figure standing beside his horse swung the ax and buried it to the hilt in Lonny's arm. Hot steaming blood splattered to the sickening sound of the steel hacking through cloth, flesh, and bone. A stunned Lonny Seed fell out of the saddle on the pony with his left arm half off. As he dropped five feet to the ground with a hard impact, gravity tore the hatchet from his bicep. He landed on his back on rock-hard frozen earth between the rows of steer hooves.

Screaming from the unbearable agony of his hacked arm, Lonny writhed and squirmed, trying to rise as a cowboy boot smashed down on his neck, the Mexican rowel of the spur slashing a spurting wound across his cheek with a savage twist of the heel.

"P-please . . ." the cowboy gagged, eyes bugging out as he stared up in the darkness at the shadow of his assailant towering above him, his dread, baleful gaze felt but not seen behind the long white hair.

Lonny recognized him.

"We killed you!" Seed choked.

"Yes. You did. And now it's my turn to kill you. But first, I want the others. All the rest. And you're going to tell me. Where are they?"

The horrible twisted claw missing three fingers in the glove held a blazing *Q* branding iron and now that mangled hand lifted it toward the felled cowboy's face . . . the red-hot metal got closer and closer, the heat growing hotter and hotter as the glowing curlicue approached the unprotected skin of his cheek, through the coil the terrified man saw the glowing red light of the metal reflected on The Brander's eyes, turning them demonic and gleaming.

"I don't know!" Lonny Seed whimpered. *"I swear! Don't burn me, mister!"*

"I want the gang!"

"It's the law you want, mister! We paid them off!"

"Paid *who* off?"

Lonny Seed gave him two names.

Then the fiend picked Lonny up by the hair, lifting him off the ground by a fistful of his grimy locks. His strength, fueled by psychosis, was incredible. The cowboy grabbed the glove holding his hair, screaming in agony feeling his own weight pull his hair out at the roots. The Brander lifted his victim's head to face the huge black bull, whose nostrils snorted steam in the frigid air, so close the tortured Lonny could kiss it. Then the fiend rammed the cowboy's face down onto the two-foot steer horn, driving the sharp tip clean through the man's eyeball, skull eye socket, and into his brain. In the moonlight, shiny black-looking blood and glistening wet matter splattered the cow's face and horns, and it *mooed* in irritation, blinking gore out of its globular eye. Tossing its head to and fro, the bull tried to shake the dead cowboy gored on its horn off, but the limp body was firmly impaled through the eye socket. The corpse just hung on the side of the longhorn's big head, dead limbs flopping this way and that like a rag doll with each toss of the annoyed steer's head.

The Brander was long gone by the time the angry bull finally shook its horn loose of the dead man by ramming him to a pulp against a fence post, then trampled him for good measure, and by the time folks came running, about the only recognizable part of what used to be a human being was the *Q* brand on his shoulder.

CHAPTER 17

The Brander sat by a campfire, reading by the light of the flames.

He had a list of names on a piece of paper.

He scratched the name *Lonny Seed* out.

Four other names had already been scratched out.

With his pen, the fiend added two new names to the list . . .

CHAPTER 18

Back in Jackson, Puzzleface wasn't talking.

She hadn't said a word for three days in her hospital bed at the clinic.

Deputy Sweet gave up trying to question her.

She wouldn't give her name.

Wouldn't answer any questions about why she was disguising herself as a man.

If she knew who had shot her, she wasn't talking.

Doc Jane had cleaned and sewn up the wound, bandaged and splinted the arm, and expected the woman who called herself Puzzleface, whoever she was, to make a full recovery.

Who she was remained a mystery.

For Deputy Sweet, Puzzleface was the biggest thing to hit town since he became interim marshal but he wished Bess was here because he didn't know what to do. This situation was above his pay grade. He was in charge, so he needed to figure it out. The lawman's guard-dog instincts told him not to leave Puzzleface's side. Whoever took a shot at her was still out there and might want to take another crack at her. So for the first three days Deputy Sweet lived at the clinic, carrying his loaded and cocked Winchester rifle and pistols on his person everywhere he went. Every few hours the deputy went out on patrols on Pearl Street, checking if the area was safe.

Twice while inside, he thought he spotted somebody through the window watching the clinic from across the street, but when he rushed outside fully armed, whoever he thought he saw was gone.

Doc Jane diligently ministered to the mystery woman's needs, changing her bandages and cleaning her wound. Infection had not set in but the bullet, likely a .45, had punched a hole through a lot of her muscle and the woman was in great pain, sobbing frequently. The doctor gave her laudanum, which helped ease her suffering, but while the morphine solution made the patient loopy, it did not loosen her tongue. The female approach Doc Jane attempted to use to question her got no answers out of her.

Until on the fourth day right after breakfast when at last finally she spoke.

"Thank you for saving my life."

The deputy and the doctor exchanged glad smiles and sat by her bed. "How 'bout you return the favor by answering some of my questions?" Sweet said.

"I can't."

"Why not?"

"I just can't."

"Can you tell us your name at least?" Doc Jane asked gently.

"Rachel."

"Rachel who?"

She smiled wanly, tight-lipped. It was all the name she was going to give and it would have to do.

"Is that your real name?"

She nodded.

"I'm here to protect you, Rachel." Sweet placed his hand on hers securely.

The mystery woman grabbed his hand, desperately. "If you want to protect me then please, please, don't tell anybody who I am, nobody can know I'm a lady. Please promise not to tell nobody I'm Puzzleface."

Sweet looked at the frightened woman and every instinct told him the way to deal with her right now was not to push. Not generally good dealing with people, he somehow seemed to know how to deal with this one. "Just me and Doc Jane is the only people know you're a lady, Rachel, and we're gonna keep it our little secret. For now."

"Thank you."

"Get some rest."

"A word?" Deputy Sweet showed Doc Jane into her kitchen out of earshot of their enigmatic patient. She made a cup of tea and they sat and drank while he explained his predicament. "Help me out, Doc. I don't know what I'm doing here. I ain't got the faintest who that woman is or why somebody's trying to kill her. This is above my pay grade. I'm just a deputy. This is a job for Marshal Bess, and I don't know if I got the experience to deal with this here situation."

The lady doctor was a good listener; she knew the overwhelmed young lawman just needed to let off some steam. "How can I help, Nate?"

"I got the badge. Means it's my job to protect Rachel but how the hell can I when I don't know who's trying to kill her or why, when I don't even know who she is? I need a few clues, a place to start. You're a doctor and you're a woman. You understand people's heads. Can you tell me anything about Rachel, who you think she might be, who might be after her?"

"I don't know any more about her than you do, Nate. Except . . ." Her brow furrowed.

"Except what?"

"I know she has been beaten. After I asked you to leave the room when I took off Rachel's clothes for the operation, I saw the marks on her. You didn't see them and I saw no reason to bring it up until now. I'd say she suffered regular physical beatings in her past over a long period of time. And the scar on her face, of course."

"Rachel ain't no train robber. Ain't no criminal of any kind. I agree she's running from somebody and whoever it is probably gave her that scar. Somebody she's scared enough of to disguise herself as a man so nobody finds out her true identity, perhaps."

"Perhaps."

"But I still don't know who I'm looking for. It could be anybody in town. You think she had a husband who was beating her, so she ran away from him and he's coming after her? And that's who's trying to kill her?"

"It might not be a husband. It could be a boyfriend. A father. A brother. A son even. Violent physical abuse against women by men is a plague out here in the West, Nate. Beatings can be fatal. Most of violence against women happens in their home. There's no law on the books against husbands beating wives. None that gets enforced anyway. Wives are seen as legal property. A man kills a whore he gets the noose. A man kills his wife he gets away with murder."

"No man got a right to lay a hand on a woman." Sweet got emotional. "Just never understood why wives just don't leave their husbands if they beat on 'em."

"The stronger women leave, like Rachel, perhaps." Doc Jane gestured to the next room where the patient was sleeping. "But so many are afraid to. Some women who have been abused develop what you might call battered-woman behavior. They won't leave. They won't tell anybody who beat them. They're too scared to fight back, so they shut down. This silence and fear I've seen in so many of these poor victims, Rachel has it, too."

"How do you explain Puzzleface?"

"I can't."

"She's two people."

"What are you going to do with both of them?" Doc Jane asked.

"Rachel can't stay here. I'm going to move her over to the Jackson Hotel while she's recovering. She can take her meals in her room and have housekeeping and all the amenities. I'll post myself in the room next door where I can keep an eye on her. There's always people around at the hotel, and less likely the shooter will try something with folks around, so I'd feel safer with her there. Hopefully she'll start talking to me and give me a face and a name on who's trying to kill her."

The lawman got a very worried look from the physician. "Be careful, Nate. Right now you still don't know who this killer is. Like you said, the person who shot Rachel could be anybody in town. What if they try to shoot her again at the hotel?"

"That's exactly what I'm counting on, Doc." Deputy Sweet checked the loads in his revolver and spun the cylinder closed with a ratcheting *whir*, giving Doc Jane a confident wink. "Because this time I'm gonna be there."

* * *

Outside the clinic, the man stood across the street smoking a cigar, watching the place. He had been there on and off for the three days since the night he followed that deputy there with Rachel, keeping the clinic under regular surveillance. The woman he shot in the back was inside, still alive. But she couldn't stay there forever. That lawman was protecting her but he'd have to move Rachel and then the man would get another shot at her.

His first bullet didn't kill her but his next one would.

The suite on the second floor of the Jackson Hotel was very comfortable. The bill for the room and the room next door was being charged to the U.S. Marshals Service because the guest was under their federal protection. The luxurious suite was the best Jackson had to offer, as swank as it got in the late 1880s. It had a window overlooking Broadway and the quaint storefronts across on the other side, and another window looking out on the town square, but Sweet told Rachel to keep the pretty lace curtains closed at all times. The four-poster bed had a plush feather mattress, silk sheets, velvet blankets, and a fluffy duvet, with plenty of room for a lady to stretch out on. The walls were lovely lavender brocade wallpaper. A large armoire stood beside a full-length mirror and a cedar chest of drawers. The floors were thick oriental carpet. The deputy did a spot-check of the accommodations, room by room. A large adjoining bathroom with a deep tub and hot running water and a bidet. A small kitchen had a working stove with plenty of wood and a teapot. The deputy had booked the best room in the hotel for a week.

Sweet chuckled to himself, picturing the look on Marshal Bess's face when she saw the expense account ledger receipts for the hotel charges. But there wasn't anything she could say about it; she left him in charge and the expenses were his to authorize, although Nate bet Bess would dock part of his pay anyway. So be it. Puzzleface was worth it.

One last detail to check. The deputy unlocked the door in the wall that connected into the adjoining hotel room where Deputy Sweet was booked, close enough to Rachel to effectively execute his joint duties as bodyguard and marshal—if anybody came to break into her room, he'd hear them coming up the hall, and if somehow they got past him, he'd be through the connecting door and into her room, guns drawn, before they got near Rachel.

"I'll be next door." Sweet gestured reassuringly at the open door but Rachel just sat like a depressed lump on the bed.

"I'm afraid to go out."

"You don't have to go out. They'll bring your meals right here."

"How long?"

"Until I arrest this guy. It would be quicker if you told me who he was."

Silence from her.

There was a knock on the door. Rachel whipped her head around with the look of a frightened deer. Sweet gave her a calm glance as he drew his Colt Navy revolver and went warily to the door. "Who is it?"

"Nate, it's Jim Gardner. Brought Mr. Taylor's belongings from the Miller Ranch like you asked me to."

When Sweet reached for the doorknob, Rachel flew into a panic. Fearful she would be seen without her Puzzleface disguise, Rachel dashed madly around the room, desperately looking for a place to hide. The sight was comical and sad. Hurriedly Sweet stashed her into the bathroom, closing the door.

Then he opened the front door and took the luggage from the cowboy standing there. "Obliged, Jim."

"Say hi to Bill for me, Nate."

"Ol' Puzzleface is around here someplace." Sweet winked. He closed the door and set Puzzleface's bags on the floor. "Safe to come out now."

The bathroom door cracked and Rachel's one big eye peered out. Seeing the coast was clear and it was just the two of them, she returned to the room. The woman had changed into a hotel robe.

Rachel plopped right back down on the bed and sunk into her depressed, defeated mind-set, the battered-woman mentality the doctor had spoken of. Rachel pulled her knees up to her nose, wrapped her elbows around her legs, and rocked back and forth, staring into space. "He's gonna get me."

"Nobody's gonna get you, Rachel. I'm the law and I'm here and nobody's getting past me." Sweet pointed to the badge on his chest. "He's not going to get you. Tell me his name and what he looks like and I'll go out there and arrest him right now." He rose and went to the window, pushed aside the lace curtain, and looked down at the street to see if anybody was watching the hotel. Didn't look like it.

Rachel sat like a discarded rag doll at the end of the bed, staring passively at her hands in her lap. "He should get me. I deserve it. I deserve whatever he does to me."

His eyes narrowing, Deputy Sweet threw her a sharp look across the room and somehow suddenly just knew. He sat beside her on the bed. "The man who shot you is your husband."

Pain flashed in her eyes and he knew it was true.

"You ran away from your husband."

She nodded.

Sweet was going to ask Rachel why she ran away but he already knew why. How badly her abusive husband beat and hurt her he could only guess, but him shooting her in the back showed what he was capable of. The deputy had seen other women in Rachel's damaged mental state when the marshals broke up domestic disputes in the territory. As Nate recognized the battered-woman behavior in Rachel, she became less of a mystery. She had the beaten wives' mental condition. The scourge of domestic violence against women was the dark side of the Old West, fanned by excesses of booze and violence, ugly acts of brutality by husbands and lovers too ignorant to know better against wives treated like property and defenseless girlfriends too afraid to fight back because they had nowhere else to go.

Nate Sweet knew the look so well.

He grew up with it.

His mother beaten by his drunken father on their farm to keep her dominated and submissive, using his belt and his fists, Nate's mother covering her little boy with her body taking the blows instead.

His mom never did stand up to his brutal dad.

It was up to Nate to do that for her.

As he sat beside Rachel, Nate felt his old familiar fury at this poor woman's abuse and with it came resolve.

This man would never hurt this woman again.

Sweet had the gun to make certain and the badge to make it legal.

The woman sitting next to him hated herself. "I was a bad wife. Whatever he's gonna do to me, I got coming."

"Don't say that, Rachel." He held her hand. "It ain't true.

No woman ever deserves to be hit. It's wrong for any man to beat a woman. My father used to beat on my mother and I know."

"He did?"

"Until I put a stop to it."

Her eyes lit up. "What did you do?"

"When I was sixteen my mother got one beating too many. I took a sledgehammer and broke both my daddy's kneecaps. My old man never walked again. Never hit my mother again, neither."

Rachel's whole face lit up. "Good."

"Nothing in this world I hate more than a man hitting a woman," Sweet said. "It's as personal as it gets."

Rachel got off the bed, her mood less despondent. Her bandaged and splinted arm appeared to be hurting her. Going to the bathroom medicine cabinet, she uncorked her bottle of laudanum and took a draft. He watched her through the door as she shut her eyes, waiting for the morphine to kick in. Its effect was immediate, and dreamily Rachel went to her luggage and opened it.

Sweet sat and watched as Rachel opened the suitcase and unpacked the clothes. It was all men's clothes, and everything belonged to Puzzleface.

His silk jacket.

His satin vest.

His black velvet trousers.

His frilled shirt.

His diamond tiepin.

Lovingly, carefully, neatly, Rachel hung up Puzzleface's clothes on wooden hangers in the armoire. Her fingertips felt the electricity touching the fabric of her male disguise, and being physically close again to the garments coursed energy back into her limbs.

When the clothes were hung, Rachel took out the circus makeup kit that made her Puzzleface and opened it, delicately running her finger over the false mustaches, beards, and eyebrows among the canisters of powder and blush. A small smile of pleasure parted her lips.

Even though her back was turned to Deputy Sweet, Rachel's face was reflected in the full-length mirror and while the features were hers, the expression he saw was Puzzleface.

CHAPTER 19

Twenty miles out from the Bar Q ranch, Joe Noose felt his insides curdle long before the last place he ever wanted to see again came into view.

It was the smells of the trees and the soil that brought memories flooding back to him. It was too long ago for the bounty hunter to remember in what season he had been branded, though he knew it was not winter, yet the white birch and pines had an olfactory-sense memory. His jaw was clenched tight as he rode in the lead with Bess on one side and Emmett on the other through a rising gradation of trees and hills pocketed with granite ravines and arroyos blanketed with snow.

He knew where he was, all right. It had been dusk twenty years ago when he and his ill-fated young friends had staked out the Bar Q ranch, and night when they had raided it only to be captured, tortured, and killed, still night when young Joe was put on his horse. But before the sun went down he had gotten a good look at the surroundings, remembered the position of the mountain peaks to the trees; it had all been burned into his memory by what came after.

"Place look familiar?" Emmett asked.

"Yeah, it looks familiar."

A new scent assaulted Noose's nostrils. Burned wood. Char. It reminded him of the smell of the vast forest-fire deforestation when he had ridden over the Teton Pass a few weeks ago—all those burned trees—but this was different; it was a smell of death.

At last, the trees parted and the three riders trotted into the Bar Q ranch, what was left of it.

"What the hell?"

They reined their horses and looked around in naked shock at the grim view. The ranch had been burned to the ground, and pretty recently. Not a structure remained standing. Not a living thing remained. The cattle stockade was empty of livestock. The buck-and-rail fencing was all burned, blackened with char, and collapsed in places from the fire damage. The snow around the grounds of the ranch was no longer white, but stained with char and ash, like a carpet of soot. A bleak carpet of black snow filled the empty floor of the stockade, gusting up in wind funnels like smoke.

The three riders slowly trotted through the ruins. Marshal Bess shook her head at the ravaged surroundings. "Man-made."

"Arson. No doubt," Noose replied. He slid a glance over to Emmett, whose expression was detached and unaffected by the sight of the burned ranch.

"What exactly are we hoping to find here?" the other marshal asked.

"I'll know when I find it," the bounty hunter replied curtly, his pale gaze hooded as he surveyed the area below his saddle with keen observation.

"The Brander ain't here," a frustrated Emmett protested.

"It's the last place he'd be. What makes you think this is where he ended up?"

"It's not where he ended up, it's where he started. For that old man, it all began here. And somewhere, in all this burn, there's clues. We're going to look around until we find them."

"Looks like one day that old man must have branded the wrong man," Bess said. "That's what comes from taking justice into your own hands."

The three rode around the perimeter of the fence and passed what used to be the barn; the wrecked structure was gutted by flames and in shambles, a rubble of broken burned boards. Noose remembered the corral by the barn was where his horse was shot from under him and he and his friends were captured and hog-tied at gunpoint. It was ashes now. "This was where they captured us, I remember."

His fierce gaze rose, following the path on the ground where he remembered the old man and his boys had dragged them to the other side of the stockade, and when Noose looked up, he saw the hanging tree.

What remained of it.

Clicking his teeth, the bounty hunter slowly trotted his horse up to the looming fire-blackened husk of a tree crooked against the steely winter sky. He stopped his horse below it, regarding the broken, charred branch where his friends once swung from ropes, the wretched dead tree no longer capable of executing anyone.

"This is where the old man and his boys hanged my friends. Right here. Twenty years ago. One of my friend's heads popped off in the noose like a cork in a bottle."

Behind him, Bess and Emmett had ridden up and sat on their horses, listening. Both the marshals were silent, respectful, and attentive hearing Noose recount the incident. The bounty hunter swung his horse around and rode past his friends to the edge of the burned corral. A round brick-and-iron fire pit had survived the flames, a blackened hole in the ground that looked like a pit leading to the underworld. Noose gazed at this from the saddle, spat into it, then lifted his gaze to his friends. "And right here, this is where they branded me."

"I'm sorry," Bess said.

"It is what it is," Noose replied.

Approaching the Bar Q ranch, the fear that had clenched Joe Noose's guts like a fist had unclenched now that he was here, his trepidation gone. A weight had been lifted from his soul. The overwhelming emotion he felt now was one of grim, savage satisfaction looking around at the old man's ranch burned to the ground, reduced to ashes. It gave him a gratifying sense of retribution to know that what went around, came around. What gave him an even greater sense of gladness was knowing that the old man had not been burned along with his ranch and Noose would still have his reckoning with Abraham Quaid, because some justice had to be hand-delivered, and Noose was determined the man who had become The Brander would meet his maker by Joe's own hand. For the first time since he had met up face-to-face with the old man, his nerves began to settle and he felt like himself again.

"What the hell happened here?" Bess wondered, looking around.

Shifting in his saddle, Emmett looked restless. "You two keep looking around. I'll go ride out to that town Consequence a few miles from here. We saw the sign back at the road. It'll have a sheriff's office. I'll find the top lawdog and ask him what happened out here at the Bar Q ranch. At least get us some answers. No reason for three of us to be up to our asses in ash. If there's anything to find here, Joe will be the one to find it."

"Suits me, Emmett." Bess nodded her approval.

Noose nodded, too.

"I'll be back directly." With a snap of his reins, Emmett Ford urged his pony into a fast gallop and rode hard past the burned corral up the hill where the snow began to whiten again and his shrinking horse disappeared over the rise out of sight.

It was just Joe Noose and Bess Sugarland now on the ranch, and whatever ghosts remained were whistling in the wind through the trees or shape-shifting in the gusts of sooty ash-black snow whipped up into what seemed like faces that disintegrated again.

"Emmett took off out of here like his ass was on fire," the bounty hunter said.

"My ass is on fire to take off out of here, too, Joe. This place gives me the creeps. I'd think it would you too, more than any of us."

"Nothing makes me happier than seeing this damned place burned to ash. I like being here to see it."

Then Noose saw something that hit him like a fist in the jaw.

"What the—?"

Releasing Copper's lead, Noose slid out of the saddle and dismounted. Then he slowly, deliberately walked step by step toward what his gaze had fixed on. When at last the bounty hunter stood over what captured his attention, he looked down in disbelief. *It was impossible. It couldn't be.*

A grave.

A plain, austere granite headstone.
Two words. Just a name.

ABRAHAM QUAID

"No," he whispered.

Bess had dismounted and walked up beside him. "That's the old man, isn't it?"

"That's what it says on the headstone."

"If he's dead then who the hell is The Brander?"

"Abraham Quaid *is* The Brander. I seen him. Looked in his eyes. Same eyes."

"Then who's buried in that grave?"

"Let's find out."

"But—"

"I need a shovel."

"You ain't thinking of . . . ?"

Noose's crazed, obsessed look told Bess that was exactly what he had in mind. She looked at him like he was nuts. "Why don't you just piss on his grave and be done with it?"

"I want to piss on his bones."

"What's the hell's wrong with you, Joe?"

But he had already grabbed the shovel from his saddlebags and stabbed it into the plot, digging up the grave . . .

An hour and a half later, Emmett Ford rode back over the hill to the Bar Q ranch.

His pouring sweat freezing to his body, Noose had been digging up the ground over Abraham's grave, hacking into the frozen soil with a pickax to break it up and using a shovel to clear the rock-hard chunks of dirt. He had dug five feet and was almost at the coffin. He breathed heavily from the exertion. It was not the first grave Joe Noose had dug and would not be the last, but with frozen ground, it was the hardest. The bounty hunter was thinking people had no idea how hard it is to dig a grave.

Bess spotted Emmett before Noose did, riding hell-for-leather down the long, tall hill like the Devil was snapping at his heels.

"He's back," she said.

Noose dropped the pickax and wiped sweat from his brow before it turned to ice. The perspiration in his long brown hair had turned to icicles. "Looks like he learned something."

Seconds later, Marshal Ford rode up and halted his horse with a jerk on the reins, hastily dismounting and walking up to his two confederates waiting with expectant looks on their faces. "I talked to the sheriff over in Consequence," he said. "He told me a year ago a gang of marauders hit this ranch. This group of outlaws who had been robbing and rustling raising hell in the territory. They stole the cattle. The rancher was alone when they hit. Sheriff said his name was Abe Quaid."

Abraham Quaid. The name to the face behind the brand that burned Noose, a name he would never forget.

Emmett went on, hardly catching his breath. "There was eight of the rustlers, one of them Quaid got a shot off with a scattergun then there was seven of them, but somebody opened up with his Henry rifle, and then it was seven to none. The gunman shot Abe Quaid dead. Or so they say."

"We're gonna find out soon enough." Noose grunted, lifting the shovel like a weapon to attack the grave again.

"Sheriff say anything else about the guy we think is The Brander?" Bess asked.

Emmett shook his head. "Not much. Said folks in the territory stayed clear of this farm while the old man was alive. Had a fearsome reputation as a dirty miserable son of a bitch recluse who didn't kindly take to strangers."

"You can say that again," the bounty hunter said, smirking.

"What happened with the gang who attacked this place?"

"After shooting Quaid, the outlaws stole the cattle and horses and burned the ranch to the ground. Their mistake was leaving the dead member of their party behind. When the sheriff and his deputies arrived, they identified the outlaw as Luke Dodge, who rode with the gang. Two days later, the Consequence lawmen caught up with the whole gang and ambushed them in a whorehouse, took 'em all into custody."

"Then what?" asked Bess.

"Here's the part that don't make sense. The gang went before the district judge on charges of rustling and murder and faced a hanging." Emmett Ford's expression darkened as he lost his composure and paused, collecting himself.

"They didn't get hanged," Marshal Bess guessed, with a sharp exhale of breath that condensed in the chill air.

Her male counterpart shook his head, incredulously. "They walked. The whole gang. The problem was there were no witnesses. And when the outlaws were arrested they didn't have any cattle or horses. Didn't have no money, either, so they didn't sell those steers off. Because there was no evidence, the judge acquitted them and the sheriff released them. But they were warned by the court to leave the territory. It was the last anybody saw of these outlaws. Rumor has it afterward the gang split up, rode off in different directions, and now they're spread across the states."

Noose brooded. "Who buried Abraham Quaid?"

"No idea. But what are you doing digging up his grave?"

The huge bounty hunter gritted his teeth as he put his immense back into shoveling the softening earth beneath the frozen crust of soil on the surface. His shoulder muscles clenched as with a final stab of the shovel, it hit wood.

"It's against the law and blasphemy against God to dig up a grave, Noose!"

"Shut up, Emmett."

The angry young lawman made a motion to lay a hand on the towering bounty hunter who ignored him but Bess stepped in between them, looking hard in the eyes of her agitated counterpart. *Back off.*

"What the hell are you looking for?" Emmett shouted.

"Answers."

Jumping down into the grave, Noose used his cattle hoof–sized bare hands to claw the dirt away from the coffin lid. Gritting his teeth, with a roar of effort, he tore the lid from the wooden casket.

Bess looked down with a gasp . . .

Emmett looked down, stunned, swallowing hard . . .

Noose looked down, unsurprised . . .

The coffin was empty!

Chapter 20

The three manhunters saddled up without conversation, for there was nothing to say—they all knew whom they were hunting. They had many questions but were certain when they caught up with Abraham Quaid, aka The Brander, they would get the answers.

Noose rode Copper in the lead, his majestic bronze horse happy to be riding up the hill away from the place of char and death. Right behind was Marshal Bess, her Appaloosa following in Copper's trail, in lockstep with the golden horse's commanding stride. Her male counterpart brought up the rear, tall in the saddle on his palomino, riding behind the other two.

Emmett Ford was remembering two hours ago when he said he was riding out to see the sheriff he told a lie. Instead Emmett had taken position in the nearby woods, undetected, to quietly spy on the distant figures of Noose and Bess investigating the grounds of the Bar Q ranch. He had tensed when he saw the bounty hunter start digging up the grave but didn't break cover. After waiting a credible amount of time, Emmett rode back down to the ranch, riding hard to tire his pony so they looked like they had traveled a considerable distance.

Even though he had not been to see the sheriff, Emmett knew exactly what had transpired at the ranch and could recount the story believably.

Most of it was true.

Part of it wasn't.

It was not the first time Emmett Ford had been to the Bar Q ranch.

Marshal Ford had a secret.

The secret was one of the many things he knew that his two companions didn't and the one thing he had to make sure they never found out; Noose and Bess wouldn't like Emmett's little secret.

That his real name wasn't Ford.

It was Quaid.

And Abraham Quaid was his father.

Emmett Quaid alias Marshal Ford's mission was not what Noose or Bess thought it was. Tracking down a mass murderer called The Brander to bring him to justice while Emmett was employed as a U.S. Marshal was merely his cover. Emmett Quaid was here as a son, his sole purpose finding his missing father, Abraham Quaid, so that when he found his dad, he could return him safely back home. Emmett didn't know the reason for his father's bloodthirsty killing spree—his father was a mad-dog killer, this he had to accept—but Abraham Quaid was still his father and nothing The Brander did made Emmett any less his son. Family is family. Blood comes first. Right now, Emmett had to find his dad, Abraham Quaid, before the law caught up with his father, for they'd surely kill him. He had only one father and Emmett couldn't face losing his dad. He'd already lost his younger brother.

He'd have nobody left in the world.

So it was his own kin that Emmett was on the trail of and desperately needed to find, not to arrest, but to bring him home.

How well Emmett Quaid remembered the night his father Abraham branded Joe Noose . . . it changed him and his little brother, Willard, forever. Made party against their will to the lynching and hanging of three boys their own ages ended Emmett and Willard's childhood in one savage stroke; their innocence had been shattered forever when the three boys swung and the fourth screamed at the end of a hot branding iron. Even now as a grown adult, Emmett still remembered the raw terror and horror he felt as those terrible events unfolded, and later the deadness he felt inside. Part of his soul was gone. Willard had borne the worst of it. Always a sensitive youth, something broke inside him that night.

The following morning, after Noose had been put on a horse and sent on his way, Abraham forced Emmett and Willard to help him burn the bodies of the hanged boys, so no evidence would remain. Willard had to collect the head that had been severed in the noose. The father made his traumatized sons dig a shallow pit. The three corpses were dragged there and set aflame with coal oil. The three stood and watched the bodies burn in the back of the ranch, until they were nothing but charred bones and ash. Then Abraham himself filled in the pit with dirt and no trace of the young outlaws remained. Nobody ever came looking for them and even if they had, they would have found not a trace. Nobody knew. Except the Quaids. And the boys would never, ever forget.

Their father, Abraham Quaid, had not always been

murderous, and certainly not the way he was now, the monster he had become.

Emmett would remember the night of the branding as the beginning of the Bad Time—those eight long, grim years of suffering for the two brothers growing up with their father on the Bar Q ranch. It was a time of pain, terror, and despair for himself and his little brother, Willard. They were subjected to the relentless torment of their father, less and less a man either of them recognized.

The death of the boys' mother, Abraham's wife, Cora, three years before had been what made their father mean. Perhaps it was the loneliness of the ranch without the comfort of the woman who had been at his side, perhaps the responsibility of raising two young sons on his own, keeping his pain and loss hidden from them, had bent the single father.

More and more tyrannical and isolated Abraham became.

Forbidding the boys to attend the local school, their father homeschooled them in the morning when they woke and later again at night before they went to bed. The Bible, the *Agricultural and Farming Journal* were their textbooks. He also taught them reading, writing, and arithmetic. He was a brutal disciplinarian.

The Q brand he used to burn Noose he now used as a cold metal rod to beat his children when they failed to measure up to his expectations or failed him in some way. The beatings were frequent. The brand kept his sons in fear of him and the loveless Abraham Quaid equated fear with respect.

By the time they were in their early teens, there were marked differences between Emmett Quaid and his younger brother, Willard Quaid. Emmett had grown up stronger and more resilient, bearing up more fitfully under Abraham Quaid's iron fist. Willard hadn't. The boy was sensitive and had severe emotional problems, given to swings of mood and occasional hysterical outbursts that brought the full force of his father's wrath down upon him, resulting in psychological and physical punishment that only made Willard worse, weaker, and more unstable.

Emmett took his share of punishment at his father's hand. But Abraham reserved a special harshness for Willard, the weaker of his two sons, who became the special object and focus of his cruelty. Their father thought his lessons did not make Willard a man. The boy was too weak, the runt of the litter. Emmett dared not stand up to his father and defy him by openly protecting Willard, but protect him he did: when Willard was unable to do his work because of his attacks of nerves Emmett did his chores for him; when the younger boy broke tools or dishes due to his clumsiness, Emmett took the blame and the beating with the rod—the cold branding iron—that followed—to this day he bore the scars on his buttocks and legs; and when in the night Willard burst into uncontrollable screams, Emmett lay in bed with his little brother with his hand on his mouth, stifling the cries so their father would not hear.

Always, big brother Emmett promised Willard he would look after him, and he kept his promise as long as he could. His younger brother was under his wing, constantly near his side, and in this way the boys somehow survived life with their father on the ranch the eight long years after the branding incident.

It all changed on the ranch when Emmett turned eighteen years of age.

He couldn't stay.

There was a world out there and he had to see it.

Emmett felt if he spent another day on his father's ranch he would die. Even now, he believed he would have. So one fateful morning, he woke before dawn and saddled his pony. Kissing his sleeping brother Willard a last time, Emmett wept as he rode out of the Bar Q ranch and never looked back. He never said good-bye to his father.

For his eighteenth and nineteenth years, Emmett Quaid traveled Wyoming and Idaho, finding work from his skills as a hardworking ranch hand and going from place to place. Drawn by a sense of right and wrong and protecting the defenseless baked into him by his family upbringing, he soon found work in law enforcement, working as a sheriff's deputy in several small towns.

It was serving as a deputy, when one day Emmett witnessed a tough group of brave U.S. Marshals rout a gang of outlaws who held up a local bank. The federal marshals had ridden in and immediately taken over from the sheriff Emmett worked for, taking instant charge with the authority the badge gave them and the fearless moral character the men had about them. Within fifteen minutes, the stand-off was over, all the bank robbers gunned down by the U.S. Marshals and slung over their saddles. Emmett Quaid watched them in awe, and at twenty-one years of age, decided he would be a federal marshal.

Turning in his deputy badge, he set off for the U.S. Marshals headquarters in Laramie, Wyoming, and filled out his application. He was accepted. There, he received training in firearms, horsemanship, serving warrants, and all manner of technical law enforcement, and by his twenty-second year, he had become a deputy marshal. At age twenty-six, he was a full-fledged U.S. Marshal stationed in Pocatello, Idaho.

In all those years, he thought of his father and his

brother less and less, tried to forget the terrible place he was from, and had nearly forgotten it all.

Then one day at the U.S. Marshal's office in Pocatello, Emmett received the letter from his father telling him his younger brother, Willard, was dead. The note, written in Abraham Quaid's terse poor penmanship, was brief and to the point: Willard had taken ill of consumption and his weak constitution had failed, causing his death. He was buried on the ranch. The letter relayed the information and nothing else, a note as cold and brutal as the parent who wrote it. Emmett never wrote back.

While he maintained his duties as a deputy marshal and continued to train, Emmett Quaid privately labored under a black depression. Racked with guilt, he believed himself to be to blame for his little brother's death; if only he had stayed home to look after Willard, the boy would be alive. During the Bad Time, Emmett had promised Willard he would always protect him but in the end he'd broken his word, and now his brother was dead. In the barracks, when the other men slumbered, he would weep himself to sleep. Emmett hated his father for a very long time until he came to accept that not only had he failed as a brother but he had also failed as a son by abandoning his father, too. The U.S. Marshals Service had forged in him a sense of duty and personal responsibility, and Emmett Quaid accepted that his act of leaving home, where his family needed him, resulted in terrible consequences because of his actions.

Family is everything, the good and the bad of it.

Several years went by and Emmett Quaid kept planning to take a leave to go back and visit his father, Abraham Quaid, but every time he was ready to, something held him back inside from going back to the dreaded ranch.

It was his father who came to him one fateful day when

a report arrived at the Pocatello U.S. Marshal's office about a killer using a Q brand on his victims.

Emmett Quaid requested the assignment to track down the murderer, and was given it.

As he rode out after The Brander, Emmett knew his trail would lead him home.

Emmett felt bad about how unfairly fate had bound his and Joe Noose's destinies together now their paths were inescapably intertwined; after what their father had done to Noose as a boy, after all this time, Emmett was using Noose to save the very man who branded him.

The worst of it was once his father was found, Emmett Quaid fully intended to shoot Joe Noose dead, and Bess Sugarland along with him, because nobody could know the truth about Abraham Quaid if his boy Emmett was going to bring his dad home and keep him safe.

Fate was cruel.

Noose had a lot of settling up to do with the Quaids in this life, Emmett readily admitted, and there would be a reckoning for all of them in Hell.

CHAPTER 21

The town of Consequence, Wyoming, was sleeping.

In the predawn hours, the sky was just lightening, and darkness hung over the small town.

The sheriff's office and jail was a one-story brick-and-mortar building at the end of the long street that ran through the settlement. The placement was conspicuous. The bunker was built like a fortress, with a heavy iron door and steel bars and shutters on the window.

The snow lay heavy on the street and boardwalk and it was very quiet. Then came the sound of hooves and three men rode up the block on three stout horses, towing a fourth gelding. One dismounted in front of the sheriff's office, while the other two remained in their saddles, cradling rifles. The three wore heavy dusters and gloves against the biting cold, and their breath condensed in thick clouds in the cold air. The temperature was in the single digits.

All of the men wore badges on their coats.

The man with the sheriff's badge who got off his horse was the hulking, heavyset sheriff Buford "Bull" Conrad, a formidable lawman in his late fifties. Beady eyes squinted out of a weathered, saturnine countenance behind a bushy brown beard. His large-roweled Mexican spurs clanked as he trudged to the sheriff's office and pulled a ring of heavy keys from his coat pocket, unlocking the door and shoving through it.

Inside, it was almost pitch-dark, broken only by a faint dawn light filtering through the windows. In the shadows, the office was one large room, one side with desks for the sheriff and head deputy next to a stove and well-armed gun rack, one side a row of jail cells.

Presently there was one occupant.

The prisoner, named Lester Wiggins, was a feral, disheveled cowboy with an animalistic aspect to his predatory, stupid features. The cowboy, alarmed, sat up abruptly upon hearing the sheriff enter, shivering equally from cold and terror. His eyes watched as slowly and deliberately, Sheriff Conrad crossed the office, spurs jangling, snatching a Winchester repeater from the rack on his way to the jail cell.

Giving the lever of the rifle a loud cock, Conrad stood in front of the bars, rearing forbiddingly over his prisoner, The lawman's grim face was shadowed, glowering eyes glinting in the dim dawn light. With dramatic effect, he just stood with a shuttered executioner's gaze and regarded the cowboy in the cell. At last, the lawman spoke.

"You're going to pay the price."

He said it as a statement and question.

The prisoner dropped his gaze, heaving a heavy sigh.

He nodded.

Moments later the door to the jail opened and Sheriff Conrad led Wiggins out in steel handcuffs, a blanket draped over his freezing shoulders. A jab of the Winchester in his back got the prisoner up into the saddle of the fourth horse.

The two hard-bitten deputies, Tom Rickey and Joe Bob Hubbard, kept the prisoner covered with their rifles as with a sneer Sheriff Conrad got on his horse. "C'mon, boys, we don't want to keep the judge waiting."

They rode off at a brisk trot and didn't have far to go.

The sun was not yet fully risen as the mounted lawmen escorted their prisoner to the local courthouse just down the street, where court was already in session.

Judge William "Bill" Black routinely started his proceedings at the crack of dawn so he could be finished by breakfast.

The thin, white-haired jurist was a patrician man in his sixties, seated at the bench of the single-room courthouse in his black robes. With a brusque, impatient manner and pitiless eyes, Judge Black presided over the proceedings with the air of a man who wanted it done with.

There was no jury. This courtroom had no jury box.

At one table, a young prostitute freshly missing an eye sat at the prosecution table. The side of her face was bandaged and the whore looked ridden hard and put away wet. She was in pain and distress, and no small state of discombobulation from taking regular nips from a small bottle of laudanum. The prosecutor had the floor, giving a vividly detailed account of an attack on a pair of local prostitutes by a vicious john that left one with a broken neck and the other without an eye. The counselor's fiery oration was suitably outraged, and the judge listened impassively, checking his pocket watch twice.

The doors opened and Sheriff Conrad brought in the accused, Lester Wiggins. Force-marching the prisoner at gunpoint past the pews with a few local spectators to the trial, the lawman dragged Wiggins to the other desk and shoved the stupid cowboy down beside an inept-looking defense lawyer, who was nodding off.

Judge Black and Sheriff Conrad made quick, covert eye contact and the lawman nodded, the jurist nodding back.

Conrad didn't stay to watch and left the courtroom.

At the defense table, the accused sat there with a dull look in his eyes as the prosecutor pointed at him and hurled invective in his direction.

The judge raised his hand to the prosecutor. "Wrap it up, Counsel."

The lawyer for the prostitute asked for a verdict of death by hanging.

Judge Black asked the sleeping defense lawyer what he had to say in his client's defense and got a snore in response.

The cowboy jumped up and shouted, "I didn't do it, Your Honor."

"She says you did," the judge replied.

"She didn't know what she saw. She only got but one eye."

"That's because you popped it out with your thumb, you dirty miserable sonofabitch!" the whore screeched.

"Order." The judge hit the gavel. "Did any witnesses see this?"

"Yeah, but he broke her neck!" she wailed.

"Then it's your word against his."

"He told everybody he done it!"

"Case dismissed for lack of evidence. The accused is free to go." Judge Black hit the gavel.

Stunned, the whore began shaking head to foot. *"What? He killed my girlfriend and he took my eye and you ain't gonna do nothing to him!"*

The wronged woman leapt up, drawing a derringer

flintlock .45 from her bloomers. Everybody dropped to the floor. Drawing a vengeful bead on the cowboy thug who cowered in terror covering his face, she righteously declared: "A bullet is the only way a whore is gonna get true justice in this life!"

Without a drop of sweat, Judge Black reached below the bench and pulled out a giant Colt Dragoon handgun stowed there. From the bench, he shot the prostitute in the side of the head, blowing the other side of her face off in a gory explosion of blood, brain, and skull that splattered the onlookers. Replacing the smoking revolver, he pounded the gavel. "Court's adjourned."

Leaving the bench, Judge Black left through the courtroom back door that instead of leading to the judge's chambers opened into the living room of his own next-door house attached to the courthouse in an adjoining structure.

The tidy living room was opulently furnished with a huge fireplace, oriental rugs, leather couches, gaslight wall sconces, and a full brass-railed bar. It looked like a San Francisco bordello down to the photos of naked showgirls framed on the wall.

Going into the kitchen, he lit the stove and took out the eggs and ham to prepare his breakfast when came a knock on the door.

He answered it. Sheriff Conrad stood in the doorway with a thick envelope that he handed to Judge Black.

"He paid the price." The lawman grinned.

"The full price?"

"Every dollar."

"Tell him he hurts another whore like that again, the price doubles."

Conrad walked away with a wink and a wave.

Chuckling, Judge Black shut the door, walked back into

the living room, and lifted the oriental carpet to reveal a large hidden safe built into the floor. He undid the combination and deposited the cash in the strongbox. The safe was already filled with a fortune in bribes: random valuables in the form of jewelry, gold, bank notes; along with property deeds, bills of sale, livestock vouchers, and all manner of barter currency.

Sitting on top of the valuables was a leather-bound black notebook. The judge made an entry in it with his fountain pen. There were pages and pages of other entries in the ledger filled with handwritten names and dollar amounts. He returned the black book to the strongbox.

Closing and locking the safe, Judge Bill Black covered it with the rug, then went to the kitchen to enjoy his breakfast.

CHAPTER 22

The three riders and horses traveled the rugged trail north, their figures dwarfed by the snowy wastes of northern Wyoming.

They had once again lost the trail of The Brander. He was out there, somewhere, but they knew not where. Wyoming was a very big territory. He could be anywhere.

Joe Noose had been doing some figuring, and when he had made up his mind he shared it. "I think Abraham Quaid ain't killing random individuals. I best believe he's killing damn specific ones."

"But if so, who?" wondered Bess.

"You ask me, he's killing the gang that robbed his cattle, burned his ranch, and shot him. He's tracking 'em all down, putting 'em six feet under. These ain't crazy kills, this is all about revenge."

"We don't know that," Bess brooded.

Emmett was suddenly overjoyed. "I'll be! Of course it is!"

"What the hell are you smiling about?" The bounty hunter lifted an eyebrow with an expression of disregard to the gleeful lawman.

"Because you're right, Joe." The marshal grinned

broadly, hugely relieved. "My—The Brander is out for justice he didn't get when that gang slipped the noose. It all makes sense now."

Marshal Bess scowled. "I don't see how murdering entire families, slaughtering women and children, makes any sense at all."

That wiped the smile off Emmett's face and he nodded soberly. "Their families are innocent. He should just be killing the men who rode in the gang, the men who actually wronged him. Left their families out of it."

Bess shook her head in fierce disagreement. "Quaid shouldn't be killing anybody for any reason!" she retorted. "Nobody has the right to take justice into their own hands. That's murder, five we know about, and it's against the damn law. Law takes a hard view of vigilante vengeance. And speaking of wrongs, we know for a fact from Joe that Abraham Quaid got away with lynching three boys who were likely not even of legal age, meaning this old man is just as bad as that gang you're saying wronged him. If that gang was acquitted, probably it was for good reason. You're telling me this sheriff you talked to says he knew the gang stole the cattle, burned the ranch? How the hell does he know that? The sheriff—what's his name, Conrad?—also said they killed Quaid and the three of us both know that's bullshit. Use your head, Emmett, you're a damn U.S. Marshal! We ain't even positively identified The Brander's victims yet, for Chrissakes. We don't know they *are* the gang. About the only thing we *do* know is Abraham Quaid is alive and on the loose and we need to put an end to him before he puts an end to any more innocent folks." Finished, Marshal Bess stared straight ahead, chin out, as she rode, figuring she put paid on the conversation.

Then Joe Noose spoke up, softly but with force of conviction. "He's hunting down the gang, Bess, I'm convinced of it. We may not have ID'd those dead men but they're the gang, all right. I'd stake my life on it. Quaid's a vigilante, not a nut, and he's killing for a reason, with a purpose. That's good for us to know if we're gonna catch him, because one thing I've learned is you got to know how your enemy thinks so you can think two steps ahead of him."

"I agree with Joe," Emmett vigorously added.

"Okay, let's say you are right and The Brander is targeting these specific individuals," Bess argued. "What's our next step?"

"We need their names," Noose replied. "That sheriff's office in Consequence or the local district court will have their names in the arrest and trial records. Then we need to find out these boys' locations if we can, and get there before The Brander does. Quaid has found some but not all of this gang, so he's a good tracker, but I'm a better manhunter than he is. I savvy where The Brander's going now, it's the places the rest of the men in that gang are. What we need to do is get there first and intercept him. You're the marshal, Bess, it's your call, but you brought me along on this manhunt for my expertise in helpin' you find this individual and I say *that's* how we find him. *That's* how we kill him."

On her horse, Bess mulled it over then rubbed her chin. "Well . . ." With a sigh, she expelled a cloud of warm breath in the cold air. "I don't have any better ideas." Shrugging her assent, it was decided.

Noose nodded, tugging on the reins to steer Copper in the right direction, and the others did, too.

"We're riding to Consequence."

* * *

Three miles on, the trio came to a large cattle ranch in a deep valley. As they rode closer, they saw the stockade contained at least five hundred head of longhorn steers. A few wranglers were riding their horses among the bulls working the huge herd.

One figure stood out, that of a tall, blond woman with flowing golden hair under her Stetson, saddled astride a mighty brown Belgian stallion that made both appear gigantic. In her long brown duster, sheepskin chaps, and matching boots, she was a vision of leathery coloration, and only the white of her pearl-handled holstered revolvers broke up the chiaroscuro of her dynamic appearance. Riding around the ranch, she gave orders to the men with a hearty confident authority. Periodically her laugh rang like a bell across the plain. The lady appeared to be the only woman on the property and she was clearly in charge. Soon her head swung in the direction of the three approaching riders, and even at a great distance Joe Noose could see the charismatic flash of her piercing blue eyes. As the three manhunters closed in, the cattlewoman rode up to meet them. The strangers received a down-home welcome from a beautiful outdoorsy woman in her thirties, her healthy strong-boned freckled face flushed with spirit and vigor. "I'm Laura Holdridge. This is my ranch, the Bar H."

Bess nodded, introducing her companions. "This is Joe Noose, our tracker." Noose nodded. "This is Marshal Emmett Ford." Emmett tipped his hat. "And I'm Marshal Bess Sugarland, out of Jackson." Opening her coat, she displayed her seven-star badge on her bosom. It glinted in the sharp daylight.

The cattlewoman's face erupted in a huge wide grin of admiration, sheer delight in her blue eyes. "A woman U.S. Marshal! I'll be damned! You're the first woman lawman I ever set eyes on, and it's about time there was one. I think that is just *damn* splendid. I'd like to shake your hand."

With a charmed grin, Bess Sugarland extended her arm across the saddles and shook Laura Holdridge's hand, exchanging a strong firm grip of feminine simpatico. "You run this ranch by yourself, Mrs. Holdridge?"

"Yes. Used to run it with my husband, Sam. Lost him last year. Now it's just me."

"I'm sorry to hear that."

"Sam, he taught me everything about the cattle business there is to know. But keeping this spread running keeps me on my toes, Marshal, that's a fact."

"My daddy was a U.S. Marshal. I was his deputy. Learned how to be a lawman from him. Kind of like you, I suppose."

"Yes, indeed."

The women laughed with an immediate camaraderie, cut from the same mold. Noose enjoyed watching them bond. *His kind of gals.*

"Well," said Laura in her gregarious Wyoming manner. "I welcome you three with open arms to stay for dinner and spend the night here at the Bar H Ranch if you've a mind to. It's getting late, and my ranch beats freezing your asses off sleeping out on the trail. We got lots of room, plenty of good food and drink, and I'd sure appreciate the company." Her eyes took on a serious look. "But I'm guessing from the purposeful attitude I see y'all have that you aren't just passing through for no reason and are on some important business. State it. How can I help you?"

"We're hunting a killer," Noose said. Laura swung her blue gaze to the big bounty hunter, and it was plain from her impressed expression she found Joe handsome—plain to Bess, anyway. "A killer who brands his victims with a *Q* branding iron," he added.

Taken aback, the mortified cattlewoman's brows knitted curiously. "A *Q* brand, you say? Brands human beings? I've never heard of such a thing."

"Our best information is it's an old man we're looking for. Sixty, seventy, mebbe eighty. Missing three fingers of his right hand. You seen or had any dealings with anybody recently fitting that description?"

"No, sir." She looked distantly out at the wintery horizon, recollecting or brooding, her thoughts hard to read. Finally, she shook her head. "Somebody fitting that description, I'd remember. He have a name?"

"We think Abraham Quaid."

She brushed a lock of gilded hair from her eyes in the icy breeze. "That name is not unknown in these parts."

"Do you know him?" asked Bess.

"Just by name," Laura replied. "Wish I could be of more help. Maybe some of my crew has seen the man you're after. Feel free to question any of my boys here on the ranch. Course, not all of them are on the ranch. Have 'em on half duty now. We're all getting geared up for a big cattle drive to Cheyenne. Have to move this stock after the thaw." She swept her arm out at the vast, sprawling stockade packed with steers stretching across the spread. A few wranglers were far off in the distance, rounding up some of the herd, like specks of black pepper on the salt white tableau of the landscape.

"Thanks," Marshal Bess said. "We'll have a word."

Seeing Copper looking longingly at the water trough a few hundred yards away, Noose tipped his hat to Laura and trotted away on his horse. The marshals and cattlewoman kept talking as he rode off a short distance.

Joe Noose watered Copper at the trough by the stockade and his horse drank thirstily. Sitting in his saddle, the bounty hunter swept his pale gaze across the large herd of cattle in the corral. He counted over a hundred. Hundreds more were grazing around the ranch. It was going to be a long, hard drive for the attractive lady cattle baron after the thaw, and she would have her work cut out for her running a herd this size across Wyoming during mud season. She seemed up to the task.

Copper was still drinking. Noose looked back across the stockade to where Marshal Bess was sitting on her horse engaged in animated conversation with Laura Holdridge. Marshal Ford had parked his mare beside her, listening intently to their discussion. From the smiles Bess shared with the cattlewoman, Noose could tell that they liked each other.

The bounty hunter swung his gaze back to the rows of steers lowing and milling in the stockade, forests of horns across acres of land. The Bar H brand was seared on their backs.

He squinted, noticing something strange.

Many of the cows bore a different brand.

Q.

Brows furrowing, he flipped the reins, leaned his hip in the saddle, and trotted his horse across the frozen ground over to where Bess and Emmett sat on their horses with Laura Holdridge. The female marshal turned her face to him as he approached, and she lost her smile when she registered the hard expression on her best friend's face. The bounty hunter's gaze was fixed on the cattlewoman as he rode up and halted Copper, but he tipped his hat politely.

"Mrs. Holdridge, may I ask you a question?"

"Go right ahead, Mr. Noose."

"I noticed there are two brands on your cattle. Your Bar H Ranch. But also a lot of your steers bear the *Q* brand." Quick glances were exchanged between the two marshals, who then looked at the bounty hunter.

"True," Laura replied.

"Back in Wind River we checked with the Wyoming Cattlemen's Association and the only *Q* brand in the territory is Abraham Quaid's ranch. Maybe you heard that a year ago his cattle was rustled and his ranch was burned down by a gang who shot him."

The cattlewoman's eyes clouded with sadness and she nodded grimly. "I heard that. My work on the ranch keeps me here most of the time so I never had cause to visit the Bar Q ranch, but word travels."

Joe Noose looked at her hard. "They never found the cattle, but I just did. How did your corral come to be filled with rustled steers, Mrs. Holdridge?"

"I bought them."

"Bought them?"

"Cash on the barrelhead."

"Bought from who?"

"Judge William Black." The widow saw by their shared glances that her three visitors did not know the name. "He's the district judge over in Consequence. Bill Black sold me the cattle last fall. I have the bill of sale if you want to see it."

With a shrewd smile, Bess nodded. "I'd rightly appreciate that, Mrs. Holdridge."

CHAPTER 23

"Right this way, then."

Dismounting and tethering their horses, Noose, Bess, and Emmett followed Laura as she climbed out of the saddle and led them across her spread to an imposing two-story ranch house of elegant gingerbread design, the brown pine exterior shining with freshly oiled boards, rising proud and weathered against the landscape. A pack of friendly golden Labrador hounds barked as they approached and the widow cattlewoman leaned down to pat them. "Ignore those rascals, they wouldn't hurt a soul."

Despite themselves, the animal lovers Noose and Bess shared a smile and both crouched down to give a friendly pat to the affectionate dogs before rising and following Emmett to the open door of the ranch house.

Inside, the living room was well-carpentered hardwood, the furnishings masculine and western but with a woman's touch evident from hand-sewn curtains and quilted throws on the couches and knitted rugs on the floor. The smell of freshly brewed coffee wafted in from the kitchen over the scents of wood and a log fire. It was good to be inside out of the cold, and Noose pulled off and pocketed his gloves, rubbing his hands to warm them. He stomped the snow off his boots along with Bess and Emmett at a pad at the front door, then walked inside.

"What a beautiful house!" Bess gushed, unable to restrain herself. It was more house than she had ever seen. She looked around the room with admiration.

The hardy blond Laura returned a warm smile. "Thank you. My husband, Sam, built this house with his bare hands, from the foundation, when we staked our claim here fifteen years ago. It has good bones. His. He's everywhere you look in this place. That's Sam." She pointed.

A large oil-painted formal portrait of Sam and Laura Holdridge hung over the massive fireplace. The impressive couple were attractively rendered dressed in fine attire standing at each other's side against the same mountain view visible outside, the ranch house in the background. Her late husband was a big, rugged, bearded, and commanding man who looked like a cattleman, she his equal in stature, and in the painting as probably in life, the Holdridges looked like a powerful couple who belonged outdoors and with each other. "He passed last winter," Laura said with softness tinctured with grief.

"I'm sorry for your loss," Bess replied. "We all are."

"Well. Let me get you that bill of sale for those cattle. My office is in here."

The trio followed the cattlewoman into a small room that served as an office, filled with ledgers and books on the cattle business. Dust motes floated in the soft daylight filtering in through the window curtains. A huge map of Wyoming, complete with topographical dimensions, was framed on the wall. Noose looked it over as Laura went to fetch the bill of sale. Beside a kerosene lamp that sat on the desk, a large leather-bound folder lay open. The cattlewoman sorted through a pile of well-organized papers and plucked one out, handing it to Marshal Bess.

"Here it is," Laura said.

Bess held the bill of sale and looked it over, Noose and Emmett peering at it over each of her shoulders. It was a standard notarized cattle purchase order, in official type-set, transferring 102 longhorn steers for the price of fifty dollars a head. It was stamped as paid. There were signatures on the line over the name of the purchaser, Laura Holdridge, and the seller, William Black.

"He's a judge, you say?"

"The only judge for hundreds of miles, Marshal. Not a lot of people in his jurisdiction out here in these parts. If there was anything crooked about this transaction I swear on the Bible I knew nothing about it. I bought the head from a circuit judge so of course I figured it was as re-spectable and legitimate as can be."

"Nobody is accusing you of anything unlawful, Mrs. Holdridge. We're just a little confused about the chain of events regarding this purchase. Probably it's all legal, but we're—" Bess paused.

Noose rubbed his chin, finishing her sentence. "Wonder-ing how this judge came into possession of stolen cattle. Best believe, Bess, we need to have us a conversation with Judge William Black, get a few things straightened out."

"Everybody round here calls him Bill. Bill Black. His house is built right next to the courthouse in Consequence. Can't miss it."

"You've been a lot of help, Mrs. Holdridge."

"Y'all still want to question my hands?"

"We'll ride back if we need to," said Bess. "First, our next stop is riding out to Consequence directly and talking to a judge about some cows."

Laura held up her hand with a bemused scolding gaze. "Now, just hold on there, Marshal Bess. It's near sundown. You'd be riding in the pitch-dark for two hours y'all head out to Consequence now. Now why don't y'all use your heads, accept my hospitality, stay the night here at the ranch and have dinner with me. Then tomorrow at first light, have a good breakfast and ride out to town." Her warm force of personality shone out of her twinkling blue eyes. "Otherwise I'll have to shoot y'all."

Dinner was served at a large oaken table in the rustic luxurious dining room before a roaring fire in a fireplace big enough for a man to stand in. Coal oil lamps hung on the walls filled the room with a gorgeous firelight. Outside the huge glass windows, the spectacular view of the towering mountains of Yellowstone Park covered with snow changed in the failing light from blue to purple to black. Then it was just moon and stars.

Around the table, Noose, Bess, and Emmett sat with Laura drinking expensive red wine brought in from the wine cellar. Noose had never tasted anything like it, his palate accustomed to whiskey and beer of the harsher variety, not the sophisticated flavors of what the cattlewoman called a pinot noir, a word he couldn't pronounce any better than he could read the French words on the label. *A man could get used to this,* he thought. He exchanged slightly embarrassed glances with Bess and Emmett, both of whom were on their second or third glasses by the time the food arrived, brought in by ranch cooks; juicy thick steaks, heaping mashed potatoes, blackened gold succulent roast corn, fresh salad, and several plates of different cooked vegetables. Laura Holdridge, their generous and expansive hostess, didn't have to tell them twice to dig in. She clearly was enjoying the company and said so.

Over dinner, the cattlewoman asked many questions of Bess about the growing town of Jackson, then about her background growing up as a marshal's daughter; inevitably that conversation led to the violent and dangerous terrible events that transpired when Bess first met Noose on the same day they both met Frank Butler and his gang, and Laura listened enthralled as Bess recounted the adventure that led to her becoming the first woman U.S. Marshal. The cattlewoman was incredibly impressed by the tale.

Turning her attention to Joe Noose, she eyed him with keen growing interest, hearing of his exploits.

Noose took the measure of the bigger-than-life cattle-woman he sat across from during dinner, and liked what he saw. Laura was very wealthy and money suited her; she was a natural aristocrat—he had met a few—who displayed a class and character and mettle that was equally down-to-earth, a self-made woman who had come from nothing and built an empire with her own hands, yet had no airs about her person. The bounty hunter knew many rich upper-crust East Coast snobs who took the train from New York and Philadelphia to Victor, then traveled over the Teton Pass and vacationed in Jackson Hole, wanting to see and get a taste of the Great American West. Many were decent folks to be sure, and a few had even bought ranches, but some rich people behaved superior to the Wyoming cowboys, farmers, and townspeople and felt their money made them better than the locals they treated like shit-kickers. Those East Coast aristocrats were soft. There was nothing soft about Laura Holdridge but her body, judging from her lovely figure, and inside she was harder than pig iron. A Wyoming woman through and through. As the evening progressed, he decided he liked her down to the ground.

Every so often in a sly look, glance, or smile, Laura reminded Joe Noose of Bonny Kate Valence.

Bonny Kate.

Who wasn't all bad.

"You ever kill a man you didn't want to, Joe?"

"What sort of question is that?"

After dinner, Noose and Emmett were sitting by the fire, playing a game of chess. Glasses of whiskey sat by the board. Bess and Laura were off in the kitchen and their laughter trickled in over the crackle and snap of the flaming logs.

"You ever have to pull the trigger on a man or a woman you didn't want to?"

"Yes."

"How do you live with yourself after?"

"It's easier for you to go on living after than it is for them."

"I'm serious."

"Why, who you planning on killing?" Noose moved his pawn.

"Someday as marshal I could get in that situation, you never know. Sooner or later, a marshal encounters every kind of situation during their career. He has to be able to handle any situation that comes up. That's why I'm asking you about this one." Emmett took Noose's pawn with his rook.

Noose lifted his pale eyes from the board to his companion. "How many men have you killed, Emmett?"

The hesitation in Emmett's gaze was just enough. *None.*

Joe smiled. "That many?" He captured Emmett's bishop left carelessly exposed when he moved his rook to take Noose's pawn.

"I was recollecting the tally. Only two. An Indian in Idaho. And a drunk who was waving his gun around in Pocatello. Actually I was with a group of marshals and a bunch of us shot him, so responsibility was shared because neither of us knew which of our bullets killed him. But those were strangers, not people I knew. I want to be sure if the time comes I ever get into a situation with no choice but to pull the trigger on a friend I don't fail, and that's why I'm asking you, how you go through with it."

"Why you asking me?"

"Because you killed a lot more men than me, Joe. You've been in a hell of a lot more gunfights and got much more experience in dangerous situations. Ain't no question who's boss steer on this manhunt, Joe. You're the toughest stud in the territory. I admire and respect you, Joe, and that's why I'm asking for your advice about how to kill a friend."

"Depends on the situation, I guess." The bounty hunter gave the marshal a look. *Your move.*

"That is the situation." Emmett was considering the board, rubbing his chin.

"Is your friend trying to kill you in this situation? That's plain old self-defense. Someone points a loaded gun at you, no matter who that person behind the trigger is, you shoot back because it's animal reflex to defend yourself."

"Let's say this friend, he ain't trying to kill you, but you have to kill him anyway."

"That'd make you an assassin and you ain't an assassin, Emmett. Those cold-blooded killers got no respect for human life, no moral conscience, and wouldn't be having this conversation. So don't worry about finding yourself in that situation."

"So let's say I have to kill a friend to protect somebody I love."

"Then you have a hard choice to make that you better make quick and not hesitate."

"You're saying because if my friend has a gun, it's kill or be killed."

"Exactly."

"And living with it after, how do you do that?"

"Like I said, you can live with anything if you ain't dead."

The marshal chuckled. "Thanks for the advice, Joe."

The bounty hunter sipped his whiskey. This subject seemed to be causing his companion no shortage of inner turmoil. He still wasn't sure of Emmett, hadn't been from the start. Over the past weeks, Noose had formed an opinion of the marshal after riding with him long enough to know a few things about him. The first was Emmett was a liar who lied easily and often; it was difficult to know which of what came out Emmett's mouth was the truth and what was fabrication. It puzzled Noose why Emmett told all these lies, and why he felt the need to. Men lied for many different reasons. Some men lied to make themselves look bigger than they were to other men. That wasn't Emmett, who was quiet, reserved, and unassuming by nature. Men also lied to cover up the truth, and Noose suspected that's what the marshal was doing. But what was he trying to cover up? It didn't make sense, because he, Bess, and Noose shared the same common goal of bringing down a mad-dog killer. But Emmett had been dead set against killing Abraham Quaid all along, even though if there was ever a man who needed killing it was that bloodthirsty degenerate old fiend. Whatever it was Emmett was covering up had something to do with Quaid, Noose guessed, and if his suspicions proved to be correct it would explain everything and affect the outcome in unpredictable ways. Yet despite all of this Joe liked Emmett. He'd felt an unexplained connection with Marshal Ford right from the start; after spending time together, his friend consistently demonstrated kindness, decency, and good humor toward his companions. Emmett was not a dangerous man.

Or was he?

All this talk tonight about shooting a friend raised doubts; as the bounty hunter took another slug of whiskey, watching the other man gazing glassily into the fire, Noose wondered if his companion was more dangerous than he looked. Sooner rather than later, Joe Noose was going to have to share his concerns with Marshal Bess Sugarland about Marshal Emmett Ford.

If that was his real name.

It was only the second time that month that Joe Noose had slept in a bed, but he had never slept in one as comfortable as he was stretched out in one of the many bedrooms on the ranch. Alone in the room, his naked body was covered with heavy layers of blankets and quilts soft as a baby's ass, wrapping him in warmth as he sank into the embrace of the mattress. *A man could get used to this,* he thought not for the first time that night. As he enjoyed the comfortable bed, knowing it was the last one he would sleep in for a while, Noose thought back on the good time he had at dinner with Bess and Emmett, the fellowship he was feeling with both of them after these weeks on the trail, the pleasure of their friendship. Suddenly, he wasn't in such a hurry to catch The Brander. Friends were hard to come by, and good to ride with, and he didn't want this ride to end.

His eyelids were growing heavy.

Deep tiredness descended on Joe Noose like a drug, a complete physical exhaustion taking over his whole body. Reaching over, he blew out the coal oil lamp and the room went dark, just the bright light from the crescent moon outside the bedroom window glinting off the .45 revolver and shells in his gun belt slung over the chair.

His eyes shut.

And that was when he knew he was being watched.

Felt someone's gaze on him.

Whose he didn't know.

Keeping his eyes half-closed, pretending to be asleep, he checked the room and it was empty, shadows and stillness.

He was still being watched.

His guns were on his right, in the chair beside the bed, and he'd reach it with a quick lunge and snatch, take him two seconds.

Slowly, he rolled over with his eyes half-closed, like he was turning over in his sleep, and there he saw the window and the silhouette of a head and face pressed against it, backlit by stark moonlight.

Noose moved lightning fast.

His right arm shot out and snatched the Colt Peacemaker from his holster as he jackknifed out of bed and in two steps reached the window but the face was gone.

With the gun in one hand, Noose threw up the window with the other, and a blast of frigid arctic air hit him in his face and bare chest as he stuck his gun, then his head and shoulders, out the window and looked.

The figure was gone.

Footprints in the snow outside the window led off across the open field and as the bounty hunter's eyes followed the trail he saw, far off, someone running away in a sheepskin coat, chaps, and Stetson hat. It was too dark to tell who it was.

His thumb eased down the hammer of his pistol from a cocked position.

It wasn't The Brander.

Somebody else instead.

Closing the window, Noose slid back into bed and under the covers, keeping the loaded revolver in his hand. He lay awake with his eyes open but the stalker, whoever he was, did not return. Still, the bounty hunter didn't sleep a wink that night.

CHAPTER 24

Later, The Brander remembers how good his red-hot brand felt burning into the corrupt flesh of Judge William "Bill" Black. Of all the guilty ones the vigilante is out to serve harsh justice on, of all the guilty ones he must punish, the judge is the worst of the worst. Savoring the jurist's hideous screams, the fiend flays the crooked old man all night. When dawn breaks, Bill Black is no more. In his final bloody gurgles, the judge gives The Brander what he requires. In the morning, the fiend rides out with it safely stowed in his coat.

In the hours before the killing, The Brander stakes out Judge Bill Black's fancy house built right next to the district courthouse, watching the place from the shadows under the hanging tree. It is just after midnight. The Brander has hidden in the bushes since sunset and now it is full dark; he has a good vantage point where through the windows of the house he can see the jurist eating dinner alone, but the judge can't see him.

The Brander is spitting distance from the porch when Sheriff Bull Conrad rides up alone and Judge Bill Black comes out with his pipe to converse with him. The men believe they are in private because no one else is in sight, but The Brander is close enough to hear every word they say above the crickets.

The chummy jurist and lawman have a terse exchange in conspiratorial tones. Black stands on the porch, eye level with Conrad sitting in the saddle of his horse on the street, as they collude.

"Bad news," Sheriff Conrad mutters. "Another one of the Jensen gang got murdered and The Brander left his mark."

"Hell you say. Who?"

"Lonny Seed."

"But Seed was holed up over in Idaho. How did The Brander find him?"

"When he killed Buck Dodge a week ago, my bet is The Brander tortured the shit out of Dodge to give up Seed's whereabouts. It's what I'd do."

"Brander, my ass! Call him by his Goddamn Christian name! We know it's that insane old coot Abraham Quaid killing Ray Jensen's gang, for God's Sake! Quaid's getting revenge for those boys shooting him, rustling his cattle, and burning down his ranch! Make no mistake. This is one dangerous old man."

"Ray said he killed that old man."

"And Quaid up and rose from the dead?"

"Ray shot him with a Marlin rifle. Gun'll drop a grizzly bear. You don't get up from getting hit by that."

"This was all a mistake." On the porch, the old jurist shakes his head, his expression pinched. "It was too big a risk letting the Jensen gang slip the noose regardless of how much they paid to get acquitted. They were animals. Tried to murder that old man and took everything he had when they stole his cattle and burned his farm. After you arrested the gang, we should have strung 'em up. The long drop for each of them. We should have taken the payoff and hanged 'em anyway."

"Folks around here is still plenty angry you let those boys off."

"Suppose I better postpone my election campaign until next year, when all this brouhaha dies down." Sighing, Judge Black throws a dark glance out at the hanging tree The Brander huddles beneath, but doesn't spot the shadowy figure in the darkness. The fiend sees the glasses in the old jurist's vest pocket by the gold watch on a fob, realizing the judge has poor eyesight; The Brander resolves to do his work close because he wants the bad old man to see every part of himself that gets burned off.

"Don't grow a conscience on me, Bill." The sheriff sputters, "This thing of ours was your idea."

"We got greedy."

"Nobody can prove nothing."

"We have made a lot of money."

"It's been a good racket, Judge. I arrest 'em, you cut 'em loose. They pay us, you hit that gavel, they walk. Ain't nobody arrests more bad guys than me and given the choice between hanging and payin', they always pay. It's all legal, a not-guilty verdict nobody can argue with. Best justice money can buy. This territory is the promised land for scoundrels."

"It's only a matter of time before everything points The Brander to us. What do we do then?"

"You worry too much."

"In case you get any ideas of going to the real law, just

remember this: I go down, you go down, and all your men go down."

"Don't threaten me, Your Honor. All that power you got can't stop a bullet, and one round will stop any conversations you'd ever have with anybody."

"I'm not scared of a bullet. I have a book." Sheriff Conrad squints at Judge Black, considers this new threat. The jurist continues, "You're in my book. It's in my safe. If anything happens to me, my lawyer will open the safe and turn my book over to the U.S. Marshals headquarters. And that's the absolute end for all of us, Bull."

"What *book* are you talking about?"

"It's all in my book, Bull. Every arrest you and your deputies ever made with the name of each man who paid us for a not-guilty verdict. Names and known whereabouts of the thirty-seven killers, robbers, and rapist who bought their freedom from us with hard cash. All the names. Yours is there. Enough to hang you and your men. And the book is a ledger. Receipts. Dollar entries next to the names. It lists the precise disbursement of funds and the two-way split of our take down to the last nickel."

Backing up on his horse, the crooked sheriff gets into a better position with his hand near his holster, ready to unload some bullets. "You miserable rotten snake son of a bitch."

"The pot calling the kettle." The diminutive figure of the corrupt district judge looks blasé. "You'll never find the safe, or the book. But if I die, the U.S. Marshal will. So I will sleep peaceably tonight, Sheriff Conrad, knowing you and your men will in short order apprehend the heinous villain Abraham Quaid who goes by the sobriquet

The Brander. Because it's your neck if you don't. Good evening, Bull."

Entering his house, Judge Black closes the door behind him and locks it. Spurring his horse, Sheriff Conrad gallops furiously off down the dirt street and disappears into the darkness, the sound of pounding hooves subsumed by the ubiquitous drone of crickets.

Beneath the hanging tree, The Brander bides his time, observing the house, clenching his *Q* brand.

Through the window, Judge Black sits alone by the fire, reading, smoking his pipe, drinking his whiskey. The Brander watches as at last he blows out the kerosene lamp, the room goes dark, and the old man climbs the stairs to bed.

It's time.

Hours ago The Brander broke the lock of the back door before Judge Black got home from court. So the fiend simply walks in.

Now he sits in the living room by the log fireplace in the empty chair Bill Black has recently vacated, his pipe left cooling in the ashtray. The Brander stokes the fire sufficiently to place the cold black metal *Q* brand on the flaming logs. A few minutes later the steel coil glows red-hot, haloed in steam.

He waits. He doesn't have to wait long.

The crooked old judge comes down the steps half-asleep.

"Who's there?"

He has a gun, a hefty Colt Dragoon held in both hands, loaded and cocked.

The living room is empty. His chair unoccupied.

Doddering confusion crosses Bill Black's pathetic aged face.

He feels the sudden heat at his back.

The judge doesn't see The Brander step out behind him and when he turns, before he can get a shot off, the red-hot branding iron is jammed against his groin in sizzling clouds of steam.

CHAPTER 25

The town of Consequence was ten miles as the crow flies.

Noose, Bess, and Emmett kept their horses at a good clip on the cold, bright Wyoming day. They crossed wintery hills and valleys with nothing but blinding snow as far as the eye could see. Three hours later, the trio reached the township.

Consequence was little more than a drinkwater outpost servicing travelers passing through and supplying the several ranches spread out around the area. Noose looked it over. It was one place he had never been. Hadn't missed much. Wasn't much to see. A sheriff's office. A feed store. A small saloon attached to a stable and a dry goods store. Squinting against the sun, which reflected sharply off the clean white snow cover on the land, he spotted a few scattered houses down roads leading out of town. His best guess was the judge lived in one of those.

Pulling her Appaloosa alongside him, Bess nodded toward the sheriff's office, the first building on the road to town. "Sheriff looks like he's in. Let's ask him where we can find Judge Black."

Emmett brought his horse beside them and the three rode up to the brick-and-wood one-story structure that housed the sheriff's office and jail behind heavily barred windows.

A big heavyset man with a huge gut in a red shirt and weathered duster sat outside the steel front door on a chair. Stetson tipped over his face, he blew on a hot cup of coffee in a scalding metal cup held in his glove, billowing steam around his head in the frigid air. The heat fogged up the silver sheriff star on pinned to his shirt. A pair of Colt Navy revolvers hung in the holsters of his gun belt. A Henry rifle leaned against the bricks within easy reach. His head raised and his unblinking pig eyes regarded the three riders as they stopped before him.

Lifting the collar of her coat, Bess Sugarland displayed her U.S. Marshal's badge. "Morning, Sheriff."

The local lawman's lips moved and his rheumy porcine eyes tried to focus and calibrate the sight. "Marshal?"

"Marshals. Two of us." Emmett showed his badge.

Noose and Bess exchanged a curious glance, both remembering Emmett had told them earlier he had already spoken to the sheriff in Consequence, who didn't appear to recognize the marshal, but they had more important things to worry about at the moment.

Bess was the one who did the talking, but the sheriff looked straight at Emmett and spoke only to the male marshal. "I'm Sheriff Bull Conrad. How can I assist you folks?"

"We're looking for Judge William Black."

"What business do you have with the judge?"

"Marshal business."

"And what business would that be?"

"We'd like it if you could point out where we can find

him, save us the trouble of knocking on the doors of your town, bothering folks."

His jaw working a piece of chewing tobacco like a cow chewing its cud, Sheriff Conrad spat a foul splat of black juice at the hoof of one of the three horses.

The wrong horse.

When the lawman looked up, he saw the huge man on the gold horse staring very dangerously at him. Conrad locked eyes with Noose but the violence radiating in Joe's fearsome gaze made him break the staredown fast; the big stud was the only one of the three who hadn't spoken and didn't need to say a word to get the point across that the marshals were expecting an answer.

"Down the street. Second road to your right. Take it to the end. Right next to the courthouse."

"Obliged," said Bess without tipping her hat.

The trio rode directly down the street, at a brisk clip.

Without moving from his seat, Sheriff Conrad's hooded eyes watched them go. The chewing tobacco worked in his mouth.

The door to the jail opened and Deputy Tom Rickey stepped out, carting a Winchester. "Who was that, boss?"

"Trouble." He spat.

Hit a bull's-eye in the hoofprint in the snow of Joe Noose's horse, Copper, filling it with tobacco juice.

The house was grand, freshly painted lime green, two stories with gabled windows and a large porch that wrapped around the front and two sides. The fourth side of the house was built into another building of red brick, white marble trim, and a tower with a widow's walk marking it unmistakably as a courthouse. The elaborate dual structure was a vainglorious construction in the backwater excuse for a town.

And it was way too quiet.

Noose sensed it riding up.

So did Copper; the coiled tension in the horse's flanks could be felt between Noose's thighs as he sat tall in the saddle.

"Something ain't right," the bounty hunter said.

The lady marshal knew enough not to second-guess her friend. She drew her revolver. Threw a sharp glance to her fellow lawman.

Emmett slid his Winchester out of his saddle sheath, levered it by spinning the rifle around in his hand to cock it.

Noose dismounted first, drawing his Colt Peacemaker and cocking the hammer, putting up a hand to the others to let him go first. Crouching to make himself a smaller target—hard to do for a man his size—he moved like a cat onto the porch, flattening against the wall between the fancy windows.

Behind him, the two marshals got off their horses. Bess gave a hand signal to Emmett and each split off to approach the house on either side.

It was silent, except for the crunch of their boots on the packed snow.

Peering quickly through the window on his left, Noose saw nothing but the darkened parlor through the window. Nothing moved. Holding his pistol at the ready, he advanced across the porch to the door and grabbed the knob. It turned easily and the door cracked open, unlocked. With the toe of his boot, he nudged it open. No bullets came his way.

What did was the coppery scent of blood, a lot of it.

And the smell of charred meat.

Joe Noose entered the charnel house.

What he found in the office made even him go pale and feel sick.

Staring down at what used to be a man, every square inch of flesh branded again and again with a Q *brand.*

"What the hell is that smell?" Bess said from the other room.

Hearing the footsteps and jingling spurs of his comrades Noose stepped to the door to bar entry for Bess. "You don't need to see this."

She pushed past him stubbornly and he let her by with a sigh. "Out of my way, Joe . . . *Oh my G-God . . .*"

"Bless my ass." Emmett had, too, now seen what The Brander had done to Judge Black.

Holstering his pistol, Noose looked around the office, peering through the doorway opening into the empty parlor and living room. "He's gone now. Ain't going to catch him standing around here. Let's saddle up. Hasn't snowed this morning. His tracks are probably still fresh."

"Wait. Joe, look." Bess crossed the room, pointing to the floor.

The men turned to look.

The oriental carpet had been ripped away, torn jaggedly by a knife.

A hidden steel safe was built in the floor, two feet wide by two feet deep.

Its door was open.

Inside, the safe was empty.

"The Brander took something, but what?"

"One way to find out." Noose grunted with a cracked grin. "Let's go ask him."

He was first out the door into the saddle.

Two minutes later, the bounty hunter and the two marshals were distant figures on the white horizon, galloping away, following the clear sign of the single horse and rider on the unbroken snow.

Two hours later, the sound of screaming reached Sheriff Bull Conrad's ears.

He had almost forgotten about the three interlopers who had ridden out to see the judge that morning. After all, it was hardly an unheard of occurrence that marshals or lawmen from other counties and districts passing through the area had business with Bill Black, who was the district judge of the territory. The most memorable thing about the trio was the mouthy female with the badge that Conrad was still fuming about. And that big son of a bitch with the killer's eyes who'd stared him down. He didn't like that stud one bit. The crooked lawman considered what such an individual was doing with those marshals.

And the sheriff wondered why he remembered the face of the male marshal. He'd seen him before. But where?

As he sat at his desk in the sheriff's office going over his private ledger, taking account of his ill-gotten gains and expenditures, Conrad was brooding about the book that Black had told him about last night. It was the first time he'd heard of it, and it changed everything. All of the names and payoffs in black-and-white. If that book ever got into the wrong hands, Conrad would be at the end of a noose. For the last few weeks, he had been planning to end the association he'd had for five years with Judge Black. It was getting too dangerous. Letting the Jensen gang off after they'd murdered a local rancher and rustled his cattle was going too far. He and Black had taken the steers and three hundred and twenty-five dollars in gold the gang had robbed somewhere as a payoff. Conrad had vehemently objected to taking the cattle but the arrogant old jurist figured he'd get away with it by selling it off. The lawman sold his share of the livestock to Black for a discount, just to wash his hands of it. The judge and sheriff's little conspiracy had worked only because the county was so spread out. They'd made a lot of money, but it was time to get out. Better not to push his luck. A man always had to know when to quit.

Across the room, the cell was empty.

Deputy Rickey was seated at the smaller desk, oiling his revolver.

Then they heard the screaming.

Bursting out the front door, Conrad and Rickey saw a Hispanic woman they recognized as Judge Black's housekeeper running down the street in hysterics, waving her arms. Exchanging glances, the sheriff and deputy rushed to her side and demanded to know why she was screaming. The woman spoke no English, but what little Spanish the racist Conrad understood indicated that she had found her employer dead.

Ordering Rickey to round up the rest of the deputies and meet him at Judge Black's house in a hurry, Sheriff Conrad set off on foot as fast as his sturdy legs would carry him.

Ten minutes later when his gang of dubious lawmen arrived at the jurist's house, they found their boss standing in disgust over the ghastly human remains. Sheriff Conrad rounded on his deputies. "Those two phony marshals and that gorilla they rode in with ain't no law. I knew it 'cause ain't no such thing as no woman marshal. They got that book from the judge and all our names is in it, boys. We need to get after them sumbitches, put 'em down, get that book back. If the law gets their hands on it, our necks are in the noose. Now, move out!"

The sheriff and his six deputies got on their horses and rode, following the tracks of the four riders on the snow heading true north.

CHAPTER 26

The muffled sounds of the hotel casino downstairs came up through the floor as Deputy Sweet folded his pair of eights when Rachel showed him her full house. The room service dishes for the dinner they ordered were piled aside to make room for the game of cards they had been playing. Ten hands of straight poker. She had won every hand. He didn't mind losing; what he won was the exquisite gleam of pleasure in her own card-shark skill that had returned some of the light to her eyes, which he had missed.

"You're a hell of a poker player. How did you learn to play cards like that?"

"My husband taught me."

"He was a card player, then."

She nodded. "A professional gambler. Still is, I reckon. A good one once. He won a lot, cheated when he didn't. We traveled all over, him and me, on the poker circuit. Tombstone. Dodge City. Wasn't a place we hadn't worked. After we got married I was always on his arm and we were quite the couple then, real pieces of work. I was very beautiful back in those days, before he cut me. We'd work the towns, me turning the heads, him slipping an ace out of his sleeve when them drunken gamblers was staring at my bosom. I'm a bad person."

"You're a good person."

"I'm a bad wife. If I'd have been a good wife to my husband and not run away maybe things would have been better—different anyway."

She felt like talking now, and he felt like listening.

"I don't know how I stayed with him as long as I did. My husband told me day in and day out I couldn't do nothing. Didn't know nothing. Swore he'd leave me and I'd have to become a sporting girl and sell my body or starve to death. Thing was, I believed him. Didn't know how I'd survive on my own. I was his property, he'd tell me. 'I own you,' he'd say.

"Round this time he had him a run of bad luck at cards and we was on the dole. He blew our money on whiskey and was drunk all the time. Then he started beating me and he didn't know about hitting a person in places it don't show. He'd just haul off and hit my face, and when the woman on his arm at the card table has a black eye, makeup don't fool nobody, so the men stopped looking at me, and one of 'em saw my husband slip an ace out of his sleeve. Some cowboys broke his hands. He couldn't wipe his own ass for a year let alone play cards. Still I stayed with him. I was scared to leave. He was so broke and crazy he got it into his head I was the only property he had, the last thing he owned, and nobody was gonna take it from him. By the time I ran away it was too late. When I finally got the guts to stand up to him he took a wire cutter to my face, saying my face was his property and he could take a piece of it anytime he wanted. When they had me at the hospital I was too scared of that man not to run away, so I did. I was so ugly I disguised myself as a man and somewhere along the line I became Puzzleface.

"But I knew he'd find me eventually, even with a disguise." Rachel's eyes were vacant, empty even of despair as she intoned hopelessly, "'I own you.' That's what he always said. He always said he'd kill me if I ever left him, and wherever I ran he'd find me and he'd kill me and said I'd never get away from him. I hear him in my dreams every night. He does own me, Nate. That's the vows you take before God when you get married. Till death do you part. I am his property and when something's your property you can do what you want with it, and if he wants to kill me, he can do it because I was a bad wife and I ran away." Rachel was sinking into the quicksand of fear and self-loathing inside herself.

Reaching over, Sweet grabbed Rachel and shook her gently but forcefully, until she raised her eyes to his, but there was nothing there. "You stop that. You hear me? You stop it. You need to stand up for yourself. You are better than that no-account man and you need to show him you're better by standing up and living your life and being all you can be. But first you gotta stop feeling sorry for yourself and stand up."

"What good will it do?" She shook her head. "I'm a woman, Nate. A woman can't stand up for herself. It's a man's world and a woman got no freedom in this world. Men got freedom. Never realized it until I put on that man's suit and became Puzzleface. When I became Puzzleface and had me a taste of life as a man my life changed. I was born again. You see, when the world thinks you're a man you can do just about anything." Rachel was grinning until she remembered. "But he knows I'm Puzzleface now and it's the end."

She hung her head.

"I'm tired, Nate, so tired. I want to go to bed."

"Sure, Rachel. Get some sleep."

When Sweet closed the door on her room, stepping into his own room to begin his long night-guard duty, the last view he had of Rachel sitting on the bed was of someone who had lost the will to live. He had never seen such a lost soul.

Washing his face and hands in the pot by the mirror, the deputy splashed water on his face and looked at his own face, facing the honest truth that he could not save this woman, as much as he wanted to.

The only one who could save Rachel was herself.

And he didn't see how.

All the U.S. Marshal could do was what he was able to by the power of his badge: patrol the hotel and see if he could flush out her husband before the man could kill his wife. Sweet still had absolutely no idea what the husband looked like because Rachel carefully refused to provide any identifiable physical characteristics.

She had, however, provided insight into the kind of man he was: a lowly, mean, insecure, insolvent gambler. The deputy might be able to spot a man like that in the place he would likely be, the casino downstairs.

Grabbing his Winchester, Deputy Sweet decided to go downstairs and take a look.

In the next room, Rachel lay in bed in the darkness, listening to the sound of the door closing on the other side of the wall and the deputy's footsteps departing down the hall.

She was truly alone now.

As she rested her head on the pillow in the total darkness, she prayed for this to stop, just wanting it all to be over.

With her eyes open, she saw just dark, when she closed them, the dark was the same.

Rachel tried to let go.

It would be over soon.

But in the silence of the room, Rachel kept hearing Nate Sweet urging her to stand up, words she couldn't get out of her skull, until she had to sit up.

Striking a match, she lit the coal oil lamp she had just blown out on the nightstand, and once again the room was bathed in bronze firelight.

The woman rose to her feet and stood straight.

She knew, quite suddenly, what she had to do.

But Rachel could not do it by, or as, herself.

Shrugging the nightgown off her shoulders, it dropped like a discarded skin around her ankles, undraping her nude body aglow with lamplight as Rachel opened the armoire where the clothes of Puzzleface were neatly hung, and she dressed herself.

The hotel casino was in full swing as Deputy Sweet entered to have himself a look around. It was Saturday night and all the tables were crowded with cowboys and gamblers busy playing poker, blackjack, faro, and roulette. The place bustled with excitement and activity. The air was filled with cigar smoke and laughter, the sound of ice and liquor poured into glasses, sporadic shouts of victory or defeat, and a rollicking honky-tonk piano.

There were six card tables, Sweet saw, three had poker games going, two had blackjack, and Sweet couldn't see the other game from his vantage. In one corner there was a separate faro table and dealer. In another corner the roulette wheel. The casino floor was filled shoulder to shoulder with people. Carting his Winchester rifle at ease in the crook of his right elbow, the lawman casually patrolled the room, his laconic gaze scanning each and every face. Many of those faces were townspeople and friends he knew, and those people he smiled at, then immediately shifted his gaze to search out faces of strangers he did not know, looking for the one who was in town to kill his wife. The deputy moved calmly between the tables, weaving his way smoothly through the crowd, his eyes constantly on the move, canvassing the place.

—There, a surly-looking long, gray-haired blackjack player in a disheveled sheepskin jacket who looked heeled. *No, too old. Rachel married a younger man.*

—There, a dapper elegant New Orleans dandy type with a pencil mustache and slicked-back hair, cleaning up at one of the poker tables. The dandy was puffing a big cigar and flashing his shark grin almost as much as he flashed his money. *Professional gambler. Asshole. Take a closer look.* Sweet started for the table to talk to the gambler, but something told him that was not the guy.

—Moving steadily on through the crowd, the deputy made a full rotation, spotting a few grungy-but-seasoned gamblers in the casino whom he was deciding to keep his eye on when his gaze fell on a big, rough-hewn man in the weathered remains of what used to be an expensive hand-tailored jacket and right away Deputy Sweet had a gut feeling this was Rachel's husband. He was sitting thirty feet away at the first poker table, pushing chips into the pot and drawing three cards. A heavy revolver was clearly visible on his dirty belt. The man's hair was long, oily, and stringy, his clothes covered with dirt stains from sleeping out of doors. The man was clearly insolvent and gave off the odor of the gutter; his nervous pawing of the cards and lunges of his head were animalistic. He twitched a lot. He was big and mean and feral. From twenty feet away, Sweet felt the man's bad energy and knew he was one of the bad ones; and he couldn't help but picture the son of a bitch taking a pair of wire cutters to Rachel's face.

It must have been telepathy because at that exact moment the husband felt the lawman's eyes on him and turned to look straight in Sweet's face, locking eyes with him.

Tension crackled in the air during that look.

Then the husband threw a crooked grin and a little nod to the deputy. *Come and get it, asshole.*

Reaching for his handcuffs, in midstep toward the husband, Deputy Sweet stopped dead in his tracks when he saw she was *here.*

Puzzleface was in the casino, wearing his suit, vest, trousers, and waxed beard and mustache. And was coming right toward them. Moving boldly through the crowd, she fearlessly closed in on the poker table her husband was sitting at. *What was she doing here?* Sweet saw the husband's back was to his wife and didn't see her coming in her elegant disguise.

At the poker table, Puzzleface pulled out a chair and took a seat directly across from her husband. She gestured for a hand of cards from the dealer while her weak hand on her wounded shoulder side tossed chips into the pot.

Behind the false eyebrows and phony mustache, her eyes were fixed on her ex-husband.

He was only three feet away across the table from her.

The husband faced away from his wife, watching the deputy staring him down, and when the deputy suddenly broke that stare to look at Puzzleface, the husband followed his gaze and that's when he saw his wife.

If he was surprised to see her, he didn't show it.

What the hell was Rachel doing? Sweet thought in alarm. Her husband's pistol was in easy reach and he looked like one of those nothing-to-lose types crazy enough to blow his wife away right here in the casino. The deputy knew he had to change position to gain tactical advantage if this thing went sideways, so avoiding sudden moves, he maneuvered himself over to the wall directly behind Puzzleface. This faced him toward the husband and kept the man in his sightline. Sweet's eyes never left Rachel's husband or his wife, watching their every move as they faced each other. Deputy Sweet was impressed. Rachel displayed unnerving mettle in her Puzzleface disguise. There she was, facing her abusive violent ex-husband, a man who just shot her in the back, and she sat across from her spouse looking him straight in the eye without a drop of sweat. He didn't think she had it in her. He was right, she didn't have it in *her*. That's when Deputy Sweet realized Rachel's plan . . . Puzzleface would be the armor of the knight she rode into battle as to overcome her abuser.

The husband was the first to speak. "Told you I'd find you."

"Hello, Ike."

"Said you'd never get away from me."

"I'm just here to play cards."

The two locked eyes, a tricky suspicious smile snaking across his face. "What's going on here?"

"Let's play cards," said Puzzleface.

"You're not good enough to play against me. And that getup of yours doesn't change anything. You're still my property. I own you."

"Not after this game."

"You two gonna talk or play cards?" Deputy Sweet said. Rachel looked over her shoulder and saw the big lawman positioned against the wall right behind her, cradling his Winchester rifle. She was safe and felt it. He literally had her back. Rachel felt brave enough reinforced by the lawman's presence. She had no fear of her abusive ex-husband, and after this game she never would be again.

Ike shot a surly glance up at Deputy Sweet standing directly behind Puzzleface, watching his every move like a hawk. The marshal would be on him the second he grabbed for a gun or an ace up his sleeve, so he wasn't going to get away with any tricks. Nothing the husband could do about it, so he slid his slippery gaze back to his disguised wife.

"I hope you don't have anything else up your sleeve," Puzzleface said.

Ike turned red. "Play cards."

There were four players at the table.

The dealer was a white-haired old man who shuffled and dealt everyone five cards. "Everybody anted up?" They all pushed in their chips to the pot.

Puzzleface picked up her cards and peered at them with a perfect poker face, keeping them so close to her chest even Sweet couldn't see them. Rachel was a pro card player who knew how to conceal her hand, keeping her cards to herself.

Ike grabbed his cards up off the table with lip-smacking swaggering confidence he would win and she would lose. Looking at his cards, the husband laughed with pleasure.

He raised. Asked for no cards.

Puzzleface doubled the raise. Asked for three cards.

The two other cowboy players folded.

With a slash of a grin, Ike dropped three kings on the table.

Expressionless, Puzzleface dropped a royal flush.

Won the pot and dragged about a hundred dollars in chips over to her side of the table. The husband couldn't believe it, seemed shaken by it.

"I win. You lose," Puzzleface said.

Ike flinched from a bolt of fear.

They played another hand.

Puzzleface won with a straight.

Then she won the next five hands. Puzzleface was up six hundred and twenty-four dollars.

Across the table, Ike was down five hundred and twenty dollars and change, close to broke. He was starting to un-ravel, losing to the wife who was beating him at his own game. Against the wall Deputy Sweet saw how agitated the husband was, and began to get worried about that revolver in his holster, thinking he should disarm him.

The other two players left the table to use the bathroom, they said, but really to get away. The poker game was now just Puzzleface and Ike. Everyone else had the good sense to know this was their game, and as people gathered around to watch it, a few spectators began to suspect this game of poker had its own set of rules.

"Well, I'll see you and raise you. Fifty dollars."

"Call."

The two showed their cards.

Puzzleface had a royal flush.

The husband had a flush.

With one arm, the wife gathered the pile of her husband's chips to the mountain of chips on her side of the table.

The next three hands went to Puzzleface.

The husband lost more of his money with every hand, going officially broke when Puzzleface raised him a hundred dollars on the next hand.

The man sweated and squirmed in his seat, checking his empty wallet. "I-I . . ."

"I'll raise you your gun," said Puzzleface.

"You want me to bet my gun?"

"Then you can call."

Full of arrogance and ugly crudeness, Ike hauled his revolver onto the table, scattering chips. "Okay, call!"

He set down three aces.

Clapped his hands.

Puzzleface laid down a full house, kings and jacks.

There was a twinge of fear on the husband's stunned face as his wife snatched his gun off the table and the man found himself unarmed.

"You know why I beat you, Ike, why I keep beating you? It's because I'm better than you." Frank." Puzzleface's taunts dismantled her abusive husband one piece at a time. "That must really piss you off, Ike. Must make you want to shoot yourself. Too bad I won your gun. Win it back. You got something to bet with."

He was listening.

"Bet your horse."

"The horse is bet."

Lost to a pair of tens and sevens.

Leaning in with a cold-eyed stare, Puzzleface chuckled to Ike. "You lost your money. You lost your gun. You lost your horse. How does it feel to lose? And lose. And keep losing. Get used to it. Because you lost everything, including your wife."

Suddenly, Ike leaned savagely over the table to whisper to Puzzleface, who leaned forward so their faces were inches apart . . . *"You give me all my shit back, I want everything back, or I'll damn well tell everybody who you are!"* he hissed. *"Under that monkey suit."*

"You won't do that, Frank," Puzzleface whispered back. *"Because then everybody will know that you got busted out by your wife, who ran away from you, and who is a woman. And you'll look like a sissy, Ike. You lost everything you have, except maybe a shred of your reputation. I'd keep what's left of it."*

In hell, jerking back upright in his chair, the husband yanked his hair then smashed the table with his fist. He pointed at Puzzleface. "I'm gonna beat you. Bad streak is all. Just keep playing. Deal the cards."

"You need credit to play."

"Yeah, that's what I need." Ike hemorrhaged sweat.

"I'll give you credit. A thousand-dollar marker," Puzzleface said. "You win the next hand, you get all your stuff back, your gun, your horse, the cash you lost, you can keep playing me, Ike."

"And if I lose I'm screwed."

"If you lose, I own your ass." A razor-sharp smile

appeared on Rachel's lips behind the false mustache. *"I own you."*

"Deal me in."

There was no money in the pot.

Souls were bet.

"Three cards."

"Two cards."

"Let's see your hand . . ."

"I'm not paying you, that's all there is to it."

In the town square across from the Jackson Hotel, Rachel and Ike stood arguing on the grass. Both were so covered with falling snow nearby children thought they were living snowmen. Deputy Sweet stood nearby, leaving the ex-couple to work things out. Puzzleface's makeup and beard had come off Rachel's face; she was clearly a woman wearing man's clothes but she didn't care right now.

"That marker is a legitimate legal debt, Ike." Rachel said. "Deputy Sweet witnessed it." She looked to the lawman for confirmation and when he nodded, she looked back at her husband. "You owe me one thousand dollars."

Pulling his pockets inside out, Ike threw his hands up in a hopeless *Where am I gonna get that kind of dough?* gesture. Then he waved her off with a broken laugh. After he gave her the finger. "What are you going to do, woman, chase me for it? Ha! You're so afraid of me coming after you, running away from me for so long, you ain't ever going after me."

"You're right."

"So I'm walking. You got my horse. My damn gun. I ain't paying that thousand dollars."

"I don't have to come after you." He kept walking and she kept talking. "I'll sell your debt. And the men I sell your marker to *will* come after you, Ike."

Her husband stopped.

"You know the kind of men those are," his wife said. "They'll get their money. They have guns and horses, Ike, and you've got neither."

Seeing the grim fate that lay in store, Ike turned weakly and walked back to her, close to tears. "Please." He fell on his knees. "What do you want from me?"

"I want you to know something."

Rachel got eyeball to eyeball with Ike and her three words made his blood run cold.

"I own you."

"Please."

He wept on his knees.

"But you can buy your way out," she said.

"Anything."

"Sell me this."

Rachel handed Ike a slip of paper. "I'll buy back your marker when you give me this in return."

He opened the paper.

One word was written on it.

Rachel

Their eyes met and he understood the price.

Ike nodded, broken.

"It's over," Rachel said.

"You'll never see me again." It was the last thing he ever said to her.

Getting off his knees, Ike walked away into the snow

on Cache Street, heading past the bar because he could no longer afford the price of a drink. Deputy Sweet watched him go, feeling pretty sure Rachel would never have to look over her shoulder again where her husband was concerned.

When he looked back, Puzzleface was gone. Hearing a woman's laughter, Sweet looked around and saw Rachel a hundred yards away, arms spread, head thrown back, tongue out, feeling and tasting the fresh falling white snowflakes drifting on her like a fairy tale. She turned round and round in childlike joy, then spun her body like a top and fell on her back in the piled snow, making a snow angel, acting like a kid again.

She was free.

Seeing Rachel happy playing in the snow was all Deputy Marshal Nate Sweet wanted for Christmas.

CHAPTER 27

The Brander can see his three pursuers a half mile back through his field glasses, but they can't see him.

They have been on his tail since he left the town after killing the judge. He's been observing them for the last two days from safe positions. At first he thinks it is three men, but yesterday realizes one of them is a woman; her hair, long and red beneath her hat, betrays her gender. The features of the three the fiend can't make out because their faces are covered with scarfs worn against the bitter cold. So he doesn't recognize two of them, not yet.

The smaller man looks vaguely familiar because of his height and his gait—his rangy stride and the way his arms swing walking—when on two occasions he dismounts to relieve himself in the bushes. The Brander can't be sure who this individual is but feels he has seen him before. But where? he wonders. It nags him, like an itch he can't scratch.

The big man of the trio, this much the fiend knows: he is the tough ornery one he fought with who gave him all that trouble several weeks ago. This bastard broke his branding iron; it had been no small difficulty finding a blacksmith to forge him a new one to replace it. It had delayed his mission and set him back days. Having his branding iron destroyed angers its owner greatly. The instrument is a family heirloom. Fearsome payback lies in store for this bastard who broke it—at a time and place of The Brander's own choosing.

But he has more important matters to deal with first.

The three riders shadowing him must be the law, probably U.S. Marshals; their eventual appearance was inevitable because of all the bodies the fiend has left in his wake, a pile of corpses on top of corpses that steadily grows. By now, The Brander wagers he is probably wanted in at least two states with a bounty on his head for his capture dead or alive. The Brander has made no secret about concealing his identity in his killings, in fact just the opposite, leaving his signature on all of his executions with the *Q* brand, and this is the point: to let them know the vigilante who is raining fiery burning justice down on the heads of the guilty; yes, he wants *all* of them to know, the whole entire world to receive the message.

His message . . .

This morning, The Brander hides in the snow with his binoculars and studies the three flyspecks of the horses and riders on the clean fallen snow of the plain, when suddenly he sees they have company.

A posse is pursuing those pursuing him.

Seven riders are tracking the three others; this could only be Sheriff Conrad and his rogue deputies from back in Consequence. The judge's black book has told him all about Bull Conrad, because so many entries bear the sheriff's name. The Brander has been reading the book on the trail since he left town after reducing Judge Bill Black to a pile of burned meat. The fiend reads each and every page. The conspiracy between the judge and the sheriff taking bribes to release criminals he already knows about. What he *is* surprised to learn is that it is Sheriff Bull Conrad who is pulling the strings, not Judge Bill Black. It's all there in black-and-white in the judge's persnickety neat handwriting. The sheriff has his hands in *everything*, making money hand over fist, running the crooks and taking a cut of their scores as well as a cut of the bribes they pay to the judge to get free. Conrad is behind the whole operation. And it is Sheriff Bull Conrad who had ordered the raid on the Quaid ranch that stole the cattle and burned the spread to the ground. This makes him the mastermind . . . and the lightning rod for The Brander's rage, the *Q* brand's ultimate target. The book gives the fiend the bull's-eye—*an address*—Sheriff Conrad has built a safe house with those ill-gotten gains he's stashed away, a hideout whose location is well concealed—but the fiend finds the address in the book and this is where The Brander now rides; it is where Sheriff Conrad will be, or soon be, and where he will feel the full wrath of the brand.

How ironic that on this fateful trail The Brander's hunters are themselves being hunted with he himself hunting them all . . . *The hunted hunting the hunters*. The elegant beauty to this notion The Brander appreciates, making him do the one thing he never ever does, and that is smile.

For now The Brander's enemies are all on their way heading like unsuspecting flies into a spider's web, his dogged pursuers riding right into his trap, where the fiend will turn the tables on them. He is supremely confident knowing the fight will be in his own backyard, the battle at a time and place of his choosing; that place lies in the mountains of the highest upper elevations of western Wyoming in Yellowstone with no other human beings for hundreds of miles, a bleak inhospitable territory so hostile even angels fear to tread. For his whole life The Brander has trapped and hunted and camped in the area and the Quaids know every foot of the terrain.

The name of the place is fitting . . .

Destiny.

CHAPTER 28

The three manhunters had arrived at the upper elevations of Destiny County, Wyoming. They had chased The
Brander here, into Yellowstone. Now Noose, Bess, and
Emmett sat on their horses and surveyed the formidable
terrain before them. Somewhere ahead lay their quarry and
there was not much farther he could go before the great
mountains stopped him.

The air was thin up here.

It was the top of the world.

Their hats felt like they touched the sky.

To the west, a staggering mountain range of towering
granite peaks reared high above them into the heavens,
mighty summits disappearing into the low-hanging cloud
bank. The crags were laden with a billion tons of snow, the
sheer size and scale of the mountains to the west was daunt-
ing to behold. This was the direction they now faced. In
the shadow of the mountains lay a frozen lake to the south.
North was impassable steep wilderness with a stretch of
the mighty Snake River traversing through it below tall
cliffs. The territory was inhospitable and unfriendly but

what wasn't obscured behind the driving sheets of winter snow was truly breathtaking to behold.

Bess whistled at the view.

Emmett looked worried by it.

Noose reached over from his saddle, plucking a piece of torn cloth from a branch. Emmett looked at the cloth, then looked at Noose and nodded. It was material from Abraham Quaid's coat. The bounty hunter looked at both marshals, pointing his finger out at the mountains above.

That's the way he went.

The Brander had to have gone either west or south. If the three were going to ride farther, hump their horses up cliffs and ridges and gorges, the going would be treacherous—no trail up here, just a steep uphill climb to where you couldn't ride anymore and man or horse could go no farther. Noose, Bess, and Emmett all exchanged glances with the same intuition.

This was the end of the trail.

It had to be.

The Brander could ride no farther.

Here was where they would take him down or he would take them down.

They spurred their horses into motion.

The three rode in, each hoping three would ride out.

Overhead, the gray clouds dumped heavy snow. Winds had picked up, the swirling snow obscuring visibility. Blizzard conditions.

It was all uphill from here.

"We need to split up," Noose said.

"Too much ground to cover," Bess agreed.

The trio of manhunters had pulled their horses together into a tight grouping and were conferring from their saddles. An hour after they rode into Destiny, the vast terrain had overwhelmed them—there were just too many places The Brander could be. They needed to divide up their manpower to search a broader area and cast a wider net in order to improve their odds of apprehension.

None of them liked splitting up the team. It had been the three of them the whole ride so far. There was safety in numbers. They were a pack, now about to become lone wolves and lone wolves were easy targets. Bess had a lump in her throat and saw emotion in eyes of Noose and Emmett, too; only now parting ways did each realize the sense of security their companionship provided each of them. *You knew what you had only when it was gone.*

But they had a job to do.

"Whoever spots Quaid fire two shots in the air," Emmett said. It would pinpoint direction for the others to ride in for backup.

"Sounds like a plan." Noose nodded.

"Then we're agreed," Bess said. "Joe, which direction you want to take?"

Noose cast his formidable gaze up at the snow-covered slope above leading into the mountains and pondered, not for long. "Brander's trail indicates that's probably where he went. Likeliest chance of encountering Quaid is up that way, I'd say. If only one of us is gonna meet up with him, it ought to be me. I'll take the west."

"Okay, I'll take the lake." From her saddle. Bess turned her head south toward the heavily iced-over body of water. "In case he backtracks."

"That leaves north for me," said Emmett. "Good chance

as any he went that way. He's so unpredictable. Could be anywhere. Remember that. And I will, too."

They ungrouped their horses, readying to split off in three points of the compass.

"Keep eyes in the back of your head," Marshal Bess cautioned. "Brander gave us enough trouble while we were all together. Now we're each on our own, so just be careful."

The men nodded.

She smiled. "If either of you boys get killed I'll kick your ass."

Grins all around.

As Noose started to ride off, Emmett called his name. "Noose."

He looked back.

"Don't kill him."

"Reckon that's up to the old man, now, ain't it?"

As Joe Noose cantered up the hill gripping his rifle, Emmett Ford had a calculating expression viewing his departure. Marshal Bess's horse was already halfway to the tree line of the lake, he saw. After another cunning glance up at the bounty hunter riding up the hill, Emmett spurred his horse and, as decided, rode north.

Then he changed direction.

CHAPTER 29

The frozen lake was one gigantic sheet of ice, Marshal Bess observed, patrolling the shoreline on her mare. It looked so thick you could ride a horse on it, she thought, but wouldn't want to try.

With a flip of her reins with her wrists, she steered her Appaloosa closer to the pine trees as they rode the perimeter of the lake, giving her more cover.

Never knew who might be watching.

Riding next to the forested rows of conifers kept the snow off her, because it was really coming down in sheets of damp white flakes and had started to sleet.

She rested the stock of her loaded and cocked Winchester on her hip, barrel pointing upward, in one glove. The reins she loosely held in the other. Her keen blue eyes made a steady scan right and left, taking in her rugged surroundings.

Detected no movement.

The frigid air felt like inhaling ice that froze her lungs every time she drew breath. Her wool scarf over her mouth and nose did little to filter it. She exhaled heavily into the scarf so the warmth of her breath warmed the cloth on her face and it helped a bit. The bitter dank cold cut through her layers of heavy clothing and chilled her to the bone. Temperatures she guessed were twenty or thirty below zero.

The marshal circled the frozen lake, keeping a sharp lookout for The Brander. Farther on she rode, aware each step of her horse took her farther from her friends into she knew not what.

The sense of oppressive vastness and utter isolation way out here in the Far West upper elevations bore down on Bess. The lady marshal was no stranger to the wilderness, having grown up in the rural mountains of Hoback twenty miles from civilization—but she had never felt so completely cut off and on her own as she now experienced in the remoteness of this place. It was like being on the moon. If you got injured out here or your horse broke its leg you'd freeze to death and nobody would come to help you and if you died, they'd never find you. A bleak thought. God, it was lonesome.

She'd been listening for the two gunshots.

Hadn't heard any.

Joe and Emmett hadn't run into The Brander.

Unless they did and . . .

Riding on nearing the far shore, Marshal Bess saw on that side of the lake fifty yards from the ice was the rock wall of a ridge spiked with forest.

It was so quiet, a dead silence save the breathy *whoosh*es of wind swaying the branches and steady *clop* of her Appaloosa's hooves. Then suddenly she thought she heard something. Halting her horse, Bess sat very still and listened for any sound.

Heard a horse *whinn-eey.*

The rattle of something metallic. A bridle, a rifle, it was hard to tell. It had an echo.

Looking for the source of the sounds drew the marshal's gaze to the other side of the lake.

She squinted to see that there was a cave at the base of the ridge.

Inside, she saw movement.

A man.

More men.

Something bigger. A horse. More horses.

Happening upon these interlopers broke the inertia—the solitude of the last half hour got her thinking too much—and Bess was grateful to have something to do. Her adrenaline began pumping as she shifted into action mode, and she wasn't cold anymore. Stealthfully the marshal dismounted—in one quick motion she slid out of the saddle and landed in a crouch, dodging behind a boulder and there took cover, a two-hand grip on her rifle. She meant business but needed to see what, if anything, she was up against.

She knew what it wasn't: The Brander. He had no accomplices.

It was a camp.

Hold your fire, she told herself.

Peering around the boulder she saw her position gave her a good vantage on the cave. Luckily, the view of the cavern entrance showed what was inside . . . six men, seven horses. The shadowy figures were masked by the darkness of the cavern, so Bess couldn't tell if she recognized any of them or not.

Hold your fire.

It could be trappers, hunters, anybody.

Metal glinted.

Guns.

Ammo.

These men were not hunters.

Milling around in the cave, the men looked to be loading firearms with fresh ammo or cleaning guns. It was hard to see, but the marshal knew from their body language and movements these boys were preparing for armed engagement.

Who were they?

What were they doing out here?

She saw one of the men come to the cave entrance and step into the light, and on his coat metal gleamed in the sun.

A deputy badge.

The sheriff's men from the town of Consequence.

Bess counted six.

Wondered where the seventh was when she felt the cold hard round muzzle of a pistol press against the back of her neck, making her hair stand on end. She recognized the voice the moment he spoke.

"We meet again."

"Reckon we do."

It was that shady sheriff from the town.

"I'll take that Winchester, little lady."

"I'm federal U.S. Marshal Bess Sugarland."

"I'll still take the Winchester."

Grabbing the rifle, Sheriff Bull Conrad yanked it from her grip and tossed it behind him, keeping Bess covered with his Colt. She was still on one knee facing away from him and didn't turn, not moving a muscle but not backing down an inch.

"I am on an active manhunt and you are interfering. Cease and desist or I *will* arrest you."

"Those, too."

Conrad leaned in. Pulling her Colt Peacemakers out of

her holsters, he stuffed the heavy revolvers in two of the many pockets of his weathered leather duster. It took him seconds to disarm her.

"I'm getting up."

"Easy."

She rose and turned to face him, her eyes steel. "You are now under arrest."

"Wrong, lady, it is me who is arresting you."

"My federal authority as a marshal supersedes yours, Sheriff, you damn well know it. I'm arresting you for threatening a federal officer, interfering with Marshal business, and obstructing a murder investigation and manhunt."

Chuckling, Sheriff Conrad's eyes twinkled with laughter as his mustached face broke into a big old grin. "Why don't you and I just each whip it out and decide this by seeing whose is bigger? Oh, wait . . ." His toothy grin broadened. "Looks like I win."

"You are an asshole."

"You are my prisoner."

"And you're making a big mistake."

"Any more guns on you I need to know about?"

She looked at him defiantly.

He shrugged. "I can frisk you. Or my men can frisk you. They'll give you a proper cavity search. I know you ain't no U.S. Marshal but you are a lady, so respecting your modesty here, ma'am, tell me the truth and come clean about any other weapons so we won't have to feel you up."

"A Marlin rifle in the saddle scabbard. That's it."

"Fair enough."

"Those Colt pistols are my daddy's guns and I want 'em back."

Covering Bess with his revolver, Conrad reached to his

belt and pulled off a heavy set of iron handcuffs. He tossed them to her. She caught the shackles. "Put 'em on."

"You can't do this. I'm a federal U.S. Marshal."

"Just because you keep saying you are don't make it so, just like having the badge don't make you a lawman. Look at my men. They all have badges. So what does that tell you? Cuff yourself, sister, or I'll do it for you."

Holding his gaze fiercely the entire time, Bess didn't look at the handcuffs once as, after fumbling with the shackles, she clumsily closed the cuffs around her wrists with a *clank*.

He gave her shoulder a rough shove and started her walking along the shore in the direction of his camp at the cave a few hundred paces away. "Start walking." The sheriff was right behind her, poking her in the spine with the barrel of his rifle to prod her along. "Faster."

"State your business, Sheriff. What are your intentions?"

"I'm taking you to the cave over there where we're going to go in and have us a friendly little chat. You and me, we have a lot to talk about. It can go easy or hard, either way; how this goes is up to you. But whether you choose to cooperate or don't, know this: in the end I will get it out of you. You will tell me what I want to know and you will give me what I want."

She was simply scared shitless. Marshal Bess did not know what to make of Sheriff Conrad and couldn't figure him out at all. What he wanted, what he was capable of, she had no clue. The only thing quite clear about Bull Conrad was he was a very bad man and a truly dangerous individual who, if she had to guess, was capable of anything. He jabbed the huge rifle in her back, not gently.

"Walk. Let's go, little lady, whoever the hell you are."

Space closed between them and the cave.

Joe Noose, where are you when I need you?

Her best friend wasn't coming to her rescue this time.

Marshal Bess Sugarland knew she was on her own, completely and utterly, facing mortal danger. Her survival was in her own hands and it was up to her to save herself. To do that she needed to keep her wits about her. She bombarded her captor with questions in the time they had alone together walking along the icy lake.

"What the hell are you and your men doing out here?"

"We've been chasing you. Caught up. Got you. We'll get the other two."

"I know why you followed us."

"Of course you do." *Not the retort she expected, but okay.*

"You're after The Brander," she said. "You want the five-thousand-dollar bounty on his head. Figured we'd lead you to him. Once we pointed him out to you, the scheme was to get the jump on us, killing The Brander first then claiming the body to collect the reward. How am I doing so far?"

Conrad said nothing, giving her another jab in the back.

"Maybe you figured on shooting us after we shot The Brander, letting us do all the work, then you boys steal the body and turn it in for the reward. Not a bad plan. Nobody would ever find our bodies out here in all this desolation."

He said nothing.

"Which is why you followed us out here. You think I don't know how you bounty killers operate?" Her laugh was a snort.

"I don't know what the hell you're talking about."

Marshal Bess gave Sheriff Conrad the side-eye and saw the baffled and confused expression on his hard face was genuine. She had read this all wrong. "You really don't know what I'm talking about, do you?"

"Nope."

"If you aren't after The Brander, then . . ."

She didn't finish her sentence. Force-marched at gunpoint past the frozen lake the rest of the way, Bess saw they had reached the mouth of the cave. The six deputies inside had stopped what they were doing and, noticing her with sparked interest, began to converge like bats waking up inside the cavern. Bess stopped and faced Conrad, and now she finished her sentence.

"Why are you coming after us?"

A dangerous look appeared on the sheriff's face as with a deadly glare, he gestured with the barrel of his Henry rifle for her to get in the cave and then spoke. "Because you have something of mine."

His eyes went dead.

"I want it back."

CHAPTER 30

The Brander recognizes the face.

When the snow clears for an instant, the features of the massive man climbing toward him become distinct; the fiend catches only the quickest glimpse before the snow obscures the figure, but it is enough.

That face out of the past, so long ago, is one and the same.

It is the boy who they branded so long ago, grown to manhood. He recognizes Joe Noose, but does not know his name, for the man had no name way back then. He named himself when he was sixteen, but The Brander doesn't know this. He just knows the face. It is the one face he will always remember. The fiend has not seen him for a long, long time.

The boy was the first time his branding iron tasted flesh—the birth of the brand; its mark burned into the boy's chest begat all the branding slayings to come.

But once marked with the brand, the boy had been left alive. They let him go. That had been a mistake. Letting him live had broken rules as yet unwritten back then but later to become law to the fiend: *Branding means death to all whose flesh bears the mark.*

From that day forward, The Brander marks with the *Q* only those whom he executes—a mortal contract sealed with the imprint of red-hot metal. The symbol is a death notice, burned into flesh. A sigil of doom. The brand sends a message. It is a signature. For all the world to see, the *Q* on a corpse means the victim was an evil man in life executed for his misdeeds. Branding means death. No exceptions. If one of the branded survives, the mark means nothing and all the other brandings become meaningless.

Not killing that boy had been a mistake, The Brander acknowledges. The brand had never tasted flesh before. It was the first time; mistakes happen. But it is time to correct that mistake.

The record must be clean.

Journeying here into the high elevations, The Brander came to kill one man; the last victim before his work is done. Now the fiend realizes there are *two* men he must kill. A last loose end must be tied up. Then the fiend can rest; the brand will cool as The Brander himself ends, disintegrating into nothingness to become no more, his soul scattering like snowflakes in the blizzard howling around him now.

The big man draws closer as he scales the mountain, his approach a white outline in the snowstorm. The Brander knows he needs a very big gun against this very big man, a gun with stopping power. Specifically, his largest-caliber handgun with enough knockdown force to drop him. The man coming toward him has as much sheer mass as a grizzly bear. The .55 caliber Remington cavalry revolver is heavy and cumbersome but a couple of well-placed rounds from it—a head and chest shot—and the big man will fall. The fiend saves the hand cannon only for special occasions. Twenty years have passed, but now fate and destiny have brought The Brander and his first branding victim back together for a final reckoning.

The first one branded will be the last to die.
Time to finish him off.
The fiend cocks his weapon and battle is joined.

Joe blinked and saw The Brander.
He blinked again but he was gone.
Noose was seeing things.
Or was he?

CHAPTER 31

"I want the book."

Inside the cave, the lady marshal was the sheriff's posse's hostage. Bess sat on a rock, hands cuffed before her in her lap. Surrounding her were seven badmen with big guns calling themselves lawmen, and the worst of them stood in front of her, growing angrier and angrier each time he repeated the same question and got her same reply. Pretty soon, she thought, he was going to use that Colt Walker revolver on her.

"We don't have the book."

"Who does?"

"The man we're hunting they call The Brander."

Exploding in rage, Sheriff Conrad waved his arms. "There ain't no Brander! You and your three friends done all those branding killings! You three are The Brander! You ain't no marshals! That ain't no real badge! I don't know why you three are butchering my men like prize hogs or why you're branding them like steers gone to market and don't give a shit. I want the book."

"For the hundredth time, me and my friends don't have the book. The Brander has the book. Joe Noose and

Emmett Ford are out there right now tracking this man down and when they get him, you get the book. *If* you let me go right now. Our business here is to take down The Brander, dead or alive. I have no business with you today, Sheriff. Release me directly before I do."

"Who are you three working for?"

"I work for federal judge John Wainright of Uinta County. Emmett Ford works for the federal judge in Idaho, I disremember the name. You can ask him. Joe Noose works for me as a bounty hunter."

"Who sent you to kill the judge and screw up our whole operation?"

"Nobody. We are on U.S. Marshal business dispatched from headquarters in Cody with orders to track down, apprehend, and subdue by any means necessary The Brander, thereby stopping his killing spree."

"And that's why you three branded Judge Bill Black over every square inch of his flesh until you killed him?"

Whirling on Conrad, Bess lost her temper and yelled in the sheriff's face at the top of her lungs.

"Are you Goddamn stupid or did your horse kick you in the head too many times? Of course my friends and I aren't The Brander! You know my badge is real! I'm a U.S. Marshal! My daddy was a U.S. Marshal!"

Hunkering down before her, Sheriff Conrad got down to her level and stared hard into her baby blues a long moment before he spoke. "Your daddy was a marshal, you say? Okay, then. I am acquainted with most federal marshals. Tell me his name."

"Federal Marshal Nate Sugarland out of Hoback."

The crooked lawman's eyes blinked with recognition.

"I know Nate. Good man. Chased me clear to Casper and almost got me back in '55. You his daughter?"

"That's right. Bess Sugarland. Marshal Bess Sugarland."

"And Nate taught you the family trade. I see, makes sense to me now why a woman comes to be wearing a marshal badge. Bet you were your daddy's deputy for lots of years, how he taught you the ropes."

She nodded tersely.

"Chip off the old block. How is your daddy?"

"Dead. Murdered by trash named Frank Butler and his pack of vulture bounty killers. My friend Joe Noose, the big man outside, he killed every last one of the Butler Gang with a little help from me in the spring of '86. It's how Joe and me met. And unless you let me go directly so I can get back to my business with The Brander, Noose will kill every one of you when he rescues me." She swept her hard glance across the tense faces of the impressed deputies. "I can see you've heard of Joe Noose and know him by his formidable reputation. Trust me, he's the last man on earth you want coming for you. And Noose already is coming for you because he's coming for *me*. When it comes to his friends, he's very protective."

Sheriff Conrad nodded, bowing his head a little. "I am sorry to hear about your father. Frank Butler was filth. Made me look wholesome."

"Oh, you two are just the same, Conrad—Butler and you—don't fool yourself," Marshal Bess spat. "You're both unscrupulous varmint killers, robbers, and thieves who would harm or kill anyone and do anything for money. You and Butler are from the same foul litter."

The bad sheriff looked stung. "Now, that's where you're wrong about me, missy. I don't murder people for money like Frank Butler did, killing folks for the bounty and all. Exceptions like Quaid wasn't supposed to happen. I rob and steal but I'm more of a businessman. That judge Bill Black, he come to me with this business proposition about me arresting criminals and getting them to pay cash to me and the judge so he lets them off. It was a good opportunity. Nobody can blame a man for taking an opportunity when he sees one. Just like you can't blame me when it became in my interest to play both sides. I organized my own gang and planned out robberies and sat in the sheriff's office while they did them. Got me a cut of the robberies plus the cut of the bribes when I arrested one or two of my boys and the judge cut them loose. Doubled my take. Right under that greedy old bastard judge's nose and he was none the wiser, at least I thought he wasn't until he told me about that book of his the night he died."

Bess was unmoved. "And Butler shot my father and framed Noose so he could chase him down for the bounty reward. You and Butler both think like criminals and you think you're so damn smart but you're both trash. At least Frank Butler did his own killing."

Rising to his feet, Sheriff Conrad rubbed his mustache and brooded, taking a few steps to the edge of the cave to look out at the wintery wasteland. "Well, talking to you now convinced me of one thing at least: that you are *not* this Brander and your friends ain't, neither. That killer out there he's somebody else, somebody real bad, somebody butchering my operatives and because he's got that book is how he come out here. He cut off one head of the snake with the judge, now he's here to cut off the other head. Me."

Inside the chilly cave, Marshal Bess Sugarland adjusted her sore seat on the icy rocks. Her handcuffed wrists were in her lap. An escape plan was formulating in her mind, but it would be risky.

Pacing back and forth, Sheriff Bull Conrad kept shooting a flinty glance out the opening at the wall of chilly whiteness of the outside world. With each metronome step, his spurs beat time to the ratchet of the cylinder of his revolver he kept turning in his finger like the ticking of clock.

"Who is that branding-iron bastard son of a bitch?" He masticated.

Bess, preoccupied, said the name under her breath.

The crooked lawman rounded on her. "What did you say?"

She raised her blue eyes to meet his. "Abraham Quaid."

"No, it ain't."

"That's his name."

"It can't be."

Her eyes questioned why.

"Because he's dead. He got shot."

"How do you know? Were you there?"

The cunning lawman grinned at her slick attempt to entrap him. "No, I was not." He spat tobacco juice on the rocks. "My men was."

"Your men shot the old man, stole Quaid's cattle, and burned his ranch?" She glared at him in disgust. "Rustling and arson."

"And murder, don't forget. That old-timer got in the way and was got out of the way with a shotgun blast in the chest, way it was reported to me."

"Your men missed. Abraham Quaid is alive and he's coming, out for the blood of every man in that raid. He's already killed most of them."

Stopping his pacing, Bull Conrad's brow furrowed. "Somebody buried him on the ranch."

"The grave is empty."

"Swell. Explains everything." Conrad chuckled and shook his head. "And now he's coming after me. That's why he's out here. It all makes sense now. It's my ass Abe Quaid really wants." Sheriff Conrad shook off his paranoid inertia, sick of standing around. Jumping into action, his blood pumping and adrenaline surging from getting ready for a fight, the bad lawman holstered his pistol, grabbed his Henry rifle, and jacked a fistful of .45 rounds in the breech, stuffed more cartridges in his pocket. "Okay, Quaid. Let's do it. Let's you and I finish it."

"You're not going out there?" Bess was aghast.

"Abe Quaid is out there right now hunting me." The sheriff pointed a heavy dustered arm out at the foreboding snowy mountain range beyond the cave opening. "I'm going to kill Abe Quaid before he kills me. He wants his fit and proper revenge, who am I to deny him? I can't wait to see the look on that old bastard's face when he looks up my barrel and knows his whole revenge was for nothing right before I pull the trigger. You want a job done right you gotta do it yourself, missy."

"Joe Noose, the best tracker in the territory, has been chasing Quaid for months, hasn't found him, and if he can't, neither can you. You'll never find him."

"I don't have to find him. He'll find me."

"You bet he will."

"I'm ready for him but Abe Quaid ain't ready for me. This time I'm going to dead that old man so he stays dead."

"The Brander ain't all that's outside this cave, Conrad. So is Noose hunting for Quaid, and I'm guessing you'll run into each other. Joe Noose is the one who you better be worried about, not that crazy old man."

"I'll steer clear of him."

"If Joe Noose can't find Quaid, what makes you think you can?"

"Noose don't know where to look for Quaid. I do. I know exactly where he's going."

"And where's that?"

"My cabin. Built me a little place up here to get away from it all a few years back. Hide out to hole up if I ever got boxed in. Can hold off an army of marshals in that cabin if I had to. The place is a secret, only Bill Black knew, and nobody comes out here this far into the wilderness. Not until Abe Quaid. He is going to the cabin for sure."

"I thought the location was a secret. How does he know where your cabin is?"

"The book. His Honor must've had the location of the cabin written down in that book of his, an insurance policy so he could turn me in if he had to, tell the law where to find me. Quaid got his hands on the book and came straight here. Guaranteed, he learned the whereabouts of the cabin from the book, which is why he come all the way out here to the end of God's creation, and that's exactly where he's going, to find me. And he's right, I will be there. I'm going to meet him directly."

"Wish I could tag along."

"To escape?"

"To watch you die."

"I'll see you soon."

Striding to the opening of the cave, Conrad turned up his collar against the driving snow, pulling down the brim of his Stetson.

Deputy Rickey's voice stopped him. "What the hell do we do with her, boss?"

"Whatever you want," was his reply, a lewd tinge to his tone. "She's all yours, boys."

Bundled against the elements, the imposing figure of the big man with the big rifle left the cave and five feet outside he was obscured by the blizzard and disappeared from view.

Handcuffed, seated against the rock, Marshal Bess drew her gaze from the cave entrance across to the inside of the small cavern itself, and felt the six sets of eyes boring into her. The deputies were looking her up and down, undressing her with their eyeballs. Her nose was always good and she could smell the men thinking about her naked—an aggressive rutting scent of animals in heat. Looking across the faces, Bess met each of the men's gazes in turn, holding their predatory stares, trying not to blink or show fear. The men exchanged questioning, sly glances.

"The boss said it was okay."

"Sounded that way to me."

"We all heard him."

"He ain't here anyhow."

"Never pass up a good thing."

All eyes were on the young woman.

"You're pretty."

"Gee, thanks."

She knew what was coming. *Let it.* The lady marshal had already decided on a desperate plan.

"Who's the best kisser?" Bess said. "I like a man who knows how to kiss."

The deputies roared with raunchy laughter.

"Me!" Deputy Rickey puckered up.

"You look like you're kissing your mama." Bess laughed. "I'm talking about a *real* kiss."

"Lady, my tongue is so long I can stick it clean down your throat." The leering deputy named Clyde Lovejoy opened his mouth and stuck his tongue way out, and it looked a foot long.

Perfect, she thought.

Adjusting her butt on the rocks for leverage, Bess got balanced, sat opened-legged like a man, thrusting out her bosom and smiling as sexy as she knew how. "You get the first kiss." Bess winked at Lovejoy. "Come and get it."

"Looks like I'm the winner, boys." Lovejoy's hands resting on the holstered stocks of his two Colt Single Action Army pistols hanging on his belt moved to his crotch, and gave himself a squeeze.

"You gonna give me that kiss?" Bess asked.

"Oh, I'm gonna give it to you. Then my friends here, they're gonna give it to you. And you, pretty lady, are going to get it but good. We're gonna pull a longer train on you than the Atchison, Topeka and the Santa Fe."

Her mouth was dry, she couldn't reply.

Behind him, the five other deputies whooped and hollered, getting ready to take turns on Bess. She knew the gang rape they had in mind and what was coming; it was all part of her plan, which depended on her being manhandled. Had the young woman let it, fear might have paralyzed her, but she did what she had to do to get the men where they needed to be for the moves she had to make.

Her life depended on the next minute or two; if the six men overpowered her she would be violated then murdered because they could not leave her alive.

The lady marshal mentally ran through where her hands would be every second, where to put her feet. Everything she would have to grab. She would need to be very, very quick.

Swaggering up to her like a king stud in his cowboy boots, the ugly deputy stuck out his crotch, staring down past his hips to her face as she sat below, his eyes bulging with lustful urge. Bess felt the redneck getting all pumped up thinking she was staring between his legs at his crotch, but her eyes were elsewhere: staring *through* his legs at the five deputies waiting in single file behind him to take their turn.

Stacked up like a row of targets in perfect shooting formation and not spread out. Good.

But before then things had to go just right.

The deputy was going to have to kiss her first.

CHAPTER 32

Whiteout.

It was a blizzard.

Joe Noose raised his Winchester and slowly turned in a 360-degree rotation, unable to see ten feet in any direction.

It was a void of white nothingness, the snowflakes swirling in a vacuum.

The bounty hunter squinted, saw no sign of The Brander, who could have been a few steps away and he wouldn't see him. The sound of his own heavy breathing in the thin air was drowned in the roaring of the wind and whooshing of the pine tree branches.

This was bad.

A distance back, Joe had tied Copper off to a sturdy tree and continued on foot because his horse could break a leg in this snowbound terrain.

Raising the repeater rifle to his shoulder, Noose looked down the gunsight and pivoted left and right at the hip, sweeping the barrel back and forth against the white. The damned sleet was getting in his eyes, blurring his vision with stinging tears. He cussed a string of profanity beneath his breath then shut up because he needed to listen. Hear what was around him.

Targeting the enemy had suddenly become much more difficult because in this mess he couldn't be sure what he was shooting at—even the nearby rows of conifers, barely discernable as faint shapes, resembled a man, the trunks the torso, the branches arms waving in the wind. Aiming had to be careful, and with caution came hesitation and a split-second's hesitation pulling the trigger in a gunfight was what got a man killed.

Trudging along the snowbound hill in a white maelstrom of thick flurries, Joe Noose kept his eyes peeled and his Winchester rifle raised. His finger off the trigger.

No time to be trigger-happy.

If he spotted The Brander it could be Emmett—the shape of a man could be anyone, identification impossible to make in the snowstorm—pull the trigger too fast, he could shoot his companion.

And the marshal couldn't see Noose any better than he could see him—if Emmett was too quick on the draw, he could easily put a bullet in Joe; the bounty hunter hoped wherever the marshal was that he was thinking the same thing and being damn careful with his weapon and placing his shots.

All of a sudden, Joe Noose felt in worse physical danger than he had ever experienced in his life. Fatal friendly fire was now a clear and present danger.

Until the blizzard died down and visibility cleared he couldn't risk a shot at any figure over thirty feet away. To shoot The Brander, Noose was going to have to be right on top of him. The fiend practically beside him. Then Abe Quaid would be close enough to touch. The old man was near, very near; the bounty hunter felt in his gut his quarry was close, and his instincts never failed him.

But Noose could not see.

He could not hear.

Did not know what direction he faced or from what direction he just came.

Panic rose inside Joe Noose as a wave of dislocation and disorientation swept over him, and he broke out in a cold sweat that instantly froze in a thin film of ice on his face. Completely losing his bearings confounded his senses and made his mind swim with confusion, disabling his gunfighter instincts. Only one thing was certain: he shouldn't be out here in this blizzard with his deadly murderous quarry; he should take cover until the snows died down, or better yet turn back.

Which way *was* back?

Noose didn't know.

There was no turning back.

He was at the point of no return.

If you can't see him he can't see you.

With that sudden realization, the big bounty hunter felt his insides unclench and a strange calm settle over him. His gloved hand on his rifle felt the weapon relax in his grip. He put his finger back on the trigger.

He wasn't going to pull it by accident.

Never had.

Putting one foot in front of the other, the bounty hunter headed off in the direction his inner compass told him to go. Didn't matter because it was all a blank empty canvas anyway, white everywhere he looked. Joe Noose resumed his hunt. He was operating by instinct, relying on his own quick reflexes.

How good were The Brander's reflexes? he wondered. How keen were the old man's instincts?

At the end of the trail now, they were about to find out.

Sheriff Bull Conrad knew where he was going.

Didn't need to see in the snow to get there.

He'd found his cabin on many pitch-black nights coming home from hunting trips where there was no moon or stars to see by. Hell, he could find his place blindfolded.

The log cabin was a quarter mile dead ahead, six degrees northeast by dead reckoning.

It wasn't getting to the cabin that worried the crooked lawman, but what or rather whom he might encounter getting there. Keeping the heavy Henry rifle raised, cocked, and loaded, Conrad bundled against the driving snow and trudged ever forward through knee-high drifts. Snow and sleet came at his face in curtains of stinging needles, and he pulled his hat down against it.

He was breathing very heavily, his lungs tight. The air was thin at these high elevations. Up here was nine thousand feet above sea level somebody had told him, but he didn't know what that meant or remember who had said it—it was just damn hard to breathe.

His big head rotated back and forth keeping a steady visual patrol of his surroundings. Saw nothing. Until he did. Three times Sheriff Conrad saw what he swore was a man out in the wastes and shouldered his rifle to target the hazy figure, but each time his finger closed on the trigger, the snow swirled away only to reveal a tree trunk two of the times and the third time an odd formation of boulders.

Should have been at the cabin by now, shouldn't he?

It was hard to get enough air. Cussing, the crooked

lawman stopped to catch his breath. Setting the rifle against a boulder, Conrad bent over, hands on his knees, wheezing. When he rose, he raised his head and thought he was seeing things.

That was a man, all right.

Occluded by the blizzard, the fuzzy snow-blown figure was unmistakable because of his height.

Only one man around here today that tall.

Joe Noose.

And not far off.

Sheriff Conrad grabbed his rifle.

The big bounty hunter son of a bitch was walking in the other direction, lost in the snow, his back facing the sheriff; Noose didn't see Conrad. Lifting his rifle, the sheriff socked the Henry to his shoulder and swung the long barrel toward the figure of the man walking away. Bull Conrad lined up the crosshairs between the back of Joe Noose's shoulder blades at the center of the spine, setting his target. This was going to be a two-hundred-yard shot in a high wind so he had to compensate his aim. Lifting the barrel two inches, gauging wind direction, its velocity and bullet drop, the lawman got ready to pull the trigger.

He had no problem shooting a man in the back.

Two hundred yards away, Joe Noose felt cold fingers on his back, a tingling sensation that told him he was being targeted.

He spun with his Winchester, dropping to a low crouch to make himself a smaller target. Here, he was exposed out in the open and there was no cover. Eyes snapping left and right, his vision tried to make sense out of the vague shapes in the sheets of snow gusting on all sides, like an unpainted backdrop on the stage of the theater of combat.

A gunshot rang out, very close.

He saw movement.

His rifle raised swiftly to his eye, finger applying pressure on the trigger.

"Don't shoot, Noose! It's me."

"Emmett!"

A blurry figure stomped through the snow toward him, flagging his rifle over his head and the familiar frame of Marshal Ford came into view.

His breath hissing through his teeth, the bounty hunter lowered his Winchester, relieved he had been mindful not to be quick on the trigger or they'd be down one Idaho marshal.

A cloud of condensed breath wreathing his head, Emmett lumbered up to Noose. His companion's discombobulated expression communicated he shared the same disorientation as Joe himself felt.

"Who fired that shot?" Noose demanded.

"I did. Saw a man with a rifle taking aim on you a few seconds ago and got off a round at him. I went over but he was gone and I didn't see any blood so reckon he wasn't hit and he took off."

"How did you know it wasn't me you were shooting at in all this shit?"

"Simple."

Noose cocked a questioning eyebrow.

"You're taller."

The two men faced each other in the snowstorm; Noose was a head taller than Emmett and now looking down on him with a certain scrutiny. For Joe, things about Emmett were not adding up.

"What are you doing here, Emmett?"

"Saving your ass. Some thanks I get."

"We agreed to split up."

"We did."

"But you're here, not where you're supposed to be." Noose had to raise his voice over the howling wind and supposed it made his words sound harsher. But something was definitely off about the marshal. He was looking left and right in a shifty, nervous way. "Got anything you want to tell me, Emmett?"

"I got lost, Joe. Look at this snow. It's a whiteout. Can't see shit, can you? I thought I was over there, I ended up here."

Maybe, thought Noose. He stepped closer to the marshal until he stood next to him, the intimidation factor high for the smaller man. Emmett was himself a pretty big guy who knew it, but Joe Noose made most men look like lesser mortals. The bounty hunter was close enough to speak normally to the marshal now that he was beside him and spoke into his ear, cupping his hand around his mouth to muffle the din of the storm.

"Two of us can't be in the same area trying to shoot The Brander, not in this blizzard. We can't see three feet in it. Two men might wind up shooting each other by mistake."

"I suppose."

"Or on purpose."

The marshal shot an angry glance to the bounty hunter, like a fired bullet. "What the *hell* is that supposed to mean?"

"It means a lot of things. Means I could get shot in the back, means you could get shot in the back, either of us could easily make a murder look like an accident. Mostly it means it ain't a good idea to shoot at anyone until this blizzard dies down and who knows when that's gonna be. And you being here, Emmett, means I can't shoot Abraham Quaid if I meet him since I can't even see you five feet away in this mess, because I might shoot you by mistake thinking you was The Brander. So you showing up here means I can't pull my trigger. And I think you know that, Emmett. You're obstructing me on purpose."

"I don't know what you're talking about."

"Sure there's nothing you want to tell me?"

"Why do you keep asking me that?"

"Because you're hiding something."

"Hiding *what*?"

"That's what I want to know."

"I don't want you to shoot Quaid if you don't have to."

"I know you don't."

"And maybe it's better if we stick together."

Noose grinned slyly. "You're thinking you being here is gonna make me not shoot Quaid or at least hesitate firing my gun, but you're dead wrong. In a gunfight, the difference between life and death is less than a second when you're touching that trigger. The man who hesitates, even for a fraction of a second, dies. Having to falter pulling the trigger for even an instant will get me killed up here against this enemy. Quaid will not hesitate for an instant. Neither will I, Emmett. Don't get in my way. I won't waver pulling the trigger, not for a split second. I can't. I see it, I shoot it. In a gunfight, there's the quick and the dead."

"What are you trying to say?"

"This: I ain't gonna let you get me killed, Emmett. So I'm letting you know. You shadow me it's your choice, but I will not hesitate to pull the trigger when I see Quaid. I will shoot to kill. You want to bird-dog me, fine, I don't have time to stop you. But if I shoot you by accident while

I'm shooting at Quaid in these damn conditions because I think you're him, tough shit. Don't say I didn't warn you. Telling you one last time, let's split up."

The marshal stubbornly stood there; he wasn't going anywhere. So Noose, who didn't have time to waste, ignored him, hoisted his gun and shouldered past Emmett like he wasn't there, his message clear:

You don't exist.

Noose trudged on up into the snow, shouting back.

"And I damn well know you're hiding something!"

CHAPTER 33

The Brander studies the cabin.

Standing like the scarecrow he often resembles, the fiend watches the place a good long time. It looks unoccupied but it is hard to tell without taking a closer look.

The Brander must be sure.

He will be coming, the man he seeks.

Or be already here.

He needs a closer look.

Gusts of snow rise and fall like a sheet lifted off and dropped on the view of the place then lifted off again, carried on the tide of the howling winter winds that make creepy banshee noises whistling around the canyon, a sonic distortion from the formation of the cliffs.

Or it could be ghosts.

The Brander isn't scared of ghosts.

They say he is one himself, he knows.

So be it.

It is a weathered log cabin of solid austere construction tucked into a cranny of the mountain affording the place natural protective cover against any intruders, surrounded as it is on three sides by granite cliffs and on the fourth by walls of hundred-foot pine trees.

The windows are dark.

No movement around the perimeter.

He has to get closer.

Then The Brander moves like the ghost others suppose him to be, floating down a snowy incline with his coat flapping around his skeletal frame. His figure is exposed as he slides down the snowbank. He keeps a close eye on the windows of the cabin where the shots will come from if they do.

No gunfire.

He hasn't been seen.

The fiend figures nobody is there to see him.

His approach has brought him a few feet from the oiled log walls of the square single-story cabin. Drawing his loaded revolver, The Brander flattens against the wall and inches to the nearest window, ducking around to risk a quick look through the window inside. He ducks back— inside the cabin is dark yet bright enough to see it is empty; the soft winter light flooding through the big dirty windows on all four walls shows a square, single-room layout. A stove. A bed. Piles of winter clothes. It is a hunting retreat from the looks.

A shabby place taking into account how many crimes the owner has committed to acquire it, The Brander thinks, crimes the fiend is about to make him pay for, here on this day, in this place.

Sheriff Bull Conrad is not here yet.

But is coming.

On his way.

Some men are in a big hurry to get to Hell.

The Brander is already in Hell. Knows its every black

corner inside his head, his brain cooking in the oven of his skull, boiling inside the bone, experiencing the heat of Hell every minute of every day.

He wants to die, wants to end it, wants it to stop, but the fiend knows he is already dead and dead men don't die.

So he keeps killing.

The only thing that makes the pain stop.

But the peace he feels delivering justice at the end of a red-hot branding iron pressed into flesh, burning, it doesn't last. He has to kill again.

Sheriff Conrad is the last one, hopes the fiend.

The head of the snake.

The worst of the worst.

The villain who planned it all and gave the orders. The one who truly must pay. Today is Bull Conrad's judgment day; The Brander will punish him in an execution that will fit the crime.

His revenge will then be complete.

After one piece of unfinished business with Joe Noose the work will be done.

And the fiend can stop.

Rotating his skeletal face upward, long white hair blowing around his face, The Brander looks up at the hazy massifs of the mountains disappearing in the clouds, a panorama of cold vacant emptiness behind blank walls of white snow. Oblivion looks good to him. It is where he will go. Walk up those mountains and vanish into the white, white, white . . . his thoughts fragment like shattering ice.

Breaking his gaze from the mountains, The Brander returns to the task at hand, and when the fiend looks back to the cabin, he sees the shed.

It is a large storage compartment, very large.

Curious, The Brander walks over to the shed and pulls aside the doors.

The fiend can't believe his luck.

Stacked inside are four gigantic rusty bear traps, jagged-jawed steel bone-crushers, oiled in good working order. Beside those are smaller, equally lethal wolf traps—smaller jaws, sharper teeth. Yes, these will work splendidly.

He doesn't need all the oil lamps but can use what is used to fill them . . . ten drums of coal oil sit in the shed. Enough to start a very hot fire Hell would be proud of.

He'd better get started now.

The brand takes a while to heat up.

CHAPTER 34

In the dank chill of the cave, handcuffed marshal Bess Sugarland braced herself for the taste of Deputy Clyde Lovejoy's kiss. And what would come right after.

Dropping to his knees on the rocks between her open legs, Lovejoy leaned in and roughly grabbed her breasts, squeezing them through her shirt. With the sudden physical sexual contact, Bess felt a stab of fear plunge through her guts.

"Kiss me." The fear must have shown because her voice sounded desperate like she was begging him.

He stuck out that lizard tongue of his, then snapped it back in his mouth like a toad. *Pig.* "You gotta give me something first, you wanna kiss from me. Want me a handful of that big titty." The deputy tore at her shirt like a child tearing open a present on Christmas Day. Buttons popped. Shoving his hand into her shirt, the deputy grabbed her bare breast. The lady marshal felt the oily skin of his palm and fingers close over her boob and crush down on it like he was juicing an orange.

It was more than she could stand.

Jerking her head forward, Bess pressed her mouth

against Lovejoy's and gave him an openmouthed wet kiss. Her lips must have been sweet because, boy, he kissed her back hard, his tongue burrowing into her mouth past her palate toward her tonsils.

She bit his tongue off.

Shrieking in raw horror and shock and holding both hands over his mouth covering the tidal flow of red blood pouring down his chin, the surprised deputy fell back but the marshal held on to him—she already had both cuffed hands on his belt, grabbing the twin Colt Single Action Army revolvers from his holsters, pressing the muzzle of one against the chain of her handcuffs, squeezing the trigger and blowing the links apart in a shower of sparks and smoke as the pistol discharged.

She was free.

Like she planned it.

Everything happened fast now as she knew it would when she came up with her escape plan.

She had six armed men to get past, starting with the one closest to her.

"You-mm bimm-tch!" Clyde Lovejoy's words came out a wet mumble from a tongueless mouth filled with blood. The maimed deputy leapt at her like a wild animal, outstretched hands reaching for her throat.

Jumping to her feet, the marshal fired her left pistol. Bess shot Deputy Lovejoy in the groin. The crotch of his jeans exploded in a bloody crater. His eyes horror holes, he clutched himself between his legs, his terrible high-pitched screams echoing off the walls of the cave drowning out the gunshots.

With the pistol in her right hand Bess shot Lovejoy between the eyes, blowing his brains out the back of his skull in a blasting shower of brains, bone, and blood that splattered the five deputies behind him, who were quickly drawing their own guns. The force of the point-blank head shot blew Deputy Lovejoy's boots off the ground, catapulting him back clean across the cave. His messy bullet-ridden corpse landed in a gory heap on the deputies, knocking two down and the other three off-balance long enough for Marshal Bess to make a break for the cave entrance.

It was fifty feet away.

Gun blasts boomed inside the cave at deafening ear-splitting decibels. Slugs screamed past her, rebounding and caroming off the rock walls in showers of ricochet sparks.

The other deputies were no longer conveniently stacked as they ran in all directions to take cover and return fire. *So much for shooting order.*

The marshal had to run the gauntlet to get out of here, directly through their line of fire to get to the cave entrance.

Her pistols had twelve bullets.

She already used three.

Nine rounds.

Time to spend 'em.

Pointing her left shoulder toward the cave opening, Marshal Bess was facing the deputies as she ran sideways toward the entrance—with a gun in each hand, she aimed straight-armed, shooting both Colt pistols in a steady string of fire, bombarding the men's positions with lead to cover her escape.

Guessing rightly that the five gutless lawmen thugs would all duck while the bullets were coming at them

during the exchange of gunfire—*the yellow bastards*—
Bess made it to the cave opening without taking any fire.

The cold fresh air hitting her lungs was a shock.

It cleared her head.

She was outside.

Running for her life

And out of bullets.

He was here.

The smoke rising from the chimney of his cabin told
Sheriff Bull Conrad that much.

Observing the log cabin from a position in the rocks
from where he knew he could not be observed in return,
the lawman saw that the window shutters had been closed.
Somebody else had lit his fireplace because he sure as hell
hadn't. And he had left the shutters open the last time he
closed up the cabin.

The Brander was in his house, right now, waiting for
him to show up, not even bothering to hide his presence.
Letting the sheriff know that he was there, in fact. *That
cocky son of a bitch.* Abraham Quaid had a pair on him,
for sure, or maybe the old man was just plain nuts. Crazy
or brave, it was hard to tell the difference with some folks
sometimes.

Either way, Abe Quaid was a dead man walking. The
sheriff was going to kill him in the next five minutes.

The Brander had pissed away his advantage squander-
ing the opportunity of picking a time and place of his own
choosing for them to shoot it out. Of all the places he could
have picked, he picked Conrad's house, choosing to fight
literally in his enemy's own backyard. The sheriff couldn't
get over how stupid he was.

As he hunkered in the rocks buffeted by driving snow, Sheriff Conrad checked the loads on his two revolvers and rifles. Best to double-check his weapons and not be over-confident or underestimate the old man who had come this far—Abe Quaid might still have a few tricks up his sleeve.

The sheriff was certain the old man could not see him. Conrad had selected the location to build the cabin he liked to think of as his castle for the natural fortifications it afforded; the sheriff knew every vantage point from which to launch or defend against any assault. Where the lawman was presently positioned could not be seen from the house.

Taking out his field glasses, Conrad cleaned snow off the lenses and brought them to his eyes, peering through his binoculars at his quiet cabin three hundred yards away. Scanning the front and right side that was exposed to him, the windows were all shuttered so he couldn't see inside his place, but he did see the mussed-up snow around the porch, like something was dragged.

What?

What would he do in Abraham Quaid's position? he wondered. Thinking tactically like the enemy was always a good strategy. And deception was the best tactic.

If Conrad were Quaid, he'd make it look like he was in the house so when he, Conrad, got there he'd see the smoke in the chimney and the shuttered windows and make an assault on the cabin—but he, Quaid, would not be in the house. He'd be outside nearby, lying in wait with a gun.

But Abe Quaid had a big surprise in store for him if he was dug in with a rifle intending to get a shot off at Conrad when he came in through the front yard.

The sheriff had a back way in.

And a secret entrance.

Time to finish this.

Holstering his pistols and scooping up his rifle, Sheriff Bull Conrad sprinted across an outcropping in the cliff leading to a declination in the rocks, and forty paces later had reached the bottom.

The stone weighed about forty pounds and looked like part of the cliff. Conrad grunted with effort. Rolling the rock away exposed the man-made hole in the ground he dropped into.

The tunnel was four feet wide by five feet high and the sheriff had to duck the two hundred feet he had to trek to bring him under the cabin. It was black as pitch, but he knew the path by feel because he dug it himself. His hand touched the ladder and he was there. The wooden rungs were covered with carpet to muffle sound. Climbing rung over rung, he reached the top.

Pushing gently with his glove against the wall, it gave, and the wooden wall swung open on silent oiled hinges. Sheriff Conrad just opened the secret panel a crack, enough to peek through without being seen by Abraham Quaid if his enemy was hiding in the cabin somewhere.

Conrad saw nothing except dark.

The heavy metal shutters were closed, sealing out the daylight, leaving the cabin in total darkness.

But that didn't concern the sheriff; he didn't need to see. He knew his way around every square inch of the place in the dark because he built the cabin with his own hands.

He would step forth and face his enemy.

Setting the rifle against the wall of the secret passageway, he pulled off his gloves and drew his two Colt Navy revolvers so he was heeled in both hands. Anticipating stepping into a game of cat-and-mouse with firearms played in the dark with the chance of getting jumped from either side, Conrad thought it wise to be able to shoot in both directions quickly; thus a revolver in his right and left hand equipped him better to do that than the cumbersome Henry rifle.

Cocking the pistols with his thumbs he was loaded and locked down. Ready.

Sheriff Bull Conrad stepped into his house, fixing for a gunfight.

Walking into the cabin, he stood in the living room in a ubiquitous darkness his eyes did not adjust to. The cozy scents were familiar and comforting. But there was another smell in the house. *What was it?* He took a few steps without a sound, avoiding by memory the wood floor planks that would creak beneath his boots. Both pistols were raised. Impenetrable gloom. Silence. Turning slowly, he rotated on his heels, a pistol pointed in each direction, searching the darkness. Saw nothing. Heard nothing. *Where was Quaid?* Wind whistling through the chimney in an eerie banshee cadence drew his attention to the rear of the cabin and the fireplace. His eyes were adjusting a little to the dark. Just enough to see the faint glowing red coats by the andirons. No, now he looked close, not coals.

A branding iron, the metal *Q* red-hot and glowing, rippling heat rising off it.

He was here.

Sheriff Bull Conrad leveled his smoke wagons at the brand and took a step toward it.

It would be his last.

CRRRRRRASSSH-ANNNKKK!

He walked right into the open bear trap. Putting the weight of his boot on the trigger mechanism set it off. Two heavy steel jaws with jagged teeth violently swung up and snapped closed—the trap closed on his legs with bone-crushing force, the sharp teeth crunching through the meat and bone of his thighs, nearly severing his legs.

Sheriff Conrad went down screaming in unimaginable agony, blood firehosing everywhere from his severed femoral artery, the shattered bones of his legs breaking apart and bursting through his skin as he toppled, hitting the ground hard, caught in the bear trap.

On his way down to the floor, Conrad caught a glimpse of The Brander standing by the fireplace, dimly illuminated in sinister bas-relief by the glimmering red glow of the brand. While the tough sheriff knew he was done, he still had a revolver in each hand as he fell, and hard and mean as he was, had a notion to put a bullet in Abraham Quaid so they could ride down to Hell together.

It was not to be.

Conrad landed on his back hard on the floor, his right arm hitting the bear trap set to one side, his left arm hitting the smaller wolf trap on the other—the former was chopped cleanly off above the elbow and that revolver was lost, the latter broken in the snapping teeth so badly the bone tore through the flesh and while the reliable Remington revolver remained in the palm, the tendons to the hand had been cut leaving the finger unable to pull the trigger.

The corrupt lawman was a bad man, a very bad man, and he died a very, very bad death, in unendurable agony and terror—his final seconds were so bad even Hell was a relief. Sheriff Conrad lay broken like a shattered doll, his life draining out of him in the gushing geyser of blood from his severed femoral, drenched head to foot in his own blood that pooled in a blackly gleaming lake around him on the floor.

His dimming eyes registered The Brander walk up to him and look down pitilessly, opening the big can of coal oil in his glove.

He poured the flammable accelerant all over Sheriff Conrad, soaking him head to foot. The dying man screamed even louder as it got into his eyes and down his throat, gagging him. When the sheriff was drenched with coal oil, The Brander splashed the remaining contents of the can around the walls and floor of the cabin.

Then, and only then, did he get the brand.

Sheriff Bull Conrad had enough life left in him to see it and feel it as The Brander approached with the red-hot Q brand, coming closer and closer until he stopped, pressing the scalding metal against his final victim's face, and the instant the blazing brand seared flesh it ignited the coal oil and Conrad went up in flames, burning alive.

CHAPTER 35

Bess Sugarland dived at her saddle. Both hands grabbed the pommel and she heaved herself up, swinging a leg over into the stirrups and driving her spurs into her Appaloosa mare's flanks, unhappy about hurting the horse but needing it to move, fast, or they would both be dead. Taking off at the full gallop, energized by the pain, the mare bolted off into the snowy tundra.

Behind Bess was loud yelling and voices over her pounding hooves and she heard the clanking and squeaking of guns and rifles being unholstered and quickly cocked. The first bullets were seconds away.

Making fast her escape but certain she would not make it, when the first gunshots sounded the lady marshal rode the only direction she could . . . dead ahead. Before her lay the frozen lake, a quarter mile of sheet ice. The surface was a foreboding frozen white and blue and black of indeterminate thickness over unseen frigid water unimaginably cold at this high elevation. Over the ice lay her crossing, the only escape route. Her horse was over a thousand pounds, a half ton. The frozen lake couldn't support the mare and the ice would surely collapse beneath its hooves moments after it stepped on it. Then both horse and rider would be plunged into ice water that would paralyze and incapacitate them, drowning them in less than a minute.

If the bullets didn't kill them first.

Between the rock and the hard place. Death by gunshot or drowning. Those were the choices. The first two slugs whistling past the lady marshal's head made the decision simple—on the ice she maybe had a chance not afforded by the sheer volume of hot lead coming at her like a swarm of angry hornets.

The mare, unaware that the vast icy flatness was a lake, galloped straight for the glassy surface without fear.

Twenty yards.

Ten.

More and more shots.

As her horse's hooves met the ice, Marshal Bess Sugarland knew a successful crossing of the iced-over lake was impossible. Unless, just maybe, she rode very, very fast.

And so she did.

Horse and rider thundered out onto the frozen lake, the animal's legs and shod hooves piledriving against the ice, leaving deep indentations in the frosted surface. In moments, they had traveled far out onto the opaque void, a discolored white emptiness. Each hoofbeat made a sharp *crack*, each successive *crack* sounding like breaking ice to Bess's ears. All Bess could hear were the staccato tattoos of her galloping mare's footfalls like hammers hitting the ice, but still the ice held.

This was a suicide ride.

At least it was a hell of a way to go.

The other side of the lake a quarter mile distant looked

farther—ahead were ominous patches of black ice indicating it was thinner there. She reined her horse sharp right. The mare leaned hard, hooves clacking across the frozen lake, giving a wide berth to the black ice.

Dropping her center of gravity, the lady marshal leaned down in the saddle and pressed her bosom against the mare's neck and withers, flattening herself as tight as she could against the animal for speed. Staring straight ahead at the approaching shore so far away, Bess kept a lookout for more thin ice as the howling winds pummeled her. Snow and sleet pelted her face and stung her eyes, and she squinted to see.

The staccato strings of gunshots rang out like firecrackers behind her, closer now, and she saw bullets strike the ice right and left of her horse, wincing each time the slugs cracked against the ice lake top, craters of splintering spiderwebs in the glassy slick surface.

Now, over the drumbeat of her own horse's hoofbeats, Bess heard a thundering of hooves behind her . . . *more horses!*

With a toss of her head, Bess swung an urgent look over her shoulder and saw the entire five-man posse had mounted their horses and ridden onto the ice, giving chase and charging after her in a horseback phalanx across the frozen lake. Recklessly emboldened by how the ice held for their quarry, the foolhardy mounted deputies chanced the dangerous ride. Hazy figures ignited by explosive flashes detonating from the discharges of their guns.

Cr-ra-ack!

That was when she saw the big crack in the ice.

A fracture in the frozen surface of the lake appeared, spreading outward from the shore, a fissure of breaking ice zigzagging in jagged advance toward the horses and riders. The weight of their combined horses, several tons, was too much for the ice to support.

Crack!

Cr-crack!

Bullets flew past Bess's head.

Thud! One round slammed into the leather of her saddle with such force her running Appaloosa almost lost its footing with the impact. It left a blasted smoking hole.

A deafening noise like splintering timber snapped her eyes face front—another deadly crack jigsawed across the glacial surface of the lake, closing in on her horse with the slow-motion dread of a nightmare. The lengthening crack in the ice was inescapable, the faster the marshal rode the nearer it got. The ice was about to collapse under her hooves at any moment. She would not be able to outrun it. Then the marshal's Appaloosa would fall with her in the saddle into the subfreezing waters to drown.

The mass of horseflesh between her legs suddenly shifted its center of gravity, her ride skidding drunkenly to and fro, saddle wobbling, Bess realizing the Appaloosa had lost its footing and was going down.

A split-second decision to make.

Her or it.

Visions of doom flashed before her eyes—w*hen the horse went under, she would get tangled in the stirrups and reins, unable to extricate herself from her saddle in the hypothermic temperatures of the lake that within seconds would numb her limbs to paralysis so she couldn't swim, if the half-ton drowning animal didn't kick her in the head knocking her out first, trapping her unconscious body under itself as it sank lifeless to the bottom of a black, cold liquid void that would be her tomb . . .*

If Bess was going to fall into the lake, it had better not be on a horse.

So she got off . . . the hard way.

Yanking her boots out of the stirrups, the marshal launched herself bodily out of the saddle, heaving herself off the horse dropping under her, throwing her arms out in front of her face protectively as she flew through the chill air, hitting the ice in a hard impact on her belly, knocking the wind out of her lungs.

The bad news was she heard one of her ribs break.

The good news was she was still on top of the ice.

Stunned, the marshal lay on the hard glacial surface facing the direction she rode but didn't see her mare, wondering where a huge horse could have disappeared to, coming to her senses when she saw a huge soaking equine head burst explosively up for air from the hole in the ice, expelling water from snout and nose, rolling eyes bulging in terror and suffocation as pawing hooves treaded water, then the head sank from view below the ice forever.

Knowing the same fate soon awaited her, Bess got off her ass. Rolling up on her boots, she made off on foot running as fast as her spurs would carry her across the glassy countertop of the frozen lake. A hundred yards dead ahead lay the shoreline and the safety of solid footing if she could just make it those last few yards. The marshal ran for her life, struggling to stay on her feet, recovering her balance as her boots repeatedly slipped on the slick unstable footing.

The ice was cracking and shattering everywhere around her now, icebergs breaking off and tilting sideways to sink. It was not more than fifty yards to the shore when behind her, Bess heard the galloping hooves and reports of gunfire way too damn close.

In all the excitement, Marshal Bess had disremembered the heavily armed five badmen with deputy badges chasing her on horseback to gun her down after she escaped their attempt to rape her.

A bullet buzzed past her ear.

It came back to her.

Throwing a desperate glance over her shoulder, she saw the five mounted gunmen bearing down to the rear, low in their saddles, driving their spurs into their galloping horses, whooping and hollering, firing pistols at her in a kill-crazy frenzy.

Had they been less trigger-happy fiends for action, the deputies would have noticed the cracks in the ice below the hooves of their steeds.

All at once the ice collapsed beneath the riders and horses, dropping them into the frozen lake in an enormous explosion of frigid water, dunking the men and horses up to their necks in it. The broken hole in the frozen surface became a splashing chaos, a knot of humans and horses tied up in each other's reins, paddling and screaming and drowning, the submerged deputies feeling brutal subzero lake waters paralyze their extremities, shutting down their bodies, and they realized they were doomed.

"Watch where you're riding, assholes!" were Bess's parting words as she ran the last few yards across the ice to shore. She exhaled in relief the moment she had boots again on solid ground, even with snow up to her knees.

By the time the marshal looked back, her pursuers had vanished from sight, drowned in the lake and sunk below the ice. Their lives had ended with grim suddenness, but it is surprising how quick you can die. *Screw 'em.* She didn't give the bastards a second thought. *Serves 'em right.*

Instead she was thinking of her two friends.

Adrenaline pumped through her veins and her limbs felt energized and powerful as Marshal Bess ran fast up the snowy embankment, heading toward the mountain range in the direction they had left the horses.

She had to find Joe Noose.

CHAPTER 36

Joe Noose had lost Emmett, at least he thought he had shaken him. Even though he cut a big figure, the lack of visibility in the snowstorm made his tricky evasive maneuver of heading in one direction then doubling back a simple but effective one; he'd gotten away from the marshal who had been bird-dogging him for reasons he had yet to figure out, though he had a few ideas. The bounty hunter was thinking about some of them as he patrolled the ridge hunting for The Brander, when an unusual light in the distance caught his attention.

Noose saw the glow of flames through the snow so he went that way. A bloom of blurry orange light was brightening behind the veils of sleet. It was a big fire. And a good bet that The Brander had something to do with setting it, the bounty hunter surmised, locking on to his target like a bloodhound on a scent.

He had no idea how far off the fire was in the howling blizzard, because distance perception ended about three feet ahead. So Noose just used the light as his guide and headed for it. Keeping his rifle at the ready, he plowed forward through the driving wind and snow. The smell of burning wood and some type of accelerant filled his nostrils as he approached so Noose knew it was a structure fire long before he reached it. He knew it was arson and who the arsonist was. Ahead, the inferno's radiant evanescence scintillated the falling snowflakes into a rain of glittering diamonds, a surreal splendor in the shooting stars of sleet illuminated from within by the reflecting flames, but for Noose it became an evil beauty as the ugly odor of burning flesh filled his nostrils and the hideous high-pitched screams of a man being burned alive reached his ears.

A few more paces brought him to the scene.

The burning cabin was completely engulfed in flames, streams of fire shooting out the doors and windows, the structure being devoured in a boiling ball of orange fire rolling up into the sky amid turbulent clouds of billowing oily black smoke. The ghastly agonized screams coming from someone inside ended abruptly when the roof collapsed in explosions of sparks.

The Brander had torched the place to burn up one of his victims and that arson fire had been set in the last half hour, Noose judged, because the victim had only just now expired. The fiend who set it could not have gone far.

Bracing for action, Joe Noose shouldered his rifle and swung his aim across the surrounding area, turning his body in a complete rotation, swinging the long barrel where his eye went, checking the perimeter down the gunsights.

Less than a second after he saw movement, his finger squeezed the trigger without hesitation.

Noose shot into the snow.

The snow shot back.

A big slug slammed into the tree behind him a foot from his head, punching a fist-sized hole in the trunk.

Winchester socked to his shoulder, Noose loosed a

volley of five shots at the spot where he glimpsed the muzzle flash when he was fired upon. Levering his repeater again and again, he loosed five more rounds into the same spot, but he couldn't see anything. Too much snow. It was like shooting into a white sheet that covered the world.

It sounded like his bullets hit *something*, but Noose couldn't tell. He had been in a lot of gunfights but never one where he couldn't see what he was shooting at. It was unnerving as hell. Taking cover behind the nearby trunk of a pine tree at the edge of the forest, he stayed low, waiting for return fire. None came. There were no more shots. Maybe he hit the son of a bitch, maybe not—The Brander knew the bounty hunter's position from where his shots came and might be changing his own position.

Reloading his Winchester, Noose kept his eyes open and his ears peeled. Wasn't much to see but white snow blowing everywhere.

It was what he heard that now made his sphincter tighten. Minutes after the bullets had been exchanged, the sound of those gunshots still echoed through the mountains above him, the fading reverberation of the discharges trailing off in endless sonic decay.

But this was a terrifying new sound: a terrible thundering rumble trembled through the titanic mountaintops over his head, as unimaginable tons of snow were being dislodged by the sound of the loud gunshots that still echoed through the peaks. The ominous low rumble was intermittent but persistent, threatening a catastrophic avalanche. If those big mountains dropped on their heads, there was nowhere to run and no escape, and it would be the end of all of them—Bess, Emmett, The Brander, and himself.

You can't fire guns up here, Noose understood now, *it can start an avalanche!* Hoping he hadn't realized it too late, Noose prayed to hell The Brander could hear that rumble and figured out about guns and avalanches, too.

Holding his position behind the tree, Noose shouted out into the white squall. "Hey, Quaid! Hold your fire! Hear that rumble? That's an avalanche about to start! We gotta stop shooting now! A slide will kill us all! The sound of our guns is gonna bring this mountain crashing down on top of us if we don't stop shooting now, so no more guns, agreed? I'm putting down my firearms! I won't shoot another bullet, you got my word! You don't shoot, either! You listening, Quaid? Can you hear me? Did one of my bullets kill you? If you're alive, say so!"

There was no response. The blizzard howled unabated. Branches rustled. Wind whooshed. The mountains rumbled but soon the rumbling stopped.

"Now I intend to kill you, Quaid, and I know you mean to kill me! Let's fight hand to hand! Finish it! Like men! No guns! Agreed?"

No answer.

"Agreed?"

"Agreed." The scary voice was so damn close it was like somebody whispered in Joe's ear.

Noose leapt up and spun around, rattled, looking everywhere around him. Nobody was there. He was surrounded by snowy oblivion, blank white space. Drawing his bowie knife, he brandished the huge razor-sharp blade, ready to stab or slash anything that moved.

Nothing did.

"C'mon!" he yelled.

Laughter floated eerily on the wind.

"Hey, Quaid. You probably don't remember me but I re- member you. I never forgot what you did to me back when

I was a kid. Now I've come for you. I'm back to settle the score. Today is the reckoning."

Wielding his knife, the bounty hunter began walking, looking for the fiend. The blizzard swirled around him, sweeping him in sheets of snow and blowing his coat like a flag. Noose strode forth into the whiteness, keeping a sharp lookout for The Brander.

"You can run but you can't hide."

A red-hot branding iron was suddenly pressed against the back of his shoulder, searing instantly through the cloth of his coat and shirt and sizzling into his flesh! Noose threw his head back and screamed in agony, rounding violently and slashing his bowie knife at the fiend who ambushed him from behind. His blade cut air. The Brander wasn't there, as if he'd evaporated. "Aggghhhhhh!" Noose screamed into the storm. Looking all around himself, he saw no sign of anyone in the snowstorm.

Joe Noose was shaking head to foot . . . the shock of being branded again by the same man brought him back to being thirteen when it happened the first time and now all those emotions came back up to overwhelm him as he reexperienced the identical raw terror and helplessness he had felt when he was a teen branded at the old man's hands, and Joe was that kid again.

Fear was all over him like stink.

Fear of Abraham Quaid.

He'd forgotten what true fear felt like.

Paralyzed by this irrational terror the bounty hunter was physically immobilized. He couldn't defend himself. Noose was thirteen Joe not adult Joe. Too scared to fight back against this man. Ready to piss his pants. What was he going to do with the knife in his hand now that he felt too scared to use it? The bounty hunter wanted to flee.

Every instinct of that thirteen-year-old kid told him to run. The scared kid was in control of Joe now. The fear that Abe Quaid put in him so long ago had returned and had him in an unbreakable iron grip. Scared to fight back.

He saw a spot of red glowing in the white snowfall.

Knew what it was.

The red-hot *Q* hissed, steamed, as snowflakes falling on the hot metal instantly melted, the sizzling drips of water looking like drops of blood in the red glow of the brand.

Noose was hypnotized by the brand, couldn't take his eyes off the disembodied red glow in the void.

His hand clutching the bowie knife lowered, his arm dropping, but he didn't notice. Hypnotized by the searing glow of the brand coming relentlessly toward him, Joe couldn't move, overwhelmed with memories as a kid of Abraham Quaid coming closer with the brand, *this brand*, reliving it all again right here, the pain, the pain . . .

The real Noose tried to push down the old fear.

Movement in the snow. The silhouette of The Brander materialized in the snow ahead of him: the clothes, the long white hair, the burning eyes of Abraham Quaid . . . and the blazing branding iron. Joe could already feel the heat coming off it.

"No," he said. Trying to raise the knife in his hand, he couldn't.

The Brander kept coming, heat from the branding iron getting hotter on Noose's skin.

"No," Noose said more firmly, his hand clenching tighter around the haft of the bowie knife, and his arm began to raise. Teeth grit. *"No."* Rage made his muscles work and Joe lifted the blade so he could stab with it.

A sudden searing pain on the back of his hand made

him drop the knife after The Brander gave him a vicious thrust with the scalding brand.

Pulling his hand back, Noose rubbed the burned flesh. It hurt like hell.

And with the pain came resolve.

This man was never going to burn him again.

Raising his dangerous gaze to stare into the depths of The Brander's shadowed face, it was time to hit back.

"You dirty, miserable son of a bitch!"

With his right fist, Joe Noose threw a roundhouse punch connecting with The Brander's jaw, snapping the fiend's head in one direction, following through with a round-house left that snapped the old man's head in the other direction, staggering him backward.

The Brander fell in the snow and before he could get up Joe Noose's boot came down on his chest hard, pinning him down. The big cowboy towered over the fiend, a force of pure vengeance. "Now it's my turn. Prepare for the reckoning, old man." He wrenched the branding iron from the fiend's grip.

"Payback time!" Noose shoved the red-hot *Q* right in The Brander's face. *Branding him!* The scalding metal seared the fiend's flesh down to the skull. Clouds of steam heat and smoke of sizzling flesh roiled into the air ringing with The Brander's anguished screams and squeals of *"No, no, no, no, no,"* as he clawed like a wild animal at Noose's arms, squirming like a pinned bug—but the big cowboy leaned into it, pressing down on the branding iron with all the might in his muscled shoulders, using both arms to increase the pressure on the scalding branding iron roasting the hide off The Brander's face. He wanted him to *feel* it. Noose tried to press that red-hot brand through the fiend's skull and *brand his brain*, burning it to ash. Wanted him

to *feel* the cranial bone cave in and *feel* the damn brand sink into his soft brain tissue . . . Joe Noose wanted to *feel* Abraham Quaid die.

Instead, what Noose felt was a blow to the head from a rock that The Brander had picked up off the ground, thrown with the desperate strength of a dying animal fighting for his life.

The rock struck the bounty hunter in the temple hard, knocking him senseless. Dropping the brand, Noose staggered back, dazed, feeling hot blood pouring down his face, his balance tripping. His boots suddenly slid out from under him and Noose fell forward, hitting the ground facefirst in the snow, the shock of cold frost on his face snapping him to his senses quickly enough to realize he was skidding backward down an icy slick incline. Looking over his shoulder, he saw he was sliding straight toward the edge of a cliff hundreds of feet high.

With no way to stop himself.

The Brander. The cowboy looked back and saw the wounded fiend was getting away. Clutching his horribly burned face with both hands, The Brander fled, staggering and stumbling off up the opposite slope, screeching like a scalded cat, his coat flapping behind him like a cape.

Noose slid backward down the slippery iced embankment, grabbing at anything for purchase, fingers skidding on the ice. There was nothing to grab on to.

He was going to die.

His final thoughts were of his worst enemy—*I got you back, you son of a bitch*—then he thought of Bess, picturing her face, and wanted to tell her how he felt about her, then over he went.

Feeling the ground disappear, Noose made a blind grab. Grabbed a fistful of air.

Then he plunged.

A hand grabbed his wrist in an iron grip, breaking his fall.

"Grab my arm!" Emmett shouted.

Noose swung his free hand up and seized the forearm of the marshal flattened on his stomach on the roof of the cliff leaning over the edge. With a strong yank and cry of exertion, Emmett hoisted Noose high enough for him to get an arm up over the ledge, then after plenty of struggle, the marshal helped the bounty hunter haul himself back on top of the cliff. They both sat on the ground gasping for breath, exhaling in relief.

"You okay?" Emmett asked, pointing at the bleeding gash on Noose's head.

"Yeah."

"You met up with him."

"Yeah, I did."

"You kill him?"

"No. Better."

Emmett looked at Noose and saw he had a savage grin.

"I branded him."

The marshal recognized the ironic justice in that and nodded, but said nothing and averted his gaze.

The bounty hunter rose and brushed himself off, extending his hand down to Emmett, who took it, letting himself be pulled to his feet. Noose was looking him square in the eye with fellowship and gratitude. "You saved my life. Thank you."

Emmett nodded with a joking smile. "Guess you're glad I stuck to you like glue now after all."

The two friends chuckled.

"Hell yes. I owe you." Noose shook Emmett's hand in a firm grip of friendship that was fitfully returned.

Through the swirling snow, the marshal spotted something on the ground and went over and picked it up.

The Q brand, cooled to a cold, dead, ugly piece of metal.

"Want to keep it as a souvenir?" Emmett joked, offering it to Noose.

Noose took it and threw the branding iron as far as he could off the cliff, into oblivion.

Then he clapped his friend on the shoulder. "We got us one last piece of unfinished business to take care of." Aiming a glance down at the snow, Noose spotted the tracks heading up the steep slope to the highest ridges atop the upper elevations where all visibility ceased. Turning to Emmett, he cocked his head to indicate where their quarry, The Brander, had fled. "He went that way. Let's go get him. Together."

The marshal beamed proudly. "You betcha. After you, Joe."

CHAPTER 37

"Lead the way. I got your back."

Drawing both his revolvers, Joe Noose advanced up the hill, trudging through the snow. Emmett Ford, his single Remington 1875 pistol in his glove, followed in his tracks a few steps behind.

Before them, the snow-and-ice-covered ridge was a wall of white in the swirling flakes. Beyond, towering titanic above, the mountain was a hazy outline of staggering scale.

A pair of tracks traipsing into them were rapidly filling with snow, and in minutes would be invisible.

The Brander was close.

They'd come to the end of the road, at the top of the world.

Noose froze as he heard the *snick* of a hammer of a pistol cocked behind his back.

"Drop your pistols, Joe."

"What's on your mind, Emmett?"

"Drop 'em. Now. Do as I say. I don't want to shoot you and definitely not in the back but I will if you force me. Drop those pistols in the snow and step away from them."

With a dark sigh, the bounty hunter opened his hands and let his twin Colt Peacemakers fall into the cold snow.

"Step away from the guns."

Noose took a few steps sideways.

Emmett moved fast, sidestepping upward and swinging down to scoop up both of Noose's revolvers, which he stuffed in the pockets of his coat.

Disarmed, the bounty hunter warily looked the marshal dead in the eye. "Slick move, Ford, or should I call you Quaid?" he snarled.

"How long have you known?"

"A while."

"You figured that out and still you let me get the drop on you?"

"Wanted to see how it played out. I know what you want to do, Emmett. You mean to save your father, but you can't. Your father is a sick animal. And a sick animal gotta be put down."

"I'm his son, Noose. He's the only father I got and I gotta try to save him, even if I can't."

"A man has to know when to give up."

"You didn't give up, Noose. Remember the story you told me about bringing your horse back to health in Victor because you loved him, because he was your best friend, even though everybody, *everybody*, told you to put it down. But you didn't. You healed him. And you brought him back."

"Because Copper could be rescued. Your father can't be. He's a sick animal."

"My father revenged himself against criminals the law was supposed to protect him from and didn't, the law those same criminals bribed to let them go free. Yes, when the law failed, my father turned to the Law of the Gun. Yes, he executed the men who stole his cattle, burned his ranch, then shot and left him for dead. Yes, he executed the crooked lawmen that protected those badmen and profited from their crimes. Yes, you're right he got revenge by taking the law into his own hands. So what? Those badmen all had it coming, every last one of 'em."

"Explain to me how their families had it coming, too, Emmett. Go ahead. I'm listening. That's right, you can't. Murdering the wives and sons and daughters of those badmen, killing women and children, that wasn't justified. That father of yours took the lives of innocent people because he likes killing people and because he's a madman. I know it and you know it."

Emmett looked down in remorse and nodded. "You're right, he went too far."

"We both know what has to be done."

"You want me to put a bullet in his head, put him down like a horse?"

"You got to put down a bad animal."

"I won't murder my father."

"It's a mercy killing, not murder. You're his son and it's right for you to be the one to pull the trigger and put him out of his misery."

"I'm taking him home."

"Even if he lets you take him home, then what?"

"Do what any son does. Take care of him."

"If you really care about your father, end him. Know this: He's never going to stop killing. He's gotten a taste for blood. All this killing turned him into a bad animal. And like any bad animal you love, he will turn on you and when that day comes, Emmett, he's gonna kill you."

"Stay out of my way, Joe."

Noose indicated the pistol Emmett leveled on him with a growl. "I'm freezing my ass off jawing out here. If you're going to shoot me, get to it."

The marshal sighed, shook his head. "Figured all along at the end of this ride only one way this whole thing could end: me killing you and Bess. Wasn't nothing personal but I couldn't let you kill my father. I'm his son. It's family. Was afraid it was going to end bad, right here, like this. Now here we are. And I can't do it, Joe. I don't want to kill you. You're my friend, Marshal Bess, too. We rode a lot of miles together. You're a good man, Joe, and my family done enough to you. So, no, ain't gonna shoot you." The bounty hunter just watched the marshal evenly. "But I'm taking my father home, Joe. And if you stand in my way, I won't like it, but I will kill you."

Noose kept his sturdy, honest, pale gaze on Emmett. "If you don't put that old man down, he'll put you down, that's a fact."

"It's family."

They locked eyes, Noose nodding. "I know."

"Good-bye, Joe."

"Good-bye, Emmett."

With that, the man Joe Noose had known as Ford but whose real name was Quaid turned his back and hiked off, up the steep hill of the ridge, heading into his destiny, swirling snow wrapping him in layers of white until Emmett was no longer visible.

Behind him below, Joe Noose stood for many long moments as still as a wooden cigar store Indian.

Then he, too, started up the hill.

* * *

Higher and higher Emmett Quaid climbed.

Leaning against the driving sleet, he marched knee-deep through the fresh snow blanketing the slope whipped up in the roaring winds. All was whiteness, an absence of everything that unnerved the marshal, creating in him a disturbing sense of dread and dislocation. It was oblivion. He kept his bearings only by following the bootprints heading upward in a crooked path. At the end of those footprints would be his father, who couldn't be far now, because there was nowhere left to go.

Ahead, the mountain face reared into the sky, a sheer wall of rock hundreds of feet high peaked by a gigantic shelf of snowpack hanging over his head. To one side was a yawning gorge plunging straight down hundreds of feet to the rocks. The other side was huge boulders too high to scale.

Another thirty paces brought him to the top of the ridge, a plateau. Visibility was hazy in the swirling snow.

There, the footsteps ended.

And Emmett saw him.

The Brander stood at the edge of the cliff fifty yards away, his back to the marshal. If he registered Emmett's presence, he didn't show it. The figure wasn't moving, a ghost in the chill evanescence of all the white space.

Emmett Quaid approached the solitary individual standing at the cliff, facing away from him, staring off into the oblivion of the gorge's abyss. The wind blew the flowing, dirty white hair.

"Pop . . ."

The figure at the edge of the ridge slowly turned and now they were face-to-face. The hair and clothes belonging to Abraham Quaid were familiar, garments now worn, tattered, and ragged. The fingers of the glove hung limp where three of the fingers were gone. The old man's shoulder-length hair was scraggly and gray, windblown across a pair of scalding bloodshot eyes gleaming with utter madness. But the face possessing that burning soulless stare was not an old man but a young one.

Willard Quaid, Emmett's younger brother!

Wearing his dead father's clothes.

His youthful features were skeletal and ravaged from hunger and savagery, transfiguring the younger Quaid into something less human, more animal.

At the startling sight of Willard, Emmett let out a shocked gasp and retreated a step.

"Willard!"

"Been a long time, big brother."

"I thought you were dead."

Noose peered around the edge of the boulder.

A hundred yards away, two men stood at the edge of the high ridge, twin tall dark figures in stark relief against the ubiquitous snow.

The bounty hunter's breath caught in his throat as he saw The Brander was not Abraham Quaid but what he guessed was his other son. Noose saw from Emmett's expression that he was just as surprised.

The Quaid brothers reunited.

"Willard, I-I'm so happy you're alive. Pop said you were dead."

"Willard *is* dead. Pop told you the truth."

"You're right here."

"I'm not Willard anymore." The Brander grinned sickeningly, his exposed teeth and gums showing like a skinned skull through the half of his face hideously disfigured in bloody charred boils in the roasted flesh of the *Q* brand wound mark.

Emmett struggled for words. "I know I left. But I'm back now. Come to take you home. And I'm never going away again."

A hundred yards down the icy slope, Joe Noose could barely hear the words spoken by the Quaids. The brothers were speaking softly. But the wintery silence up in the high elevations was so profound and complete, the bounty hunter caught most of what was said. Looking down at his empty holsters, Noose knew even if he had two loaded pistols he couldn't use them. He had no concern about drawing down on them before they returned fire, that was not his problem . . . Looking up, Noose saw the titanic crags of the mountain towering into the low cloud cover around him, piled with countless tons of snow in a monumental shelf. The unsteady rumble of the unstable snowpack could occasionally be heard. It was an avalanche waiting to happen.

One loud gunshot was all it would take.

The mountain would come down on their heads.

Shooting either of the brothers was not an option, and the bounty hunter damn sure hoped neither was thinking of shooting the other. It didn't look like it. Gunplay not being an option for Noose subduing the Quaids—he would have to use his bare hands or his blade.

Reaching into his belt with a gloved hand, he quietly unsheathed his heavy steel bowie knife from his scabbard and slid it into the back of his belt for easy access.

Now he huddled against the boulder, peering around the edge at the two men a hundred yards away, listening, watching, biding his time, and waiting to make his move.

Emmett stood a few feet from Willard, carefully closing the space between them with a conciliatory aspect to his stance.

It was a final reckoning between the brothers. Willard looked grotesque wearing his father's corpse's clothes and the wig of long white hair. The deranged younger brother's face was twisted in emotional anguish.

"Why you wearing Pop's clothes and hair, Willard?"

"Don't you see? I'm doing what Pop would have wanted to be done to the men who murdered him and burned our ranch and stole our cattle."

"That's why you burned them with his brand."

"I knew you'd understand, Emmett." His moods changing with shocking violence, Willard's face broke into a psychotic sickle grin. Even from this distance, Noose could see the horror and remorse at the state of his troubled brother on Emmett's face.

"What happened to your hand?"

"I took an ax to it, like Pop did to his. I always wanted to be like Pop, Emmett. Wanted to live up to his standards. Follow the example he set for us as men. For the longest time, I didn't, but when he died, I knew I always did want to be just like him. He never thought I measured up because he always told me I didn't, and he was right, so to do what needed to be done, I gave up being me and became Pop. Don't you see? I feel him in me. His spirit carries on and gives me the strength to do my work. The work is done. They're all dead, the badmen who wronged Pop and took everything from him. Including his life. But he's not dead, you see . . . I'm still Pop."

"Let me take you home."

Emmett took a step closer and touched Willard's arm.

The younger brother violently recoiled and yanked his arm away, screaming at the top of his lungs in the older brother's face.

"You left me! You know what he did to me? Pop hurt me, Emmett! Every day he broke my body! Because you left, he took it out on me! The way he hurt us as boys, that was nothing! Nothing! Where were you? You made a promise to me, big brother! Promised you'd always protect me! Said you'd always look after me! But you left me! You abandoned me! To him!"

Emmett's face was screwed up in the pain of remembrance. "I-I couldn't stay. Not on the ranch, not with him. I had to go."

"You said you'd never leave. You lied. We were brothers. You were all I had, we were all *each* of us had."

Emmett was so racked with guilty remorse he could barely get the words out. "I'm sorry. But I came back. I-I found you. We can start again. I'll make it all up to you, I swear. We *are* brothers."

"Emmett . . ." His tortured younger brother broke down in sobs and hung his head. The sound of his weeping was like a mewling dog.

"Let's go home," his older brother said.

Emmett embraced Willard.

Hugged him hard.

Over his shoulder, his younger brother's eyes were blank. "It's too late. Pop was right. Everybody is guilty. You, me, everybody in the whole entire world is guilty. Only one thing to do. *Kill 'em all.*"

Willard pushed Emmett off the edge of the cliff.

* * *

Far below them Marshal Bess Sugarland was climbing hand over fist up the sheer natural trail in the rock face when the body fell past.

It was only a quick glimpse of the flailing, tumbling figure but the plummeting Emmett Quaid's doomed gaze caught hers, his horrible screams filling her ears as he clutched at dead air then he was out of sight below. She covered her ears when she heard the wet *smack* of his body hitting the rocks.

Noose grimaced hearing the fading echo of the screams until the soft *thud* of impact an impossible distance below when the screams abruptly ceased.

He stepped out from behind the boulder.

Willard was standing at the edge of the cliff looking down, when he heard Noose's boot on the snow and whirled fast, quick-drawing his revolver from his side holster with surprising speed.

"Willard Quaid! Don't fire that gun!" Joe Noose yelled.

Surprised the stranger knew his name, the psychopath kept the gun lifted but his head was cocked in curiosity.

Noose stood his ground, his hands open and empty, the bowie knife out of sight jammed into his belt behind his back. The men stood twenty feet apart on the edge of the precipice over the snowy abyss. Too far for Noose to rush Willard. The silence was oddly deafening, punctuated by the tics of falling snowflakes and a periodic ominous rumble of the ice and snowpack on top of the mountain poised to be loosed from the gunshot.

"Don't shoot, Willard. The sound of a shot from that Colt up here will start an avalanche and bring this whole mountain down on our heads. You shoot me, you kill us both."

The bounty hunter saw he might as well be talking to a wild animal from the unreasoning raw predatory look in The Brander's eyes—murder was in his bloodthirsty nature. Noose kept him talking, taking a step closer, knowing this was the final face-off.

His whole life had brought him to the top of this God-less mountain and it was probably all going to end right here.

Willard Quaid kept the Colt Peacemaker pointed directly at Joe Noose in a lock-elbowed straight-armed grip, but the hammer wasn't cocked.

"Look. I'm not armed, Willard. I'm not going to shoot you."

The Brander stared hard at the bounty hunter, scrutinizing him.

"You know me, boy," Noose said. "Look at my face. It'll come to you. It's been a long time. Remember back twenty years. I was the boy your father branded at your ranch. I still have the mark on my chest. I'd show it to you but it's too damn cold for me to open my shirt."

In the mad, anguished whorls of Willard Quaid's eyes the spark of recognition flashed. Joe Noose saw it, his gaze locked with the psychopath's.

"That's right. You and your brother, Emmett, held me down while your father Abraham put the brand to me. Yes. I'm that boy, Willard. Me and my friends tried to rustle your cattle, but you caught us. You father made you help him hang my friends. There were three. You put 'em on horses, put ropes around their necks. I know you and Emmett didn't want to be part of that hanging, Willard.

You was just kids. We was all just kids. Your daddy made you do murder and I saw how bad you felt about it, how bad both you boys felt about it. And I know you hated to watch him brand me, before you put me on a horse and sent me away. But I lived, and I grew up, and here I am now, you and me face-to-face, at the end of the world."

"You." Noose saw Willard knew who he was now, watching the last living Quaid's eyes widen with shocked recognition, remorse, rage, and confusion all together in his broken, twisted gaze. "You had it coming," Willard snarled. "You *all* had it coming."

"We had punishment coming. Jail time for sure. But not hanging, not without a trial. And not branding. Not for any reason. That was torture."

Willard thumbed back the hammer of the gun, cocking it. "You're guilty. You're all guilty. You all have to pay. Everybody has to pay."

"This ends now, Willard. I don't want to kill you. This ain't all your fault. It's your father's fault for what he done to you boys. Give me the gun, Willard. You can't shoot it. Not up here."

Seeing movement out of the corner of his eye, Noose glanced quickly left and saw Marshal Bess quietly sneaking up the ridge, hugging the rock out of Willard's line of sight. Happy to see her safe, the bounty hunter's stomach clenched knowing she was now in danger from an avalanche if Willard fired his gun.

Noose kept his eyes fixed on The Brander, who was watching him down the gunsights of his big revolver. Willard held the pistol bare-handed, fingers blackened from frostbite and the bloody skin peeling off against the frozen metal of the gun. "I killed my brother."

"It wasn't all your fault. Hand over the gun."

The realization that he ended Emmett's life came over Willard in a flood of sadness and bereavement, as he comprehended what he had done. His posture slumped and finally the pistol lowered.

Noose dared a few steps forward and put out his open hand.

Willard started to hand over the still-cocked Remington cavalry pistol.

Below, a sudden cry and *thud* of impact.

Head whirling, Willard saw Bess slipping on the icy steep slope and taking a tumble on the snow.

"Bess!" Noose called.

Willard swung his awful gaze back to Noose, his mad vulture eyes dripping with malignance, letting out a high-pitched insane shriek of raw accusatory fury. *"You tricked me!"*

The Brander drew down on Noose, finger closing on the trigger.

Reaching behind his back, the bounty hunter drew his hidden bowie knife with blinding speed and threw it with deadly accuracy in a flash of steel.

Crunch.

The heavy blade impaled Willard Quaid between the eyes, burying to the hilt, the tip bursting out the back of his skull.

Dead on his feet Willard stood, shivering, body going into convulsions, his blank eyes staring into space.

The gun lowered, his arm dropping.

Noose and Bess exchanged a relieved glance.

The cocked revolver discharged into the snow in a thunderous pistol crack and flash of flame and smoke—

the deafening gunshot echoed through the mountains in booming reverberations, amplified by the granite walls, until a new terrifying sound drowned it out: the earthquake rumble of the snow-packed mountainside above collapsing in a towering avalanche.

Noose looked up. "Oh hell."

CHAPTER 38

Willard Quaid sank to the ground.

Noose didn't bother to collect his bowie knife from the sprawled corpse's head. No time.

"Avalanche!" Noose grabbed Bess's arm and just ran, yelling at the top of his lungs. "Don't look back! Run, Bess! Just go!" He didn't look back, either—those were seconds they didn't have to waste. "Go! Go! Go!" The man and the woman held hands to hold on to each other as they ran and jumped and leapt down the side of the mountain, boots hitting snow and ice and rocks.

Behind and above them, where Noose and Bess dared not look, they heard the mountains fall. In the seconds beforehand, the air thrummed, trembling with sonic vibration, a roaring rolling thunder gathering force and timbre, until the peaks exploded in muffled cracking and booming impacts as monumental shelves of snow and ice broke loose of the peaks in giant slabs, crashing down onto the hill the tiny figures of the man and woman fled down, showering them with snow. The collapsing ice shelves shook the earth. The ground rocked below Noose and Bess's feet, throwing them off-balance as they tripped and fell. Rolling over and over, the man and woman tumbled head over heels down the steep mountainside—neither let go of the other, holding hands the whole way. The fall was almost straight down but the snow was very deep, safely cushioning their bodies from bouncing off boulders. softening landings after sudden fifty-foot drops as the man and woman literally fell down the mountain.

The thundering rumbling roar of the avalanche was a complete deafening cacophony of ceaseless noise as, after the ice shelves collapsed, the million tons of snow they once held back was released like water from a burst dam. Those tons and tons of snow fell down the mountain in landslides of gargantuan size, crushing and burying everything in a relentless path of destruction.

Half a mile down, the tiny figures of the bounty hunter and the marshal were directly in its deadly path. Joe Noose could hear the avalanche above them breathing down their necks. Bess Sugarland clung to his arm with both hands, holding on to her friend with all her strength and he didn't let her go. Feeling the same raw terror so plain in her face.

Locking eyes and exchanging desperate looks as they held hands, Noose and Bess felt themselves picking up speed during their tobogganing descent riding a landslide of snow. More snow came down on them every second and they were getting covered with it. Still they didn't look back. Just at each other. And held tight to one another, holding on for dear life.

Exploding down the mountain, the disastrous landslide snowballed in size and mass with every inch of its unstoppable advance, death by a million tons of snow bearing down on Noose and Bess. The bounty hunter could hear and feel catastrophe closing in. There wasn't much time.

A flash of gold caught his eye.

Copper was still tethered to the tree Noose hitched him to, now a few hundred yards distant. The horse was looking up at the avalanche. Joe knew Copper could have chewed through those reins and been long gone after the avalanche started but the horse was waiting for Noose, would wait as long as it took for his master to get to him, even if it meant the stallion getting crushed in the avalanche. But that was one scared horse looking up at the mountain coming down on top of it.

"Bess!" He pointed to his stallion. "Copper!"

Get to his horse.

If anything on earth could get them out of the path of the avalanche, Copper could.

It was only a short distance on foot to the horse to saddle up . . . they might make it.

"Now!" Noose threw his arms around Bess and heaved both of them off the landslide, tumbling onto the snowpack where the man and woman made for the horse in a dead run through snow up to their knees.

The snow was just too deep.

They had to trudge through it, Noose and Bess pulling each other, plowing through the snow using their knees to push the stalling weight of it out of their way, moving in slow motion as the mountain crashed down above them. Copper reared and pawed his forelegs in the air, warm brown eyes wide in urgency. It actually bellowed. In horse-speak that meant *Move your ass!*

Because behind them reared an avalanche about to bury them under nature's fury.

As the awesome shadow of the landslide rose up and its darkness fell over them, Noose and Bess reached the saddle. The woman already had the knife out so she cut the tether, the man already up in the stirrups on the horse, grabbing the reins, reaching out a hand to haul her up, and she took it just as Copper launched into a hard gallop, the horse's velocity lifting her boots off the ground, catapulting her up into the saddle, where her ass landed on the back behind Noose. Bess wrapped her arms around Joe and held on for dear life as he leaned into Copper, the good, fast horse giving them all it had, charging hard to get ahead of the avalanche chasing them, trying to outrun a falling mountain dropping on their heads.

The stallion galloped through the snow in high powerful long strides, Noose and Bess tight in the saddle. The snow-covered terrain ahead was steep and uneven but Copper negotiated the hidden ruts in a display of prowess, taking leaps and jumps and tight turns, fleet on his hooves.

"Go, boy, go!" yelled Noose, urging Copper on. His horse gave it more speed. The man's voice was drowned by the wind and sleet blasting their faces and clothes. Looking over his shoulder, Bess was heartened by open country ahead.

Feeling confident they had outrun the avalanche, Bess Sugarland did the one thing Joe Noose warned her not to: *She looked back.*

And what the marshal saw was so terrifying she nearly fainted and fell out of the saddle, her face the color of ash "O-Oh. My G-God."

"What's wrong?"

"W-W-W—"

"Spit it out!"

"We're not going to make it, Joe!"

It was a split-second decision Noose made, as the

rushing shadow of the avalanche fell across them again. Even Copper couldn't outrun Mother Nature but the courageous galloping stallion kept trying. Swinging his gaze in the saddle, Noose looked east and saw the top of the canyon bluffs drop off. Out of view, a hundred feet below lay the Snake River's powerful rapids raging through the mountains.

Pulling on the reins and leaning hard, Noose steered Copper in a sharp left, straight for the cliffs.

"Hold on tight, Bess!"

"Look out! We're riding straight at a cliff!"

"Yeah, we're jumping! The Snake River's down there! Ain't our first rodeo, Bess! We done this before, remember?"

"That was in the summer!"

The edge of the bluff rushed up at them as Copper closed the space between the cliff and them at full gallop. A hundred feet . . . seventy feet . . .

Behind in the wake of the horse, the landslide rose and roared and blocked out the sun, crashing ice and snow coming down on them in detonations behind their stallion's hooves. Thirty feet . . . twenty . . .

"That avalanche is gonna kill us in about ten seconds, so listen up! When Copper jumps, get out of the saddle, fast! Fall as far away from the horse as you can, so he doesn't land on top of you in the river. Once you're in the water, swim back to Copper as fast as you can and hang on good and tight! Big rapids down there! And try not to hit the rocks when you land!"

"You're crazy, Joe!"

"Here we go!"

In a mighty jump, Copper leapt over the edge of the cliff with Noose and Bess in the saddle. A dizzying drop opened up yawning below them. And then they were falling fast through dead air, the roar of the avalanche in their ears, the thunder of the river rising in volume, the smell of the icy fresh water rapids filling their nostrils. Noose pushed Bess out of the saddle at the same time as he threw himself off his horse. Seconds later, the man, woman, and horse hit the white water simultaneously in an enormous splash.

They missed the rocks and landed in deep white-water rapids whose raging force swept them violently downstream, somersaulting head over heels. The chilling temperature of the water was such a stunning shock to their system Noose and Bess almost lost consciousness. The woman choked from the bite of the frigid water. Noose let out a roar and reached out to grab for her, his big fist closing on her wrist as with his other hand he swam for Copper, the horse paddling its legs and neighing, trying to stay afloat. Fighting the currents with all his strength, in a few powerful strokes the bounty hunter reached his horse and grabbed an arm around the saddle. Pulling Bess to him, he helped get her arms on the saddle and they both clung to Copper, gasping for breath. The three rode the icy rapids swiftly downstream, bursting waves of white water hitting them in the face, the bracing cold bringing them back around to their senses.

The deafening roar of the raging avalanche exploding over the cliffs filled their ears. It was a narrow escape. Noose and Bess clung on to Copper's saddle, carried downriver in the frigid rapids, teeth chattering and soaked in subzero river water. The bounty hunter and the marshal were glad to be rid of the cold desolation of that place neither hoped they would ever return to.

Looking back, they saw the bluffs behind them disappear under a million tons of avalanche snow, as farther and farther the Snake River took Joe Noose and Bess Sugarland out of the frozen place in the high elevations of Wyoming called Destiny, where some fulfilled their destiny and others wished they hadn't.

CHAPTER 39

Beginning their long journey home, Noose and Bess rode side by side across a winter plain, taking their sweet time, in no hurry to get back.

The marshal had purchased a fresh horse, a lovely chestnut mare, from a small stable they had ridden past, and once she got saddled, Bess named her new horse Scout. Copper was instantly smitten with Scout whose tawny color complimented its own bronze coat, and the two horses had been flirting.

Somewhere on a snowy road thirty miles south of Consequence, Joe saw Bess was looking over at him with a considering gentle gaze.

"Penny for your thoughts, cowboy."

"Thinking about Emmett."

"Poor guy."

"He was a friend."

"I liked him. He tried to do his best, I think, but, I don't know. For him, with his father, his brother, it was all so complicated. Too complicated in the end. But, yeah, he had a good heart, Emmett did, I do believe that. But he was a puzzle."

"I feel sorry for him, Bess. He was a good man who came from bad stock, that's all. He wanted to do good but all his good intentions got twisted up and tied in knots because of his family upbringing. Kinda like light through cracked glass. Being a Quaid, Emmett never had a chance. But he would have if he could. I always saw the struggle in him to rise above the bad in himself, the Quaid side, to find the better angels of his nature he knew he had in there. Guess he reminded me of me, Bess."

"I can see that, a little, I suppose. But Emmett wasn't you, Joe, not even close." She threw him a glance. "He got to you, didn't he?"

He shrugged. "We were both branded by the same man, Emmett and me, in different ways but branded just the same. That night I got the hot iron we all did, Willard included. The same bad thing happened to all of us but we took it different, went different paths when we grew up, and I'm alive and they're dead. Been asking myself how I come through and they didn't, having the same thing done to us and each of us turning out so different. Think I know."

"Go on."

"It's not what happens to you, it's what you make of it. What you do with what life hands you makes you what you are. My brand made me who I am, because I chose to do the right thing because of it. My actions aren't because of an old flesh wound, but because of me." He shrugged.

"Of course."

"It was on my mind."

"What else is on your mind, Joe Noose?"

"Family."

"Well, there's good ones and bad ones. I had a good one with my pop. Quaid boys had a bad one. Abraham Quaid was the devil. He destroyed his two sons. You, too, nearly, when you were a kid."

"Yeah, he branded his own sons like he branded me, but I was lucky, I see now. I could get away and they couldn't. I wasn't kin. They were. Emmett and Willard had it worse than me because they were branded inside, for life. My brand was a flesh wound, Emmett and Willard got their souls branded and souls don't heal."

"I don't know about that, Joe."

"Been wonderin'. Is that what family does, brand you? Never had me a family, never even knew my folks. You know all that."

"Sure I do."

"So I been thinking. Time was I thought that not having no parents or knowing who they are was a bad thing, now I ain't so sure. Got to be the man I wanted to be because my family didn't stop me 'cause there wasn't one. Now I'm glad I never had a family."

Noose felt Bess's eyes on him.

"You do have a family, Joe." He looked at her, fell into her strong and steady gaze. "You're riding one and riding beside the other."

"Family is who you ride beside. I like that." Joe Noose had to smile, couldn't help himself. The man felt a flood of warmth through his entire body, from his fingers to his toes and it started at his heart.

Right then, the sun came out.

Two days later at the town of Wind River, Marshal Bess found a telegraph office and sent a wire to the U.S. Marshal's office in Jackson Hole three hundred miles south.

She checked in with her deputy Nate Sweet to see how things were back in Jackson the whole time she was away. He telegraphed back promptly that the town was quiet except for a few cattle and sheep rancher disputes he had to intervene with, but nothing he couldn't handle. Reassured that her competent new lawman hire had things under control. Bess wired back that her mission was over and the killer was dead, and that she was riding back, although with the weather conditions, it could take several weeks. Sweet told her not to rush, and they agreed to check in with each other by telegraph at several terminals that her deputy had already identified, aware of his boss's movements over the preceding weeks.

After Bess and Noose had reprovisioned and ridden out of Wind River into the northwestern Wyoming hill country, Joe Noose saw his friend Bess Sugarland seemed more relaxed about things regarding her job and responsibilities in Jackson Hole. That turned out to be a good thing, because they were about to experience a few delays.

The following week, the bad chest cold and chills that had dogged Bess since their difficult ride down the freezing rapids in Destiny resulting in her weakened condition on the ride back, got the better of her. Despite being hardy and tough, the woman was suffering from exposure. One morning, seized with an attack of chills, she simply fainted and fell out of the saddle.

Luckily for them both, the lady marshal's collapse occurred ten miles out of the town of Sawyer, Wyoming. Noose got Bess back on her horse, and with Scout in tow, galloped for the town without stopping. Copper, somehow sensing Bess's dangerous condition, ran with exceptional power and stamina and got them there within two hours.

The growing mining town had an excellent doctor, and Noose carried her into the hospital in his arms. She was given immediate excellent treatment. For the next two weeks, Bess was confined to bed rest and a steady diet of liquids, soups, and vitamin concoctions of some kind. Noose spent most of every day at her side and, even though he checked into the local hotel, visited her several times every night. Her friend knew his presence was a great help to her. While they never talked about it and he didn't bring it up, Joe Noose knew it wasn't just exposure that had made Bess Sugarland sick, but the built-up tensions and stress of their dangerous hunt for The Brander her body only now was able to deal with because she couldn't in the midst of it.

And there was something else bothering Bess, making her distant and brooding. Noose didn't ask her what it was as he sat by her bed ten days into her hospice. He knew she would tell him when she was ready. They had been quiet for several hours, looking out her window at the people passing on the street, when a bluebird lit on the windowsill outside, and at last she came out with it.

"I killed six men, Joe. One by my gun. The rest by my direct action."

"It was them or you."

"Why don't that make me feel better about it? You killed a lot of men, Joe. How do you live with it?"

"Just do."

"That doesn't help."

"It comes with the job. You and me have different jobs, but we do the same thing. We are the law against men and women whose only law is the Law of the Gun. Those men you killed, the men and the one woman I killed, they died by the law they chose to live by: the gun."

"True. That's a good way to look at it."

"If we hadn't been there, they'd have killed a lot of folks who couldn't protect themselves, the ones we take responsibility to protect."

"Also true."

"Did you ever ask your daddy how he felt?"

"I did not. And I don't know if he would have told me."

"And these bad guys we bury, there's one last thing to remember, even if you forget all the rest."

"What's that, Joe?"

"If you didn't kill the bad guys, somebody else would."

She laughed. He did, too.

"So you gonna quit?" He cast a glance at her badge on the table beside her.

"What? No! Why the hell would I do that?"

He raised an eyebrow at her. *Because of what we just talked about.*

"That'll be the day."

That afternoon, Marshal Bess Sugarland was out of bed and back in the saddle, and with Joe Noose at her side, they had put twenty miles between them and the town by sundown.

Homeward bound, they were taking the ride slow.

Four days later, fifty-two miles farther, Noose and Bess rode through empty hill country. They could smell cows. As their horses crested a rise, the sprawling view of a big valley opened up before them occupied by five hundred head of steers standing stationary on the plain. Noose and Bess had happened upon a cattle drive but the gigantic procession of horns and hooves stood at a dead standstill spread across the plain. Off to the right, unmanned wagons were parked. Fifteen horses, saddled and riderless, were hitched to them.

"Where are all the people?" Bess wondered.

Noose pointed. "There."

Far off across the valley at the edge of the forest, a group of wranglers stood in a circle, hats off, heads bowed, somber figures very small at this distance. The ramrods were all men, but there appeared to be a female in their midst at the head of the circle. Her blond hair beneath her Stetson was recognizable even at this distance.

"Is that?" Bess wondered.

"I best believe it is." Noose grinned.

"Let's say hello."

The two of them spurred their horses and rode down across the plain, galloping past the enormous herd of cattle the size of which became more impressive the closer they rode. Noose and Bess cleared it, cantering toward the grim gathering of the wranglers, who now saw them coming. A pall hung over the group and the faces who watched their approach looked sad.

But Laura Holdridge smiled, her face brightening like the sun, as she whipped off her Stetson and flagged it over her head at Joe Noose and Bess Sugarland as they waved back and rode up to her. "Joe Noose and Marshal Bess Sugarland. I'll be damned. What are the odds of running into you way out here?"

"Good to see you, Laura." Bess leaned down to shake hands. "I see you're getting your cattle to market."

"Yeah, well, hoping to, anyhow. It's a long way from here to there to Cheyenne." The cattlewoman's gaze darkened as she slid a sidelong glance at her wranglers. "We ain't exactly off to an auspicious start. Did you catch that man you were after?"

"We did. Up in Destiny."

"But . . ." Laura had noticed Bess's shuttered expression.

"It was complicated."

"Weren't there three of you before?"

"I'm afraid now there's just two."

"I'm sorry."

"We are, too."

Joe Noose observed the men were standing around a grave. It was freshly dug, shovel stuck in the ground. He saw the Bible in Laura's hand. It became clear to him. She and her crew had been holding a service when they had been interrupted by his and the lady marshal's arrival. "Looks like you lost one of yours, too," he said.

"Four. So far," Laura replied sadly. "One a day out of my ranch near Consequence. One back in Sweetwater Station. One by Muddy Gap. Ox Johnson, Jed Wade, and Clyde Fullerton were their names. Luke McGraw here today makes four." Bess exchanged glances with Noose. *What the hell?*

They both swiveled their gazes down to Laura Holdridge, who stood planted on both boots, fists on her hips, looking back and forth fearlessly up at both of them on their horses, taking their measure. The cattlewoman's mind was working behind her eyes. "Take a ride with me." It was less a request than a friendly order and her tone broached no refusal. Noose and Bess shrugged and nodded, and Laura mounted her horse in one swift, strong motion. She tossed the Bible down to one of her ramrods, who caught it. "Curly. Finish reading over Luke. Rest of you men, pay your respects and be back in the saddle in fifteen minutes. We're moving out in twenty."

Spurring her horse and riding in the lead back toward

the herd. The marshal and bounty hunter rode after her. Laura slowed her mare so Noose and Bess could catch up on either side of her saddle. She didn't speak until they were well out of earshot of her crew. "Those deaths were no accident. My four drovers were murdered. Somebody on my crew is killing my wranglers. I can't prove it. I don't know who the killer is. Somebody doesn't want me to get my cattle to market. I believe this individual or individuals will murder every one of my outfit including me to be sure these steers don't make it to Cheyenne. So I'm asking for your help."

Bess looked at Noose.

Noose looked at Laura.

Who was looking at him.

"You're a bounty hunter, Mr. Noose. A damn good one, I understand. I will pay you five thousand dollars cash reward for you to discover the killer on my crew and stop these terrible murders. A dead-or-alive bounty."

The lady marshal raised her eyebrows.

The bounty hunter tightened his jaw, swinging his glance back at the receding figures of the drovers standing around the grave. "You positive your drovers were murdered, and it wasn't just accidents?"

"Five thousand dollars positive."

"Saying your suspicions are true, it ain't as easy as just asking them which one of them is the killer, Mrs. Holdridge. I'd have to ride along with you a spell, sniff around, for starters. *You* know I'm a bounty hunter. Do any of them?"

"No. They'll recognize the marshal here as the law because she was wearing her badge, but they don't know who you are."

"What are you thinking, Joe?" Bess asked.

"I'm thinking I sign on with Mrs. Holdridge's cattle drive as a replacement wrangler, go undercover, and find me a killer."

"Do you know the first thing about cowpunching?" Bess laughed.

"I've done a little."

"When?"

"Ten, maybe twelve years ago."

"Joe."

"Nothing to it."

"You will be kicked in the skull or trampled or gored by a bull the first day out, *if* whoever the killer is on this drive doesn't put a bullet in your back first."

Noose gave Bess that look and she rolled her eyes. He swung his gaze to Laura, his pale eyes steady as he extended his hand. "I like you, Laura. Think you got guts running these cattle and crew to Cheyenne by yourself and I don't want to see you fail. I'll take the job."

Laura Holdridge shook his hand with a firm grip, brushing her windblown blond hair out of her beautiful, stormy eyes. "Thank you."

"Thank me later."

"We move out in ten minutes," the cattlewoman said, all business. With that, Laura brusquely yanked her reins and swept her horse around, riding hard back to the livestock and wagons, as her men turned from the grave back to their horses and mounted up, ready to move the herd.

Noose looked at Bess, who, with a big old grin shook her head at him.

"Joe Noose, what the hell are you getting yourself into?"

*Keep reading for a special early excerpt of the next
Joe Noose western!*

THE CRIMSON TRAIL
by ERIC RED

On the long ride back from tracking down a killer in
remote Wyoming, Joe Noose and Marshal Bess
Sugarland come upon a large cattle drive. The trail boss,
the ruggedly beautiful and tough cattlewoman rancher
Laura Holdridge, tells Noose that four of her wranglers
have died under mysterious circumstances on the cattle
drive since she started moving the herd weeks ago.

She suspects a killer in their midst but doesn't know
who or why. Learning Joe Noose is a legendary bounty
hunter, Laura Holdridge offers him a five-thousand-
dollar bounty to ride with the cattle drive across
Wyoming, uncover the assassin, and capture him,
dead or alive.

***Look for* THE CRIMSON TRAIL,
*on sale this summer.***

CHAPTER 1

The cattle drive set forth after the thaw with five hundred steers, sixty horses, and twelve wranglers but after a hundred miles, the number of hands had dwindled to nine because the rest had been murdered.

That's what ramrod Luke McGraw believed.

Even if the rest of the outfit thought the deaths were an unlucky string of unfortunate accidents.

McGraw didn't believe in accidents and damn sure didn't believe in coincidences. Three men dead in two weeks was no coincidence.

He rode beside the herd of cattle moving across the plain still covered with the last snows of winter. He shivered. It was getting warmer, but not by much. Unlucky, like everything else on this doomed trail so far. As he sat in the saddle of Jenny, his big chestnut brown mare, the rugged cowboy reflected on the troubling sequence of unfortunate accidents that had plagued the cursed cattle drive from the moment they had departed the Bar H Ranch in Consequence, Wyoming, west of Wind River, driving the steers four hundred miles southeast to Cheyenne, on the other side of the state. The herd had to be delivered to the big Cattlemen's

Association auction in just over a month, and the long winter had delayed their departure. Still, they had enough time by the trail boss's reckoning; covering ten miles a day, it should have been a five-week journey, but the deaths had put them behind schedule.

First there was drover Ox Johnson, who fell off his horse and broke his neck. They blamed it on the whiskey, for the man was a rounder known to drink on the job.

Then a week later, driver Jed Wade was gone; healthy as a horse, then one day complains his stomach hurts and next thing anyone knows he's frothing at the mouth like a rabid dog and five minutes later, boom, stone-cold dead. They couldn't blame that on the whiskey because Wade was a teetotaler who didn't drink. And it sure wasn't the chow from Fred Kettlebone's chuck wagon that killed him, because the whole crew ate that, and Fred was the best cook anybody had ever ridden with. Snakebite was what some of the outfit were blaming for the cause of Jed Wade's untimely demise, but McGraw had never seen or heard of anybody dying that way from getting bit by a snake. However, he'd heard tell of some poisons that would do it to you, and Luke's suspicions were raised.

Both wranglers got a Christian burial on the trail because the trail boss insisted, even though she wasn't a religious woman; the great outdoors was the cattlewoman's church and McGraw figured she wanted to bury her men in the earth under the open sky where she herself felt close to God. The wrangler put no stock in men who refused to work for a woman because Luke McGraw had nothing but respect for Mrs. Laura Holdridge, his boss at the Bar H Ranch. All of the men in the outfit did. Or did they?

As Luke McGraw sat on his horse, guiding the long

march of longhorn steers across the rolling hills, listening to the shouts and yips of the eight other ramrods driving the cows, McGraw looked around for Mrs. Holdridge, but she was nowhere to be seen. He spurred his horse and sat tall in the stirrups, seeing two of the bulls were getting into an altercation and locking horns in the middle of the herd. The combative animals needed to be separated before the outfit lost a steer, because while that would have meant steaks every night for the crew and lots of good eating on the trail, Luke knew Mrs. Holdridge couldn't afford to lose a single cow and it was his job to make sure she didn't.

A week ago, McGraw took his trail boss aside and shared with her his suspicions that the deaths in their outfit were not accidental but deliberate. She listened attentively and then simply asked, "Why?" And he had no answer, just a gnawing conviction these were not accidents.

The Sharps rifle exploding in cowpuncher Clay Fullerton's hands and blowing his face off two days later was no damn accident, no misfire like everybody assumed. Fullerton was zealous about his guns, oiling and cleaning his rifle and revolvers every night. He could take a firearm apart and put it back together. Clay's death made three, and nobody in the outfit really thought anymore the experienced wranglers' deaths were accidental. Now everybody was watching their back and looking over their shoulders, sleeping with one eye open, if they slept at all. A few were sleeping in the saddle, catching some shut-eye on the trail. A palatable sense of dread had settled over the crew, and suspicion and tension between the men was tightening like a noose. All of the wranglers hated to camp now, fearing getting murdered in their slumber. Everyone felt safer out on the trail saddled on their horses driving the herd, with nothing but wide-open spaces around in every direction where you could see what was coming at you.

The two argumentative bulls needed to be separated directly; an expert horseman and seasoned cattle wrangler, Luke McGraw skillfully eased his horse into the herd, staying calm though surrounded by thousands of tons of fast-moving steers, their hooves thundering across the tundra. When he reached the middle of the moving mountains of cows, he felt his mare miss her step so he tapped his boots in his stirrups against her flanks to speed her canter to keep pace with the herd. Then he reached out from his saddle and separated the two bulls that were snorting and going at each other with their four-foot-long horns. One of the angry steers tried to gore the horse, but it wasn't McGraw's first rodeo; he grabbed one horn in each glove and wrestled the head of the bull in the other direction, diverting its attention and using his horse to force the steer away from the one bothering it. Soon, the whole herd was moving smoothly again, torrents of cattle stinking like a river of cow shit rushing past on both sides of his horse. Luke took off his hat, wiped sweat from his brow, and looked at the distant open eastern horizon, the direction they headed.

It was a long way to go to Cheyenne, their destination where the steers would go to auction at the big cattle show. Three hundred miles across hard, frozen tundra.

With the outfit dropping like flies, the ramrod was thinking they were never going to make it, when a lasso looped over his head and shoulders and jerked taut, catapulting him clean out of the saddle. Luke McGraw hit the ground hard and the last thing he saw were hundreds of hooves coming at his face before he got trampled to death.

CHAPTER 2

"Luke was our friend and our brother, part of our Bar H family. We're going to miss him . . ." As Laura Holdridge said a few words over her late wrangler Luke McGraw's grave, the cattlewoman was wondering whom to send his back pay to, only to realize she had no idea if the man had a wife or children. In fact, Laura realized she knew almost nothing at all about the wrangler she had employed all these years, or any of the wranglers who worked for her, for that matter.

The eight somber faces of her other drivers stood in a sad circle around the grave, as she spoke softly. "He loved the outdoors. He loved animals. Loved animals more than people, we all figured. We hope wherever you are, Luke, that dog of yours Blackie is up there with you, because everybody knew how you loved him and how much you missed him . . ." Laura eyed the faces of her drovers, wondering how much she really knew any of them now.

All the lady trail boss knew was four had died on the cattle drive the last couple weeks, and at this rate, all her crew would be dead before they got the herd to Cheyenne. Laura had to get her livestock to market at the Cattlemen's auction. Every cent she had was in these prime steers, and if she did not get a good price for her cattle she was going to lose the ranch she had been struggling to run since her cattleman husband passed away and left her a widow.

That had been a year ago. She had been on her own ever since, independent-minded and self-sufficient, getting by on pure grit and stubborn determination, running a working ranch of twelve men and making a go of it. Laura Holdridge was a Wyoming woman born and bred, hardy and fit, damn beautiful with long blond hair and a well-built statuesque figure that turned heads when she went to town; at thirty-one years of age, the cattlewoman knew how desirable she still was, but there had been no time for romance because running the cattle ranch took up every waking moment. And that's how Laura Holdridge needed things to be, because she missed her husband, Sam Holdridge, so much she couldn't bear it sometimes, and running the ranch kept her mind off his loss that had left a hole in her. And her outfit kept her from being alone.

"Good-bye, Luke." Finishing her speech at the shallow grave, Laura looked up into the faces of her wranglers circling the plot, hats in hand, forming an oval of mourners. Wearing a poker face, her eyes traveled from one face to the next, observing each of the eight cowboys' expressions very closely.

One of her wranglers was a killer.

The murderer stood five feet from her.

Who he was, she did not know.

How could she not know? Laura wondered, how could she not have some clue who the killer was when she knew these hands who worked for her and lived at her ranch who she saw every day? But she obviously didn't know them at all, and now she better be careful.

It was one of the eight, but which one?

Curly Brubaker, Wylie Jeffries, Joe Idaho, Charley Sykes, Frank Leadbetter, Rowdy Maddox, Billy "B.J." Barlow, and lastly, Fred Kettlebone; friendly faces she knew as well as her own, or so she had thought.

Most of the wranglers' eyes were downcast, grieving, in an ill-tempered, dismal mood. They would be taking the foreman's death very hard. McGraw was well liked among the cowboys and she wondered who would want to kill him. Two of her ramrods, Brubaker and Sykes, met her gaze, then looked away, not like they were guilty, just subservient to her like all the cowboys in her outfit were; she made sure of that, had her crew well trained. As a woman in the West, and a cattlewoman to boot, respect was everything and she had to work twice as hard as a man to get it. But all that being said, Laura knew her men loved her, and she loved them right back, because she was loyal to her outfit, they were like a family to her. She paid them well and fed them well and they would do anything for her, she knew. Now she had lost four of them.

The woman's heart was breaking losing Luke McGraw. She wanted to cry but she couldn't in front of the men. She always had to be strong. Her heart may break, but Laura Holdridge never would.

They had buried the foreman in a shady copse of white birch trees at the edge of an airy open plain. She had helped dig the grave herself. The crew had voted on the selection of the spot but the whole outfit knew it was a place of peace and quiet their fallen friend would have appreciated, and in life would have enjoyed spending time in. He would be spending a lot of it here.

'You boys go on and say a few words now, say your good-byes." Taking off her sweat-stained Stetson, Laura heaved a huge sigh, turning away from the grave to face the open plain. The gigantic herd of cattle was standing as far as the eye could see, it seemed, grazing on the tall grass near the parked wagons. The sight of the herd daunted her now. Behind, she heard the soft, quiet words of the wranglers each in turn saying their piece over their departed saddle mate. A few wept. The lady trail boss thought the sadness in their voices couldn't be the voices of men who murdered McGraw, or Johnson, or Fullerton or Wade. But one of them did.

When Laura recovered the trampled corpse of Luke McGraw, what was left of it, off the hoof-trodden muddy plain, she knew he didn't fall out of the saddle and his death was no accident. The cowpoke was born in the saddle and the best rider her ranch had, and the cattlewoman was no fool. *Why didn't she listen to McGraw when he warned her a week ago?* Sometimes she was too damn stubborn for her own good and his warning didn't make sense to her then, but it sure did now.

McGraw's clothes were bloody, muddy rags so the cattlewoman respectfully removed them from his person for burial. She washed the body and cleaned up his remains doing the best she could because his condition would have meant a closed-casket burial back in civilization, but this wasn't civilization, it was the open trail. And it was dangerous, with no law for hundreds of miles.

She saw the raw rope burn across what was left of his upper body and knew he had been lassoed off his horse. It had taken skill to throw that rope in a moving herd of cattle. Her ramrod Brubaker was a stud with a lasso, but that didn't mean anything because the other wranglers could also throw a rope and any one of them could have pulled Luke McGraw off his horse with a good toss.

That the killer would strike again was a dead certainty, the only question was who was next. For some odd reason Laura Holdridge did not fear for her own life, having an intuition she herself was not the killer's target, her men were. Why? She trusted her instincts but that didn't stop her from strapping the massive Colt Dragoon revolver under her coat and lately keeping it under her pillow.

The five hundred head of prime Wyoming beef stood before her scattered out across the plain, giving her bovine looks that seemed to say, *Let's get a move on.* It was time for the outfit to get back on the trail. They had to make time. It was over three hundred miles to Cheyenne and the outfit had a schedule to keep if they were going to cross that considerable distance, the whole of the state of Wyoming, and get there in time for the two-day Cattlemen's auction three weeks from now. The murders of her wranglers had slowed down the whole cattle drive, already costing several days dealing with the burials. Getting the herd to Cheyenne presented an impossible task now there was a killer in the outfit picking off her wranglers, and there seemed to be nothing she could do about it.

What the hell was she going to do?

She knew what she *should* do. Go to the law. Report the killings. Ride back to the local sheriff in Wind River or ride ahead to the U.S. Marshal, report the deaths, and let the authorities investigate. And the minute she did that, her outfit and the cattle would be detained for an investigation. Guaranteed then she would not make the auction and by this time next year, would have lost the ranch, everything she and her husband worked for, and her men would be unemployed. Going to the law was the right thing to do. But it was suicide for her ranch and those in her employ. She had discussed it with the wranglers earlier in the day before the burial, and they were all agreed to report the deaths once they made it to Cheyenne; it is what McGraw, Johnson, Fullerton, and Wade would have wanted, too.

There was one other thing she could do.

Quit.

Turn the herd and abandon the cattle drive, put them back in her corral. Pay her wranglers what she could. Sell the cows at a huge loss after the auction. Her outfit would lose money but keep their lives. Perhaps then the killings would stop.

Laura didn't know what to do at this moment, had never felt so helpless and overwhelmed in her natural life. The entire combined weight of the massive herd of steer filling her field of vision suddenly felt like it was sitting on her bosom—a crushing weight of those tons of cows bore down on her, and Laura couldn't catch her breath; her heart was pounding, her pulse racing. *Pull yourself together, woman!* she excoriated herself inside. *You will not fall apart in front of your men! Be strong!* Through sheer force of will, Laura Holdridge settled down, regaining her composure. Inhaling deep refreshing breaths of the clean Wyoming air into her lungs, Laura willed herself to stand straight and be calm, and her panic attack was carried off in the wind.

The cattlewoman was not a quitter. She never quit once in her whole entire life. But she had the lives of eight souls she was responsible for as trail boss. She had to ask them whether they wanted to turn back or push on.

She walked back to the men at the grave. "Listen up."

Eight pairs of eyes immediately locked on her, she had the full attention of the hardy cowpokes standing before her. She was the boss.

Laura Holdridge addressed the drovers as the first among equals, looking each man directly in the eye as her gaze swung across their attentive faces while she spoke. "Boys, we all know we have a killer in the outfit. He's murdered four of us. That pisses me the hell off, as I'm sure it does seven out of the eight of you. What burns my ass the most? That's he's one of you. I trust all you boys with my life, each and every one of you, but unless one of you fesses up now, I got no idea in hell which one of you has our outfit's blood on his hands."

As she stood before them by the oak tree, Laura witnessed paranoid, distrustful glances traded by men who had always been friends. It broke her heart to see. But she remembered what her mother always said: *Nothing wrong with a broken heart so long as it don't break you.* The cattlewoman looked perspicaciously into the eyes of each and every cowhand—not one had the eyes of a killer.

For the first time Laura doubted her faculties.

"How do we know it's one of us?" Leadbetter asked, looking at his fellows. There were a few nods.

"We don't," she replied evenly. "But who else could it be?"

"Not us."

Laura hadn't thought about that but now she did. "You mean a killer who's not part of the outfit, not riding with us, but shadowing us, watching our every move, and when our guard is down and this individual sees an opening, that's when he strikes."

"Could be."

"Smells like Injun to me," Kettlebone, the cook, offered. "Them Injuns is so quick when they attack they don't make a sound and you never see 'em. One minute you're reaching up to scratch your hair, the next minute you've been scalped, your hair and skin is gone on the top of your head, and all you is scratching is skull bone." A few of the men groaned in disgust. "I have seen Apaches do this with my own eyes, boys."

"Ain't no Apache in Wyoming, Fred," Brubaker argued. "Just Shoshone. And that tribe ain't warlike and they don't scalp. I count a bunch of 'em as friends."

Laura shook her head. "Brubaker's right. The Apaches are three states away, our cold doesn't agree with them. Like the man says, the only Indians we have around these parts are the Shoshone and they're a peaceful tribe. Nope, this isn't Indian trouble. It's something else, or someone else."

The wranglers all muttered agreement.

"Boys, maybe it is a killer stalking our herd murdering us, or maybe the killer is one of you boys, though I hope it ain't because I'd hate to have to hang one of you boys. Except for *you*, Leadbetter." She pointed at the youngest wrangler, Frank Leadbetter, a hulking kid probably no more than nineteen, whose beard was just growing in. She was teasing him to lighten the grim mood and shake off some of the dread they all were experiencing as best she could.

"It don't make no sense," Sykes mumbled.

"Why is this happening?" Idaho moaned.

"Ain't it obvious?" Laura faced her men soberly. "Somebody doesn't want us to get our cattle to market. They'll do anything to stop this cattle drive. That's what's happening. What do you boys think?"

Every head nodded in agreement.

"Who you think is behind it?" asked Kettlebone.

"We all know who's probably behind it," Laura spat. "Calhoun, who else? But I can't be sure. Don't make no difference, it doesn't matter who it is. Somebody's got it out for us. That's the situation. Way I see it we got two choices: turn back or push on. We can go home. That's one choice. The other choice is we get the herd to Cheyenne or die trying. I'm putting it to a vote."

"It's your herd, Mrs. Holdridge. You're the boss," Curly Brubaker, the new foreman, insisted. "It's your choice."

The cattlewoman shook her head, fairness in her gaze. "It's your lives. It's your choice, too. The Bar H Ranch isn't just me, boys, it's all of us. We ride or die."

"Ride or die!" several drovers repeated. Moved by her words, the wranglers' spirits were lifted, the outfit's morale boosted by fellowship and cowboy orneriness.

"Let's vote," the cattlewoman said.

"Wait." Billy Joe Barlow put up his hand, looking at the others. "Sorry, ma'am, didn't mean to interrupt, but if I may, before we vote, if it were just up to you, Mrs. Holdridge, if it was, what would you do?"

Laura Holdridge was on the spot. All eyes were on her. She searched her soul before she spoke, and when she did it was what she truly believed with all her heart. "If it was just up to me, I'd think to myself: This is my herd, am I going to let any man stop me from getting my herd to market like I got a right as a free American to do? And I'd answer: Nobody is going to take away my freedom. I'm moving my herd and if they want to stop me they'll have to shoot me, and let them try, because I'll shoot right back because I'll fight to the death for what's mine. You asked me what I'd do if it was up to me, Barlow? I'd drive these longhorns to Cheyenne. Ride or die."

The outfit's faces had not a dry eye.

"Okay. Let's have us that vote." The cattlewoman took a deep breath. "Anybody wants to turn back, raise your hand."

No hands went up. Not one.

"Votes are counted." Laura grinned. "We're going to Cheyenne."

The entire outfit let out a huge cheer, throwing their hats in the air, and Laura Holdridge never loved her boys more than she did right then.

The mood grew somber once more as they gathered again around Luke McGraw's shallow grave, because Billy Joe Barlow and Rowdy Maddox hadn't had the chance yet to say their piece, and Rowdy was going on and on.

It was then Laura saw something that caught her attention. Stepping away from her men, the cattlewoman looked out across the valley, raising her hand to her brow to block the sun so she didn't have to squint.

Far in the distance, two horses had crested the rise above the sprawling valley across the five hundred head of steers standing stationary on the plain. She swore she recognized the two riders.

Could it be them?

What were the chances of running into them again, out here of all places?

The cattlewoman had eyes like an eagle, and sure enough, she recognized the two riders as Joe Noose and Bess Sugarland, a bounty hunter and lady U.S. Marshal, who had stopped by her ranch a few weeks ago, and she had liked them very much. They'd stayed the night in her house and left the following day on U.S. Marshal business tracking a killer. Joe Noose had left quite an impression on Laura. A third man had been their companion, another marshal, Laura recollected, but she disremembered his name or anything else about him. Whoever that man was, he wasn't with them now. Laura could see Noose and Bess up on the rise looking in her direction but figured they couldn't recognize her from this distance so she'd better catch their attention before they rode off.

Laura Holdridge smiled, her face brightening like the sun, as she whipped off her Stetson and flagged it over her head at Joe Noose and Bess Sugarland, and they waved back and rode down the ridge toward her.

Feeling a weight lift off her bosom, the cattlewoman heaved a sigh of relief. It was the perfect time for a talk with a friendly U.S. Marshal, given everything that was going on with the murders in her outfit. Plus Bess was a woman, the only lady marshal Laura had ever met, and the two of them had gotten along famously at the Bar H Ranch. Maybe the law could help. Laura kept her gaze fixed on the small figures of the riders and horses as they approached at a comfortable stride, growing larger in her field of view as they skirted the sprawling herd and rode her way. Friendly faces.

The bounty hunter Joe Noose was a very big man, she had almost forgotten how big. The mountain of a cowboy rode tall in the saddle toward her, a formidable figure who would physically intimidate lesser mortals. Nobody would mess with this man, Laura thought admiringly. Today the bounty hunter wore a heavy leather coat over a bright blue denim shirt and a yellow kerchief. He was close enough now that when his broad brown Stetson hat lifted, his pale blue eyes flashed in hers and Laura remembered the kindness and goodness she saw in that gaze when they had last met, because beneath his tough dangerous exterior, the biggest thing about the man was his heart. Laura was very glad to see Joe Noose.

His riding by was the first stroke of good luck the cattle drive had enjoyed since departing on their unlucky journey. Joe Noose was exactly the man she needed in her most desperate hour.

If she could only convince him to stay.

That gave her an idea.

Slipping into her big cowgirl personality as easily as a pair of blue jeans, Laura became her loud and gregarious extroverted self as the two rode up to her. "Joe Noose and Marshal Bess Sugarland. I'll be damned," the cattlewoman hollered out. "What are the odds of running into you way out here?"

"Good to see you, Laura." Bess leaned down to shake hands. The cattlewoman exchanged a warm grin with her. "I see you're getting your cattle to market."

"Yeah, well, hoping to, anyhow. It's a long way from here to there to Cheyenne." Laura's gaze darkened as she slid a sidelong glance at her wranglers. "We ain't exactly off to an auspicious start. Did you catch that man you were after?"

"We did. Up in Destiny."

"But . . ." Laura had noticed Bess's shuttered expression. *The third man who wasn't here now.*

"It was complicated."

"Weren't there three of you before?"

"I'm afraid now there's just two."

"I'm sorry."

"We are, too."

Laura saw Joe Noose observing the drovers standing around the freshly dug grave beside the shovel stuck in the ground. She saw him glance at the Bible in her hand. His somber expression made it clear he understood the outfit had been holding a service interrupted by his arrival. "Looks like you lost one of yours, too," Noose said.

"Four. So far," Laura replied sadly. "One a day out of my ranch near Consequence. One back in Sweetwater Station. One by Muddy Gap. Ox Johnson, Jed Wade, and Clyde Fullerton were their names. Luke McGraw here today makes four."

Bess traded *what the hell?* glances with Noose.

As they swung their gazes down to her, Laura stood planted on both boots, fists on her hips, looking back and forth boldly up at both of them on their horses, taking their measure. The cattlewoman's mind was working behind her eyes. "Take a ride with me." She made it less a request than a friendly order and her tone broached no refusal. Noose and Bess shrugged and nodded, and Laura mounted her horse in one swift, strong motion. She tossed the Bible down to her foreman, Brubaker, who caught it. "Curly. Finish reading over Luke. Rest of you men, pay your respects and be back in the saddle in fifteen minutes. We're moving out in twenty."

Spurring her horse and riding in the lead back toward the herd. The marshal and bounty hunter rode after her. Laura slowed her mare so Noose and Bess could catch up on either side of her saddle. She didn't speak until they were well out of earshot of her crew. "Those deaths were no accident. My four drovers were murdered. Somebody on my crew is killing my wranglers. I can't prove it. I don't know who the killer is. Somebody doesn't want me to get my cattle to market. I believe this individual or individuals will murder every one of my outfit including me to be sure these steers don't make it to Cheyenne. So I'm asking for your help."

Bess looked at Noose.

Noose looked at Laura.

Who was looking at Joe.

"You're a bounty hunter, Mr. Noose. A damn good one, I understand. I will pay you five thousand dollars cash reward for you to discover the killer on my crew and stop these terrible murders. A dead-or-alive bounty."

The lady marshal raised her eyebrows.

The bounty hunter tightened his jaw, swinging his glance back at the receding figures of the cowboys standing around the grave. "You positive your drovers were murdered, and it wasn't just accidents?"

"Five thousand dollars positive."

"Saying you're suspicions are true, it ain't as easy as just asking them which one of them is the killer, Mrs. Holdridge. I'd have to ride along with you a spell, sniff around, for starters. *You* know I'm a bounty hunter. Do any of them?"

Remembering Joe's stay at her ranch, Laura thought back about any encounters the bounty hunter had with her hands, and didn't remember any offhand. "No. Don't think so. They'll recognize the marshal here as the law because she was wearing her badge, but they don't know who you are."

"What are you thinking, Joe?" Bess asked.

"I'm thinking I sign on with Mrs. Holdridge's cattle drive as a replacement wrangler, go undercover, and find me a killer."

Laura's heart leapt in her chest with hope and beat faster with excitement, but the cattlewoman didn't want to say the wrong thing and screw this up so she kept her mouth shut and let the two friends talk among themselves.

"You don't know the first thing about cowpunching." Bess laughed.

"I've done a little," Noose replied.

"When?"

"Ten, maybe twelve years ago."

"Joe."

"Nothing to it."

"You will be kicked in the skull or trampled or gored by a bull the first day out, *if* whoever the killer is on this drive doesn't put a bullet in your back first."

Noose gave Bess a knowing look and she rolled her eyes. He swung his gaze to Laura, his pale eyes steady as he extended his hand. "I like you, Laura. Think you got guts running these cattle and crew to Cheyenne by yourself and I don't want to see you fail. I'll take the job."

Laura Holdridge shook his hand with a firm grip, brushing her windblown blond hair out of her eyes. "Thank you."

"Thank me later."

"We move out in ten minutes," the cattlewoman said, outwardly all business but inside so excited she could bust. She wanted to throw her arms around Noose and Bess and kiss them, so happy and relieved was she. But habit and prudence told her to keep her feelings hidden behind her boss lady demeanor. And with that, Laura brusquely yanked her reins and swept her horse around, riding hard back to the livestock and wagons, as her men turned from the grave back to their horses and mounted up, ready to move the herd.

Behind her back as she rode off out of earshot, the last words Laura overheard the marshal say to the bounty hunter were, "Joe Noose, what the hell are you getting yourself into?"

Plenty, the cattlewoman thought as she rejoined her wranglers and the herd, yelling, "Move 'em out!"

"Guess this is farewell for now."

The time had come for them to split up. Joe Noose and Bess Sugarland sat in the saddles of their horses and said their good-byes.

"Come with me on the cattle drive, Bess. It'll be an adventure and I sure can use your help."

"I can't, Joe. I'm a U.S. Marshal and I got a sworn duty to uphold. I've been away from Jackson for three months. If my daddy were alive he'd have had my badge for taking that long a leave of absence. But it had to be done and we got our man. It's okay, my deputy Nate Sweet is a good man and he's covering the office, but it ain't fair to him, neither, his taking care of all my responsibilities. It's a two-week ride back to Jackson so I need to get a move on and get home. Got a town to protect. Gotta earn my salary." She trailed off.

"I know." He nodded. Her sense of duty was one of the things he most admired about her.

"Buck up." The lady marshal took the bounty hunter's hand and held it in hers. "You don't need my help anyway. After The Brander, how bad can this killer be? You'll flush out this villain in that outfit in two days and be back in Jackson a couple days after me. You'll see."

"I hope so." Joe noticed Bess's expression change when he added, "I'm doing this for Laura Holdridge. She deserves my help." He saw she had let go of his hand.

Bess looked off at the mountains, gathering her thoughts. Breaking his gaze was unlike her since she was so direct. When Bess turned her face back to him, Joe noticed it was flushed and not from the weather. "You like her, don't you?"

Joe saw the flash of jealousy in Bess's face, a pain in her guileless expression she didn't understand or know how to hide. Realizing he hurt his best friend's feelings pained Noose inside more than a bullet in the gut. "I like her, Joe. She's a good woman."

The worst part was Bess had it all wrong, but Joe didn't know how to tell her. The two companions sat on their horses on the rise looking at each other with so much they couldn't say, but now it was time for their farewells. "See you in Jackson," Joe said, tipping his Stetson.

Bess searched his eyes. "You got something on your mind, tell me, partner."

Joe wanted to tell Bess how he felt about her, but somehow the thought of that scared him spitless. "I hate good-byes, Bess."

"This ain't good-bye," Bess said softy with a smile, her eyes wet, a hitch in her voice. With those parting words, the lady marshal snapped the reins and turned her horse away from him to begin her long ride.

And Joe almost said it.

He wanted to. The words were on his lips.

Bess, you have nothing to be jealous about.

But Joe knew if he said that, he'd have to say the next part.

You're the only woman I want to be with.

And then he'd have to say the rest.

I love you.

So Joe Noose said nothing.

As Bess Sugarland rode away, a piece of Joe Noose rode with her. His heart.

In its place, on his chest above his heart, the bounty hunter felt the old scar of the cattle brand burned into his flesh start to tingle and sting like a phantom pain, the way it always did when there were wrongs to right, justice to be done, and he had to act. The white-hot cold fury of the brand filled the empty hole where his heart felt it was missing, adrenaline pumped through his body and he was ready for action, his purpose clear for today: help the Holdridge woman track down the killer in her outfit and stop him from murdering her wranglers so she could get her cattle to Cheyenne.

It was going to be a hell of an adventure, Joe Noose thought, tearing his eyes away from the distant speck of Marshal Bess Sugarland on the plain, swinging his gaze over to the valley where the procession of longhorn steer on the march moved out with the covered wagons, the drovers and their horses driving the herd with whoops and hollers and cracks of bullwhips. Laura Holdridge rode gloriously out front of the herd on her wagon, her golden hair blowing in the wind. The valley rang with the voices of the men as the ground shook with the thunder of hooves, sounds of jubilation and life. It was quite a sight.

Joe was going to miss the woman he loved.

But he'd see Bess in Jackson soon enough. Sure, it wasn't going to be the same without her. For now, he had a job to do, and for a while at least, that was enough.

The cattle drive was on the move.

He better get on after them.